THE SK

THE

SKY

VAULT

BENJAMIN PERCY

WILLIAM MORROW
An Imprint of HarperCollins*Publishers*

THE SKY VAULT. Copyright © 2023 by Benjamin Percy. All rights reserved. Printed in the United States of America. No part of this book may be used or reproduced in any manner whatsoever without written permission except in the case of brief quotations embodied in critical articles and reviews. For information, address HarperCollins Publishers, 195 Broadway, New York, NY 10007.

HarperCollins books may be purchased for educational, business, or sales promotional use. For information, please email the Special Markets Department at SPsales@harpercollins.com.

FIRST EDITION

Designed by Diahann Sturge

Library of Congress Cataloging-in-Publication Data has been applied for.

ISBN 978-1-328-54441-4 (paperback)
ISBN 978-0-358-33155-1 (library edition)

23 24 25 26 27 LBC 5 4 3 2 1

For Lisa

PROLOGUE

t begins with a comet.

Decades ago, an infrared telescope captured the thermal emission streaking through the solar system. Eventually it was determined to be 300.2 kilometers wide and orbiting the sun in an elongated ellipse that would bring it within five hundred thousand miles of Earth.

The moon, by comparison, is 238,900 miles away. This would be, scientists said, a beautiful light show that everyone should enjoy all the more knowing that we'd narrowly escaped planetary annihilation.

The official name of the comet was P/2011 C9, but most people called it Cain, the surname of the astronomer who'd discovered it. Twenty years later, it burned into view and made its close pass by Earth.

People took off work. They gathered at soccer fields and in parking lots, on rooftops and along sidewalks, setting up lawn chairs and picnic blankets and grills and coolers as though readying for a fireworks display. Everyone suddenly owned a telescope. Vendors sold comet T-shirts and hats and key chains and plush stuffed toys. Surfers stacked up on beaches waiting for the big waves they believed would come from the gravitational flux. At least two cults killed themselves off, announcing this was the end of the world and the comet a gateway to the vault of heaven.

Professors and scientists and religious leaders became regular guests on cable news shows, where they talked about how comets had long been associated with meteorological and human disasters—tsunamis, earthquakes, and droughts. In 44 BC, when Caesar was assassinated, his soul was said to depart the Earth and join the comet flaming overhead. In AD 79, a comet aligned with the eruption of Vesuvius. In AD 684, when Halley's comet passed by, the Black Death broke out, and in 1066, when it made another appearance, William the Conqueror won the Battle of Hastings. Celestial judgment and providence. Or an instrument of the devil, as Pope Callixtus III called it.

"Heaven knows what awaits us," one professor said. "It is a reminder of our irrelevant smallness and accidental existence in the universe, a glimpse of something violently outside the bounds of human existence, as close as you can come to seeing God."

Local news reporters interviewed people on the streets. "I don't know—it's just kind of cool," one man said. "Special. Once-in-a-lifetime sort of deal. You want to be able to say, *I was there.* It's almost like we're living this two-dimensional life, and now there's this sense of it being three-dimensional, if you know what I mean."

Cain looked like a roughly drawn eye, some said. Or a glowing animal track. Or a slash mark in the fabric of space. A wandering star.

For a few days, the comet made night uncertain, hued with a swampy green light. And by day, the sky appeared twinned with suns. And then—gradually—the comet trailed farther and farther away, and people forgot all about it.

Until one year passed. The planet finished its orbit of the sun and spun into the debris field left behind by the comet. The residue of Cain's passage.

This June, the sky would fall. That's what the newscasters said.

The meteor shower was not as long-lasting as August's Perseids, but for several nights the sky flared and streaked and wheeled, the constellations seeming to rearrange themselves with ever-shifting tracks of light. At first hundreds and then thousands and then hundreds of thousands and finally an uncountable storm of meteors.

The ground shook. Windows shattered. Grids of electricity went dark. Satellites shredded. Radio signals scrambled. Dogs howled and people screamed their prayers. Many of the meteors dissolved in the atmosphere, but many struck the earth, sizzling into the ocean, splintering roofs, searing through ice, punching craters into fields and forests and mountainsides, like the seeds of the night.

It was then that everything changed.

THE SKY VAULT

1

Sometimes, when Chuck Bridges takes a long, hard look at his life, he feels like a time traveler who ended up in the wrong place, one of those alternative futures where things went haywire. He should have hair, for one. His hair had been glorious. Thick, inky curls that gave off a kind of light, like an oil puddle in a parking lot or something. Also: He should be a well-respected mayor or an important scientist guy or maybe the beloved host of one of those programs about UFOs and Bigfoot on the Discovery Channel. Also: He shouldn't be in a cell.

He'd been arrested before—a New Year's DUI, a fistfight at a county fair, a protest march in Anchorage—but not for years and not for anything serious. Not like this. Port Authority had been waiting at the end of the jet bridge, and as soon as the plane engines quieted to a whine, the flight attendant unlocked the cabin door, and the cops marched in.

They found Chuck in his twentieth-row seat, and when he said, "I don't know what you're looking at me for. I didn't do nothing wrong," they yanked him up and twisted his arms behind his back and cuffed his wrists. "You should be thanking me!" he said. "I was trying to save their lives! I'm a goddamn hero!" They escorted him up the jet bridge and along the concourse and through a locked door and down the stairs and into a hall that ended with a windowless cell in the basement of the Fairbanks International Airport.

He tries telling them the same thing he's been telling everybody else. But they won't listen.

It goes like this:

Cumulus. Cirrus. Altostratus. Nimbostratus. Clouds have names, right? But even though the sky is ever shifting, the cloud atlas doesn't change. It's more like the color wheel than the dictionary or star charts. The labels and order are firm. There is nothing more to discover.

Except that there is. Chuck believes he has identified a new formation. On six different occasions—six!—he has documented its existence. The photographs and videos on his cell are not comprehensive, in part because he really needs to order a new phone—the screen on this one is so cracked, it doesn't function properly—and the weather events have been short-lived, dispersing after less than a minute.

"But you should see it," he tells everyone. "It's wild, man." Its appearance in the clouds at first resembles a stormy sea, with sharp gray waves and pulpy black troughs—and then something shifts and tendrils lower, like those of a jellyfish. A puckered swirl forms at the center, what could be described as an eye or a mouth.

Then, just as quickly as it began, it dissipates. *Briefly apocalyptic* is how he describes it. He has sent his files and arguments to both the National Weather Service and the World Meteorological Organization, and they have dismissed him. Not once, but repeatedly. Because he won't let up. Several scientists and meteorologists have blocked his phone number and e-mail and a few even filed for restraining orders against him because they are—in their words—"Exhausted by the insane ramblings of a hobbyist and conspiracist."

Of course he takes offense. Not at the conspiracist jab—that's fine. It's the hobbyist label that bugs him. He is in fact a meteorologist for 93.3—the Grizz—the fifth-biggest FM market in north-central Alaska. Or maybe *meteorologist* isn't his official title—he's a classic rock disc jockey who also acts as the janitor for the station. But by God, he's been reporting on the weather for more than twenty years—thirty-second updates every half hour—and that's got to count for something.

What hair Chuck still has he grows long. His wiry beard matches it, running halfway down his chest. He's long-limbed and bony except for a prominent belly that makes him look like he's smuggling a basketball beneath the Hawaiian shirts he favors with his jeans and cowboy boots. He sometimes has at least three pairs of reading glasses on him—cheaters, he calls them—one perched on top of his head, another on the tip of his nose, another dangling from a cord around his neck, because he misplaces them so frequently.

And yes, it's true that he has a blog—called *The Truth Is Out There*—that is responsible for inquiries into cloned celebrities, faked moon landings, microchipped vaccines, mind-control television programs, alien lizard people, Sasquatch, and the Bermuda Triangle of the North. But so what? So what! There's nothing illegal about any of that.

The truth of the matter is this: He should get credit for discovering a new cloud system. But he won't because he made the mistake of telling the NWS that something in the sky was trying to communicate with him. At least he thinks it's in the sky.

The first time he noticed it—the whispering in his headphones when he cued up Zeppelin—he wondered if he was picking up another frequency. And then he got this feeling—this tingle-at-the-back-of-the-neck feeling—that made him tear off his headset and spin around in his chair to make sure he was alone in the studio. That's when he saw it. Out the window. The darkening sky. The lowering shoots. The swirling nexus.

It happened again, and again, and again. Over the course of several years. Not on any regular schedule and not with any steady connection to the temperature or pressure system or moisture index. He recorded the whispers and played them for others, including his wife, but she only said, "Maybe it's the wind?"

This was in their kitchen, where slices of Spam sizzled on a stovetop pan. "Maybe it's the wind!" he said with a mean laugh. "That's what the stupid people say in horror movies before they get killed!"

She shut off the burner, and the meat continued to spit and pop. She crossed her arms and gave him a hard stare. "So I'm stupid, am I?"

"No!" he said, realizing his mistake, stepping back. "No! That's not what I meant."

Her name was Janey and she kept her hair and her nails cut short to avoid the fuss. She worked at the credit union as a teller and could butcher a deer in less than an hour and didn't like much in the way of nonsense outside of the sitcoms she watched at night to relax. She had a way of inclining her head, like a boxer lining up a shot, that usually tipped him off to the fact a big fight might be coming. She was doing precisely that now when she said, "Then what did you mean?"

"I meant . . . I'm frustrated is all. I feel like something's happening, something important, but I'm the only one who believes it." He walked over to the kitchen table and flopped down in a chair and put his head in his hands. "I'm sorry."

She found the spatula and scraped the Spam slices off the pan and onto a plate. She laid a paper towel over them to soak up the grease. Then she walked over to Chuck and rubbed his back and told him it was all right. But she was worried about him.

"You think I'm crazy, don't you? You always think I'm crazy."

"I don't always think you're crazy. I think some of your ideas are a little *out there*."

"This is different. This isn't some theory about Jack Parsons and the Jet Propulsion Lab. Or Area 51. Or the hodag or Mothman or any of that."

"How is it different?"

"Because I saw it! I heard it! There's no distance or speculation. This is raw data. A firsthand account."

She said, "I think you should listen to the recording again."

"Fine. Let's do that." He set his phone on the table and called up the recording and hit the Play button and they both leaned in. It was as if one of his ears heard it as a whispering urgent voice, and the other heard it as a scratchy recording of the wind. "Maybe I should play it for Theo when he gets home."

"You should not play it for Theo."

"Why not?"

"Because he's fourteen and he already thinks we're aliens and spends all his time with his friends. There's no reason to give him another excuse to roll his eyes."

He squeezed the phone in his palm and stared at his ghostly reflection in the black screen. "The whispering is one thing. But how do you explain the clouds?"

"Well, the TV signal doesn't come through as sharp when the weather gets rough. I'm guessing the same can be said for radio."

"I've been working at that station for how long? And there's been some enormous weather. Some serious howlers. But I never noticed this—never—until we put up that omnimetal antenna."

"What are you suggesting?"

He stood up from his chair and went over to the window. This was September and the lawn was yellow weeds. "I don't know."

"Well, until you do, maybe you should just take things down a notch."

But he couldn't. He sent off more e-mails and made more phone calls. He brought it up at his favorite bar—the Broken Mirror—and ended up getting a bowl of peanut shells dumped over his head. He brought it up on the air during his morning shift and ended up in trouble with the station owner. "The world is a strange enough place right now, don't you think? People don't need another reason to be scared, and they sure as shit don't need an excuse to turn the dial to another station. Give them the news, the weather, and a few laughs. Then shut the hell up and let the rock and roll take over."

Chuck had become a regular on several Reddit boards and Facebook groups devoted to weather, and it was here that he learned about an upcoming meeting of the American Meteorological Society. The conference would take place at the Red Lion Inn in Portland, Oregon. There were several research meteorologists who would be presenting on subjects like predictive algorithms, atmospheric geophysics, NOAA leadership, and apps like Radar-Scope. But there was one thing in particular that caught his eye. A scientist named Dr. David Hyuck who taught at the University of

Florida and had written a book called *Synoptic Analysis* was lecturing on the increase in extreme weather since the meteor strikes. Not just droughts and flash floods and hurricanes and tornadoes and blizzards but peculiar phenomena, like a rainstorm of blood in central Texas and a thunderstorm that lasted for ten weeks in Carbondale, Illinois.

Chuck had reached out to him before. Many times before. In fact, Hyuck was one of several scientists who had filed a restraining order against him. Which made no sense. It's not like Chuck was jerking off on his lawn or threatening his dog or something. So what if he'd found Hyuck's unlisted address by making a few calls to the Gainesville DMV? So what if he'd gotten hold of his private cell number by tricking the department secretary at the university? Chuck just wanted to talk. If the two of them could meet in person, things would be different. He was certain of it.

So he booked a flight to Portland. He polished his cowboy boots and wore a corduroy jacket over his Hawaiian shirt and even trimmed his nose and ear hair. Because he was going to make a good impression. But upon arriving at the hotel, he discovered that the conference was taking place in an annex that he couldn't access without registering. To get through security, he needed a name tag, which he could easily acquire if he was agreeable to paying the two-hundred-dollar same-day fee. But he was not agreeable. He had just blown a month of grocery money on the flight down here. He didn't see the need to register for the same reason he hadn't seen the need to book a room. He didn't want to attend any of the panels and lectures. He just wanted to speak to Dr. Hyuck. All he needed was an hour. His flight home was later that afternoon. He would be in and out, so if they could point him in the right direction?

It didn't take long for things to escalate. Chuck had a habit of speaking loudly—it was part of being a DJ—and sometimes people mistook this for yelling. The security guards gathered around him, asking him to please lower his voice, and as they were guiding him away from the annex, he broke free and made a mad dash past registration.

His feet pounded as he negotiated the maze of carpeted hallways looking for ballroom 1A, where he knew Dr. Hyuck would soon be taking the podium. He could hear the guards huffing and yelling, "Stop!" He knocked over a ficus tree, thinking that might slow them down. He dared a look back, and it was then that a catering cart rolled out of a conference room. He ran into it with a crash. Plates shattered. Coffee urns overturned. Linen napkins fluttered like doves, and water chestnuts wrapped in bacon bulleted the wall.

He tried to scramble up and keep running, but the guards had caught up to him. They weren't so accommodating this time; one jammed a knee into his back and threatened him with a Taser when he screamed, "Dr. Hyuck! Dr. Hyuck!"

A few men in tweed blazers gathered to watch as he was dragged away.

Three hours later, he was back at the PDX airport. He wasn't about to pay the fee for a flight change, and the cops promised not to charge him if he just got the hell out of their jurisdiction. He had broken his glasses and torn his jacket and lost four hundred and thirty-five dollars to Delta for nothing. So he decided he might as well get drunk.

Six tiny bottles of vodka and six hours later, he was on a plane roaring past the white fang of Denali and over the forested nowhere of central Alaska. He couldn't concentrate on reading or watching a movie. If he had worn a tie, he would have loosened it. He could feel the worry creases in his forehead aching from too much use. His tongue felt numb and his chest was slippery and warm. His window shade was open, but his eyes were unfocused, so the world unscrolling beneath the jet blurred.

He had lied to his family. He had told them he had an important meeting scheduled. Said scientists had finally agreed to review his findings. They wanted answers as much as he did and would likely name the new weather formation after him. The *Chuck* didn't really work, but *Bridges* sure did. The Bridges Paradox. Yes, it was pretty much a done deal. Maybe he'd even end up on the front page of the newspaper. It didn't feel like a lie, because he honestly believed it would happen.

Janey had always supported him. He had a tendency to get really passionate about something and then lose all interest and conviction. When he'd liquidated their assets into silver. When he'd signed up for courses at the U in economics, Mandarin, astrophysics, figure drawing, and creative writing, then dropped out of all of them halfway through the semester. When he'd bought books on coding and the equipment to build his own computer. When he'd rented a backhoe and dug a hole in their yard and begun construction on an apocalypse bunker he planned to pack with canned goods, propane tanks, water jugs. But lately she had grown more impatient with him and he knew that he was facing a week of stony silences and banishment to the couch. He deserved it. He was a big, dumb idiot. He was a—

He didn't know how to articulate it, but whenever the clouds gathered and the whispers issued from his headphones at the radio station, he felt . . . something. Something *electric* that couldn't be captured through audio or video. Like his nervous system was expanding outward from his body and wiring its sensors into the very air. This same sensation bothered him now.

He tried to stand up but his seat belt caught him. He twisted one way, then another, as if there were somewhere to go. Then he stilled and cocked his head and cupped a hand to his ear. Because he heard it—maybe spitting and hissing from the overhead speakers—a voice. The words too soft and ephemeral to catch.

"Do you hear that?" he said to no one in particular.

The man beside him had meaty thighs and wide knees that jammed into the seat in front of him. He wore an eye mask and a neck pillow, and he was snoring softly with his mouth open. Chuck reached for him to give a little nudge, but the whispers rose in volume and urgency and made him unclip his seat belt and spin around. A few curious and annoyed gazes flitted toward him, but most everyone else seemed to be lost in a book or a screen.

He ducked down as a chime sounded over his head. The seatbelt alert. The pilot's grainy, boxy voice followed, asking passengers take their seats and make sure their belts were fastened because there was a storm system up ahead that had the potential to cause some severe chop.

He slumped back into his seat, buckled his seat belt. His heart thudded in his chest. He must have simply heard some interference in the comm before the pilot's voice sounded—that was all. A flight attendant hurried by and he motioned to her. "One more?" he said and held up his plastic cup, a single ice cube rattling on its bottom.

"Sorry," she said. "We're supposed to buckle in, and we're not too far from our descent anyway. Enjoy that last sip."

He tipped back his head and knocked the cup against his mouth until the ice cube came loose. The medicinal residue of vodka was soaked into it. He leaned his head against the cool glass of his window and scrunched shut his eyes. A couple minutes of sleep would be a nice escape. A narcotic blackness.

The first rumble of turbulence hit the plane. A few nervous laughs sounded after the flight stabilized. Then a hard jolt made several people cry out and grab their armrests. The fuselage groaned and quaked. A baby wailed.

The sun was an hour from setting and the light outside was hazy, so it took Chuck a moment to feel certain of what he saw. "No," he said. "No!" The plane was shuddering its way into pulpy, swirling, bruise-shaped clouds lit with sudden cracks of lightning that made it appear as if the sky were opening up.

The pilot's voice came through the intercom again, but it was interrupted and unclear this time. "Don't," he seemed to say. "Look."

"Don't," Chuck said. "Don't, don't, don't."

The man next to him tore off his eye mask and studied him blearily. "What's your problem, buddy?"

The air suddenly tasted like hot cardboard. Chuck twisted the valve above him, trying for a fresh blast of oxygen, but his lungs felt like they couldn't fully fill. He closed the window shade and immediately opened it again.

Because there were shapes in the clouds. They were not like the giraffes or alligators a child might imagine in a puff of white. They were tentacles coiling and oozing throughout the black thunderheads. Here was a giant eye in a flickering ball of lightning. Here was a gaping mouth, miles wide, its breath powerful enough to make the plane tremble.

"Don't you see," Chuck said, tapping at the window with his finger.

He didn't wait for a response. He unclipped his belt and climbed over the man beside him and raced up the aisle. He tripped over a foot. An elbow knocked his thigh. He lurched into a seat, got up again. "We're going to die if you don't get us out of this system!" Chuck said when he finally arrived at the cockpit door. He pounded at it with his fists. "Do you hear me! We're all going to die!"

It was then that the cabin lights went dark. The plane banked hard before settling into a steady shuddering line. Everyone's cell phone lit up, and a scratchy static like the popping of an old vinyl record started to play from all of them. And the whispers began.

That's more or less what he tells the Port Authority cops in the interrogation room at the Fairbanks International Airport. There are two of them: a big Alaska Native guy with sleeve tats, a ponytail, and acne-scarred cheeks, and a short woman who chews gum like she hates it and has the kind of red hair that comes from a bottle. It is puffed up on top and clipped short along the ears and runs to her shoulders in back. His name is Ted-O and her name is Diane. They keep their arms crossed and their eyebrows raised.

"I just honestly don't know why you're treating me like a criminal. I told you before, I didn't do nothing wrong. In fact, I literally probably saved the lives of everyone on board that plane."

"Saved their lives, huh?" the red-haired one says.

"Yes."

When Diane speaks, he can smell the puff of mint from several feet away. "How exactly did that work?"

"The pilot changed his course. He listened to me. And here we are."

"Here we are, all right," Ted-O says. "You done?"

"I guess."

"Ain't you gonna ask for a lawyer or something?"

"Would I have to pay him?"

"Lawyers are rich, right? Reason for that."

"I was a prelaw major for a few months," Chuck says. "I think I'm perfectly capable of representing myself."

Diane pulls the gum from her mouth and sticks it to the underside of the table. "Do you know that flight-crew interference can come with a fine of up to two hundred and fifty thousand dollars and twenty years in prison?"

"Then," Ted-O says, "there's fines the FAA can hit you with."

"Plus you're probably going to be banned from Delta."

"My advice?" Ted-O says. "You plead temporary insanity." He poses the question to his partner: "Don't you think? Insanity? Temporary?"

"Temporary?" she says. "He's *still* acting crazy. When does the temporary end?"

"I'm not crazy," Chuck says.

"Said every crazy person ever."

"Flight-crew interference." Chuck straightens up and combs his beard with his fingers. "Is that what I'm being charged with?"

The Port Authority cops shrug their shoulders as one. "Up to the feds, man," Ted-O says.

2

There was a time when Theo would hold his father's hand when shopping at Big Ray's or the Bentley Mall. He would imitate his style, wearing cowboy boots with Hawaiian shirts. He would listen to the radio every morning when he ate his Froot Loops and mimic his father's voice when he transitioned into commercial breaks, saying, "Thanks for listening to the mighty roar of the Grizz, your source for classic rock!" He didn't question the existence of Bigfoot or UFOs for the same reason that he didn't question Santa Claus—if his father said it was true, then it must be. Because dads were giants; dads were gods.

But that was before. His whole world changed the summer he graduated from middle school; that's when puberty finally kicked into gear and he shot up six inches and gained fifty pounds of bone and muscle. Nobody recognizes Theo. Theo doesn't recognize Theo. And that dumb little kid who worshipped his father? He's the past. He's a ghost.

These days, at fourteen, a high-school freshman, Theo finds himself rolling his eyes and blowing sighs at everything his dad says and does. "Can you not call me *buddy*?" Theo says. "*Buddy* is such a weird, old-man word." And "Can you knock before you come in my room? I could be naked or something, and even if I'm not naked, it's weird. It's just weird having you barge in." And "Can I get an unlimited data plan already? Everybody else's got one." And "You have food in your beard. It's disgusting. Also, you have food in your teeth." And "Don't come to the door when you pick me up at my friend's house, okay? Just wait outside and text me." And "Don't ask if I have a girlfriend." And "Don't burp." And "Don't have sex with Mom when I'm in the house. I can hear you. It's revolting." And "Also, don't walk around without a shirt on. Also, don't ever, not ever, not in a million years, touch my phone."

Theo's Hawaiian shirts have been replaced by a camo coat and thrift-store vintage tees. He purged all Zeppelin and GNR from his phone and replaced them with Luke Combs and Drake. He scrapes his fork across his plate as quickly as possible, finishes his dinner, and asks to be excused so he can hide out in his room and get on-line with his friends to play Fortnite and Apex Legends. They no longer had family game nights or movie nights, and they no longer went on hikes or camped. Because Theo was busy with school or busy with his friends, which was another way of saying *not in the mood*. "I feel like we hardly see each other anymore, buddy," his father sometimes says. "I feel like I hardly know who you are." In response to which Theo can only shrug while thinking: *Good*.

He knew that everybody's parents were embarrassing. Jim Jim's dad rode around in a Buick with moose antlers anchored to the hood. Frannie's mom didn't have but three teeth in her mouth. The Ranson twins were always driving their drunk parents home from the bar. The Trachtenberg and Berdahl parents were always screwing each other and swapping houses. If Theo thought about it, just about everybody over forty was a total weirdo and disaster.

But there was something different about his father, even by the standards of Fairbanks, a place where you could live in a yurt or a school bus or a house made of welded-together shipping contain-ers and nobody would blink an eye. His loudness was the problem. People didn't like being told what to do or think around here. They kept to themselves. Even Theo knew that, and he couldn't even drive yet. Whether his father was on the radio or at the bar, his voice was always dialed up to eleven, and what he was broadcast-ing made people glance his way and shake their heads in pity or annoyance or judgment.

Now—Monday morning at Lathrop High—the other students are bending their eyes toward Theo and giving him that same look.

Because this weekend, all the gate agents and luggage handlers and janitors and Port Authority cops and TSA officers at Fairbanks International headed home, pulled up their chairs to the supper tables, and reported that crazy old Chuck Bridges had gone totally off his rocker on an inbound Delta flight. Some said he was drunk and some said he was high and some said he was completely sober. Some said he tried to bring down the plane. Some said he was convinced a goblin was clinging to the wing or that a flying saucer was going to beam them all up. Who knew with that guy? Port Authority tossed him in a holding cell, and federal charges were expected before EOD Monday. But really, they ought to pretzel him into a straitjacket and send him straight to the loony bin, right? Right.

Lathrop High is a series of rectangular slabs cored with long hallways, cinder-block walls painted white, and skinny windows that didn't let in enough light. The floors are a purple tile that grow filmy with salt in the winter. There are glass trophy cases celebrating the rifle and cross-country teams. Every classroom is a cold cube of fluorescent light with different posters tacked to the walls depending on the subject: Shakespeare, Einstein, Miles Davis, Thomas Jefferson, Frida Kahlo.

In first-period English, Mrs. King moves up and down the aisles during a quiz and gives his shoulder a squeeze when she passes him. He looks up at her, and she gives him a pinched smile and whispers, "Are you hanging in there?" In American History, after he takes his seat but before the bell rings, he hears somebody a few rows back saying, "He was trying to go full 9/11. Take out the whole downtown." In the restroom, he catches two kids staring at him in the mirror while he washes his hands, and when he says, "The hell are you looking at?" they race out without rinsing the soap from their knuckles.

As a young kid, Theo had always been big, but he was chubby. A-pack-of-Oreos-in-a-single-sitting kind of child who preferred an elastic waistband. Aside from a few clumsy attempts at baseball and soccer, he avoided sports. But now his body is in overdrive. Hair everywhere. Bad smells. Growing pains that make his bones feel like they are marrowed with lava. He drinks three gallons of milk a week. He hit six feet over the summer, and his mother guesses he has a few more inches in him before he tops out. He let his brown hair grow down to his shoulders. Girls have started smiling at him, talking to him between classes and in line at the cafeteria, but he isn't so good at talking back. His grandfather says he has the build of a grizzly bear. He doesn't really know what to do with all this extra body. Most of his time is spent slumped in a chair or staring at himself naked in his closet mirror.

But he finds a use for his size today. Fifth period. Phys ed. They're running the mile. For lunch, the cafeteria served meat loaf and mashed potatoes, and Theo made the mistake of returning for seconds, and now he feels like he's ready for a big hot puke and a long nap. He slogs along, his feet slapping the track, two laps down, two to go. The September sun brings sweat to his forehead that burns his eyes.

The teacher, Mr. Reuben, who also coaches the football and track teams claps his hands and yells bland encouragement from the sidelines. "Let's go, folks! You got this!" He is a box-shaped man who always wears a purple hoodie with the malamute mascot on his breast. He clutches a stopwatch and periodically calls out how much time has passed. "Five and thirty. Five and thirty, everybody. Go hard."

Maybe it's just the sweat blurring his vision, but Theo thinks he sees something. For just a moment. North of town, a chain of hills rises into the White Mountains, and a few gray, cottony clouds cluster there. As Theo takes a couple more lumbering steps, the clouds swirl and solidify into the shape of an eye. His gait stutters; he nearly trips. A few girls giggle as he rights himself, and by then, whatever he thought he saw has gone.

He worries a lot about genetic inheritance. Some sloppy puree of his parents makes him *him*—that's inarguable. He can't control his eye color (green, the same as his father's) or the quality of his fingernails (flat and brittle, like his mother's). Maybe he'll go bald. Maybe he'll get heartburn and precancerous moles. Maybe he'll unavoidably develop a number of their traits. But he's doing everything he can to avoid becoming their shadow otherwise. The crazy, especially. He doesn't want that wrinkle in his brain that carries his dad's breed of crazy. And yet here he is, seeing shit that shouldn't be seen.

Theo has twice been lapped by Chris Peters, one of those honor-roll kids whom parents and teachers love but who is actually secretly a giant dick. Student council, cross-country, choir, golf. Blond hair, white teeth, white sneakers, muscles tight as rubber bands, wearing the same smug smile every hour of the day. He crosses the finish line now—no doubt breezing in under six minutes—kicks the lactic acid out of his legs, paces around, and scoops up his water bottle and sprays some over his head before taking a sip. He watches the other runners pass him, offering up a few high fives and an occasional "Way to go." His eyes settle on Theo as he approaches, and something twists and lights up in his expression. "Junior terrorist here looks like he's moving in slow motion," he says.

Theo jogs five yards past him and stops running. He doesn't know what he plans on doing, but his body takes care of that decision for him. He spins around and charges and wrestles Chris into a hug, then he uses the momentum to swing the boy up, almost over his head, and slams him down on the grass.

Chris's eyes bulge, his face reddens, and his body goes rigid; from his mouth comes a choking sound. For a moment Theo worries he might have paralyzed him. But then the boy gasps and sucks air into his lungs, and Theo realizes he only knocked the wind out of him. Theo balls up his fists, waiting for a fight, but the boy curls into a ball, sputtering and blinking rapid-fire as if he can't quite focus on what Theo has become.

"Hey!" Mr. Reuben yells. "Hey, that's enough, you guys!" He sprints across the track and puts his body between the two of them and bellies Theo back a few steps.

Theo doesn't say he's sorry, but he holds up his hands to make it clear he's done.

"You going to live, Peters?" Mr. Reuben says to the fallen boy, but before he gets a response, he clamps a hand around Theo's right biceps and says, "You and me, let's go take a walk."

The runners keep circling, but many of them slow their pace and crook their necks, watching Mr. Reuben lead Theo to the center of the field. Here—out of earshot—the teacher lets him go and lowers his voice: "I heard what he said to you."

Theo doesn't know what to say to this, so he drops his eyes.

"I don't know what's going on with your old man, okay? He's obviously in trouble. But he's him and you're you. You can't let his shit get mixed up in yours. You gotta be your own man. Understand?"

"I guess." This isn't the way Theo expected the conversation to go.

Mr. Reuben clicks his tongue a few times and walks around him in a circle and gives him an assessing look. "You're quite the bruiser, aren't you? Picked Peters up like he was made of paper."

Theo's shoulders rise and fall in a shrug.

"What do you weigh? Two thirty? Two forty?"

"Don't own a scale."

"Why didn't I see you at football tryouts?"

"Don't know how to play."

"It ain't rocket science, I can assure you."

"Not really a sports guy."

"Then what kind of guy are you?"

He shrugged again.

"You know it's a good thing, being part of a team. You've got a support system. You make lifelong friends."

"I got friends."

"Yeah, I've seen your friends."

More and more students cross the finish line and stagger off to stretch or flop themselves on the grass. Mr. Reuben glances at the stopwatch and beeps it off and tucks it in his pocket. "You're probably going to be figuring some things out over the next few weeks, but I could sure use you as a lineman."

"Aren't you going to suspend me?"

Mr. Reuben has small eyes, made smaller now as his eyes pouch in consideration. "No, I don't think so. And if you sign up for the team, of course I'll be much more inclined to keep this between us." He slaps Theo on the shoulder. "Now, go on. Shower up. Get changed. I don't want you and Peters in the locker room at the same time. Not until you both cool off."

An hour later, Theo is seated in study hall, a paperback open before him. He's trying his best to read *The Talisman*, but the words keep crawling away from him; his mind is distracted. He tries to puzzle out the paragraph he's in the middle of—something about jumping between worlds—then flips back a page for context, then another page, then all the way to the beginning of the chapter.

He's still buzzing from what happened in gym. He's never been in a fight in his life, and it felt kind of amazing to completely own someone like that. Especially a perfect little bitch like Peters. Theo hasn't known power many times in his life. Maybe, if that sort of feeling is bottled up inside him and waiting for release, he *should* sign up for football and fuck some shit up. Fucking some shit up turns out to be fun.

High school was supposed to be a new beginning, and here he is, a month in, still hanging with the same dumb friends and play-ing the same dumb games and quoting the same dumb movies. *You gotta be your own man*, Mr. Reuben said, and that line keeps looping through his brain. Every now and then as his mother was reading a novel or watching a TV show, she'd say, "Now that's a good line," and go write it down in this leatherbound journal she called a commonplace book. If Theo had one, he'd put that *Gotta be your own man* shit on the first page. He even imagines it as a sweet tattoo in, like, a barbed-wire font, probably running around his biceps. And then, when he was playing football and slammed another player to the grass, he would stand up and flex the tattooed biceps—like, showcasing it—and Mr. Reuben would yell from the sidelines, *That's what I'm talking about!* Yeah. That would be pretty badass. He can almost see the white flash of the cheerleaders' panties when they did cartwheels celebrating his hugely important tackle.

Alaska doesn't have a baseball or football or basketball team of its own—not outside of the universities—so maybe that's why Theo doesn't care about sports. He knows plenty of people who cheer for the Seahawks (because they're the closest franchise) or the Braves (because they're always on TBS), but it just never clicked for him. The same as religion. He could watch a game or attend a service and make the same motions everybody else did without actually believing in any of it. Cheer here, pray there, "Hallelujah," "Great game," blah-blah.

But maybe that isn't fair. He's completely in love with all things Marvel and DC. He wishes he attended Hogwarts and lived in Middle Earth and piloted his own Millennium Falcon. He and his pals play Magic, Warhammer, Dungeons and Dragons. Sure, at a glance, the jocks and geeks seem like they belong to separate camps, but when you get right down to it, they're more or less the same. The people who love sports and the people who love sci-fi and fantasy both wear face paint and costumes and pretend themselves into heroes. Their day is ruined or made depending on whether their team—the Avengers or the Trailblazers—pulls off a win. They obsess over minutiae, trivia: This is the batting average of David Justice in 1994, and also did you know Wolverine made his first appearance in *The Incredible Hulk* no. 181? Fandom just means you want to be part of something bigger, and what's wrong with that? Because whatever you've got going on at home isn't nearly as exciting or high stakes as what might be inked on the page or projected on the screen, so you transport yourself elsewhere. He can get behind that. If his heart rate spikes when dwarfs battle goblins in a cave system beneath the mountains, he can't blame people for cheering when gladiators clash on the football field or basketball court. If he knows what a Beholder is and how to cast a healing spell, he can figure out when to blitz and the difference between a smashmouth and pistol offense. He can become a sports dude. Maybe he already is a sports dude? He should probably buy a jersey or something.

Really, it's his dad's fault that he doesn't already play football. That's something you're supposed to be exposed to growing up. The old man should have invited Theo into the backyard to work on his spirals. He should have tuned in to ESPN at dinner and shared stats off the sports page. Theo is missing an essential strand of American DNA thanks to his father, who is a constant and total disappointment and—

"Theo?"

The voice startles him to attention, makes him go rigid at his desk. The principal—Mrs. Carthright—is standing in the doorway. She—and everyone else in the room—is looking at him. "Can I speak to you a moment? In the hall?"

He shoves his book in his backpack and loops its strap over his shoulder and mazes his way through the desks. He figures Mr. Reuben decided to report him after all. Or someone from phys ed said something to somebody else and the news traveled down the halls and made its way to administration. Whatever brash certainty he felt a few minutes ago quickly deflates when he stands before Mrs. Carthright in the empty hall. He's a kid again. Just a stupid sucky kid.

She wears round owlish glasses and a fleece vest over a gray cotton dress. Her hair is wound in a long silver braid, and she smells like lavender soap. She says, "Theo . . ." and lets his name linger in the air between them. Adults always slow down their sentences when they want to pry out a confession or lay down the guilt.

"I'm sorry," he says, and he is. He's never been in a fight, and he's also never been so much as late for a class, so speaking to the principal shrinks him down to about two inches tall.

"Sorry?" She tips her head. "What do you have to be sorry for? I'm the one who's sorry."

"Wait." He readjusts his backpack and neatens his hair behind his ear. "What?"

"It's your father, Theo."

"What about him?"

"He's in trouble."

"I know he's in trouble. All anybody ever wants to do is tell me how he's in trouble."

"I mean his health. He's at the hospital now."

"No, he's in jail. Or airport jail. Whatever you call that. He gets these crazy ideas in his head sometimes and . . ." His voice slows and grows shaky. "Is he really in the hospital?"

Mrs. Carthright nods, her face creasing in sympathy. "Your mother is on her way to pick you up." She reaches out and cups his elbow with her palm. "I hope everything turns out for the best."

"But what's wrong with him?"

"That's unclear."

"You don't know or they don't know?"

"Nobody knows."

3

Rolf keeps forgetting he's old. His license might say he's seventy-one, but in his head, he's living somewhere in the neighborhood of forty-five. Time lies. Somebody wound the clock of the world wrong.

He should be able to spend a Saturday splitting a cord of wood without throwing out his back. Hell, he should be able to put on his shoes without sitting down and climb the stairs without running out of breath. And eat a cheeseburger with fried onions without worrying about heartburn and diarrhea. And enjoy a book without reading glasses perched on the end of his nose, for God's sake.

That's his predicament now. A few minutes ago, he climbed into bed with a mystery novel and a tumbler of bourbon, but he forgot his damn glasses. Rather than get out, he's squinting hard, holding the book at arm's length, then bringing it within a few inches of his eyes, trying to decipher the text. They printed things too small is the problem.

The landline rings. The bedside clock reads 11:32. His wife does not stir—her arms are folded across her chest and her eyes are covered with a pink frilly sleep mask—but she says, "Don't you answer that."

The phone rings again, its shrillness shivering the air.

"Don't you dare."

His eyes dart around the room with his thoughts. A fan wobbles overhead. A Terry Redlin print of a black Lab fetching a shot-down duck in a morning marsh hangs on the wall. A Pendleton blanket is folded on top of a pine chest. A spider spins a web in the horns of a deer mount. His holster lies on top of the bureau, and his uniform is draped over the back of a lacquered-log chair. The phone rings again.

"World's not going to come to an end," she says. "I can promise you that, Rolf Wagner. Either they'll give up or they'll leave a message on the machine. And then you can figure it out in the morning."

He's been planning on retiring as sheriff of North Star Borough, but he just can't quite make the announcement. For twenty years, he's been in charge of an area roughly the size of New Jersey, and if you think that sounds impossible, it is. There's the glad-handing at pancake fundraisers and salmon-fishing tournaments, and there's the politics of press conferences buttressed by microphoned podiums, and there's the ugliness of domestic disputes and car chases and overdoses and homicides that send him deep into the bush and directly into the concrete heart of Fairbanks. His phone never stops ringing and his e-mail never stops pinging. He's tired, but he's addicted to the tired.

Doreen knows it and she made him promise to shut off his cell at eleven every night now that his time is winding down. Mostly he's made good on that promise. But this caller is bugging them on their unlisted landline, and that's not something you can just ignore.

"What if it's the kids?" he says.

"It's not the kids. The kids call Sunday."

"What if it's an emergency that made them call?"

"They're fine. You let the machine do its job."

"What if it's work?"

"That's what this is really about," she says. "Work. You won't be fooling me with your kid-emergency nonsense."

"Well . . ." He rolls over, the bed shaking with his weight. He's staring at the phone as it rings once more.

"Rolf Wagner," she says.

He grunts at her and hooks the receiver in his hand and brings it to his ear. "Yeah?"

"Emily here." No *I'm sorry it's so late.* No *Hope I didn't wake you up.* A few decades ago, he and Emily Katoo worked as detectives for the city police, and they developed a shorthand they still share.

"What's the news?" he says.

"You ain't going to believe it."

"I don't know," he says. "I can believe a lot."

"And I'm telling you, you ain't going to believe it."

"That kind of lead-up, you better deliver. Where are you?"

"Downtown. Roof of the Westmark."

"Be there in fifteen," he says and drops the receiver into the cradle.

His wife pulls up her sleeping mask and eyes him blearily. "I told you it wasn't the kids."

"You were right." He swings his legs out of bed and hitches up his boxers. He gives his uniform a sniff before pulling on the shirt and snapping the buttons into place. "You're always right."

"You want me to put some coffee on?"

"Nah," he says. He yanks on his pants, struggling to balance on one foot, then the other, and fumbles with the holster. "You know me. I get wound up this time of night anyway. Second wind." He finds his hat and fits it on his head.

She pulls the mask back down and cozies her head into the pillow. "Tomorrow's going to hurt."

"Usually does," he says. He approaches her side of the bed and bends to give her a quick peck on the lips.

But there's nothing to kiss but the pillow.

A pillow that still smells like her rose-scented shampoo. Because even though he still talks to her daily—even though she still lives in his head—she's been dead six months. Time, once again, is a goddamn liar.

The late nights and full days have caught up to him. People probably assume he's a hundred fifty years old from the look of him. He's long and gray with a walrus mustache bending his mouth into a perpetual frown. His face is as wrinkled as a tissue pulled from a pocket. His systolic blood pressure regularly cranks up into the 170s despite the Losartan he pops every night before bed. His fingertips and teeth are stained yellow from all the cigarettes he burns through in a day. His left knee looks like a rotten cauliflower and clicks with every step.

Rolf imagines that if he peeled back his skin, he'd find, instead of nerves, tangles of frizzed-out fishing line with the barbs broken off the lures. Didn't used to be this way. Back in the day, you could have bottled up his blood and sold it as an energy drink. But he supposes you just get to a certain twilight hour in life when the easy chair beckons. His body is sure ready to quit, and his mind is right behind it. He can eat an entire meal without tasting it. Movies leave him feeling nothing more than mild amusement. Maybe that's what happens when a stroke kills your wife in her sleep. Or maybe that's what happens when you've been lied to and spit at, when you've shaken a million hands and cuffed a million wrists. He's pulled too many bodies out of lakes and crashed cars and burned trailers. There's been too much over too many years, and although he knows he's ready for a rest, he can't quite find the gumption to quit.

He understands the attraction of retirement. The only things occupying his mind would be a fly rod and a cold can of Coors. People could take care of themselves, and he would look after numero uno. Sounds nice. But it's possible he'd be miserable. Work is the only thing that gives him a reason to live. He can't remember the last time he felt wonder. He can't remember the last time he felt surprised or happy or anything, really, other than some constantly exhausted and headachy version of alive.

Tonight, though. Tonight might have dang near done it. After he takes the elevator to the eighth floor of the Westmark Hotel and climbs the service staircase to the roof, he can feel his pulse behind his eyes. He steps into the cool night air and says, "Well, isn't that the damnedest thing."

He logged ten years as a patrolman, twenty years as a detective, and he'd made a promise in his first campaign for sheriff that he would continue to actively work cases so he wouldn't forget what it meant to wear a badge. He didn't want to become a hornless moose, as he put it. He's stayed true to that promise. The papers and politics are the necessary focus of his days, but he still shows up at crime scenes at three a.m. to help deputies unspool crime tape, bag evidence, and interview witnesses.

Emily Katoo comes over to stand beside him. The night is cool enough that she wears a parka. She has a round moon of a face and short steel-colored hair. She doesn't say hello, just launches immediately into an update: Eagles apparently started congregating on the roof earlier today. Circling the sky, zooming past top-floor windows, squatting on the air-conditioning units like gargoyles. Folks assumed they were building a nest, given the hotel's closeness to the river. The manager sent up security to chase them off with a broom, and that's when they found it.

An elk. A dead elk. Six-by-six rack.

No floodlights have been set up. Forensics isn't bagging evidence. A few officers stand around with their hands on their hips, but nobody seems sure what to do. Emily watches Rolf circle the elk, pausing now and then to shake his head or poke at the carcass with his boot.

"What do you think?" she says.

"Don't know what to think."

"A prank? Teenagers? Disgruntled employee?"

"But how?"

She says, "Only way up is through the same staircase and service door we used. I imagine that's how."

"They got cameras at the entrance. I guess you can review the security footage. But . . ."

"But?" she says.

"But look at them horns. That's a good forty-inch spread. Don't go real neat through a doorway."

"No, it don't."

"And that's not even accounting for the animal itself. How much you figure he weighs?"

"Shot a big bull two winters back," she says. "Nine hundred and change."

"That's not something you transport whole."

"No, sir. You gut and quarter it where it lies."

"So to get a whole animal up here, you need seven, eight men—big men—doing the hauling."

"Or . . . there's the possibility the elk was still alive."

"Or it was still alive," he says. "Nice and tame, elk is. Just lead them on a leash or offer them a carrot, they'll do exactly what's said. Fetch. Sit. Roll over. Come up on the roof and die."

"I detect some sarcasm in your voice, Sheriff."

"You certainly do."

"There's no blood on the stairs, of course."

"Not that I saw, no."

He squats down—wincing at the firecracker pop in his knee—and examines the carcass further. "You seeing any bullet wounds?"

She shrugs. "Eagles."

The hide is torn and shredded in many places from their burrowing beaks, making it unclear whether the animal had ever been shot or stabbed. White gravel coats the roof and a bloodstain skirts the elk for a good two feet on either side of it. The darkness of the blood initially hides the fact that the gravel is collared up around the edges of the elk. He pokes at the berm. "Huh."

"*Huh* what?" Emily says.

"If I'm not mistaken . . ." He stands up and takes off his hat and looks up at the sky. "That's an impact crater."

"What are you saying?" She follows his gaze up. "You saying it fell?"

"I'm saying . . . what in the name of heaven, Emily? What in the goddamn name of heaven?"

They stand there in silence for a second or two. She says, "How you holding up? We haven't really spoken since the funeral."

He takes a moment to respond. "Let's not talk about that," he says. "Let's focus on the work."

4

Joanna Straub grew up on building sites. She could operate a backhoe before most of her friends learned how to drive. She got a new pair of steel-toed boots every Christmas. Wet concrete or hot tar splatters stained all her clothes. Her knees and palms were as callused as the soles of a child's feet after a shoeless summer. She started off playing on sites—scaffolding was her jungle gym, ten-ton concrete pipes were forts, rebar was a sword, and bulldozers were dragons. Later on, as a teenager, she joined work crews, learned how to frame and drywall and roof. She drove trucks, hauling loads of lumber, copper piping, dumpsters packed with debris. Electrical. Plumbing. Zoning. It all became second nature to her. She majored in business management at UA while working part-time as a supervisor. And eventually she oversaw, as a contractor, the construction of a Home Depot, a Walmart, a sawmill, an elementary school, a hotel, a housing subdivision called Eagle's Roost, and several dormitories and lecture halls for the UA.

Her uncle Harry Straub raised her. A lot of people refer to Alaska as the Island of Misfit Toys. It is a place for people who don't belong. It is a place people go to escape—from the law, the government, old debts, broken hearts, themselves. Sometimes when they show up here, they make a mess. Her family is a mess. Her mother didn't want to be a parent, and her father got a job working on an oil platform in the Caribbean and never came back. She has no memory of either. There was always only Uncle Harry.

He began North Pole Construction back in the eighties, and even when she was managing the day-to-day operations, he remained the face of the company. He closed the deals. He took the calls from the major clients. He hung out at the VFW and the Elks Lodge and accepted awards from the Rotary Club and sponsored three tables every December at the Greater Fairbanks Area Chamber of Commerce gala. Harry was only in his sixties, but his blood type was a stew of beer and ham gravy that clogged up his arteries and finally loosed a clot that knocked him flat with a major stroke. Now he spends his days drooling in front of the television over at the Frontier Nursing Home. So here she is—at thirty-three years old—running his business.

Her business. It's *her* business. She still hasn't wrapped her brain around that fact. A part of her can't help but feel like she's second in command even when she's the one signing the checks.

The way construction bids work, North Pole had a year and a half of jobs already on the docket when her uncle had a stroke. But since then—since she asked him what was wrong as he sputtered and gasped in a bowling alley parking lot and collapsed with a pop-eyed face redder than Mars—she hasn't been able to secure more than a handful of contracts. Clients never say why they're choosing to go with Callahan or Great Northwest instead of her, but she knows damn well the reason. When she pulls up to a lot, climbs out of her Dodge Ram, and offers her hand to shake, she sees it in their eyes. She's a woman. North Pole is a woman-owned construction company, and who in the hell ever heard of such a thing? Nobody in Fairbanks, where the good-ol'-boy network is alive and well.

All of her supervisors quit on her, so she scrambled to recruit others from Anchorage and the Lower 48. She is now starting to get desperate—laying off a dozen members of her crew, selling off a demolition crane, agreeing to renovation gigs that would have been beneath the company a few years ago.

The phone rings. At first she thinks it's a telemarketer or a crank call. There is silence followed by a click and a hazy, windy murmur. "Hello?" she says. Normally she would hang up, but the back of her neck prickles as if something electric has passed through the line. "Hello?" There is a soft chittering then, like the mandibles of many insects moving at once. "I'm going to hang up now."

But she doesn't. The line goes hollow, and a hissing pop sounds, as if a seal has broken. Then a voice begins talking. His name is Thaddeus Gunn, he tells her, and he has a proposal for her.

There is a razor-blade edge to the way he speaks, every word cleanly cut from the air and delivered to her. He sounds like graduate degrees and *Masterpiece Theatre* and C-SPAN congressional hearings. When he asks if she would sign an NDA before they continue their conversation, she says she has never heard of such an arrangement.

"The link should arrive any second," he says. "Refresh your inbox. Open the document. And sign."

"I gotta say, you're being a bit presumptuous, mister."

"There's no reason to pretend you're in charge," he says and again she feels that static charge to the air. The fillings in her teeth seem to be ringing. Her fingernails feel like they might curl back and fall off.

North Pole's offices are located in an industrial park at the edge of Fairbanks, and down a long hallway from the entry and showroom, she's sitting at her desk, and there is something about his voice that makes her feel like he already knows this. She spins the chair around as if he might be hiding among the rolls of blueprints, the messy stacks of permits and paint samples, the trash can overfull with empty soda bottles, the filing cabinet with a grease-stained tool belt on top of it. Then comes the *ding* from her desktop, indicating an e-mail.

"Is it there, Joanna?"

"Yes." There it is, at the top of the inbox, above messages from the housing authority, a building inspector, two electricians, and some spam advertising pills for erectile dysfunction. She wonders if this is one of those phishing schemes. Maybe the moment she clicks on the link, her computer will be owned by ransomware. She checks the address—it's .gov—and at a glance, it looks legit.

"How do I know you're not—"

"How do you know I'm not a scammer? A Russian or a Nigerian looking to pilfer your meager savings? I admire your caution. A quick Google search of my name should suffice."

She nudges the phone between her shoulder and ear and types in *Thaddeus Gunn*, and a series of articles unscroll before her. West Point– and Harvard-educated. A long history in the private sector and government. Frequent visits to the White House and Pentagon. The *Washington Post* believed he had been named to head a task force in the Department of Defense devoted to the geopolitical crisis brought on by the comet. There aren't many images of him, but the few that she sees do line up with his voice. He's short and soft and smug and buttoned into a three-piece suit. The search also turns up Reddit threads and magazine features reporting research outposts springing up throughout the world, including in northern Minnesota, the location of the richest omnimetal strike. Several anonymous sources have been cited in a *New York Times* article, but no one inside the government will respond to press queries. In one discussion forum, he is rumored to be dead. "Is what I'm reading true? Obviously it can't all be, but—"

"Sign the NDA, please, and we can continue our conversation." A slightly mocking tone bends his voice when he says, "Unless, of course, you're too busy . . ."

She clicks on the link and cringes, expecting the worst, but the screen doesn't go dark. Instead, a new window floats into view with a Department of Defense seal along the top and a long bulky block of text, beneath which is a box highlighted for her electronic signature.

"I'm afraid *I'm* the one who's terribly busy," he says, "so if you could please sign your name, we can move on with the business at hand."

"I don't even know what I'm reading." She tries to focus on the density of the language, but it feels equivalent to a new tool's fifty-page user manual or a new phone's terms of agreement. Her eyes never want to do the work.

"Ms. Straub?"

"Just a damn second, please," she says. A half-eaten Subway sandwich attracts a fly. Down the hall, at the front of the office, a door opens and closes. She can hear a dump truck *beep-beep-beep*ing in the lot outside as it backs up. "Fine. Whatever." She dashes out her name and clicks Done and flops back in her chair. "Tell me already."

"Very good," he says, and his voice seems to grow as large as a song sung in a cathedral.

She pulls the phone away from her ear.

"Ms. Straub?"

Slowly she returns the phone to her ear. "I'm here. You just sounded . . ."

"I just sounded what?" His voice is normal now, perfectly crisp.

"It must be a bad connection. You keep sounding weird." But it's more than that. A bad connection is an irritant. These spurts of whispers and megaphone loudness soak into her, make her guts twist with nausea. "Where are you calling from?"

"Someplace far away," he says, sounding vaguely amused, letting the words linger. "Now . . . I need you to build me something."

"Figured."

"This is a project that requires ambition, competence, and discretion."

"I'm listening."

"There is a plot of land," he says. "North of Fairbanks. Forty miles away, roughly. Five hundred acres in the foothills of the White Mountains."

"If you expect me to know the area you're talking about," she says, "know that Alaska is bigger than Texas, California, and Montana combined. People who don't live here forget that."

Her e-mail chimes again with another message from him. "I've pinged you the GPS coordinates."

She clicks on the link, and a satellite view of thick woods greens her monitor. A dotted fluorescent line indicates the boundary of the land.

"The Last Frontier, yes?" he says. "That's your state's motto."

"So says the license plate."

"Which is what makes Alaska the perfect location for a project such as ours. Because our world has gotten a little larger, stranger, and more exciting lately, wouldn't you say?"

"Because of the comet?"

"Just so."

"Hasn't really affected lives up here. It's just something we read about in the news."

"Oh, but skyfall had an impact on us all. It's affecting you right now in ways that you don't yet understand."

"If you say so. We kind of go our own way up here."

"Alaska has always been the edge of the map," he says. "Geographically but also spiritually. It's like the boundary that explorers could only guess at, writing in the margins *Hic sunt dracones.*"

"'Here there be dragons.'"

Surprise inflects his voice. "You speak Latin, Ms. Straub?"

"No, not really, but I got a fondness for the History Channel."

"Ah."

"So you're saying this project's got something to do with the comet?"

"Indeed."

"Why here?"

"That doesn't concern you. Blueprints concern you. Deadlines concern you. Moving dirt and hauling steel and punching nails into wood concern you."

"All right," she says. "So you've got this land. And you want me to build—what? Some facility?"

"That's one word for it."

"Well, that's going to be a heck of a job, all right," she says. "The roads that exist up that way—mostly loggers—aren't exactly accommodating."

"You'll take Highway Six to Country Road Two. From there, you'll turn off onto a Forest Service road that—"

"I got it open on the screen. I can see that."

"But what you *can't* see, Joanna, is the gated entrance or the fenced perimeter. Or the offshoot road that will need to be cleared of deadfall and fresh growth before it's regraded and graveled."

"So you're saying this isn't undeveloped land."

"Precisely. It needs to be *re*developed."

"You actually been there?"

"No. But I have camera feeds."

Back in the 1940s, he explains, a government lab was there. An atmospheric sciences lab. But the campus had been abandoned long ago.

"You've got surveillance going on a 1940s lab?" she says.

Here his voice grows big and echoey and warped. "There is nowhere that is not seen anymore."

"Okay," she says as if it were two words.

"You should assume, in this day and age, that you're *always* being watched."

Again her eyes flit about the room. This feels like a threat, but she decides to deflect it, make it a joke. "I always wondered what dumb-shit things my tax dollars were being spent on."

"Now you know."

"You talking teardown? Or a reconstruction? If this thing was built back in the forties, it's going to be in rough shape."

"No, no. Neither of the two. You can leave the old lab to the weeds and the owls. We'll be building fresh. There's plenty of space for an adjacent property."

She once again wanted to ask, *Why there of all places?* If Fairbanks was the middle of nowhere, that was the edge of nowhere. "I suppose the atmospherics—or whatever you call them—are better the farther you get from the light pollution and whatnot?" she says.

Some static again works its way across the line or maybe it is a little cough of impatience. "Nails and steel and wood, Ms. Straub. That is your concern. Now, I've just sent over the plans along with the pricing, and you'll—"

"I'm sorry," she says. "Mr. Gunn?"

"Dr. Gunn," he says, again with the little cough.

"Dr. Gunn, that's not exactly how this whole thing works."

"Oh? Please tell me how *this whole thing* works."

"You see, you tell us what you need, then our architect will draft some plans—or coordinate with whoever you got at the drawing table—and then we can talk about a bid. Everything's more expensive up here in Alaska, see. Whether it's a gallon of milk or a bag of concrete mix. So whatever you *think* is proper pricing—well, frankly, the Lower Forty-Eight's got no clue."

Her computer chimes again as a third e-mail pops into view. "As I was saying before you interrupted me," he says, "I've sent over the plans along with the pricing, and I believe the money will exceed your expectations."

"I—okay." She rolls her eyes and slaps her hand on the desk. "I guess I can take a look. What's your ideal date for breaking ground?"

"Construction will begin next week."

Now she stands up, nearly tipping over her chair. "Next week?"

"That is correct."

"I don't know who else you're talking to, but that's impossible."

"I am talking to no one else. Only you."

"Why me?"

"Because you need me as much as I need you."

To this she has no response.

"Now, please review the documents and respond within the hour. If you agree—and I have every expectation that you will—an associate of mine will arrive in Fairbanks shortly to oversee your progress."

"This associate got a name?"

Colonel Mason Purdin wears fatigues and boots polished to an obsidian shine. He keeps a gun holstered at his side. He stands with perfect posture, often with his hands clasped behind his back. But his age makes him look like he's wearing a Halloween costume. Joanna can't be sure how old he is, but if she were working the counter at a liquor store, she'd sure as hell ask for his ID.

He's waiting for her when she muscles the wheel of her Dodge up a steep, rutted grade of a Forest Service road. He stands beside an olive-green Humvee. He appears comically small beside it. She parks beside him and yanks the emergency brake.

Here the road ends at a rusted vine-choked gate. NO TRESPASSING, a gunshot sign reads. GOVERNMENT PROPERTY.

She climbs out of the truck and says, "Morning."

He makes a show of looking at his watch. "I thought we agreed on zero eight hundred."

"It's eight-oh-seven," she says.

"Exactly."

She fights the urge to say, *I'm sorry.* A few years ago her uncle told her she used the phrase too much. She ought to save the apologies for the moments that count. This isn't one of them. "Long drive and a rough road, but I'm excited to get to work."

His left cheek twitches. His eyes blink constantly. His neck carries a red splotchy rash from razor burn.

"I'm Joanna. You probably guessed that already." She sort of puts out a hand for a shake but then second-guesses the gesture and lamely waves instead. "What should I call you? Mason? Or—"

"Colonel Purdin," he says hurriedly. "Now, I'm not going to be here every minute of every day. I have a lot of very important responsibilities. So I think we need to establish expectations up front. Because we are on a tight schedule." He pulls in his jaw and strains his neck when he speaks, as if he's making an effort to lower his voice a few octaves.

She motions to the gate. "Let's get digging, then."

He nods. From his Humvee he withdraws an envelope. Out of it falls a set of tarnished brass keys. He approaches the gate and fits a key into the lock. Though the lock is stubborn with age, the metal teeth click into place. The gate swings open with a shriek. The road ahead is a mess of debris. Fallen trees, clumps of devil's club, knee-high grasses. No one has traveled this way for years. For decades.

She looks up and scans the fence line and spots the red eye of a camera blinking at her. It is stationed on a high metal post and angled down toward the entry. "Looks like somebody's keeping track of us." She gives it a two-finger salute. "Hi there, Dr. Gunn! Is that you, Big Brother?"

Mason—no, Colonel Purdin; she's going to have trouble with that—seems to find no humor in what she says.

"Hey, so every time I talk to your boss—" she begins.

"Dr. Gunn is my superior."

"Well, every time I talk to him, he sounds weird. Like he's got a terrible connection or something. What's with that?"

At this Colonel Purdin's cheek twitches again, but not in the beginning of a smile. He must have a tic. "Dr. Gunn's current position is privileged information."

"What? Is he, like, reporting from some bunker underneath a volcano or on a top secret satellite station in orbit or something?"

"Do you think this is a joke, Ms. Straub?"

"I—um—well, no. Just trying to, you know, lighten the mood a little."

"Because none of this is a joke. In fact, it is deadly serious."

"Right. Okay." In the distance she can hear the rumble of engines as her crew slowly catches up with her. "Here comes the cavalry," she says to him even as she wonders what the hell she's gotten herself into.

LOGBOOK: GEORGE C. WARNOK

ENTRY 3

November 17, 1942

I used to dress up as a soldier for Halloween. I would stage battles on the living-room floor with tin army men. The neighborhood boys and I would toss pine cones and pretend them into grenades and employ sticks as rifles.

Now a world war has come—and I am not where or who I dreamed I would be in these circumstances. Some days I feel I am looking in the wrong mirror.

The soil of Europe shakes with bombs, and the waters of the South Pacific foam with blood, but I am far, far away from all that madness, showered and rested and uniformed in spectacles and a starched white lab coat. A scientist, not a soldier.

There is not an hour that passes that I do not feel guilty about this. And this is a good thing, I've decided. Because guilt is a powerful motivator. The faster I do my work in the laboratory, the swifter our victory in the field—God willing, if all goes as planned.

It would be so easy to focus entirely on my research—to allow the walls of the lab to muffle the raging noise of the world—but I feel it is my obligation both to acknowledge my privilege and to suffer for it.

The newspapers arrive weeks or even months late here, but I read them with care, front page to funnies. I am not allowed off the grounds, so reading is my only way to travel. The *Times* has been publishing the names of dead Americans, and I have taken to cutting myself once for every dead soldier. It is my own way of acknowledging their sacrifice and reminding myself why I do what I do. My forearms and calves are bandaged thickly beneath my lab coat and trousers.

We are all fighting this war, and everyone is doing his or her part, whether it's rationing food or donating old tires, but I can't help but feel soft and spoiled in my current position.

My "battlefield" has no muddy trenches or tangles of barbed wire. My hands and belly are soft, and my skin is pale for want of sun. "Your mind is a weapon," I was told by Major General Tusk when I was first conscripted. "Put it to use—not just for our country, but for the world." Grand words and ambitions, but I hardly feel inspired by them anymore.

In the Great War—what was *supposed* to be the war to end all wars—my father fought under the command of Major Benjamin Berry at the Battle of Belleau Wood as part of the Third Battalion, Fifth Marines. He doesn't understand what I'm doing up here in Alaska, and because of the classified nature of my work, I'm unable to tell him.

A few months ago, when the Japanese bombed Fort Mears and the naval base, when they occupied the Aleutian Islands, he seemed thrilled that I was here. Alaska was suddenly important. He could justify to his friends at the Harvard Club why I was stationed all the way up in what he called "Timbuktu." He speculated that Hirohito was expanding his eastern defensive perimeter, and I was no doubt in the thick of it. *You show them what the Warnoks are made of,* he wrote. *Fight them into the sea until the waves roll over red.*

It's difficult to know what he considers currency in this war. If it is discomfort and the spectacle of battle, then I am impoverished.

If it is danger, well, I am rich beyond belief. But the threat I face is different than the kind posed by a bullet or bayonet.

There are thirty of us stationed here. Twenty of those are guards, fifteen are staff. Only five are scientists. We are a top secret operation running in tandem with Los Alamos. Theirs is known by the code name the Manhattan Project.

Ours is called the Alaska Project.

5

heo's mother has always called him a dreamer because of
the novels and movies and TV shows and video games he
seems to prefer over this gray reality. And because of his
tendency to stare out windows or space out during conversations
so she has to snap her fingers and say "Hey. Where did you go?"

Weekends, he sleeps twelve to fourteen hours a night, and his
dreams are so vivid he sometimes has trouble forgetting them,
and their details get mixed up with actual living. He has dreamed
of blizzards and felt surprised when he stepped outside and onto
a bare, browning lawn. He has dreamed of eating Froot Loops
and looked for the box that didn't exist in the cupboard. And
then there are the sexual dreams that tug at his mind constantly,
day and night, an erection throbbing to life whenever he thinks
about classmates or teachers or neighbors or really anyone with
breasts. He can't stop thinking about breasts. They are his passion.
Mrs. Fetero—his teacher for study hall—wears tight sweaters and
he spends an inordinate amount of time imagining her naked, so
when she says hello, he often blushes and stammers because he's
certain she knows about his breast-filled dreams as surely as if he
painted them on a wall.

But then there are the bad dreams too. The ones in which he
pretends himself into somebody tougher or meaner than he is.
Maybe he beats the living piss out of James McDonall, the student
council president. Or he slashes the tires of the brand-new Bronco
that fucker Tom Franklin in his Spanish 1 class drives. Or he

envisions his parents dead when they scold or discipline him. His mom will slip and fall in the shower. His dad will get in a car accident and fly through the windshield. He hates that his brain produces those kinds of images, but he can't seem to stop that machinery from grinding to life in his sleep when he's angry.

He knows it's stupid, but he can't help feeling that he's responsible, that he caused something to happen to his father. "What's wrong with him?" Theo asks his mother on the way to the hospital.

"I don't know."

"They must have told you something."

"I don't know, I don't know, I don't know." His mother drives a Subaru with a rusted-out carriage, and it creaks and moans with every turn as they hurry. The amount of salt the city dumps in the roads every winter—to fight the ice and the snow—rots cars from the rims up, and that's a little how his brain feels right now. Pitted with guilt, flaked with resentment, barely held together. His mother bumps a front wheel up and over a curb with a chirrup. She nearly runs a red light, slamming on the brakes at the last second. She almost nudges a motorcycle off the road when she changes lanes. "Mom," Theo keeps having to say. "Mom!" And then she corrects the steering wheel or clicks on her signal and says, "Sorry."

"Why is he such a disaster?" Theo says.

He knows her mind is elsewhere, worrying over what awaits them. "What?"

"Everything he does—it all goes wrong."

She glances back and forth between him and the road. "Why would you say that? Don't say that." She always gnaws on her fingernails, keeps them chewed down to clean half-moons with a nub of flesh on top, but now she's bitten them to blood. "Shit," she says, her index finger welling red. "Can you see if there's a napkin or something in the console?"

Theo digs through the pens and tampons, a wrinkled copy of *People*, a dusty surgical mask, some broken sunglasses, and finds some old napkins from McDonald's. "Thanks." She mummies her finger with it.

A concrete-gray slab of clouds rolls over Fairbanks as they pull into the hospital parking lot. She rips out the keys, reaches for the door handle, and pauses.

"What?" Theo says, unclipping his seat belt. "Shouldn't we go in?"

"In a second."

"What?"

"I know things have been tense between you and your father."

"You guys aren't exactly getting along either."

"But I love him and I've stuck with him." She reaches for his hand, but he pulls it away. "That's what you do with family." She snaps her fingers and makes a grabby motion with her hand. "Are you really not going to let me hold your hand? Stop being such a teenager."

He flops his hand toward her and she squeezes it so tightly, one of his knuckles pops. "Look. I get all that. But—why does he have to be so weird?"

"Is he any weirder than Jeff Parker down the block? That guy washes his car every day and mows his lawn three times a week."

"Yes. He is, actually. Because Jeff Parker isn't getting arrested."

"We know plenty of people who have been arrested. Half this town has probably been arrested."

"Not on federal charges. Not for something like this."

"Theo."

"Do you realize how embarrassing this all is?" His voice cracks with emotion. "I am embarrassed. I am ashamed of him." It felt at once horrible and great to say.

"Theo . . . no."

"I know that's terrible and wrong of me or whatever, but it's true."

"Stop. You've got to stick with family. Always. Always."

"Okay. Great. Can I have my hand back now?"

She releases him, and he opens his door and steps out into the day. The air smells like exhaust and rotting leaves. "I'm sorry, but he sucks. This sucks. Everything sucks."

His mother gets out and studies him over the roof of the car. "Your father would take a bullet for you. I would take a bullet for you. You know I'm not exaggerating when I say that."

"I know." He gestures with his chin toward the big beige complex. "We should probably go in."

She tries to bite her thumbnail and gives up. "Everything's changing so fast."

"What?" He notices the tears slipping down his mother's cheeks. "Mom, jeez." He walks around the hood of the car but doesn't really know what to do. "Come on. We need to go."

She uses the bloodied napkin to dab her eyes. "You know, there was a time when we celebrated milestones with you. Like your first step. And your first word. And the first time you—I don't know—slept in a big-boy bed. But we don't celebrate that kind of stuff anymore. You know why? Because the milestones all suck now. That's what sucks. Your behavior. You stopped telling us things. You want to be in your room alone instead of with us. I mean, we knew all of this was coming, but that doesn't make it any easier."

He starts toward the hospital, then spins around, hurries to her, and gives her a crushing hug. She feels so small in his arms—not just smaller than she looks, but smaller than the mother who still exists in his head. "You're so big now," she says damply into the breast of his camo jacket. "My big boy."

"Hopefully he's okay," Theo says.

"Hopefully."

They start at the emergency department—that's where they were told he was—but the woman at the screening desk says Mr. Bridges has been transferred. She has a lipless slit of a mouth, and she seals it now rather than offering them more information.

"Transferred? Where?" Theo's mother asks. "Transferred why?"

"If you could hold on just a moment." She picks up the phone and punches a button and brings the receiver to her ear.

"Hello? I don't understand. I'm his wife." She grabs Theo by the sleeve and pulls him forward. "This is our son. We're family. We were told to come here. We're family, and you have to tell us."

"Hi," the woman says into the phone. "You said to call when Mr. Bridges's family arrived. Well, they're here. Mmm-hmm. You're welcome." She hangs up and gives them a pinched smile. "If you can wait over there, someone will be with you shortly."

They stand there for a moment, wavering. His mother seems ready to argue further, but then she turns in a circle and points at a few chairs lined up along the wall. "There?"

"Right over there, yes."

There is a television anchored to the wall tuned to CNN. Theo blinks and a wildfire is blazing. He blinks again and a hurricane swirls off the Gulf, sending storm surges that drown neighborhoods. Everything seems to be in peril. The waiting room is empty except for a couple in their eighties. Theo can't tell which of them is sick because they both look ready to call it quits.

Maybe a minute passes—maybe ten; everything feels sped up and slowed down in the limbo of not knowing. Maybe his father was transferred because he felt better. Or maybe he required a specialist in another wing. Or maybe his father is dead. Maybe *transferred* is just a nice way of saying his body is cooling on a slab in the morgue. Neither he nor his mother says any of this out loud, but of course she must be thinking the same thing. Theo wishes, more than anything, that he could take back what he said in the parking lot. He feels poisoned by the sense that he caused this.

An ambulance comes wailing up to the entry, flashing its red and blue lights. The rear doors swing open and a rolling gurney unfolds. The burly EMTs hoist it out and lock the legs into place. A tall man in a business suit is strapped to it. When they roll him through the automatic entry, his head lolls sideways—his eyes half closed and his mouth hanging open—and Theo sees something he can't quite process.

Just like that, the man's face tears away like a mask, revealing a flash of a skull. Or maybe that's the wrong way to put it. He's there one second and transparent the next, like somebody slid him through an X-ray filter. The flesh of his face returns, but just as quickly vanishes again, revealing a glossy collection of muscles and veins and nerves. His face returns, then the skull flares once again, and then something deeper reveals itself, sodden and wrinkled, the wet walnut of his brain—followed by the skin pinkening and packaging everything up. This happens in the space of an impossible second. And then the gurney passes by and punches through the swinging doors into the ER. Something like a thin stream of smoke or fog lingers in the air, the only indication that anything might have happened.

Theo stands up from his chair to follow.

"Where are you going?" his mother says.

He doesn't answer, but she doesn't care, because a doctor with a willowy build has entered the reception area. "Mrs. Bridges?" he says in a gentle voice, a voice meant to deliver bad news.

Theo leaves them behind. The double doors to the ER have windows in them, and he peers through. He hears the EMTs talking to the nurses about an erratic heartbeat and wild blood pressure variations. "He was talking to us at first but got real quiet about two minutes ago. Sounds like he's from out of town. Here on business. Collapsed in the middle of the hotel lobby." They say they hit him with aspirin and nitro. Had the monitor on him but he never needed the defibrillator. "I know you don't want to hear this," the EMT says, "but there's something else. I'm worried he's . . . like the other guy."

One of the nurses has purple braids pulled back in a ponytail. "The other guy?" she says.

"The one we brought in from the airport."

"No. Nuh-uh. No way and nohow," the nurse says and makes the sign of the cross. "I've had enough of this nonsense for one day."

That's when a figure walks through a far door. A man in military fatigues. He has a baby face, and he seems to be compensating for it by scowling darkly. His boots clap the floor. He exchanges a few unintelligible words with the medical crew. The nurses and EMTs step away from the gurney, and the officer pushes it down some far hallway.

Theo's face is pressed up against the window so tightly that his breath fogs it. His vision of the emergency room hazes over, but he doesn't wipe the glass clean because behind him, his mother continues to repeat the word "No" louder and louder until it becomes a keening and the doctor tries to comfort her with his gentle voice.

6

The car looks like any other car, and that is the point. A beige Buick sedan. Too boring to draw more than a glance, too worthless to steal. Dead bugs speckle the grille and cataract the windshield. The wheel wells and doors are faintly splattered with dirt from the long drive.

South of Fairbanks, the car follows a switchback road that zigzags through a dense black spruce forest. The car does not look like it belongs here, both because the road is too rough for a two-wheel drive and because the car moves with a slowness that makes it appear lost.

The trees open up into marshland. Here the car brakes, then moves forward, brakes, then moves forward. Finally it parks and the engine coughs off. Out of the car steps a woman. Short black hair with bangs, watchful eyes, a petite build hidden beneath a trim gray coat with a military cut and many pockets. Some fox sparrows flutter by, chirping, but otherwise she is alone. She offers only a passing glance to the last blooms of purple aster, the clusters of willows, and the thick wall of spruce before focusing her attention on a handheld GPS unit.

She doesn't bother closing the door to the car. She steps off the road and into the marsh. It is mostly dried up as summer fades into fall, but sudden puddles form around her shoes as she progresses through the clearing. There is a loamy smell to the air. On the screen, a location pings, pings, pings, giving off ripples of light like a stone tossed in a sunlit pond. She takes a few steps in the wrong direction and course-corrects before deciding she is in the right place.

She turns in a slow circle, studying the ground. She locates what looks like a fist-size puncture in the spongy matting of peat. She scuffs it experimentally with the toe of her boot. Some brown water burbles up. She kneels down and peels back the bog's matting like a damp carpet. Then she digs her hand into the muck below, scooping dirt and roots aside, searching. Her fingers close around something solid. And she withdraws, with some sucking difficulty, a transponder. She stands and wipes it clean as best she can. "Found you," she says, but her search has only begun.

A rumble sounds. She looks up. A jet cuts across the sky almost directly overhead, a white contrail scoring the blueness behind it.

When she rolls into Fairbanks an hour later, evening is coming. The sky is a dying violet, the streetlamps buzzing to life.

She does not stop at the Ramada or the DoubleTree or the Hampton Inn; she pulls into the lot of the Klondike Motel. The asphalt sparkles with glass where it isn't potholed. The sign advertises FREE HBO and AIR-CONDITIONING. There are two rusted-out trucks parked here, the lot's only occupants. She spots a grill. Lawn chairs. This is the sort of place people stay long-term when they get kicked out of their homes by their spouses for drinking or cheating.

She locks the door with a bleep of the fob. Her boot heels click the pavement as she moves toward the front office.

A light buzzes on and off with the sizzle of bad wiring, but the man seated behind the front desk doesn't seem to mind. He wears an unbuttoned flannel with a mustard-stained T-shirt underneath. His hair is flattened on one side from being slept on. He sits on a stool and watches a countertop TV with rabbit-ears antenna. *Jeopardy!* is playing when the woman pushes through the glass door.

"Who is Amelia Earhart?" she says.

The clerk's eyes drift toward her and his shaggy eyebrows raise. "What's that?"

"Who is Amelia Earhart?" one of the contestants says, then moves on to the next category, taking Shipwrecks for four hundred.

"Oh, the TV," he says and lowers the volume. "Are you interested in a room?"

"I assume you'll accept cash."

"All cash, no questions." He flips open a binder, snatches up a pen, and pauses it over the paper. "But . . . you sure you want to stay here?"

"I'm sure, yes."

"Because," he says and clears his throat and adjusts his glasses. "Well, hope you don't mind me saying, but you just don't look like the standard clientele."

"How much a night?"

He looks toward the parking lot and finds her sedan and scratches his whiskered cheek. "Fifty." Then he takes in the sight of her again and corrects himself: "Sixty."

She unbuttons one of her coat pockets and withdraws four hundred-dollar bills and lays them neatly on the counter. "Let's say this will cover the week."

He scoops up the bills and disappears them into a drawer. "Let's say sure." He picks up the pen again. "What name should I put down? Because I gotta put down something."

"Then put down . . . Ripley, Tonya."

"Ripley don't sound Chinese to me," he says with a chuckle as he scratches down the name.

She tips her head up and narrows her eyes. "And what makes you think I'm Chinese?"

He doesn't chuckle so much as let out a long vowel of nothing. "Well, I don't know what you are, but you're *something*."

The overhead light buzzes off. She reaches into a different coat pocket and her hand closes around something. But then the light buzzes back on and she reconsiders.

"Every room's the same," he says. "Two twin beds. Hope that suits you." He tosses a key attached to a red plastic triangle embossed with the number 9 onto the counter. "And if you're up to any trouble in there, it better not come back to me. Or you're out. Capisce?"

She snatches up the key. "Capisce."

From her trunk, she removes a black roller suitcase and a silver briefcase. She scans the windows of the motel before walking to her room. The door opens with a moan. She flips the switch and an overhead lamp bottomed with dead bugs lights up. The air smells like ash and bug spray. The bedspread is a quilted brown, the carpet has cigarette burns and chewing gum mashed into it, and the popcorn ceiling is water-stained in the corner. A framed painting hangs crookedly above the bed. The glass is cracked, so it takes a second for her to recognize the moose feeding on duckweed at the edge of a pond.

She closes the door and bolts it. She pulls the luggage stand out of the empty closet and sets her suitcase on it. Then she goes to the TV and clicks it on and *Jeopardy!* fuzzes into view. She cranks up the volume as loud as it goes. She sets the silver briefcase on one bed, gets down on her knees, and peers under the other.

There is no dust ruffle. The floor beneath is clotted with dust bunnies. She spots a candy wrapper and a condom wrapper. She reaches into the second jacket pocket and removes a knife from it. Her thumb swivels out a six-inch serrated blade that locks into place. She stabs it into the gauzy underside of the box spring and slides the knife, forming a twenty-inch slit. She folds the knife away. She retrieves the silver briefcase from the bed behind her and nudges it into the gap. It vanishes into the guts of the box spring.

She heads to the bathroom next. Mold rimes the tile. The toilet tank drips. A frizzy nest of dental floss waits at the bottom of the garbage can. The varnish is worn off the knobs of the sink. She cranks on the hot water and unwraps a bar of soap as small as a chocolate mint and scrubs her hands and dries them on a white hand towel that's been washed so many times, it's gone gray.

She returns to the room and opens the black suitcase. She doesn't unpack the neatly folded clothes but unzips a compartment and removes a manila envelope from it. She shakes this out onto the bedspread, making a colorful mess of more than a dozen badges and licenses and passports, all featuring different names but the same photo of her. She picks up the one that reads DEPARTMENT OF TRANSPORTATION, flicks the plastic with her fingernail, and tucks it away in one of her many pockets.

7

You take care of yourself. That's a standard Rolf has known his whole life. It's ingrained in you as an Alaskan. You can't count on Triple A rescuing you off a snowbound highway, so you better carry chains, water, flares, and sleeping bags in your trunk. You can't count on the grid to stay lit through a blizzard, so you better have three cords of wood stacked and a gas-and-propane gennie on deck. Grow your own vegetables. Raise your own hens and collect the eggs. Know how to clean a rifle, patch your jeans, change your oil, sharpen the chain on your saw.

That's why he can't figure out why he agreed to this, what he's doing here. His kids insisted on it. They have a way of talking to him lately—like he's the child. *Have you been eating three squares? Are you getting enough sleep? Are you drinking too much? Did you change the sheets on the bed this week? When's the last time you visited the dentist?*

He knows they mean well, but it's demoralizing. He wiped their asses, and he's still the goddamned sheriff. A few months away from hanging it all up, but come on, now. Afford him some respect. He still has a bit of swinging dick yet.

He parks two blocks over. He doesn't want his car associated with this address, 232 Poplar. It looks like a house, and it is a house—a blue Cape Cod with wind chimes and Tibetan prayer flags dangling from the porch—but it's also an office. For Dr. Judith

Cleary. A woman with long silver hair, many scarves, and a flowing purple dress. Her glasses hang on a lariat of colored beads.

She greets him at the back door with a warm smile and a blast of air spiced with lavender incense. "Welcome," she says and motions for him to enter.

"Thanks," he says.

She might be younger than him by a few decades, but he can't help feeling like a student shyly walking into class and hoping the teacher doesn't yell at him. Normally he's the one in charge, big-bellying folks around, but right now he feels shrunk down, small enough to lose in a purse.

"Shoes off, please."

"Oh," he says and looks down at his scuffed Red Wings. "Sure. You bet."

He settles onto a bench and leans over his gut and puffs his breath as he fumbles free the laces. Nearby is a basketful of bedroom slippers of all sizes and colors, and she tells him to select a pair and make himself comfortable.

He doesn't own bedroom slippers. He has no desire to wear bedroom slippers. But when he removes his boots, he realizes that his big toe is fully revealed through a hole in the sock and he's a month overdue in clipping his horned yellow nails. So a pair of teal fuzzy slippers it is.

Her office is softly lit by a floor lamp and a lamp on her desk. A patterned tapestry hangs on one wall, a painting of an English garden on another. A chair is stationed opposite a couch. Between them is a shaggy white rug with a coffee table on it.

"Should I take the chair or the couch? Probably the couch. That's how this works, right? Couches."

"Would you like some coffee? Tea? Bottled water?"

"No, I'm—" The couch has more than six pillows on it, and at first he tries to simply flop down. "I'm fine." But there's not enough room, so he scoots one way, then another. "My wife, she always liked having a lot of pillows around." He shoves some of the pillows aside and stacks up the others, trying to make room for his bulk.

"Never done this before," he says. "I mean, I've sat on a couch before, obviously. But I've never done *this*. Not before now."

She is already seated in the chair, a leather notebook open in her lap. She wears many rings, and her pen looks like it's made of the same swirly stone as the bowling balls at the alley.

"Why are you here, Rolf?"

He opens and closes his hands. "You know why I'm here."

"I know your children set up the appointment."

"One of them's in Minneapolis. Another one's in Tacoma. They're far away. They want to make sure I'm all right. And they believe in . . . things."

"Things?"

"You know. *Things.* Organic food. Electric vehicles. Those kinds of things."

"You'd put me in the same category, then?"

"I don't know. Sure. This is all a little . . . outside my comfort zone."

"Woo-woo?"

"Woo-woo. Sure." He barks out a laugh. "Let's hold hands and sing around the campfire." The laugh turns into a cough and his mouth suddenly feels so dry. "Maybe I will take some of that coffee."

"Of course." She rises from the chair and goes to a small table with one of those single-serving coffeemakers on top of it. "Dark, medium, or light-bodied?"

"Dark, please. My wife liked it light and sweetened with loads of cream and sugar. But it's dark as dirt for me."

She pops in a pod, punches a button, places a mug on the plastic tray beneath the drip. "You keep referring to her as your wife. Instead of using her name."

"Doreen. Her name's Doreen."

"How does that feel? Sharing her name with me?"

"Well." He bites down on a corner of his mustache. "Feels a little raw, guess you could say."

"By saying *my wife,* you feel like you're distancing her from this?"

"Like I said, I never done this before."

The coffeemaker chugs to life. A mechanical groan is followed by a spluttering hiss as the mug fills. She brings it to him, trailing steam. "Doreen needs to be in here with us. For this to work."

His eyes rise over her shoulder to where his wife stands. She wears a gray sweater and blue jeans. She has her arms crossed and she's looking at him over the top of her glasses. The way she did when she was disappointed. "You're the doc, Doc."

Dr. Cleary settles back into her chair as he blows and sips on the coffee and makes contented noises. "You like it?"

"Got one of those machines at the station. They do an all-right job." He isn't looking at her, but he can feel her eyes on him. He decides to wait her out but gives up after a half a minute. "So how does this work?"

"We talk."

"And after the talking's done, I'm supposed to leave feeling better about myself? I'm supposed to not be as sad or something? That it?"

"I can't promise that, no."

"Or you just give me a happy pill? Something that makes me forget everything?"

"I'm not a psychiatrist; I can't prescribe drugs. I'm a therapist."

"Then what's the point of all this?"

She scratches a few notes with her pen and he leans forward and angles his head. "What are you writing down? That I'm a reluctant witness?"

She taps the pen tip on the paper, punctuating a sentence, and says, "Your children say that you're carrying on conversations with Doreen. That you see her everywhere."

Doreen takes a step closer to Dr. Cleary as if to announce herself.

"I knew I shouldn't have told them that." He sets the mug on the coffee table. "They caught me at a bad moment."

"It's perfectly normal."

"Talking to ghosts is normal?"

"Do you believe she's a ghost?" When he doesn't respond right away, she continues. "Do you believe in an afterlife? Do you believe there's something else besides . . ." And here she twirls the pen around in a circle, indicating the room, the house, the world.

It's always been hard to know what death means. Maybe it is darkness. Maybe it's light. Maybe you live permanently in the place you visit when you're dreaming. Or maybe you start over in this world—or another.

All he knows is, when you love somebody a long time, the two of you become one. You're in two places at once, sharing a heart and mind. And when that other person goes away, the second half of you starts to diffuse, to feel vacant.

His eyes jog back and forth between Dr. Cleary and Doreen. "I don't know what I believe. But I know what my kids think. This is a phantom-limb pain kind of deal. Arm gets cut off but the body still feels like it's there. That's where you come in, I guess. Telling me to get over it already, that I got no arm."

"Tell me about Doreen."

His wife inclines her head as if to say, *Yes. Tell her all about me.*

He wants to tell Dr. Cleary about the way they'd read novels to each other every night, passing the book back and forth every ten pages to keep their voices strong. He wants to tell Dr. Cleary about how much she liked board games and would whoop when she won and pout when she lost. He wants to tell Dr. Cleary about the time they went halibut fishing outside of Seward and a whale broke the surface of the water a few feet away from their boat and a big wave came rolling off it that soaked the deck. He wants to tell Dr. Cleary about the elk bourguignon she made every Bastille Day, an Alaskan take on the French recipe, and how they'd spend hours in the kitchen together, chopping vegetables, scrubbing potatoes, sampling the red wine they needed for that good, rich sauce. He wants to tell Dr. Cleary about how his wife played the piano, so now he always turns on the classical-music station in the car because it makes him feel like she's there with him. He wants to tell Dr. Cleary about how he woke up that last morning and reached for her hand and found it cold and already stiffening. There are a thousand things he wants to tell her, but it all feels stuck in his throat like a bunch of wet newspaper.

Doreen reaches out a hand and sets it on the back of Dr. Cleary's chair, and her skin is a purple-blue. Maybe he can smell a faint sweet rot in the air under all that lavender.

There is a box of tissues on the table. Dr. Cleary nudges it toward him, and he realizes his cheeks are hot and his eyes are brimming. He picks up the tissues. The store-bought cardboard container is tucked inside a fancier box, a wooden receptacle with an elk carved on it.

"What are you thinking?" Dr. Cleary says.

And all of a sudden this room dissolves and he's once again on the roof of the Westmark Hotel with Emily Katoo studying the dead carcass of the elk. He felt so alive then. So focused. So needed. So purposeful. There were mysteries to be solved in the world that were a hell of a lot more interesting than the troubles banging around in his head.

"Rolf?" she says.

"I'm thinking I got work to do." He sets the box down on the coffee table, heaves himself off the couch, and heads for the door. "You can keep your tissues, thanks very much."

LOGBOOK: GEORGE C. WARNOK

ENTRY 14

January 1, 1943

We walked outside—each of us toting a bottle of champagne—
and stared in wonder at the northern lights. They had come out
just for us, to give us a show for New Year's Eve. That's what we
said. We knew better, of course, as scientists, but scientists are
also humans, and humans can't help but believe they are the stars
of their own movie and not bit players in a vastly complicated and
infinite narrative. Anyway, we were drunk and happy and singing "Auld Lang Syne." Some of us wore pointy foil hats and blew
noisemakers. Wiggins had somehow dug up a boa he wore around
his neck.

Alaska was the tippy-top of the world, a summit that reached us
into space. And from that vantage, we believed with all our hearts
that surely, surely, there were other worlds than ours. A new year
awaited us. New discoveries too. There was magic in that drunken
night—but it was gone the next morning. The blistering headaches
and the fluorescent lights washed away all wonder. We returned to
the cold calculation of our work. Decimal points were more important than dreams.

Compared to the work at Los Alamos, our research is different in its approach but similar in its aim. We are focused on the atom, yes. We hope that science will win us the war, yes. We hope to unlock hidden powers and develop a new military arsenal, yes. Because, as hopeful as Roosevelt's rhetoric might be, there are those in this world who will respond only to force.

But Los Alamos hopes to split the atom. That is not our strategy. Our strategy is something else entirely.

We hope to *spin* the atom.

We are a long way from success. In fact, we are plagued by failures. But I trust in our work. I trust we will find a way.

An article from this morning's *Post*—or rather, last month's *Post* freshly delivered to our isolated laboratory—fascinated me. There was a diagram of a fighter plane with a series of dots on the wings and tail indicating damage from enemy fire. This data was culled from the eastern front by mechanics charged with repairing damage from antiaircraft fire. The military initially believed their engineers ought to work on reinforcing these damaged sections of the plane. But a Jewish Hungarian mathematician named Abraham Wald informed them their strategy was upside down. The damage they were calculating came from the data pools of planes that made it home. The military should instead reinforce the areas of the planes that had no markings at all, because *that* was what destroyed the flights that never made it home.

Wald referred to this logic error as *survivorship bias*. This is when you focus your research on what survived rather than what didn't.

I need to keep this in the forefront of my mind. Because even when the experiments fail, there are answers in those failures.

So that we might arm ourselves for a stronger future.

8

few days ago, in the common room at the Frontier Nursing Home, Joanna sat down with her uncle Harry. There was a big birdcage full of parakeets that fluttered and twittered, and their chairs were stationed side by side before it. His eyes vaguely followed the birds' bright shapes. He wore flannel bedroom slippers, sweatpants, and a Seattle Mariners hoodie. He didn't eat a lot anymore, so the fat and muscle had melted off his big body. Some drool glistened on his chin. He could say only one word: *bucket*.

"I got a job, Uncle Harry."

"Bucket."

"A big one. Government contract."

"Bucket."

"I'm going to do you proud, okay? I'm going to make sure North Pole keeps in the black. And when I win one of those Chamber of Commerce awards, I'm going to dedicate it to you, okay?"

"Bucket."

"But the next few months are going to be crazy, so I wanted to let you know you won't be seeing much of me, but it's for a good reason."

His hair was sticking up and she licked her thumb and tried to neaten it. But it slowly bent upright again. She leaned in and kissed his cheek. "Bye. Love you. You take care."

"Bucket."

Barely any time has passed since then, but it feels like a hundred years and a thousand miles ago. Because Joanna has been moving constantly ever since.

Chain saws buzz. Bulldozers rumble. Surveyors shout out readings as they mark off the perimeter and spray-paint the outlines into the dirt. *Clear this area, dig here, dump there. Set up the trailers. Set up the porta-potties. These are the specs on excavating, laying the concrete for the foundation, arranging the I-beams, and on and on. Put in an order for commercial-grade glass. Make sure the electricians are here in a week to bury new lines. Make sure the plumbers are here in two weeks when we drill the new well. Make sure the HVAC guys are here in four weeks for a consult when the foundation finally dries.* And so on. An endless list, a constant sprint. They're fifty miles from the city building a fifty-thousand-square-foot facility with winter not far enough away. Seven days a week, overtime as the norm, a rotating crew for day and night shifts—that's her life for the next few months. All hands on deck from here the hell on out.

She's not afraid of the work. What she's afraid of is a future where she runs her family's business into the ground and ends up picking up the scraps of the construction scene: working shitty remodels, kicking out mold-stained drywall, ripping up cat-piss-stinking carpet.

There will be complications—there are always complications: shipping delays, shitty weather, broken equipment—but if all goes relatively well, she'll net not only a few mil but also the respect of the industry for handling one of the biggest and most lucrative gigs Fairbanks has known.

Colonel Purdin. He's a complication as well. When he is on-site, he expects her full attention, but that's something she can't provide except in quick bursts, because when you're overseeing a project of this scope, the questions and commands are constant. *Sign here, dig that, move that, dump that, cut that, clean that, paint that, sand that, that, that, that.* A parade of distractions. The word *multitasking* doesn't begin to cover it. She is juggling a thousand flaming chain saws. Thankfully, the colonel is needed in Fairbanks as well, so she can do the work without his strict oversight. But he insisted on leaving several soldiers as guards.

"Guards?" she said. "We're in the middle of nowhere. Nobody's going to steal anything."

"It's not a point of negotiation. They will patrol the site twenty-four/seven. They'll be watching. And so will others." Here he motioned to one of several cameras mounted near the construction site. Their red lights blinked a steady rhythm.

She worried the guards would be in the way, pestering her with questions like Colonel Purdin, but she hardly notices them. The two soldiers spend most of their time standing like sentinels near the gate, checking everyone as they come and go, but a few minutes ago she spotted them marching through the site toward the un-explored back end of the property.

Phones barely work up here, so the crew is outfitted with walkie-talkies. Hers is chirping constantly at her belt as she hikes after the guards, curious where they're headed.

She's done her research. There are a number of privately and publicly funded labs in Alaska. The high altitude and steep latitude make the Arctic ideal for researching ecological and at-mospheric sciences, radiative processes, climate modeling, and biogeochemistry.

There are government facilities in Barrow, Oliktok Point, and Juneau. There are university labs in the areas surrounding An-chorage and Fairbanks. And all of the atmospheric sciences labs, she discovered, have controlled airspace above them.

That's the case with this Department of Defense facility. It's a no-fly zone. Maybe the designation was meant to protect the integrity of the research—the people who worked here were studying the sky, after all—or maybe it was to maintain secrecy. She suspects secrecy. This whole thing stinks of it: The NDAs. The refusal of Dr. Gunn and Colonel Purdin to answer any of her questions. No matter what she plugged in to the search engines, she came up with nothing but crumbs about what the campus might have been researching in the 1940s. The best leads were unverified rants on Reddit threads about top secret World War II labs scattered throughout the country.

Last week she called the Geophysical Institute at UA Fairbanks. She had taken a bio course with a Professor Butler there what felt like a thousand years ago, and she'd never really thought of him as anything other than a teacher. But much of his time was spent outside the classroom, she learned, at the Poker Flat Research Range.

"So you're studying the atmosphere and such?" she asked him over the phone. "Like, sky stuff?"

"Yes, including space weather." He had one of those voices that sounded like corduroy and beards.

"Space weather? Like moon hurricanes and Martian monsoons?"

He chuckled as he said, "It does sound a little made-up, doesn't it?"

He talked her through the lidar research that was his specialty. *Lidar* stood for "light detection and ranging." "It's a remote-sensing tool. It uses light—pulses of light—to measure various Earth systems. Most often it's used on the land or the sea to create infrared maps. But we use it on the sky."

"So your job is you shoot lasers into the sky?"

"That's a simplistic way of putting it, but yes."

"Isn't that dangerous? Shooting lasers?"

"Dangerous to whom?"

"I don't know. Makes me nervous when folks fire guns in the air on New Year's. I'm always worried when and where it's all going to come down. Guess the same goes for lasers. You're basically shotgunning energy into the heavens."

"I assure you it's perfectly safe. We aim at a target. We fire high-frequency blasts, thousands of them a second, then it's all reflected back to us with information."

"Information like what?"

"Oh, data about air molecules, aerosols, particulates—anything, really."

"So it's like looking into a really good mirror."

"Like a really good mirror of the sky, yes. A sky mirror."

"Why up here? Why Alaska?"

"Well," he said, "Antarctica would do just as nicely, but they don't have fast-food chains and movie theaters. We're a little more accessible here. A little more livable. But you've got to be near the poles. The poles are where change begins."

"The bad kind of changes, you mean? Beginning-of-the-end stuff? The way people are talking about where the planet's headed, it doesn't seem like we're going in the right direction."

"There's not a lot of good news to report, I'm afraid."

"So," she said. "Do you know about any research facilities in the White Mountains?"

"No," he said. "But you're welcome to visit Poker Flat anytime."

"What about old labs? Like from way back in the day?"

"How far back in the day?"

"The 1940s."

There was a beat of silence. "You know . . . I do remember hearing something, now that you mention it, about some World War Two research that took place in the mountains. But that's a dusty bit of information on a back shelf in my brain."

"Interesting. Okay. Any idea what kind of research they were doing?"

"I don't know. I'm sorry. But please, tell me—why are you asking?"

"Can't say."

"You mean you're not allowed to tell me?"

"That's correct. Lips are sealed."

"Well, now I'm intrigued. You said you're in construction. Are you . . . building something?"

She almost told him. Almost. But then she remembered the NDA she had signed. And the cold current of Thaddeus Gunn's voice. She studied the black screen of her computer and saw her reflection in it and felt suddenly seen. Observed. She said, "Thanks so much for your time, Professor Butler," and hung up.

Here's the thing she doesn't understand: the blueprints themselves. She knows next to nothing about laboratories and atmospheric sciences, but she does know something about buildings. And no matter how specialized they are, they all have a recognizable skeleton. Her uncle Harry said they were like people in that way. Doesn't matter if you have Cher here and Barack Obama there and Pee-Wee Herman over there. As unique as each might be, their bones and organs are all put together in roughly the same manner.

That isn't the case with this job. There are a few standard design elements, like a reception area and offices and bathrooms, but other than that, she feels like she's constructing something artistic or experimental. The arrangement as a whole looks like a giant door set on its side. There are superconducting electromagnets, vacuum seals, liquid-helium cooling coils, an omnimetal battery grid, and omnimetal antennas. She repeatedly asks for more information about what this thing is exactly, and she is repeatedly denied. She argues that she can do her job better if she's not working blind, and Dr. Gunn tells her, "You don't need to know about this facility any more than a pool builder needs to know how to swim."

All day, the clouds have swirled overhead, dimming the sun. The light grows weaker still as she follows the guards off the construction site and onto an old, rough road that cuts through the trees. Pine needles carpet the ground and hush her footsteps. The noise of trucks beeping and engines growling grows fainter. She steps over fallen logs, ducks under branches. The guards must be up ahead, but she's lost sight of them.

She's lived in Alaska her whole life, but she doesn't fish or hunt, rarely hikes, never camps. Work defines her. The wilderness has always been something to distantly appreciate or raze at a construction site. Wild places make her feel disoriented. There are no plumb-straight lines, so she can't quite blueprint nature in her head. She prefers the smell of hot tar to wildflowers, and she'll take a pile of sun-warmed lumber over a stand of shadowed pines any day.

Lichen clings to her hair. Some devil's club tears a gash in her jeans. A crow cackles in the sky and draws her eyes upward, where she notices something odd.

All of the old-growth trees here have fallen or are missing their tops. She supposes a straight-line wind might have ripped through the area decades ago. Younger pines and cedars grow upward through the old ruined forest. She remembers seeing a program about Mount Saint Helens, and the wilderness surrounding it after an eruption appeared much the same as this.

She's distracted by a structure in the near distance. The old lab. She would have noticed it much sooner except that the mold staining it and the vines engulfing it made it look like a veiny cliff with trees and shrubs crowning its top. It is the size of a big-box store but windowless and, other than a door, featureless, a wrecked concrete slab.

The two guards stand outside it. They are pointing at something in the doorway. She can hear their voices faintly. They enter the building and disappear from sight.

Her walkie-talkie bleeps to life. "Joanna? You copy?" This is her project supervisor, Bryce. "Joanna?"

She takes a moment before she unclips the device. "Yeah, I'm here."

"Here where?"

"I took a walk up the road to check out the old lab."

"And?"

"It looks like a haunted house. Maybe we'll have to explore it later."

"Later, sure. But right now, I need you. We just uncovered a big slab of basalt that's going to get in the way of leveling. Not sure if you want to dynamite it or if we can adjust the placement of the footprint."

"How far?"

"Shouldn't be more than thirty feet or so."

"Be right there." She takes one last look at the old lab and the fallen forest around it before starting back the way she came.

9

Her name is Sophie Chen but the motel guest book has her down as Tonya Ripley, and the Department of Transportation ID badge clipped to her chest reads BARBARA TURNER. Sometimes it's hard to keep track; the names are like cards she's shuffling behind her back, hunting for the right suit.

At the desk in her room, she sits before a laptop. On the screen, a Tor browser is open. In a dark-web chat room, she types—in Mandarin—that she has located the transponder along the flight path. No anomalies were detected on-site. She will proceed with the investigation as planned.

When she leaves her room, she hangs up the DO NOT DISTURB sign, locks the door, and checks the knob. This is midmorning, and the wild-haired, unshaven clerk stands outside sucking on a cigarette and staring at his phone.

He glances at her as she approaches her car. "How'd you sleep?" he says.

"I don't need housekeeping."

"That's not what I asked, but okay." He ducks his head and makes a funny little gesture with the cigarette, like a butler in an old movie inviting people into the ballroom. "You're the boss."

The airport is a ten-minute drive away. Fairbanks is the sort of city where everything is a ten-minute drive away. There will be surveillance cameras on-site, so she parks in an outlying lot and takes a shuttle. She wears sunglasses and carries a satchel. When the driver says, "You sure you didn't forget something?" she says, "I'm sure."

She gets dropped off at Arrivals but doesn't go in; she continues along the sidewalk a hundred yards or so to a two-story building the color of old, once-white socks that houses the TSA and Port Authority offices. Inside, a big guy with a ponytail and sleeve tats fills a cup with coffee. His blue shirt is untucked. It's difficult to tell if he's coming on or off a shift. "Help you?" he says, toasting her with the Styrofoam cup.

She flashes the badge, but he doesn't pay much attention to it. That's how it usually works with her. That's one of the reasons she runs point for her team on most of these operations: she slides past suspicion. "I'm here on behalf of the FAA." She tells him they've requested an investigation into Delta Flight 3469, Portland to Fairbanks, arriving two days ago.

"Your colleagues beat you to it."

"I'm sorry?" she says.

"There have been a lot of suits and even some military folks around here lately."

She tries not to stiffen. She tries to keep her smile steady. "May I ask who? I'd love to reach out, compare notes."

"I get all of you all mixed up." He squints as if he can see something materializing in the air. "What was it? Department of . . . Defense, I think."

"Are they here right now?" She tucks the badge away in a pocket and looks over her shoulder as if expecting someone to walk in behind her.

"Not now, nope. You got the place to yourself."

"That's a shame," she says and feels the muscles in her neck unbunching. "I would have loved to talk to them."

"They all wanted to know about the guy me and my partner brought in, about the flight, about what happened."

"Tell me more about this guy."

"Loony Tunes? He's gone. We shipped him off to the hospital in an ambulance."

"The hospital, huh? What happened?"

"Sick. I don't know. Heart attack, maybe. I'm no doctor."

"Remind me, what was his name again?"

"Hank Bridges. No!" He snaps his fingers. "Chuck Bridges."

"Chuck Bridges. You're sure?"

"Hank, Chuck. Middle-aged-guy names, right? But yeah, Chuck Bridges. Hundred percent. Guy went crazy during the flight and started talking about how they were all going to die and how there were faces in the clouds et cetera."

"Here's a strange question," she says. "Have you had any queries as to the whereabouts of any other passengers?"

"What do you mean?"

"Like, people calling and asking why somebody didn't show up for their scheduled arrival?"

"Don't know nothing about that."

"I'd like to examine that Delta plane if it's still here."

He takes a sip of the coffee and makes a face at its bitterness. "What's the plane got to do with anything?"

"No stone unturned, as they say."

"Huh." He doesn't care enough to question her further. "Well, okay, you're in luck. The thing shit the bed."

"Do you know what's wrong with it?"

"Just like I'm no doctor, I don't know nothing about planes. Electrical issue, maybe? Something. Mechanics have been bitching about it. It's in the maintenance hangar, but I suppose you already guessed that."

"Will you be so kind as to show me the way?"

There are three jets parked in the hangar. Some mechanics are busy taking apart the wing engine of an old regional plane that looks like it's held together with wire and duct tape. Their tools clink and echo in the vast space. A wind cuts through the open doors and chills the air.

When the Port Authority officer—Ted-O, he calls himself—introduces her to them and explains why she's there, the mechanics just wave distractedly and tell her to have at it. The 737 is in a state of undress; several plates are unscrewed and set aside, the underside of its jaw revealed.

"This is my lunch break, so I'm out," Ted-O says and shambles toward the exit. "Good luck with your whatever."

"You too," she says. "But Ted-O?"

He spins around but keeps walking backward. "Yeah?"

"One more favor. If you could drop by the Delta counter and pick me up the passenger manifest, I'd be indebted to you."

"Didn't you hear me? I'm on break, man!"

"I didn't want to mention it, Ted-O, but I'm going to have to pull rank on you. You don't have a choice."

He stops walking, holds up his arms as if to argue, then lets them fall. "But I'm on break!"

"It's a matter of national security."

This makes him straighten his spine and suck in his gut. "Fine."

There are rolling toolboxes and wheeled ladders scattered everywhere. She finds one of the taller ones and pushes it, creaking, across the oil-stained concrete until it aligns with the cabin door of the 737. She locks the brakes in place and climbs the steps. At the top, she pulls the handle up on the door and slides it to the left. There comes a stale gasp from inside the fuselage. It smells like hot cardboard and sweetly rotting garbage.

She steps into the shadowed hull. Some of the window shades are closed, others open. She removes a penlight from her pocket and snaps it on. Row by row, she sweeps the seats.

The plane hasn't been cleaned because it began registering irregularities before landing. There are napkins and newspapers and candy wrappers and half-drunk water bottles shoved into pockets or left on the seats. An abandoned set of headphones. A forgotten stuffed bear. A ball cap for the St. Paul Saints.

Row 8. Row 12. The beam of her flashlight pauses. She removes a quart-size Ziploc bag from her satchel, turns it inside out, and uses it as a glove to pick up something from the window seat. She seals the bag and holds it up to examine. Three teeth. Unbroken. All the way to the roots. One with a silver filling that gleams.

She uses a Sharpie to label the row and seat number on the bag.

Then she tucks it away and continues her search. She gathers eight more specimens. Sometimes it's unclear what she's found. One item looks like a dried worm on a sidewalk. Others are more obvious: a toenail, a finger bone, a glass eye, a pacemaker.

The deeper she travels into the plane, the more severe the rotting smell. Here, at row 24, she finds the source. She changes over to a gallon-size Ziploc bag. At first glance, it looks like a spoiled plum. Upon closer inspection, it turns out to be a kidney. She makes a note, tucks it away, and continues.

She briefly checks the toilets, then enters the attendant's station at the tail of the aircraft. She opens several cabinets before finding what she's looking for: A panel labeled FDR. She withdraws a multi-tool from her pocket and unfolds the screwdriver. With this, she removes the panel. Inside she finds the black box, which is neither black nor a box. It is a flame-orange container shaped like a small keg. FLIGHT RECORDER/DO NOT OPEN, the metal canister reads on its side.

"Gotcha," she says.

LOGBOOK: GEORGE C. WARNOK

ENTRY 24

May 3, 1943

In a way, living and working in this remote laboratory is an experience in sensory deprivation. I see the same people in the same place doing the same things every day. When that happens, you observe small things more closely, vividly. A colleague of mine, Wiggins, has a way of curling his upper lip that annoys me. The second stall of the second-story bathroom is the best one to use in the morning because the sun has warmed it through the window. My mattress chirps like a cardinal when I roll to my left. The boiled potatoes served in the cafeteria taste like they've been seasoned with chalk. I could go on with these slow, everyday observations.

I experience things more deeply. I marvel at things more readily. That includes the sky. I have made a habit of going out nearly every night, no matter how cold, to study it. It isn't merely the spectacle of it—the visual feast of all those burning pinpricks of light and the hazy sleeve of the Milky Way curdling the black. It is also . . . the humility I feel alongside the awe.

The brass tries to keep us motivated by constantly lauding our accomplishments. The exceptionalism of our team, the exceptionalism of our country. All that rah-rah jingoism you'd expect. But when I look at the night sky, when I take in the unguessable expanse of the stars . . . I feel the opposite. The sky counters any notion of American or even planetary exceptionalism. It reminds me I'm an irrelevant speck, which I find strangely soothing.

I've memorized the craters of the moon. I've learned to find all the planets and constellations. But the stillness of the sky always gets me thinking about a paradox. Given the infinite reach and uncountable age of the universe, there really *should* be life elsewhere. Not just others like us, but those who are well beyond our development. Whether they're airborne squids or intelligent algae or a single computer mind, I don't know.

But . . . where are they? Shouldn't the sky be teeming with as much life as the ocean is? It should.

That must mean one of two things: Something consumed them. Or they destroyed themselves.

I consider myself an optimistic person, but the longer we focus on the weaponization of the atom, the more I wonder . . . will the work we're doing here or in Los Alamos bring us closer to that same black fate?

10

◎

Theo's mother pulls into the garage and shifts the car into park but doesn't unbuckle or twist the key. She has the radio tuned to the Grizz. Her husband's station. His father's station. Chuck Bridges should be the DJ for this shift. They should be listening to the swaggering baritone of his voice. A rock anthem by Journey is playing. She turns the volume up and says to Theo in a bruised voice, "I just want to hear this. I just want to sit here a little longer."

"I'm going to go."

"Okay."

Theo leaves her there and hurries through the cloud of exhaust the car coughs out. There is a workbench against the wall where his father screwed around with old radios as a hobby. The bench is a mess of tools, wires, and radio equipment, an assortment of ham, solid state, and tubes. They used to play around here together, tuning in to stations around the world. His father would play Japanese jazz out of Tokyo and death metal out of Sweden. He would broadcast weather reports from Greenland, the rantings of a cult leader from South Africa, the synth and chimes and sitar of a New Age network in India. "There's a million other worlds out there," he would say, "if you just listen."

Theo pauses before the workspace for a moment, studying it like you would a tableau in a museum, then pushes through the door to the kitchen and bangs it shut behind him. He heads straight to his room and twists the lock. His whole body feels like a clenched fist.

His lungs are so tight, he can barely find his breath. He feels like if he doesn't do something, his bones might break with the tension. His eyes flit around the room. There are bookshelves overstacked with Wizards of the Coast fantasy novels. Posters of Batman and Wolverine and Han Solo. Pop-head figures from horror and Pixar movies. A plastic lightsaber. A Nintendo Switch. An Archie coffee mug packed with colored pencils. It all looks suddenly and incredibly stupid. Kid stuff.

He starts by pulling a book off a shelf and chucking it across the room. Then another, then another. Then he sweeps an arm across an entire shelf, and the paperbacks tumble with tearing flutters and meaty thumps. Then he pulls hard on his whole bookshelf and it slowly topples like a felled tree. He rips down his posters. He punches his pillow again, again, again, again, and swings it against the corner post of his bed so hard that the fabric punctures. Down feathers puff out of the gash. He tears the pillow open fully, gutting it, and feathers snow the air. He hoists up his bed frame and flips it. He snatches his lamp and smashes it against the wall; the light bulb shatters with a pop. He rips down the clothes in his closet and rips out the drawers in his bureau. He wheels about in a circle, looking for something else to destroy, then drives his fist into the door over and over, punching it until the knuckles on his right hand split open and blood smears the wood.

"Dad," he says. "You stupid fucking idiot. You stupid fucking— Dad, Dad, Dad. Goddamn it, Dad." He collapses into a heap, breathing raggedly. His pulse whines in his ears. Sweat soaks his armpits and forehead. But he doesn't cry. He scrunches his eyes shut, as if to keep away even the possibility of tears. Eventually his body stops shaking. He stands up, surveys the wreckage, and leaves the room.

His mother is coming in from the garage as he heads out the front door. "Where are you going?" she says.

"To see my friends," he says and walks into the afternoon gloom.

Just over a thousand kids attend Lathrop High, but Theo spends most of his time with two of them, Jackson and Little Head.

Jackson is stick-thin and wears shorts all winter. He has a faint unibrow and big dribbly eyes that make him look like he's always on the verge of crying, even though everything makes him happy. His dad is a Pacific Islander and jumps back and forth to Hawaii constantly to work on charter fishing vessels, and his mom manages a Ponderosa buffet sixty hours a week, so Jackson is a latchkey kid who always hangs out at other people's houses.

Little Head has a little head. His legs are long and hairy, and his shoulders are broad, but the skull screwed onto his neck is tiny, and he has a tiny face with bug eyes that make him look like his parts got mixed up in the factory bin. As an infant he was diagnosed with some rare cancer and given a 2 percent chance of making it, and after a thousand surgeries, he lived, but something went developmentally haywire and his skull didn't grow much bigger than it was when he was one.

If you didn't know Little Head, you might think he didn't have much in the way of brains, that he was a few neurons away from being a babbling drooler, but he's the smartest kid Theo knows. He doesn't have social media or a column in the school newspaper, but he nonetheless refers to himself as the king of hot takes. His voice is screechy and fast when he goes on a tear about why time-travel movies make no sense, why Reese's Peanut Butter Cups are the best candy, why Superman is unrelatable, and why Gandalf is a terrible wizard.

A familiar tirade involves the pizza cut into squares in the cafeteria. He believes square pizza to be an abomination for three reasons: (1) The crust is supposed to act as a handle. Like a burger or a hot dog, pizza is meant to be a casual, handheld food, but a gloppy square with cheese and sauce pouring off all sides means you need to eat it with a fork and knife. (2) Squares are far more difficult than triangles to quantify in terms of how much you have eaten, whereas everyone knows that two or three triangular slices of pizza is an ideal serving. And (3) Square pizza is aesthetically displeasing on a round plate. A triangular slice neatly arranges itself on a rounded plate, an echo of the full pie itself.

And don't get him started on werewolves. The dumbest monster, in his opinion. "What happens when a werewolf bites a wolf? What happens when a werewolf bites a guinea pig? What happens when a werewolf bites a goldfish? I mean, is the mythology like the xenomorphs in *Alien*? They change shape depending on their host? If so, that's cool. Awesome. I will watch the shit out of that movie with the wolf guinea pig and the wolf goldfish. But the fact that the mythos completely ignores this kind of super-important and obvious complication makes werewolves dumb. Vampires win. Immortal sexy life every time."

Theo kicks off his boots at Little Head's front door and as he goes down to the basement, he can hear his friend's voice buzzing like an angry bee. "It's absurd that they call rescue dogs *rescue dogs*, and it's even more absurd that people refer to them— proudly—as their rescues. 'Oh, this is my *rescue*,' they'll say. Or 'I was walking my *rescue* the other day,' they'll say. Give me a fucking break."

He and Jackson are sprawled out on beanbags in front of a seventy-inch TV that displays their split-screen play. Little Head's avatar is Yoda while Jackson plays Chewie. Their thumbs mash the controllers as storm troopers fall like dominoes all around them. "Did you swing across a pit of molten lava to get your *rescue* dog? Did you climb the staircase of a burning skyscraper to get your *rescue* dog? Did you fight off great white sharks to get your *rescue* dog? No? Then shut up with the rescue bullshit and stop acting so proud of yourself." More thumb-tapping. "*Rescue*, my ass. That dog is from the *pound*. It's branding, man. Branding and virtue-signaling from the bougies."

Neither of them glances Theo's way, their eyes sharp on the screen, but both say, "Hey," when he slinks down the final few stairs and plops onto the couch. Little Head is an only child, so the basement is his alone. The Bat-Cave, he calls it. His mother is a surgeon, and she is the only one who calls him by his name, Junius; and she dotes on and fusses over her Junius, buying him whatever he wants. There are three shelving units packed with DVDs, video games, comic books, board and role-playing games. Framed posters of the Lord of the Rings movies. A coffin-size aquarium darting with candy-colored fish. An unmade king-size bed and a couch with pen marks and spilled soda dirtying the arms. On his desk is a custom-built computer.

Normally Theo explores the space, picking things up and marveling at them, wishing he had a Switch, asking if he can borrow the latest issue of *X-Men*, but today he just feels numb. He stares at a half-eaten Pop-Tart on the floor as if it were the most interesting thing in the world, not wanting to talk to his friends but knowing he has to unload all these mixed-up feelings or else scream into a pillow.

Little Head seems to sense this. "Just let me kill one more guy," he says as Yoda leaps and spins and slashes his green lightsaber. "Just one more. Okay, two more. Maybe three more, and—" Here he pauses the game. "There. My Jedi bloodlust is satisfied. For now."

"Dude! Why are you stopping the game?" Jackson says.

Little Head stands and stretches his body into a big X and says through a yawn, "Because I need the hot goss. I want to know all about what happened in gym class between big fella here and Chris D-Bag Peters."

"Oh, shit. Oh, right," Jackson says, and he's smiling when he scooches his beanbag chair around to face Theo. "Did you get suspended? I can't believe you were in a fight."

"It wasn't really a fight."

"Look at his knuckles," Little Head says, and Jackson says, "Look at your knuckles!"

Theo holds up his hand. It shakes slightly. The blood has caked over. His fingers are red-streaked. The sleeve of his army coat is stained.

"Don't be getting your diseased blood all over my couch," Little Head says. "You have hep C and gonorrhea written all over you."

"I heard you pile-drived him, man!" Jackson says. "Did you pile-drive him?"

"I didn't pile-drive him."

Little Head says, "He didn't pile-drive him, idiot. Pile-driving is when you station the guy upside down between your thighs and drop his skull to the mat. By all accounts, what Theo did was more of a body slam."

"You were like the Undertaker," Jackson says and claps his hands. "You were like Stone Cold Steve Austin. You were all WWE and shit. That's awesome."

They don't know about his father. How would they? They're still living in another time—the time before—and he wishes he could join them there. He wishes right now didn't exist. "Guys . . . I don't want to talk about that." Every word feels as heavy as a boulder. It takes so much effort just to push out a full sentence.

"Then what do you want to talk about?" Little Head says.

"My dad," he says and puts a hand over his mouth as if to catch the words before they fall. But then he lets them go anyway. "My dad's dead."

They're smiling. They're waiting for the joke, and when it doesn't come, their mouths begin to tremble and fall open. "What?" Little Head says.

"Oh, shit," Jackson says. "Wait. Are you for real? He's dead? Like, *dead*-dead?"

"What are you talking about, Theo? Are you being serious? I can't tell if you're being serious or making some weird fucking joke."

Theo keeps waiting for the tears to come, but he's got nothing. Just numbness. Like his brain is buried in a snowdrift. Maybe a minute passes. Maybe an hour. "I'm being serious. And I need your help."

"Yeah, sure," Little Head says, his voice uncharacteristically quiet. "Anything."

"Anything," Jackson says. "Whatever you need, man."

"Your mom works at the hospital," Theo says, not a question.

"So?" Little Head says.

"What kind of access does she have to their security system?"

"Why?" Little Head says. "Why are you asking that?"

"You know how when you're a kid, adults think they can talk around you, and you won't notice what they're saying? They try to hide things, but they're bad at it."

"We're still kids, Theo," Jackson says.

"This is like that. There's something weird going on in Fairbanks. And the hospital is trying to hide it. And I want to see for myself what happened."

11

very October before the snow started flying, Rolf used to drive up into the foothills of the White Mountains with his pickup bed packed with rice, beans, and propane. He would dump everything in a faint driveway rutted into a fire-grass meadow surrounded by trees posted with sun-faded signs that read KEEP OUT and NO TRESPASSING and THIS HOME IS PROTECTED BY THE GOOD LORD AND A GUN. Then he would lay on the horn for a few seconds and drive off.

The Lavenders lived up there. Off the grid. A family of survivalists. Sometimes they sold elk meat or mushrooms and berries they'd foraged at the farmers' market, and sometimes they sold hides and antlers and doeskin gloves along the side of the highway, but mostly they kept to the woods. They poached. They didn't pay taxes. They didn't have a mailbox or any plumbing beyond a well crank or any electricity outside of a sputtery generator.

The land had originally belonged to one Samuel Lavender, a soldier stationed in Alaska during World War II when the territory was a lend-lease transfer station and the North Pacific stronghold for U.S. military forces. Samuel was from Alabama but he fell in love with the land and bought a fifty-acre parcel that he used for hunting trips. When he died, his son Moses inherited the acreage. He drove a school bus onto it, welded it together with a singlewide trailer, and set to work dropping trees to build a collection of cabins and outbuildings and treehouses linked by rope bridges.

The thing about Alaska was, people came here because they didn't fit in anywhere else. It was as far as you could retreat without falling off the edge of the world. You want to live off the grid or own a million guns or escape your ex-husband or reinvent yourself after quitting your job or serving ten years at San Quentin? Great. But do it quietly. Don't make a fuss and don't ask a lot of questions. People lived here because there were a lot of places to hide in the woods.

The first time Rolf visited—thirty years ago, back when he was a peach-cheeked deputy—he didn't make it ten paces from his squad car before a divot opened up in the ground close enough to him that the dirt sprayed his calves. The crack of gunfire followed. He had expected trouble. He didn't run. He didn't reach for his holster. He just yelled out, "Going to pretend that was an accident. Now, come on out, look me in the eye like a man, and let's have a conversation."

There was a rustle among the trees, and Moses stepped into the sunlit meadow. He had a mossy red beard that reached to his chest. He wore raw denim jeans and an elk-hide jacket. In his hands he held a rifle, but after a squint-eyed moment, he shouldered it. With a knuckle, he tapped one of the NO TRESPASSING signs. His voice was rusty as if from lack of use when he said, "Guess you can't read."

"I'm here about your daughter." One of the Lavender kids— Olivia, a girl with a dirt-smeared face, burrs in her hair, and a pair of patched-up overalls—had apparently been tempted out of the woods by the play equipment in someone's backyard. She'd kicked her legs on the swing with fearless abandon, going up so high that it seemed she might loop the chains over the top of the set. The homeowners approached her, but she jumped off and backed away. When one of them reached out and touched her on the shoulder, she bit his hand and ran off. They'd called Social Services, which was what led to Rolf paying the Lavenders a wellness-check visit.

Rolf explained all this while Moses watched him silently and finished by saying, "Now, if I go back without nothing to share except you threatening me with that thirty-aught, then I can promise you that before dark, you're going to have a whole swarm of badges up here."

"Then maybe you don't go back," Moses said. "Maybe you just disappear." He rubbed a hand along the stock of his rifle. He and Rolf were not that many years apart, but Moses's face was already deeply wrinkled from sun exposure, so it was hard to pin down his exact age. But he was clearly trying to mean-uncle Rolf away.

Rolf wasn't playing that game. "Genius plan," Rolf said, "if you want to go down like Ruby Ridge. Here's a less dumb idea: Maybe you convince me you're doing all right by your family and we part ways as pals."

"That sounds like a false promise made with a forked tongue."

"My uncle and aunt raised their kids on a sailboat traveling from port to port around the world. I know there's other ways of living than what most choose."

Moses worked his jaw as if testing a loose tooth. Then he whistled a two-noted song and his wife and kids came creeping out of the brush. There were five children altogether, all gingers like Moses, all long-haired, so it was difficult to tell boy from girl. None had birth certificates or Social Security numbers, but they could all read and write. They learned math from old textbooks and studied the Bible every evening. Their water came from a crank pump and a nearby pond-size spring. Nobody was malnourished; their bellies were full of nuts and venison and salmon. They farmed an acre-size garden and filled a root cellar they had dug into a hillside. They liked the old ways best, and they wanted to be left alone, and nowhere but Alaska could you get away with taking such a stand.

Occasionally Rolf stopped by to check in or to donate a rifle or a brick of ammo seized in a raid, and he dropped off a load of provisions each fall. Years passed. The Lavender kids eventually grew up and broke away and carved out their own lives. Moses's wife died of breast cancer she refused to let doctors treat, and he burned her body rather than let the wolves dig her up. Now the old man was up there alone, with three teeth in his head and probably a dozen words spoken in a calendar year.

Never, not once, had Moses asked anything of Rolf. But last week he'd called from a pay phone and left a message. Rolf could hear the rush of the traffic in the background when the old man said, in his rusted-out voice, "When you get a chance, better come up to the camp. There's been something funny going on up here in the woods. Something I don't quite believe." At that point, a semi blasted its horn and drowned out most of what he was saying, but Rolf picked up the word *elk*. Moses didn't give his name. He simply said, "You know who this is," and hung up.

In a normal time, maybe a week or two would have passed before Rolf followed up on such a call, but today, no sooner had he sat down at his desk and played the voice mail than he stood right back up and told his secretary he was leaving.

Her name was Aimee and she was a short round woman who taught Sunday school, wore sweatshirts with kittens on them, and brought baked goods to work. She looked up from her desk and said, "But you just got here."

"Don't I know it."

"What about your ten o'clock with the DA?"

"Reschedule."

"Well, aren't you going to tell me where you're going?"

He pulled on his leather jacket, the sleeves still warm from when he'd hung it up a few minutes ago. "Way up yonder to the Lavender camp."

"What's going on at the Lavender camp?"

"I aim to find out."

Sometimes when he was working a case, a detail would pop. And he'd know—he'd just know—the hunt was on. Maybe he zoomed in on a photo and nabbed an address off the collar tags. Maybe he isolated the background noise of a voice mail and caught the announcement of a bus leaving a station. He has that same focused feeling now as he rumbles out of Fairbanks and up into the foothills of the White Mountains. What happened on top of the Westmark Hotel and what's happening out at the Lavender camp—they're connected. He doesn't know how he knows, but he knows.

The road angles upward and a fogbank descends. At a distance it appears as a milky wave splashing down from the sky and seeping into the forest. Soon the tops of trees are no longer visible. Then wispy strands cling to the lower branches. Then the road itself becomes a soft mystery. He slows his speed to forty, then twenty-five, then ten. At one point, a big logging truck comes blasting down the mountain, there and gone in a roaring instant, but otherwise he encounters no traffic.

Long ago Moses told him to lay on the horn whenever he visited. "I don't like getting snuck up on," he said. In the meadow now, Rolf leans on the steering wheel, giving it a long honk, before stepping out into the clammy air.

He can't see more than twenty yards ahead. When he moves, the air moves with him, like stirred cobwebs. The fog does strange things to sound, making his crunching footsteps seem like somebody else's. "Moses!" he says. "Hey! Moses!"

The trees close around him. Their trunks are plastered with signs that flash in and out of sight as he continues forward: KEEP OUT, GO BACK, VIOLATORS WILL BE SHOT, NO TRESPASSING, NO TRESPASSING, NO TRESPASSING. The light glooms. A branch pops; a chipmunk chitters; a bird flits in and out of sight. Then everything hushes.

He says, "Moses," one more time but at barely more than a whisper. There is a chapel-like atmosphere that makes him slow and quiet his steps.

He can see the rusted school bus and trailer that were the original homestead. The windows have a dusty sheen and the wheels have long since rotted away like black socks. Beyond them another twenty yards he knows he'll find the full-scribe log cabin Moses built for his family. But in front of that there is a skinning rack from which Moses hangs his kills. Something dangles there—only faintly seen in the fog—like a cocoon.

Flies buzz. Rolf approaches and slowly makes out the doe. She is hung by a hook at the pelvic bone. She has been gutted; her torso flaps open. There is a dented metal bowl beneath her, catching the blood. A drop blips now, dimpling the surface. The skinning has just begun; the hide was peeled back to reveal the candy-slick muscle before the carcass was abandoned.

Rolf isn't fast enough to spin around when he hears a twig crunch behind him, and a bloody hand clamps down on his mouth. He tries to wrestle away, but Moses's voice is in his ear saying, "Shhh, shhh," like a hot wind.

When he speaks, his voice comes as a harsh whisper: "You need to be quiet. Or the clouds will hear you."

12

oanna will sleep on-site. Driving back and forth to Fairbanks every day makes no sense when she doesn't have any pets or kids to worry about. Just Uncle Harry, and he's well taken care of at the home. The lot is outfitted with generators and big spotlights tentacled with wires to accommodate work done at night. They even dragged in a mobile cell tower to help boost the spotty signal here because the e-mails and the calls are becoming a twenty-four-hour problem.

There are three trailers. One will serve as her home, the other as the office, and the third is for the guards. But for now, she appears to be alone.

Rain, which wasn't in the forecast, has driven the crew home. A few inches fell and the ground grew muddy and they couldn't accomplish much else without making a mess. She called Colonel Purdin with the news and he said, "That is unfortunate. There must be something you can do."

But there isn't, really. The area has been cleared, a massive hole half dug. Hopefully the walls of the foundation won't slope in. They need to get ready for the pour. Two weeks from now, once the concrete settles and everything gets framed, the work will be varied and nonstop, but for now, it's all about establishing the footprint.

She hasn't seen the guards since they entered the old facility. Their trailer is dark. She supposes they left for Fairbanks along with the construction crew and will return when work resumes.

Her trailer—a rental—smells like stale plastic and urine. Maybe it's because she got soaked earlier, but the air in here feels refrigerated. She rubs her hands together and cranks up the heat, and the catalytic heater ticks and brightens orange.

She hasn't yet unpacked, is living out of her duffel bag. She unzips it now and figures she might as well settle in. But when she opens the closet in the bedroom, she finds its shelves dotted with mouse shit. She goes to the kitchen and tears open a fresh package of paper towels and wets one and returns to sweep up the pellets.

She pauses and cocks her head as the radio turns on. The clock radio on her bedside table. A rock anthem plays through churning static on 93.3, the Grizz. She wonders if an old alarm got triggered, but the screen glows with a time—10:23—that hardly seems like something programmed.

She punches the radio off. But she hasn't gone two steps before it sounds again. Wailing guitar riffs. Distant drumbeats. She recognizes GNR, "November Rain," but the static is dominant, like churning water or whispering voices.

Slowly, she turns around. Slowly, she approaches the radio. Slowly, her finger depresses the radio button. Silence comes—except for a rain-pelleted gust outside that pecks the windows and makes the trailer shake.

She hesitates, her hand hovering an inch above the controls—and sure enough, the radio turns on and the noise returns. This time the music is even farther away and the hush of static dominates. The feeling like ants seething in her ears makes her hurry to yank the plug from the wall.

Right then a noise sounds in the kitchenette, where she left her cell phone plugged in on the table. A watery sizzling. Like a frying pan freshly laid with bacon. She looks behind her twice on the way down the hall. The phone screen offers nothing but a faint green glow. No ID on an incoming call, no inventory of apps. Just a cosmic light.

She picks it up and brings it to her ear and then pulls it back a few inches because the noise is too oppressive. "Hello?"

The connection cuts off.

She punches the Home button. Swipes the screen. Nothing. Beetle black. Unresponsive.

Another gust of wind shivers the trailer and the walls feel suddenly paper-thin and insubstantial. She glances at the window, and a pale face stares back. She jumps, then claps a hand over her mouth and laughs when she realizes she's seeing her reflection. She doesn't like the way the glass makes her feel spotlighted. She drops the blinds, clapping away the blackness of the night. She goes to pull the string on another set when she sees something. Beyond her own ghostly reflection. Out in the dark. A light.

Her Ram truck. A light glows inside it.

She doesn't know what to think. Maybe she carelessly left a dome light on or maybe there's some sort of electrical disturbance brought on by the storm. Or maybe something else. Something she can't wrap her mind around just yet. But she can't risk a dead battery. So she pulls on her boots and Carhartt jacket, snatches up a Maglite, and steps outside. Rain falls, but in a spitty way. The faint moisture seems to come from all directions, and the beam of her flashlight swirls with something like a mist. The air is chill, tinged with the smoky rot of fall.

The ground squishes and splats with every step as she trudges through the night. She swings the flashlight about, taking in the dark hulking shapes of heavy equipment, the messy pile of stumps and branches they need to burn, the gaping cavity of the foundation with streams of water pouring into it.

She doesn't know why she didn't park closer. The thirty yards she travels now feels like a mile, the way before and behind her lengthening with every step. She runs the yellow beam of her flashlight the length of a front end loader, pauses, and hurries it back to the cab. Because she saw something—she could swear she saw something—crouched on top of it, eyes glowing. Not the two eyes of a raven or a possum or whatever it is that might be casually perched up there but several eyes, too swiftly seen to count, seven or eight or more, glimmering like candle flames.

But now they're gone. She catches nothing more in the trembling reach of the flashlight beam except wisps of moisture. Some water seeps through the sole of her left boot and coldly dampens her sock and she realizes she's standing in a puddle. She hurries on, feeling as though she's walking through a cloud.

The truck is close now, only ten paces away. She didn't leave the dome lamp on—that much is clear—so it must be the touch screen in the dash that's glowing. A swampy light greens the windows.

Something hits the ground behind her with a heavy slap, followed by a quick *smack-smack-smack*—the mud sucking at what sounds like hurried footsteps. She doesn't bother spinning around. She just bolts. Rushes the truck.

One foot slides out beneath her, then she straightens her gait. Her fingers hook the handle and she jerks back and nearly knocks herself down. She can't hear anything over her own panting breath. She throws herself inside the cab and drags the door closed beside her and hits the locks. They fall with a collective *shunk*.

Nothing hits the door. Nothing tries the handle. Her breath and body heat immediately begin to fog the windows. The touch screen in the dash glows a digitized green. She punches the power button and it goes black. She grips the Maglite like a weapon. She pats the front pocket of her jeans, reassuring herself that the keys are there. She pushes the ignition button and the engine roars to life.

She doesn't have a plan beyond—what? Get away. Get away from what? This gooseflesh feeling, more than anything. She hasn't actually seen anything. But right now she can't imagine another second spent up here alone. So she puts the truck in reverse and that's when the touch screen lights up again, solidifying this time into an image broadcast from the backup cam.

She screams at what she sees.

13

At the Klondike Motel, Sophie sits in the car for a moment, listening to the engine tick. She habitually scans everyone and everything she encounters. In a second's pause, she'll account for twitchy eyes, ringed knuckles, a skull tat, the bulge of a shoulder holster. At this intersection, there is a cop in an unmarked vehicle, and in that park, there is a man pretending to be asleep. In this restaurant, there is a steak knife within reach and an ice caddy that could slicken the floor and a wine bottle that could double as a bludgeon and an exit through the kitchen. Her mind is ceaselessly running through an inventory of potential violence.

Here, in the motel parking lot, she surveys her surroundings. The day is overcast, the clouds low and gray-bellied with the possibility of rain. The traffic on the road is sparse. The security camera nested over the front office probably stopped functioning ten years ago. The curtains on all the room windows are drawn shut. And the same two vehicles from this morning remain in their spaces. One of them—a compact Toyota with all the letters but the YO painted over on the tailgate—must belong to the clerk. The other, a rust-scalloped Nissan pickup with a flat tire, appears to belong to the toothless man presently seated in a sunken lawn chair outside his room. He wears a stained canvas jacket with the hood pulled up over his bald head. A grill smokes beside him. With a fork, he pokes at several hot dogs.

The toothless man watches as she exits her car and crosses the lot and pulls her key from her pocket. "You want a hot dog? Got plenty," he says.

She doesn't bother responding. In any given day, anywhere from dozens to hundreds of people will try to steal your time. They'll push a flyer for a strip club into your hand, ring your doorbell and ask if you've been saved, beg for change on a street corner, send you an e-mail marked *urgent*, ask if you'd mind filling out a survey, holler that you're a sweet-looking thing, call you and offer you mortgage relief. Every one of them nibbles away at the clock and your mind. If words are currency, she gives nothing to the world that doesn't pay dividends immediately.

She opens her door and stands in the gray rectangle of light, studying the room: The paper cup of water on the nightstand. The nappy trail of worn carpeting that leads to the bathroom. The dust coating the bureau and television. The placement of her suitcase on the luggage rack and the location of the zipper slider—both wrong.

She enters the room, closes and locks the door. She checks to make sure the bathroom is empty. Only then does she kneel beside the bed and pull up the dust ruffle and reach beneath the box spring. Her hands search for a moment and then withdraw. She purses her mouth and narrows her eyes.

She stands from her crouch, neatens her hair, and marches to the door. Outside, the toothless man again asks her if she wants a hot dog. The coals of his grill burn orange. Smoke bends in the breeze. "Got plenty," he says again and spears a wiener with his fork, pinches a bite of it, and mushes it down with his gums when she walks past him and into the front office.

The clerk has his hands behind his head and his feet up on the counter. There is a tear in his shirt near the armpit that reveals a hairy yellowing strip of flesh. He wears flip-flops with his jeans. The television is on. A news program reports on the Pan-Asian Alliance that's currently being negotiated in Beijing.

"What can I do you for, little lady?" he says.

She doesn't bother with any sort of discussion. She walks around the desk. Out of her pocket she pulls a Taser. She jams it into his neck. There is a zapping sound. He flings up his arms and shudders and says, "Ack-ack-ack." The chair topples over and he goes with it.

She checks the window. The toothless man has not moved from his chair. He remains fully invested in his hot dogs.

The front office stinks suddenly of urine. The clerk has pissed himself. His eyes are unfocused. His breath comes in gasps. But he's beginning to stir, bending his knees, scuffing his feet back and forth, losing a flip-flop. A moan escapes him. She hits him again with the Taser, this time in the ribs. His body goes as rigid and humming as a baseball bat swung into a brick wall.

She tucks the Taser back in her pocket. She neatly arranges his hands above his head, then takes hold of his wrists and drags him into the storage area behind the desk. She closes the door. She yanks open drawers until she finds a roll of duct tape. With this, she binds together his ankles and then his thighs, wrapping them ten times over. His arms she twists behind his back and wraps those at the wrists. He's beginning to garble out curses at her, so she snaps a strip over his mouth as well. His nostrils flare and whistle with each breath.

She removes his wallet from his back pocket and notes that his name is Garry Pitcher. A wrinkled Social Security card is tucked behind a Discover credit card, a Walmart Visa, and an Applebee's rewards card.

An old desktop computer sits on a counter stacked with paperwork, skin magazines, and empty soda cans. She shakes the mouse and the screen awakens. She spends the next half an hour logging into all of his accounts—medical, financial, insurance, entertainment, even the porn sites he frequents. She sits in a rolling chair and when she spins around, she sees that Garry is watching her with bugged eyes and a red face colored by some combination of rage and fear.

She joins him on the floor, sitting cross-legged. "I'm going to take this gag off your mouth. When I do, you're not going to yell. Yelling won't accomplish anything except upsetting me. I dislike loud noises. No one will be able to hear you anyway. Do you understand?"

He blinks several times before nodding.

"Are you going to yell?"

He shakes his head no.

She grips the edge of the duct tape and rips it off, taking several tufts of facial hair with it. It's a struggle, she can tell, for him to keep his voice to a whimper. The duct tape remains attached to his cheek and flaps when he says, "What the fuck is wrong with you, man?"

"Let's talk about why you went into my room."

"I didn't go into no room."

"Oh? I think you did."

"Maybe I did. Just to drop off some fresh towels. It's motel policy."

"I don't like liars, Garry."

His tongue makes a crackling noise inside of his mouth as he debates what to say. "I didn't. I didn't take nothing."

She cocks her head. "You didn't take anything?"

"I didn't. I swear."

She returns the duct tape to his mouth, pressing it firmly in place despite his protestations as he tries to pull away. Then she reaches into one of her pockets, not for the Taser this time but for the multi tool. She slides it out of its leather case. She folds it open, brandishes the pliers. He tries to struggle away from her, but it's no use. She rolls him onto his belly and takes hold of his thumb with the tool and squeezes it until it damply crunches.

Garry lets out a scream, but the duct tape muffles it to a high-pitched whine. She waits maybe two minutes for him to settle down, then says, "I'm going to continue to hurt you. I can get pretty creative. Have you ever had a toenail peeled off? Or a cigarette put out in your eye? Or a clump of your pubic hair torn out? Things will only get worse from there. Do you understand?"

Tears leak from his eyes when he nods. She unpeels the duct tape again.

"Where is it?"

"I don't have it."

"Where is it?"

"Rhonda's. Rhonda's got it."

"Is Rhonda your wife?"

"Girl—" His voice trembles and cracks. "Girlfriend. She came by and took it over to the garage where she works. To see if she could open it up. We couldn't get it open."

"I hid it. And once you found it, you couldn't get it open."

"Yes."

"So you thought, *This must have something valuable inside.*"

He nodded in such a way his head seemed unhinged from his spine. "Yes!"

"And you were right."

He stops nodding and his lips tremble.

"That's why I'm going to get it back."

She explains then that she now controls his entire life. Not just physically, but digitally. "I know your name, your physical address, your IP address, your router number, your credit card and Social Security numbers, your prescriptions, all your passwords. And everything—all of it—has now been uplinked to a remote server operated by a colleague of mine. This colleague is very good at his job and not somebody you want to fuck with. You're being watched. And if you make one wrong move, something will happen. Maybe ten tons of kiddie porn will get downloaded to your hard drive. Maybe a SWAT team will arrive at your apartment at midnight and blow you to bits while you sleep. Who knows? Just like with these pliers," she says as she holds up the bloodied pincers of the multi-tool, "I can get pretty creative. In a matter of minutes, I can guarantee you'll be dead or in prison for the rest of your life."

He's doing a coughing-sob thing she finds irritating, but she lets it go on for a minute so that the dread sets in and he appreciates what she's about to offer him. "You can go to prison for the rest of your life, Garry. Or you can do *exactly* what I ask of you."

Sled Dog Auto Repair is two miles away, down an industrial road lined with rust-stained warehouses. Night has fallen. Streetlamps burn, the only light. The sky is moonless, starless, smothered with clouds. Sophie drives past the garage twice. The sign shows a sled dog pulling a crumpled, smoking car. The business closed an hour ago. Several cars are parked out front, but she guesses they're being worked on. She spots among them a crushed fender, a shattered windshield. In the side lot—which she assumes is reserved for the staff—she clocks a wrecker and an SUV with mismatched tires and a primer-gray door.

She parks two addresses over at an air-conditioning manufacturer and walks back through the weed-choked lots that separate them, keeping to the shadows. The collar of her jacket unzips into a hood that she uses to cowl her head.

The garage stalls are closed. The entry is locked. But through a door she can see a light is on in back. She circles the building and finds an open loading door near the dumpster.

Inside, the air smells of oil. There are shelves stacked with parts, tool benches busy with torque wrenches, socket wrenches, oil caddies, and grease-smeared rags. A truck with its hood open is parked in one stall. A car is hoisted up on a lift with all of its tires stripped. She steps around an air compressor, steps over a snaky tangle of extension cords.

In a side office, she finds Rhonda. Sophie checked out her social media accounts before coming. She's a square-shaped woman with a cap of salt-flecked hair. She wears work boots, jeans, and a hooded sweatshirt with a Harley-Davidson logo on the back. She likes moose hunting, chicken wings, Taylor Swift, and *Survivor*. The briefcase is open on a desk. There is no combo or key lock, only a small square keypad along the top with fingerprint recognition. Tools lie about—a hammer and chisel, a vise, a welding torch— and Rhonda has cracked her way inside. A silver-blue light pulses from the briefcase, haloing her.

Sophie approaches, but Rhonda either does not notice or does not care; all of her attention is focused on the light. Two paces away, Sophie scuffs her shoe against a screw and sends it skittering across the floor. Rhonda tips her head slightly. "We're closed," she says in a dreamy voice.

"I know," Sophie says.

She stands just behind the woman now. She has so many pockets in her coat, and she knows what is in each of them. Her hand closes around the grip of a pistol now.

"What do you think it is?" Rhonda says.

"The end of the world," Sophie says and fires a bullet into the back of Rhonda's head.

LOGBOOK: GEORGE C. WARNOK

ENTRY 33

July 26, 1943

I thought I knew everyone involved in the Alaska Project. How could I not? We are utterly isolated. Though we are but fifty miles from Fairbanks, we might as well be posted in Antarctica or on the moon.

But I saw someone new the other night.

Or maybe *night* is the wrong word. There is little darkness at this time of year. A kind of occlusion or gloaming occurs in the two hours after midnight. There is still light, but it's a special sort, as if you're seeing the world through a black veil. Everything softens and loses its detail, like in a dream.

I have difficulty sleeping. We are each assigned to what you might call dormitory accommodations. The walls are made of cinder blocks painted egg white. My small closet of a room has enough space for my single bed, a bureau with books on it, and not much else. Most of my time is spent working, so I don't necessarily require anything more in my living area, but things can get rather claustrophobic. That's why I like to get outside whenever possible to walk the grounds, take in the woods and the sky.

There is a small window in my room. I would normally appreciate the view, but the constant sunlight that pours through it is maddening to my circadian rhythm. A white metal rod is screwed above it from which a brown curtain hangs. The fabric is unfortunately thin, and though I've tried sealing its edges to the wall with masking tape, still the sun seeps through.

So sometimes I pace my room when I should be sleeping. And sometimes I go for a stroll outside. It's not that my mind is sharp and busy. I'm barely awake; I'm just not asleep. *Fogging*, you could call it. I am fogginess incarnate. Moving helps, somehow. My footsteps act like a metronome and I fall into a kind of walking slumber.

So maybe, because I was fogging, I shouldn't trust my eyes. But as I walked in circles around the compound, spiraling out, spiraling in, I happened to glance up, and I could swear I spotted a figure on the roof. It was a man. An old man with silver hair and a face cragged with age. He smoked a cigarette and puffed thick gray clouds from his mouth.

I barely registered this at first because, as I mentioned, my mind was running at half speed. But when I paused and angled my gaze upward once more, I found the space he had occupied a moment before empty.

I've been wondering about him ever since. Was he a figment of my imagination? A specter? Or—perhaps—a man among us I had never laid eyes on before? The last honestly seems the most unlikely.

*Note: As a follow-up, I mentioned the smoking man to some of my closer associates, such as Wiggins, this morning in the cafeteria. Several reported seeing him as well—down a hall, through a window. But none could identify him.

14

◎

n the basement, Theo, Jackson, and Little Head sit on the couch staring at the ceiling, listening. At four o'clock every Monday, Mrs. Castor goes for a jog with her friend Debbie. Their three-mile route ends with a cooldown walk followed by a glass of chardonnay at Debbie's. From the time Mrs. Castor leaves the house, the boys will have one hour. One hour to find and hack into her hospital laptop.

"This is our only shot," Little Head says. "If she's home, I can't go upstairs without immediately getting compromised. She always wants to, like, bake me cookies or play Monopoly or some shit." This is true. Mrs. Castor babies and worries over Little Head, and they know it's because she almost lost him. She thinks he could die at any moment. And for the first time, Theo understands that maybe she's right. Death has never been real to him until now.

Little Head holds up a finger as if testing the wind. "Wait. I think I hear . . ."

The footsteps thump down the staircase to the second floor. The soles of her sneakers squeak across the hardwood as she heads into the kitchen. A cupboard door creaks open. Glasses chime. The faucet hisses. She glugs a few swallows of water, then clicks the cup down in the sink. More footsteps, along with off-key humming. The front door creaks open and booms closed.

"Go," Little Head says, and they spring off the couch and charge out of the basement and up to the main floor. "Go, go, go."

"Where?" Theo says, wheeling one way, then another. "Where is it? Where do we even go?" His experience in Little Head's house has been limited to the kitchen and the basement. Everything else is a maze of cream-colored furniture, vanilla-smelling candles, dried flower arrangements, and abstract art that looks like a bunch of random shapes crushed into silver frames.

"Top floor," Little Head says as he uses the banister post to swing around and pound up the next flight of stairs.

"This is awesome," Jackson says.

Once on the top floor, they slow their movements and hush their voices. The hardwood gleams like honey. The light fixtures are the same silver as the picture frames. The light switches are all fat-buttoned with dimmers, and the outlets all feature USB ports. Theo marvels at everything as if he's in a showroom.

Jackson pauses before a framed black-and-white photograph of a round-cheeked baby with rolls of fat creasing its arms and thighs. "You used to be pretty cute, actually."

"Used to be? I'm *still* cute," Little Head says and enters the master bedroom. "She always keeps the laptop in her work bag. It's like a leather satchel kind of thing."

Theo pauses in the doorway. The bedroom is too much to take in. Here is a walk-in closet, a bathroom with a marble Jacuzzi tub, and floor-to-ceiling windows along one wall. A four-poster bed with an ivory duvet and too many pillows that makes Theo think with shame of the waterbed his parents sleep on that's heaped with quilts made of fabric scraps and a fleece blanket patterned with the Seahawks emblem. And then the shame gives way to sadness as he envisions the hollow spot in the pillow where his father's head will never lie again.

Something starts to well up inside him, but he chokes it down by thinking about Little Head's mother, Mrs. Castor. She's tall and athletic with bottle-blond hair that makes her look younger than her fifty-three years. She smells like she just rolled around in rose petals. Theo always has trouble looking her in the eye. Minutes ago, when she changed into her jogging outfit, she'd tossed her work clothes on the bed. Jackson rummages through them now. "Holy shit," he says and holds up a lacy white bra. "Look at this!"

Part of Theo wants to knock the bra from his hands and another part of him wants to stuff it in his pocket. Everything about his body feels so easily triggered these days. The way he can swing instantly to anger or glee, grief or lust—it's like living with constant whiplash. Everybody is constantly saying *Hormones* this, *Frontal lobe* that, *You're acting like a teenager,* and blah-blah-blah. He always wants to give them the middle finger. But maybe there's something to it. He thinks about the way he can gorge himself at lunch and feel bottomlessly hungry an hour later, the way he can wish death on his parents one minute and then feel horribly guilty about it the next, the way horniness can own him so wholly that once in the middle of math class, he had to ask for a hall pass to rub one out in the bathroom stall. It's like his body is trying to sabotage him. He knows he should be focused on figuring out what happened to his father, but for the moment all he can think about is Mrs. Castor's boobs.

Jackson holds the bra up to the light as if studying a gem. "This is awesome."

Little Head emerges from the walk-in closet. "Put that down, you disgusting perv," he says and hoists up a satchel. "Got the goods. Let's get to work."

But just then, downstairs, the front door swings open with a rattle and a creak—and the three boys go statue-still.

"What do we do?" Jackson whispers, his eyes so wide they bulge white.

"Maybe she forgot something," Little Head says. "Maybe she'll leave again."

"If she forgot something, it's probably up here," Jackson says. "We should hide. We should definitely hide."

He doesn't wait to see if the others will follow; he chucks the bra across the room and drops to the floor and rolls under the bed. Little Head sneaks back into the closet and draws the door closed behind him.

But Theo remains in place. He doesn't know what compels him—a wild gut feeling, like when he hoisted up Chris Peters and slammed him to the ground—but he starts toward the hall. He wills his ears to open more fully, to accept any and every sound, like an aperture on a camera starved for light. Because he could swear he can *almost* hear something. An oversound. Like that high-pitched tinnitus whine that's always in the background if you listen for it. This was softer, though. Like a constant hush of breeze or an endless whisper.

He creeps onto the landing. Cold air from outside pushes upstairs. His skin tightens. Another creak sounds below, what he assumes to be the hinges as the wind nudges the open door. Maybe no one is there after all. Maybe Mrs. Castor simply didn't pull the door closed fully when she left.

A few gray wisps rise from below, curling like smoke, and when he peeks over the banister, he sees their source. He sees that he is not alone. Fog or mist or a cloud—he doesn't even know what to call it—has poured into the house. Like a slow-motion wave, it splashes against the walls and froths up the stairs and eddies in the foyer. He can hear voices in it. And maybe—maybe—he can see faces.

Fifteen minutes later, they're back in the basement, and Theo is seated on the couch with his head in his hands, pressing at his temples as if he's trying to hold on to the memory of what happened.

He had screamed at the fog. He had thrown his body away from the banister and against the wall with such force that the baby picture of Little Head fell off its hook and shattered on the hardwood.

"I saw—I saw—I saw—I saw," Theo said when his friends came rushing out of the bedroom to see what was wrong. "I saw—I saw." That was all he could manage at first, because what did the rest of that sentence even look like? A ghost? Had he seen a ghost? He didn't have the vocabulary for it. The entryway was churning with fog and maybe there was an eye and maybe there was a mouth or a tentacle or, or, or—he doesn't fucking know. It wasn't solid but ever-shifting. A gray shimmer. A wave of cobwebs.

Little Head peered over the railing and said, "There's nothing."

"But I saw . . . I saw something."

Jackson hurried down the stairs and shut the door, clapping away the darkness. "Nothing."

Yes, fog clung to the lawn and frothed the air outside, but that wasn't so unusual with the temperature swings of fall and spring.

Somehow they helped Theo up and dragged him to the basement, Jackson offering up generic encouragements like "Let's go," "Come on," "You've got this," and "You've been through a lot."

They deposited him on the couch—and there he remains.

Jackson runs upstairs to fetch a glass of water and Little Head hovers over him uncertainly. Normally he speaks with machine-gun rapidity and aggression, but his voice is hesitant and softened by a weird sympathy when he says, "You know how when you look at clouds, you see shapes? You kind of bend them into whatever you want? Like there's a dragon or there's a train or whatever. Maybe this was like that. Your old man was seeing things in the clouds. You're really, really missing your old man, so you're seeing what he saw. It's like a sympathetic connection. That makes sense, right?"

"Clouds," Theo says.

"What's that?" Little Head says. "What did you say?"

Clouds. When Little Head mentioned clouds, it was like a lightning bolt ran through Theo's mind. The other thing people say about clouds is that your head is in them. Your head is in the clouds. That's what people had always said about his father. What does that expression even mean? That clouds are like dreams. Unreachable.

It's as if his father took the expression literally when he began his quest to prove a new cloud formation had repeatedly appeared over Fairbanks. He made a thousand phone calls, sent a thousand e-mails, ranted about it on the radio station, brought it up to strangers in the supermarket, even traveled to a meteorology conference in Portland to share whatever so-called research he had gathered. And now he was dead.

But maybe—it has never occurred to Theo until now—maybe he was also right. Maybe when your head is in the clouds, you actually have a higher vision. His father knew something was going on, and even though it sounds crazy to even consider, it's as if he's trying to share that with Theo now.

A glass of water comes into focus before him. Held by Jackson, who is a little out of breath with flushed cheeks. His hand is wet from hurrying the glass down the stairs.

"Thanks," Theo says, accepting the water.

"That's such a parent thing to do," Little Head says, "Parents are always pushing water on kids after they freak out. Why is that?"

"I don't know," Jackson says.

Little Head's voice starts to ramp up again to its normal volume and speed. "It's not like you ever say you're thirsty. If you say you're thirsty, they make you get the glass yourself. Instead it's like: 'I'm so disappointed I failed my bio test.' 'I'm so sad I'm going to miss Christmas at Grandma's because I have the flu.' 'I'm so pissed I can't get a PS Five for six months because it's on backorder.' You drop a few tears and I guess they think we're suddenly dehydrated? Or—wait—do you think it's because they slip something into the water? Like Benadryl? To calm us down?"

Theo, without really thinking about it, empties the glass with a chug and sets it down on the coffee table.

"That was the same glass Mrs. Castor drank out of," Jackson says. "I found it in the sink." A smile trembles on his lips as if he's afraid for it to form. "So you basically just made out with Mrs. Castor."

Little Head hits him on the shoulder. "You're sick and disgusting. You're like a future sex offender."

"You made out with Little Head's mom! That's awesome."

"Speaking of Mom." Little Head plops down on the couch and opens the laptop. "We now have approximately thirty minutes until she gets home." The screen lights up as the computer chugs to life. "Let's get hacking."

But Theo can only half tune in to the conversation and keystrokes that follow because his mind keeps rewinding to ten minutes ago, trying to find the right focus on what he saw in the open doorway.

15

When Joanna was a kid, Uncle Harry, to pass the time while they drove around town visiting construction sites, would tell her stories. A fifteen-minute chapter here, a five-minute scene there. The stories built over days, weeks, sometimes months, before he'd conclude them or pivot into a spin-off narrative. He had a big booming delivery and liked to vary his cadence and try out different voices for the characters, which he sometimes got mixed up—a squeaky child here, a rust-throated grandma there. He often gestured dramatically with his right hand while gripping the steering wheel with his left.

He never acted silly around any of the adults he worked with. He preferred a gruff voice, a businesslike attitude, a backslap, a handshake, a "Good job," "You betcha, consider it done," "Get your ass moving," "How much is this going to cost?" She liked that he shared a part of himself with her that he never showed others. He might have been a square-shaped guy with a weather-hardened face who always had a black fingernail and a canvas jacket and concrete splatters in his hair, but he could also be a big friendly teddy bear of a guy.

One of her favorite stories of his involved the Roof People. They were lost souls. The dead who didn't want to depart the Earth. Spirits who lived between worlds. They occupied the attics and roofs of houses, and they spent their existence studying us, sometimes kindly, sometimes cruelly. If you saw the pale hint of a face in the window or if you heard a thump in the ceiling, the Roof People were nearby.

Uncle Harry returned to the mythology often. Once he shared the tale of two brothers who grew up with a monstrous father, and when the elder died in an accident, his spirit lingered on the roof to watch after and guard his little brother. And then there was the story of the Roof People who discovered an attic cluttered with mannequins and trunks of old clothes, and they inhabited them and flopped about whenever the owners weren't home, pretending at life.

Joanna had always been fascinated by and terrified of the Roof People, and now a part of her wondered if Uncle Harry was already among them. His body might be alive, but his soul seemed absent. Maybe it was scrambling along some spire or gable.

What she sees in the video feed of her truck's backup camera is the kind of face she has always imagined for them. Monstrous but vaporous, like something spun from rotten clouds. A big face, like a bear's, with gray tendrils spilling out of its mouth. She couldn't quite focus, like she was trying to relive a nightmare that dissolved when you woke screaming in a cold sweat.

At the sight of the thing, she stomps on the accelerator. Her tires had sunk into the mud already, due to the heavy rain, and when she hits the gas, she only digs in farther, splattering a fan of mud, scooping out a divot that won't let her go. She yanks the gearshift between reverse and drive several times. She punches on the all-wheel drive. Nothing works. "Fuck, fuck, fuck," she says under her breath.

She swings her head around, checking the mirrors and windows. The dark offers her nothing except wisps of fog licking at the truck. She listens to the rumble of the engine and the splatter of the rain and the breath gusting from her mouth. She thinks about getting out and making a run for the trailer. But she can't find the courage. So she kills the engine and double-checks the locks on the doors and lies across the bench seat and curls up in her coat, and eventually exhaustion takes over and she falls into a fitful sleep.

She wakes to a tapping. She opens her eyes to the bleary gray light of morning. She tries to rise up, but her right arm is asleep and her back feels like it is barely held together with duct tape. She always bruises easily, and she can tell from the hot feeling on her hip—where the seat belt dug into her all night—a purple-black splotch will stain her skin.

She gives a one-eyed squint out the driver-side window. A figure stands there, but he's distorted by the foggy glass. Her breath during the night has warmed and dampened the cabin. Moisture dribbles down the glass.

At first she's certain it's Colonel Purdin, here to question and lecture her. But when she wipes her hand across the glass, in the smear stands Bryce Silva, her site supervisor. He's in his midthirties, solidly built. He's never without a baseball cap, so she's actually uncertain if he's bald or not. His eyes are as brown and moist as rain-soaked soil. He has a porcupine of a beard that makes it look like it would hurt to kiss him. She might have imagined doing exactly that on more than one occasion. Not that she has time for those kinds of complications.

"Hey," he says through the glass.

"Hey." She runs her hands quickly through her hair, neatening it as best she can. She fumbles for the handle and pushes open the door. He takes a few steps back, hopefully not for the smell. The inside of the truck must reek like a stale mouth.

"You okay?" he says

"Yeah." She tenderly scoots and swings her legs out over to the running boards, but she doesn't stand. Not yet. Every joint in her body feels mortared with hot ash. "Fine." She hopes her cheeks aren't reddening with the blush that sometimes afflicts her.

Rain isn't falling so much as misting; the air is full of fine particles that dew Bryce's beard and spot his jacket. "Looks like you're dug in," he says, motioning to the truck tires.

"Yeah. You'll have to pull me out. We can drag some sheets of plywood over here to help."

"You bet." Her eyes track the thermos of coffee in his hand. He notices. "You want some?"

"That's okay."

"If you slept in your truck, you're definitely needing some diesel." He unscrews the cap, pours it full, and hands it to her.

She takes it gratefully. "Thank you."

They both blow and sip at their steaming coffee for a minute. All the supervisors left when her uncle had the stroke. Bryce was the first person she hired, a recent transplant from Anchorage. She doesn't feel like she knows him, not outside of work, but on the job, he's been nothing but a pro. Never questioning her, always on top of the crew. She tries to come up with some sort of excuse for sleeping in her truck but in the end she's too tired to bother and she supposes she trusts him enough to be honest. "I know this is going to sound stupid, Bryce, but I got a little freaked out last night."

He cocks his head. "You see something?"

"I . . . I thought I did. But it all seems a little embarrassing now that it's morning."

"Don't be embarrassed."

"I am."

"What happened to the guards?"

"They went home with everybody else, I guess."

"But their rig is still here." Bryce sees the confusion on her face and points toward the entry, where the Humvee is parked.

"Huh. I haven't seen them since yesterday."

Bryce's truck is the only other one on-site.

"Joanna?" His eyebrows puzzle together. "What did you see?" He's always spoken and moved in a manner she initially mistook for slowness but has come to realize is actually gentleness. It's as if he's afraid he might crash into something and do harm or cause offense.

"I don't know. Maybe it was nothing."

"It's okay to share."

She lives in a neighborhood development. She works around a big crew of people every day. She isn't used to being alone in the dark in the wilderness. Probably she was just imagining things. Probably it was just the exhaust thickly curling from the tailpipe.

"I could have sworn it was . . ." she says. "Something."

"Bears. Wolves. There's plenty out here that can gobble you up. Something probably came close for a sniff, wondering what you were doing in its backyard."

"Maybe a bear, but I don't know." She finally climbs out of the truck. She bunches a fist into the small of her back and leans into it. Vertebrae pop, pressure relieves.

He keeps looking at her shyly, like he should be the one embarrassed. "I tell you about the time I got bluff-charged by a grizzly and her cubs? Happened this summer. They followed me on the Angel Rocks Trail. Maybe for fifteen minutes, but it felt like fifteen hours. Never been so scared."

She appreciates what he's doing, trying to make her feel like they're in this together, but she has a hang-up she inherited from her uncle. He never allowed himself to become friends with his crew. "They should always be mildly afraid of you," he once told her. "That's when they do their best work. You can buy them a case of beer for Christmas, but don't drink it with them. You can laugh at their jokes, but make sure the joke is never directed at you." The worst person to have on a crew is what Uncle Harry called the rank dog. The guy who was too eager, too friendly, rubbing up against you. "Acting like my buddy before you're my buddy is not the way to become my buddy," he always said. He once fired a construction worker for hooking an arm around his shoulder and calling him pal.

She knows this isn't the same thing, but she guards herself closely, given that she's a woman leading a company on the brink. "Let's get this truck unmoored," she says. "Then we'll update the scheduling software to account for the delays. Not sure what the forecast says, but assuming this rain quits, I'd like to start in on some gravel staging to help fight the mud."

But while she talks, she wanders around the truck checking the ground for tracks. Her boots leave clear mucky prints. But the overnight rain has made every other impression in the mud floppy and uncertain. She finds something the size of a catcher's mitt near the back bumper that could be a track. Could be. She turns in a slow circle, taking in the site and the forest beyond.

"I hauled up a load of dynamite," Bryce says. "Figured we could take care of that rock shelf at least."

"We need to wait on the explosives crew for that."

"I'm actually certified, remember? When I worked for that quarry out of Anchorage, that was my deal. I'm a blaster. So . . . let's have a blast?" He says this like a shy joke, and she gives him a smile in return, but she still feels bothered.

It is a day so damp and cloudy you can taste the gray. Somehow, without any sun, shadows still collect beneath every aspen leaf and spruce needle, and their darkness carries cold in it. The woods are cold. Her eyes settle on the back road that leads to the abandoned facility. A light breeze lifts and waves the branches, and they seem to either beckon or waft their chill at her as if trying to make her shiver.

"Joanna?"

She startles. "Yeah?"

"You good?"

"I'm good." She claps her hands together. "Let's get to work. Let's blow some stuff up."

16

Rolf always believed that whatever trouble and weirdness was afflicting the Lower 48—comet-worshipping cults and electrical disturbances and whatnot—it didn't apply here. Alaska operated by its own rules, even in a planetary crisis.

But now he's not so sure. He and Moses sit in silence in a root cellar dug into the side of a hill. The air is cold, loamy. At first everything appears black and uncertain, but then his eyes catch up with the gloom and the shapes around him begin to solidify. Herbs hang from the ceiling like desiccated veins. Railroad ties sweetening the air slightly with creosote brace and column the walls. Squash and turnips and onions and garlic cloves fill baskets on the shelves. There are mushrooms like corpse ears and red potatoes like dirty hearts. Every time Rolf tries to say something—"Can we please talk about what's going on here?"—Moses hushes him.

Because of the clouds.

A part of Rolf feels like he is humoring a disturbed old man. Another part of him believes. In what? He isn't yet sure. The fear evident in Moses's voice and watchfulness—that's real, and that's a truth worth exploring further. There's something wrong in the air. He knew that when he stood on top of the Westmark Hotel. He knew that when he answered Moses's call. He knows it now and he's hunting for answers.

The floor is dirt, hard and polished from years of footsteps. Three stone slabs lead up to the thick wooden door. A pale line of sunlight frames it, and sometimes it flickers uncertainly, as if something is passing by. Then it transitions from a faint white to a thick gray to a hard yellow.

Moses approaches the door, his boots softly scraping the steps. "Think it's passed," he says. "It always passes."

"What does?" Rolf says.

The door creaks open, letting in a wedge of sunlight. Moses staggers out into it and turns in a wide circle with the rifle aimed before him. His body relaxes when he encounters no threat. He clicks on the safety and loops the strap over his shoulder.

"What does, Moses?" Rolf says again.

Moses clears his throat and speaks in a grander tone: "'When he opened the sixth seal, I looked, and behold, there was a great earthquake, and the sun became black as sackcloth, the full moon became like blood, and the stars of the sky fell to the earth as the fig tree sheds its winter fruit when shaken by a gale. The sky vanished like a scroll that is being rolled up, and every mountain and island was removed from its place. Then the kings of the earth and the great ones and the generals and the rich and the powerful, and everyone, slave and free, hid themselves in the caves and among the rocks of the mountains, calling to the mountains and rocks, "Fall on us and hide us from the face of him who is seated on the throne, and from the wrath of the Lamb."'"

His voice echoes through the cathedral of trees. He holds up his arms and lets them fall. "Or something like that, anyway. I tend to butcher my scripture."

"Sounded pretty convincing to me."

It was unsettlingly quiet when he first got here. A forest goes quiet when a predator is near. Now the birds are beginning to call to one another again. A squirrel pokes its head from a hollow, sniffs the air, pulses its tail, then acrobatically leaps to a neighboring branch. Rolf takes his cue from the animals and follows Moses outside.

"You're talking Revelation," Rolf says. "Trying to tell me the world's coming to an end?"

"I am just a witness, not an apostle," Moses says and taps at his eyebrow. "I see the signs."

The forest is threaded with trails from all the years Moses and his family have hiked and hunted and foraged in it. He moves surprisingly fast for a man his age, dodging past stumps, hurdling over a log, and Rolf has trouble keeping up. It's not just the weight he carries in his feed sack of a belly, it's his knee, his damn old knee, grinding like glass with every step.

Moses doesn't ask if he's okay but pauses every thirty yards or so, allowing Rolf to catch up. And when they pass by a spring dribbling from a cloven rock, he instructs Rolf to drink from the cold clear water that tastes like a glacier's tears.

"You going to live forever, drinking this good water right out of the mountains, aren't you?" Rolf says, slurping a palm full and then splashing his face.

"Didn't help Jenny none."

"No," Rolf says and grunts with effort as he rises from a kneel. "Don't suppose it did."

This would be the point to tell him about Doreen. About the nauseating loneliness he feels every time he comes home to an empty house or wakes up in a cold bed. About how he finds evidence of her everywhere—a ginger ale in the fridge she never finished, a silver clump of hair clogging the drain, a tube of lipstick in the glove box. He doesn't know the right way to communicate what's broken inside him. How does Moses carry on? Is that what he wants to know? How can you live in a future that feels broken?

But Moses is already hiking away from him, the ferns slapping his shins, and Rolf follows in silence.

Rolf once read in an article that the average person knows around six hundred folks. He's got a hell of a lot more than that in his Rolodex. Thousands upon thousands. That's a part of the job. But knowing that many sometimes feels like it thins out the intimacy. He's not close to anybody, really. Not outside his family. If he's grabbing a coffee or a beer, if he's meeting up for a meal, there's always business mixed up in the conversation. He doesn't know Moses well, but it occurs to him there's never been any agenda between the two of them. Maybe that's some version of what a friendship is, even a small one.

They go another hundred yards before Moses stops and aims a finger skyward and says, "How's that for a revelation?"

Rolf's pulse pounds in his ears and his breath bellows from his throat, so it takes him a moment to settle into his surroundings. At first he doesn't hear the crows. They cackle and hiss and scrape and flutter, filling the branches of the trees above them. Rolf also makes out a bald eagle. No, two. Along with a buzzard. And they're not merely roosting. They're feeding.

The breeze puffs and carries something rancid in it. Rolf shades his eyes with his hand, trying to make sense of what he sees. Flaps of skin. Bones. Entrails. Antlers. Some of them are caught in the branches thirty feet up. Others seventy feet up. They're in the larch before him. The paper birch a few paces away. The white spruce beyond that. The trees are ornamented with carcasses and the underbrush is spotted with dried and blackened blood.

"Whole herd of elk, near as I can figure," Moses says. His voice follows Rolf as he walks among the trees, looking up until his neck aches. "They didn't climb. Not that I need to point out such a thing. They fell. You can see it in the branches that broke under their weight. And you can see it in the way some of them got speared through."

A few made it to the ground, though. Moses says they were fresh enough when he came upon them that he gutted and butchered them. Smoked the meat.

Rolf spots something in the moss and picks up a broken bit of antler. He keeps looking up and down as if he's lost all sense of space.

"You know what I'm noticing?" Moses says.

"What's that?" Rolf tosses aside the broken antler.

"I'm noticing not once have you said, *That's impossible.*"

Rolf hooks his thumbs on his belt. "I really don't know what to say."

"You know something."

Rolf smooths his mustache with his hand. "More likely I don't know a damn thing. That's what I'm starting to realize. I think I'm here to learn from you."

"These woods have always been haunted."

"What do you mean by that?"

"Heard and seen things my whole life I couldn't explain. Whispers in the wind. Ghostly figures wandering among the trees."

"Ghosts?"

"Angels, demons, ghosts—I don't know. I always kept my distance. But lately." Here he pauses and watches a spearhead of geese pass overhead. "Lately it's like somebody flipped a switch. Lately it's like I'm living in some kind of purgatory. An in-between."

"Tell me more."

Moses grunts. "Why tell you when I can show you? This ain't nothing. Just wait until you see what's coming next."

17

◎

Sophie Chen grew up as Chen Sū fēi, the daughter of fish-mongers. She worked at their booth at the Huanen Mark throughout her childhood, changing out ice, carving fillets, wrapping in newspaper eel, shad, bream, perch, turbot, silver and black and grass and bighead and crucian carp. She was especially good with a knife, and people would stop to watch her hands flash with steel.

The smell of fish was always in her hair, her clothes, her skin, and the other children would tease her about it. China was supposed to serve all its citizens, but sometimes she looked at the Apple phones and Burberry scarves and Gucci purses of her customers and knew that some were served better than others. She knew this could be the story of her life—scales forever jeweling her thighs, slime always beneath her fingernails, counting out change with a smile and a "Xièxiè nǐ."

But then one day at school, the People's Liberation Army visited, and in the concrete courtyard, the students and teachers gathered for an assembly. The soldiers offered up patriotic speeches and stories of adventure that made her imagine a life beyond her one-bedroom apartment and fishmonger stall.

Sophie signed up the day she turned eighteen. She vowed never to eat fish again. But she continued to work with a knife, then a 5.8 mm pistol and QBZ-191 assault rifle. Eventually her body became a weapon.

Five years ago, she was a member of a special forces unit known as the Black Dragons. They were involved in deniable missions and trained in night actions, sniper attacks, fast-roping helicopters. When her unit was tasked with a false-flag operation—taking out a Tanzania orphanage and making it look like a Congo rebel group was to blame—she refused.

They were already in field, set to deploy. It was a swampy hot night and her entire body was sleeved in sweat. Skyfall had begun. Meteors burned through the atmosphere in quick flashes, like skate marks on a frozen black pond. It was an evening when anything seemed possible, and maybe that was why she chose to take her stand. The rotor of the helicopter was beginning a lazy rotation and the engines were whining up to speed. Her unit commander was a man named Huang Lixin. He had acne-pitted cheeks but a mouth like a rosebud. She remembers it pinching out the words telling her she didn't have a choice. She would follow orders or she would go to prison.

Up to that point she hadn't realized she had an uncrossable line. She had planted IEDs, poisoned wells, dropped bombs, popped skulls with bullets fired from four hundred yards. But here was her limit. "I can't kill children," she said, and he said, "The only code you must follow is that of your country." This had been hammered into her since birth, and she believed it. She had recited the oath "No matter where I was born, the blood of my motherland is always flowing inside me," and she had sung with full-throated enthusiasm "Cup of Gold" and "Praise the Dragon Flag." She had waved flags in parades, the red flags she had been taught were soaked with the blood of martyrs. Blood. It always came down to blood. And it had come down to blood once again: the blood of children considered disposable in the name of oil. This operation was meant to increase Chinese military protection in Tanzania, a generosity that would allow her country to take advantage of the thick juicy oil reserves waiting to be tapped.

"Do your duty," Huang told her and she said, "I respectfully cannot." She didn't know then that the meteor showers would change the world, but her life had shifted dramatically when she drew her pistol and shot out his kneecap and sprinted into the night, abandoning the PLA forever.

She was not disloyal to China but to nationhood. These same sorts of deniable operations were happening with the United States. And Russia. And Mexico. And, and, and. Soldiers in every country saluted flags that hung high from poles while conveniently ignoring the fact that a flag was something you draped over a coffin twisting with worms and rotted flesh, a costume for death and terrors. Every country wanted the same things: power and profit. They held rallies and press conferences in the sunshine, but they did their bloody work in the shadows. She decided to do away with the sunshine and become a shadow country of her own. She would answer to her own constitution, her own code, and if she killed, the coin that came from it would fill her own pockets.

In this spirit she founded an organization known as the Collectors.

Now she is in the parking lot of a Fred Meyer in Fairbanks, Alaska, fitting on a black ball cap and sunglasses. She enters the store, and there are cameras nested in the ceiling so she keeps her head low when she rattles a cart through the hardware area and picks up a magnifying glass, screwdrivers, wire cutters, needle-nose pliers, an external caddy, and a USB cable. She realizes she might not be leaving her motel room for some time, so she also swings through groceries and snatches a rotisserie chicken, a premade salad, a bottle of mineral water, a sleeve of Oreos, and a pack of instant coffee.

When the clerk observes the strange variety of items rolling down the belt, he says, "You must have something special cooking in that kitchen of yours."

She pays in cash.

She drives a mile down the road and turns into a residential area and finally parks in front of a cottage after studying the porch and confirming it isn't outfitted with one of those camera doorbells that are becoming so ubiquitous. She pulls her coat off the black box in the passenger seat. She digs through her shopping bags and withdraws the screwdriver. The device is double-wrapped to protect it from harm, so it takes some time to remove one layer of titanium casing and then the other to finally reveal the guts of the mechanism. With a knife, she disables the internal power supply so that the pinger goes dark. She removes the transponder and lowers the window and tosses it into the gutter. Only then does she drive to the Klondike Motel.

The light is on at the front desk and she can see the familiar shadow of the manager seated there. She keeps the black box hidden among the shopping bags she carries to her room. She locks the door behind her and sets everything on the bed and checks under the box spring to make certain the briefcase is still there.

After she sweeps the room for hidden cameras—checking the alarm clock, the light fixtures, the power outlets—she gets to work. She sets the black box on the desk beside her laptop and removes the SSD made bulky to withstand a crash from thirty thousand feet. She drags the lamp over and snaps on the light. With a magnifying glass and needle-nose pliers, she removes the printed circuit boards and chipsets. These she installs into the external caddy that she connects to her computer using the USB cable.

She uses a Tor browser to get online via the motel Wi-Fi and then connects to the dark-web chat room. *Ready*, she types in Mandarin.

Transfer and scan under way comes the immediate response in German.

How long?

Could be thirty minutes. Could be five hours.

She turns on the television and flips through the channels until she finds a nature show about the strange sea life that has been washing up on Australia's shores ever since skyfall, including a pod of phosphorescent whales, and about the rumored existence of a sentient life-form made of sand. She takes off her jacket and places a bath towel in her lap and eats the rotisserie chicken with her bare hands. She licks the grease off her fingers and washes the chicken down with half a bottle of mineral water. She is about to tear into the bag of salad when the computer chimes an alert.

She returns to the desk and receives the following message: *The data from the black box reveals that for thirty-five seconds and 9.2 meters, the plane was not present on Earth or in its atmosphere.*

LOGBOOK: GEORGE C. WARNOK

ENTRY 37

August 18, 1943

Here at the Alaska Project, there has been much excitement about our new visitor. The Smoking Man, we've nicknamed him. As it turns out, he is not only an "invaluable scientific consultant" who will oversee and advise us on our atomic research—he is also a Russian.

Major General Tusk is the one who sat us down for a briefing. The cafeteria is the only space in which we can all fit, so in this windowless room that smelled of tomato sauce and fryer grease, we observed the boxy officer as he stood at attention. His head was mostly bald but his knuckles were thick with black hair. He had a paunch, but he kept it sucked in while puffing out his chest. Tusk was a regular visitor—our military overseer—but he spent most of his time in the Pacific theater. Whenever he dropped into the compound, he took to the woods with his rifle. His hunting costume was the green sweater and wool pants tucked into black boots that he wore now.

He spoke in a barking manner when he said, "I know there's been a lot of whispering and gossiping going on, which is never a good thing. You all are like a goddamn henhouse. So I figure I might as well put an end to the speculation. I'm going to come right out and say it. Dr. Devinor has been imprisoned for the past two decades in a Russian gulag. We tried to negotiate a prisoner swap with Stalin, and when that failed, we sent a strike team in and retracted the asset. Yes, the asset. He knows a great deal about your atomic experiments. In fact, you could consider his research to be the urtext of what you're working on now. He is, frankly, in poor health. It's amazing he's still alive, given his age and the conditions he's been living in. So we're going to be gentle with our asset, but we're also going to squeeze from him every bit of knowledge we can." He lifted his chin a little higher and eyed us down the length of his nose. "This is all highly confidential, of course."

Why he bothered telling us that last part, I don't know. Everything we were doing was highly confidential. We had signed a contract as dense as a book that essentially threatened us with a firing squad if we ever so much as whispered a detail of what happened here to a chipmunk in the forest. But there was something about the way he spoke of the Russian that seemed especially explosive.

"Dr. Devinor has been recovering in his private quarters while reviewing your research. Now, I'd much rather get on with my day, but I suppose some of you busybodies won't be able to refrain from asking me some obnoxious questions. So go on. Get it over with."

A hand went up and Tusk's eyes narrowed. "Yes."

The hand dropped. "It's not a question, sir, so much as an observation."

"If you must."

"Dr. Devinor . . . he's a Russki."

"What's your name?"

"Charles Kubert, sir."

"Are you afraid he's going to cut your throat in your sleep, Kubert?"

"I . . ."

"He's an old man with a big brain. You'd be wise to learn from him. As I understand it, we're not exactly winning up here. Your experiments keep failing. Get your thumbs out of your asses and keep an open mind or those Los Alamos fucks are going to show us all up."

Charles shifted his feet. "But what if he's . . . I don't know . . . here to spy on us? Or lead us in the wrong direction? Or . . ."

"Or what, hmm? Spit it out, Kubert."

"I don't really know, sir. It's just . . . this is a time of enemies. And *he's* the enemy."

Tusk looked at the rest of us. "Dr. Devinor will be visiting some of your labs later today. I suggest you ask smart questions and take smart notes and ignore whatever cockamamie bullshit Kubert here is talking about. Because if you had to spend twenty years in a gulag, I guara-goddamn-tee you, you'd spend those twenty years plotting revenge against whoever put you there."

18

heo's mother tells him he doesn't have to go to school, and he almost says, *Why?* Then he notes her eyes are moist and red-rimmed from crying. And he remembers, *Oh, right, she thinks he's dead.* Her husband. His father. Dead.

Theo should be in bed right now, staring at the ceiling and listening to classic rock and cuddling one of his dad's old shirts or something.

Instead, the same as every weekday morning at 7:15, he's sitting at the kitchen table spooning up his third bowl of Lucky Charms. He taps his school iPad as he finishes the final few calculations of his math homework.

His mother wears a flannel bathrobe loosely knotted at the waist over yesterday's clothes. Her hair is mussed with sleep. She stands waveringly between the hall and the kitchen with the overhead light inking dark shadows down her face. She just wants to go back to bed, he can tell, and avoid all the horrible checklists that await her. Talking to life insurance reps. Setting up a meeting with a lawyer about his father's last will and testament. Calling the funeral home. Thinking about an obituary.

If only she knew what Theo knows . . .

But he can't tell her anything, not yet, or she'll get in the way of what they have planned.

"You go back to bed, Mom. You rest. You need your rest."

"You should stay with me," she says in a croak. "You should stay home."

"Too much to do."

"Whatever homework you have due, whatever tests you have to take, I promise you, the teachers will give you an extension."

"I want to go."

"But your room," she says and drops her eyes.

"I'm sorry about that. I was angry. I cleaned up most of the mess. I'll do the rest later."

"You don't have to apologize." She takes his hand, the scabbed, bruised one, and runs her fingers along it. "I understand."

"I want to go to school, Mom."

At first she shakes her head back and forth, indicating she doesn't understand or doesn't approve, but then she slowly shifts into an up-and-down nod. "Okay."

"Can I do something for you, Mom? Can I make you breakfast or something?"

"That's what I'm supposed to . . ." She puts a hand over her mouth, and her face crumples. "That's what I'm supposed to say to you."

"Don't worry about it. I'll make you breakfast, okay?" He stands from the table and directs her to his chair. He can feel her body shivering under his hands. "I've still got fifteen minutes until the bus comes." He yanks open the fridge, pulls out a loaf of bread, a carton of eggs. "Plenty of time." He puts bread in the toaster, drops a pan on the stovetop, cranks a burner, knifes in a pat of butter. The toaster ticks and hums orange. He snatches a plate and a glass from the cupboard. "I've got you."

He remembers his mother yelling at him just two weeks ago because he stayed up too late and slept in too late. He stared at his phone too much. He didn't pick up his dirty clothes from the bathroom floor or empty the dishwasher or make his bed or eat a vegetable unless she asked him to. Why wasn't he more responsible? How was she ever going to send him off to college? How was he ever going to learn to take care of himself? Her voice was jagged with pleading and disappointment and fury. He remembers hating her then while also recognizing that maybe she was right.

Now he's the one hurrying about the kitchen and fussing over her as she sits slumped in a chair, gnawing at her bitten-down fingernails. Guilt propels him. So does motivation. He never really felt like he was doing anything important before. He was just floating, getting by, living in this weirdly transitional zone of not-boyhood. Now he has a purpose. Stakes. Responsibility.

Because he thinks his father might still be alive.

"You'll feel better when you eat," he says, laying the plate before his mother and kissing her forehead. He's performing a kind of theater, he knows, but it's a deception that feels good and right.

"Thank you." She catches his hand before he can scoop up his backpack and head out the door into the dawn light. "My little man," she says. "I don't know what I'd do without you."

Once outside, halfway down the block, he turns back once. He can see her black silhouette standing at the window as if the shape of her has been scissored out of existence. He needs to hurry if he's going to make her whole.

Normally he would catch the bus at the corner, but he hangs a right instead and half jogs the mile to the alley behind the Value Village where he and his friends are supposed to meet. The sun still isn't up, but the sky has a peachy blush to it. His breath fogs the air.

Hearing his approach, Jackson steps out from behind a dumpster. He always wears athletic gear even though he doesn't play or watch sports. Today he's in an Adidas tracksuit. His black hair is hidden beneath a stocking cap with a Nike swoosh. His smile looks anxious when he says, "Never cut school before."

"Me either."

"I feel nervous, even though there's no reason to be."

"What do you mean?"

His shoulders rise and fall. His smile wavers. "It's not like anybody's checking up on me."

Jackson's father is a different sort of gone: In Hawaii. Piloting a charter boat. Baiting the hooks of tourists who drop a thousand bucks to bring home a swordfish. And his mother is another kind of absent: Supervising the breakfast buffet, ordering the kitchen to cook more bacon, refilling the basket of strawberry jam packets. "I think that's why I never skipped. Why would I want to stay home and be lonely?"

"Yeah."

"But this—this is worth skipping for."

"Hope so," Theo says and they stamp the cold out of their feet. "Still no Little Head, huh?"

"You think he chickened out?"

Before Theo can say, *He'll be here,* the noise of an engine grumbles toward them. A white Ford Explorer turns the corner at too fast a clip. A tire chunks into and out of a pothole. The SUV lurches up to speed and then nearly skids to a stop before them. The window drops and Little Head looks at them and pops his eyebrows. "Get in, losers."

"Epic," Jackson says and claps his hands. "Awesome."

Theo looks around as if he thinks they might be overheard and then approaches the vehicle and says, "What are you doing?"

"What am I doing?" Little Head says in a mock-innocent voice. "I'm chauffeuring your delinquent asses."

"You can't drive."

"Of course I can drive. That's what I'm doing now. Driving."

"You know what I mean."

"Come on. I've got my permit."

"Even with a permit, you're supposed to have an adult in the car."

He points at Theo and then at Jackson. "Fifteen plus fourteen equals a basically middle-aged dude with lower-back problems wearing pants he bought from Costco. The math works out. We're good. Besides, did you know in Iowa, you can drive to school on your own starting at age fourteen? Fourteen! It's fine. I've got like twenty hours in. I know what I'm doing. Basically."

Jackson races for the passenger door, yelling, "Shotgun!"

"Get in," Little Head says and his voice takes on a more reasonable tone. "What are we going to do otherwise? Hitchhike around Fairbanks? It will take forever and somebody will call the cops on us for truancy."

Theo hates driving. When he started practicing, he expected it to be as intuitive as Mario Kart or Grand Theft Auto, but his body hasn't yet learned to compute all the different sensory details flowing past him. Crosswalk. Speed limit. Yield. Yellow light. Flashing lights. Car turning on the left; car passing on the right. Blinkers. Roundabouts. Google Maps spouting directions. Mom or Dad seizing the handle above the door and screaming "Slow down!" or "Oh, sweet Jesus!" Maybe that's what it's like to be an adult. You have a thousand things coming at you—crying babies, overdue bills, grocery lists—and you've got to somehow keep track of it all to function. Part of Theo wants to charge right into his twenties, and another part of him wants to retreat back to ten.

Not Little Head. He seems completely at ease with who he is. One hand grips the steering wheel, the other adjusts the rearview so he can eyeball Theo as he climbs into the back seat. "You ready to rock 'n' roll?" he says.

Jackson and Theo clip their buckles into place.

"All right," Little Head says. "Let's go figure some shit out." He stomps on the gas, but the Explorer remains in park, so the engine roars but they remain stationary. "Oops. Hold on."

He fumbles the gearshift into neutral and tries again, only to rev his way nowhere. "Almost there."

He finally locks into drive and they lurch forward, screeching and rocketing down the alley. "Hold on to your butts and nuts!"

Last night in Little Head's basement, they opened the stolen laptop and punched in the passwords his mother kept written on a pad of paper and navigated the medical portal for Fairbanks Memorial. Accessing the hospital's patient-information system required a password that Mrs. Castor hadn't written down, but the VPN offered a back door to what Little Head referred to as a Mickey Mouse security system.

"How do you know how to do this stuff?" Jackson asked him, and Little Head said, "I could hack this shit with my feet."

"But how?"

"These are the sort of skills you acquire when you're a dedicated indoorsman. I chat on the boards. I watch YouTube and Twitch tutorials. And I figure things the fuck out." He smashed a finger against his temple. "Because I'm smart."

His fingers were long, and they spidered across the keyboard as he accessed patient records. Thousands of names scrolled before them. He plugged in *Bridges* and more than two dozen entries popped up, among them Charles. "There he is." A mouse click revealed a drop-down menu of patient history. Doctor visits dating back to the eighties. Prescription refills. Diagnoses of high blood pressure, high cholesterol, pre-diabetes. A removed mole, clipped tonsils. An MRI. A colonoscopy. An ingrown toenail. A frozen wart. And then a record of his visit to the ER at 10:08 a.m.

But when Little Head clicks on the record, nothing loads. A window pops up that reads *Files no longer available.*

"The hell is this?" Little Head said.

He tried again and again and again. But the same window challenged them each time: *Files no longer available.*

"Why won't it load?" Theo said, and Little Head said, "I don't have the slightest fucking clue. It's there but it's not there. Like all the information was uploaded and then deleted."

He kept trying for another minute and then searched elsewhere for an autopsy report but he admitted that they sometimes took weeks or even months to get into the system due to backups at the coroner.

"How do you know that?" Jackson says.

"Because I basically have a PhD in cop shows. *CSI: Las Vegas* is a favorite." Little Head leaned back in his chair and drummed his fingers against the armrests. "Hmm," he said and then made *Hmm* into a kind of song. "Hmm-hmm-hmm-hmm-hmm."

"Now what?" Theo said.

"Now things get trickier." Little Head rolled forward again, leaned over the desk. He clicked his way back to the main page of the portal and banged out some commands, and the screen went dark except for a few lines of code. Not much changed over the next few minutes. Little Head typed, deleted, typed, deleted. Whenever they asked him a question, he told them, "Shut up. Just shut up for a second."

Then the screen brightened, displaying a blueprint of the hospital with alphanumeric tags. "There we go, baby," Little Head said. "Big Brother's watching." He clicked on one of the tags, and it opened up a window live-streaming a nurses' station. "Lights, camera, action!"

He explained that there were only so many feeds due to patient privacy and people dropping their gowns and pulling out their junk and such for doctors to examine, squirt ointment on, slice open, whatever. "But we can get some idea of what was going on around the edges of it all."

He pinned the cameras at the entrance to the ER and the reception area. Then he opened an archive featuring hundreds of folders. He nosed the mouse around, studying troves of MP4 files. "Looks like they backlog for a week before erasing." More clicks and swipes. "The intake form for your dad? It said ten something, right? Ten oh four? Ten oh eight?"

Every MP4 was half an hour long, and Little Head scrubbed his way through two of them before an ambulance rolled up and two EMTs leaped out and pulled a gurney from the back. "There!"

There he was. Unmistakably. Black-bearded. Wearing a corduroy jacket over his signature Hawaiian shirt and jeans. Strapped down and handcuffed to the safety bar. Little Head ran the footage at a quarter speed, so everybody moved as if through syrup. Somebody else jumped down from the rear of the ambulance. A cop. A short woman with a mullet, her arms swinging widely to avoid the pistol and walkie-talkie on her duty belt. She followed them inside.

"Wait," Theo said.

"What?" Little Head said.

"She looks like a cop but not like a cop."

Little Head zoomed in on the paused image. The pixelation corrected itself. PORT AUTHORITY, her badge read. "A different kind of a cop. An airport cop."

"Is there a camera inside?" Theo said. "There must be."

"You betcha," Little Head said. He backed out of the current footage and entered a new portal for the ER reception area. It took a moment of scrubbing to find them, but the light was clearer here, their images sharper.

The double doors opened. The gurney rolled inside, flanked by the EMTs. Theo's father swung his head back and forth, his mouth a black O of pain or confusion. And then something impossible happened. He vanished.

"What?" Theo said.

"What the actual fuck?" Little Head said.

He was there, and then he was not there. A black padded cushion, still molded by the weight of his body, remained.

"Maybe it's just a glitch," Little Head said. But no. One EMT and then the other stutter-stepped and let go of the gurney as if it were burning hot. Another few seconds of slow-motion disbelief passed as they swept their arms through the air and mouthed, *What the hell?*

And then the body once again materialized in the frame. Now he was on the floor behind them. He continued to swing his head back and forth, but his arms were free of the handcuffs and he tore at his shirt so that the buttons popped, revealing a black thatch of chest hair over a pale onion of a belly. A kind of vapor hung in the air around him, like a magician left behind onstage when he popped up from a secret compartment.

A few more seconds of confusion followed before the EMTs recovered, helped him back onto the gurney, and shoved their way through the swinging doors that led to the ER.

The boys watched the video five more times in stunned silence before Theo said, "Look something else up for me, would you?"

"Okay." Little Head dangled his hands over the keyboard. "Shoot."

"Can you look up the hospital's incoming and outgoing calls?"

"I think so." He backtracked through the data system and began typing. "What are you looking for?"

"Any sort of communication with, like, anything and everything military."

"How do we know if it's military?"

"My dad taught me a lot about radios and transmissions and stuff. We sometimes listened in to frequencies we shouldn't have. Anyway, there's this thing called the DSN. The Defense Switched Network. The Department of Defense controls it. It's all their voice data. The Alaska area code for it is three one seven."

And there it was, only fifteen minutes after his father's admission: an incoming call from a 317 number.

"Write it down," Theo said.

At the airport, the sky is a porridge gray and the lot is half empty. Little Head parks the Explorer at a messy diagonal, taking up two spots. When they climb out of the SUV, Theo lingers, examining the space. "Shouldn't you try to park again?"

But Little Head is already marching away. "It's better this way. Two spots for the price of one. Nobody parks close to you and bangs you with their door."

Jackson walks backward, toward Little Head, away from Theo, his loyalties torn. "Come on, let's go."

Theo follows, head down, his hands shoved deep in his pockets. He should be leading the way, he knows. This is his problem, *his* father. But his feet feel suddenly heavy. And the open air of the parking lot makes him feel small and exposed. They're no longer in Little Head's basement, the staging ground for an uncountable number of D and D' campaigns and video-gaming marathons— they're within a hundred yards of the place where his father was arrested on federal charges. A jet screams, a noise like sheets of air ripped in two. The wind tastes like aspirin and kerosene exhaust. There's no more make-believe. He can't just act like he knows what he's doing as he did with his mother this morning.

He jogs until he catches up to his friends. They walk in a hunched cluster. The wind bites at them. A single flake of snow swirls down and dies on the pavement.

"I heard there's a storm coming," Jackson says, his words swept away by the wind. "I heard we could get our first snow. That could be fun, right?"

"I wish I lived in California or Texas or Tahiti or something," Little Head says. "*Winter* is a bad fucking word."

"We could go sledding," Jackson says, but his enthusiasm isn't catching.

"Sledding is for diaper babies," Little Head says.

"Oh," Jackson says.

Little Head pulls out his phone and checks the time. "Hurry. Her shift just ended."

They jog the rest of the way to the airport, crossing a road that crawls with traffic. Here people are getting picked up and dropped off. The boys dodge around hugs and goodbyes and *So good to see you*s. They see suitcases hurled in and out of trunks. This is as close as Theo has ever been to getting on a plane, and the airport's buzz and movement make him feel even more puny and insignificant. People wear suits. They speak urgently into cell phones. The three of them are the youngest people here by a decade or more. Theo has never been out of this state. He barely knows anything or anyone or anywhere. He's just a dumb, powerless kid who's probably seeing things, no different than a boogery seven-year-old who swears he hears sleighbells on the roof and a monster in the closet. He almost trips over a suitcase. He bumps into a man. Moving among all these adults—some of them staring at him with suspicion or annoyance—he can't help but feel like that speck of snow that got knocked around by the wind and then extinguished on the pavement.

"You guys," he says, but nobody hears him. "You guys, maybe we should go."

They walk past a baggage-claim door, and its electronic eye registers their movement and yawns open. Jackson pauses here in the warm exhalation of air. "I smell Cinnabon!"

"You smell my ass," Little Head says.

"Let's go inside? Can't we just go inside? I swear I smell Cinnabon."

"There is no Cinnabon at this airport," Little Head says. "I am the supreme authority on this, as the only one of us who has ever been on a plane."

"I swear I smell it though."

"This was a mistake," Theo says, but Little Head says, "No," grabs them both by the arms, and leads them away. "You both look like overgrown kindergartners. Act like you've got somewhere to go. We don't know what her route is through the airport. She could get past us. Besides, we'll attract too much attention in there."

Five minutes later, they're standing on the sidewalk outside the building that houses the TSA and Port Authority offices, huddled together on a gray square of concrete. Jackson pulls the hood of his sweatshirt over his wool hat. Theo tucks his hands up inside his sleeves. Little Head loses himself in his phone, scrolling through ten-second videos that blare pop songs as people crash on skateboards, bounce around in bikinis, fail to blow out candles on cakes.

"Is that her?" Jackson says. "The lady from the video?"

"That's her," Little Head says, tucking his phone away.

A uniformed woman in a blue jacket is walking toward them. Her penny-red hair is clipped above her ears but runs long in the back in a mullet. She takes short, hard strides, like she's trying to crush a trail of ants. She slows as she approaches them. Her jaw works at a stick of gum. "You here to sell me Boy Scout cookies or something?"

"Are you Diane Ryall?" Little Head says.

She chews the gum open-mouthed, and Theo can see it is the same green color as her eyes. "What's wrong with your head?"

"It's little."

"I can see that."

"There's nothing *wrong* with it."

"If you say so."

"You shouldn't say shit like that. It's rude. What if I said, *Hey, what's wrong with your haircut?*"

She touches her hair. "You think there's something wrong with my haircut?"

Theo has let Little Head lead the way until now, but he can feel things spinning out of control, and despite his doubts, he needs for this to work out. He ignores the sick twist in his stomach and steps forward. "Ms. Ryall?"

Her eyes shift to him, slitted with suspicion. "How do you know my name? And shouldn't you little shits be in geometry class right now?"

They don't know what to say to this.

"I'm one radio call away from reporting your asses. Seriously. Bunch of creepy weirdos. You look like you're members of some kind of school shooters' society."

Theo thinks about lying to her, telling her they're working on a research project or intern program, but he can't muster the energy. "We've got some questions we were hoping you could answer. About my dad?"

"Your dad?"

"He's the one you arrested the other day. He's the one who . . ." But he can't finish the sentence.

Her voice is softer when she says, "That was your old man, huh?" She walks to the edge of the sidewalk and spits her gum into the road. "Jesus. I been thinking about him." She shakes her head and puts her hands on her hips. "I don't even know what to say to you, kid."

"Can you," Theo says, "can you please tell me what happened? At the airport. At the hospital. Please?"

She blinks at him a few times. She barely has any eyelashes, which makes her face appear all the more blunt and scared when she says, "I could lose my job. Talking to you. They made me sign a . . ." A jet takes off with a shredding roar and she follows the sight of it. When the clouds swallow it up, she says, "Do you know the Grizzly Hangover?"

"Think so, yeah," Theo says. "Over by the ice arena?"

"Meet me there in an hour."

LOGBOOK: GEORGE C. WARNOK

ENTRY 58

February 16, 1944

We didn't know a lot about what was happening in Los Alamos. Not outside of the occasional nugget in the month-old newspapers delivered to our outpost. But one day, when General Tusk was on-site, I approached his office to deliver a briefing and, with my fist ready to rap at the door, heard Dr. Devinor talking. The floor was the dirty spotted white of an egg, and the door was a cheap pale grain that could not hide their voices. I stood there but couldn't quite bring myself to knock. Instead, I listened to scraps of their conversation.

Dr. Devinor's voice had a depth to it, refined by age and cigarettes. It could veer sharply between a bassoon's bellow and a violin's quiver. It was a fine thing to listen to, especially when embellished with the music of his accent. He was in the middle of some heated diatribe that I couldn't quite follow, but it concerned the nature of what we were doing here, the dangerous games we were playing with the world. "You think you are gods. Not merciful gods either, but gods of thunder, gods of blood sacrifice. Do you really think history will look kindly on your efforts here?"

The major general muttered something in response, and Dr. Devinor's voice rose again as he went off on a wild tear. "You don't strike me as a man who reads, General Tusk. But you do seem like a man who enjoys moving pictures. Have you seen the Universal monsters? You probably see Boris Karloff and refer to him as Frankenstein, like everyone else. That's wrong, of course. If you'd read the novel, you'd know better—you'd know him as *the creature*. But nonetheless, everyone now calls the monster Frankenstein. They call him that even though that's the name of the doctor. Do you know why? It's because you are what you create. There's a lesson there. You are not Major General Ambrose Tusk. No. No, you have a new name if you continue to carry out this plan of yours. You are *War!*"

I checked the hallway behind me, not wanting to be caught, then bent closer to the door. Now Dr. Devinor was speaking of Los Alamos.

Nuclear tests were under way in the Southwest, Utah and Nevada mostly. Sometimes the bombs were buried. Sometimes the bombs were dropped from an aircraft. The seismic shocks could be felt hundreds of miles away. Windows cracked. Framed photos fell from walls. Porcelain figurines danced off shelves and shattered on the floor. People began to take note of when and where these tests took place. They weren't angry. They were curious and even delighted. It was all in the name of science and the war effort, yes? So the military stopped trying to keep them away and instead designated areas where people were permitted to watch the tests. Families would picnic and snap photos and applaud when the warheads bloomed in the desert. And then one blustery day, a ten-kiloton atomic bomb melted the skin off a gathering of fifty people. A downwinder, it was called.

The press had not reported on it—the military had so far been able to keep the story quiet—but Dr. Devinor knew and he was furious. Had they learned nothing? Was the utter failure and disaster that came out of Tunguska not enough of a warning? If the U.S. military was acting this reckless already, then what would they do once they harnessed the power of—

It was at this point that the door flew open and I was caught in the light of the office. Dr. Devinor stood there, his hand on the knob, his eyes peeled back white, his mustache bristling. He paused there only a moment before shaking his head and saying with finality, "You're going to make these boys into unwitting murderers." And then he pushed past me. Wherever he went, he left behind the toasty smell of cigarette smoke.

"Come on in, Warnok," General Tusk said.

"Yes, sir," I said and held up the stiff stack of papers in my hand. "I came to give you the briefing, as requested."

"How much of that did you hear?"

I took a seat across from him. His desk was bare except for a coffee cup and a jar of pens. He wasn't present at the facility often enough to put much of a mark on it, but he had hung up a mounted set of antlers. When I sat, he stood, positioning himself in such a way that the horns seemed to grow out of his head.

"Nothing, sir."

"That's bullshit."

"The only thing I understand is that you and the doctor had a professional disagreement."

"That's a fine pile of bullshit you're serving me." He stood there breathing fiercely through his nose another minute before telling me to carry on, then. He was ready for his briefing, and he hoped like hell I had good progress to share.

19

One of Uncle Harry's favorite sayings was "Why sit around wringing your hands when you could keep your fingers busy building something?" He trained Joanna to never sit still. That's why the past few months were torturous as she competed for and repeatedly failed to land contracts. She'd rather drive a dump truck than sit at a desk. She'd rather fire a nail gun than punch texts into a phone. So she keeps busy now. Even with the rain, which has given way to a sleety mix.

She and Bryce lay plywood down in the mud. They rope the tow hooks of her truck to the hitch of his company Ram. They both gun their engines at once. The trucks roar and rock. And, finally, she lumbers forward. They smile at each other through their spotted windshields.

Then they get to work. A ten-ton load of gravel is mounded at the edge of the site. She fires up the front end loader and spends an hour shaking out buckets to skirt the entry while Bryce rakes it out. This won't make any difference today, but it might help them tomorrow or the next day. The sooner the site dries out and stabilizes, the sooner her crew can get building.

Her phone buzzes. She pats her pocket in confusion before she pulls out the phone, thinking maybe it's that phantom feeling she sometimes gets, because even with the cell tower, she hasn't gotten much of a signal since the weather rolled in. Maybe it's that omnimetal antenna Verizon was advertising. Supposedly it has a reach like no other. The number is unlisted and the voice on the other end is warped and patchy with static. Thaddeus Gunn.

"Why isn't your crew there helping you?" he says, his voice solidifying toward the end of the question until it's almost shrill.

"Because you can't dig when it's damp," she says.

"There must be something they can do. *You're* working."

His knowing tone makes her remember the camera stationed at the entry. She wonders if there are others. The black screen of her phone suddenly feels like an insectile eye burrowed into the side of her head.

There is a sound she can't quite comprehend, like a hundred throats moaning, and she pulls the phone away from her ear for a moment, then tentatively returns it. "Hello?" she says. "Hello, did you say something?"

"I said"—his voice fuzzes in and out—"I'm deeply disappointed in the delay. I don't know how much longer I can . . ." And here his words fade to something that sounds like whispers.

"We're on it, all right," she says, not because she believes it but because that's what you say to clients. "I said I'd get it done and I'll get it done."

His voice rings out loud and clear when he says, "See to it."

She isn't sure if he hangs up or if the signal drops.

Bryce is walking across the slab of basalt that interrupts the footprint of the building. It's the size of a McMansion. She climbs out of the payloader and joins him, trying not to slip. The shear of the wind brings tears to her eyes that mix with the precipitation on her cheeks.

She shouldn't complain—she's the boss—but she can't help but motion with her phone and say, "These people are something else."

"The colonel?"

"No, the big boss. The colonel's been tattling on us, I think."

"Why do you think they're in such a rush?" he says.

"Competition, I'm guessing? I mean, you think about the Russians and Chinese and U.S. all racing to get to the moon back in the sixties. Is it something like that?"

"Yeah," he says. "Yeah, I suppose." His face flinches almost in apology. "Or maybe it's more dangerous."

"Why would you say that?"

"We are dealing with the military. Weapons are kind of their thing."

"Ugh." She chews on her lip a moment. "Anyway. What do you got for me?"

Bryce's ears are red with the cold and his ball cap has an inch of sleet on the brim. He talks her through some of what he's looking for—mud seams, joints, fissures, contours, bedding planes. It's all about pressure points and reading the rock. Shock energy and gas energy. He has a can of red spray paint in hand. When he shakes it, the ball inside makes a sound like hail hitting a window. He makes some marks to designate the shot areas. The color immediately bleeds and dribbles in the damp.

She drums her feet on the ground for warmth and he flexes his fingers to bring the blood back into them. "Not ideal weather for blasting," he says. "But we're racing the clock, so we'll make it work, right?"

"You're a man after my own heart, Bryce," she says and he looks at her with a bright flash of teeth and says, "Yeah?"

"I just mean . . ." She starts to correct herself, but changes the subject instead. "Do you need me to go fetch the drill?"

"That would be great. I just need a few more minutes to map out the blast. We'll take it out one section of a time."

She recently purchased a rotary drill with an omnimetal tip. The pounding force of it with the kinetic charge is supposed to outperform all other equipment on the market. It looks like a space-age blaster, with a long silver rod poking out of its muzzle. It weighs sixty pounds and comes with a shoulder strap. When she returns to him lugging the tool, he says, "That looks like a fun toy."

They tuck orange foam plugs into their ears. Bryce puts the strap over his shoulder and spreads his legs to bear the weight. He bores five deep holes into the slab. This takes the better part of an hour. The air shakes. The ground shivers through Joanna's boots. She covers each hole with a piece of plywood to keep the water out.

When Bryce speaks again, his voice is muffled, and she realizes she still has the plugs in her ears. She picks one out and the forest suddenly seems louder than any city with its branches creaking and sleet hissing and wind gusting. "What?"

"I said, what do you think? You want to blow some shit up?"

"You bet I do," she says.

Mushy snow clings to their shoulders. Water dribbles down their chests. The air tastes like a mountain stream. She's cold to her marrow, but they have only an hour of daylight left, so she can't quit now.

The dynamite is stored in a silver trailer with an orange explosives placard on the rear door. Sleet drums the roof when they step inside. The air has the burned-caramel smell of nitroglycerin. "Okay," Bryce says and claps his hands together.

And it's as though the clap summons more bad weather. A tinny roar sounds, filling the trailer with an impossible noise. The weather has surged. Outside they see curtains of rain mixed with snow falling.

"Okay," he says again. "Okay, maybe this actually isn't happening today."

She gives the floor a soft kick and says, "Goddamn it," under her breath. Her brain feels scorched from the lack of sleep. Her body feels cold down to the marrow. She herself could crack apart like that slab of stone at any second. This job has to work out, but it's already turning into a shitshow.

"Hey," he says, wiping a hand through his beard to wring out the moisture, "I got an idea. Let's go inside the trailer and warm up. I'll make us some grilled cheese sandwiches and tea. How does that sound?"

"Yeah." She pinches the bridge of her nose and takes a cleansing breath and says, "That sounds good, actually. Let's do that."

Inside the trailer, the gas burner lights with a small *foomp* of blue flame. She sits at the dinette while Bryce digs in the cupboards for a pan and in the fridge for cheese, bread, butter. He hums to himself. Their jackets hang by the door, dribbling a puddle onto the linoleum. She has damp hair and wrinkled fingertips. Her skin is clammy enough that it feels like she could peel it off. She has traded her wet socks for a fresh pair of Smartwools. She pulls her sleeves over her hands and tucks them under her thighs for good measure. She looks out the window. Through the sleet-smeared glass the bare branches of the aspens rake at the air and she feels intensely happy to be out of the weather for a moment.

"So I keep looking at the plans," Bryce says as he knifes butter onto the bread.

"Yeah?"

"I know we're not supposed to ask. But it's kind of hard not to ask. You really don't have any idea what the hell it is we're building?"

"Not really."

"Some of the components make it feel like we're rubbing up against hadron-collider territory. You know that particle accelerator they have in Switzerland or wherever?"

"The thought has occurred to me, but . . ."

"But?"

"Those tunnels go on and on and on for like fifteen miles."

"And this thing is powered by an omnimetal battery grid that could light up a city." He drops the buttered bread in the pan to sizzle and hurriedly rips open a package of sliced American cheese. "So this is different." He fills two mugs with water and pops them into the microwave. "I can't really decide what it looks like. You said a door. But I was thinking it's maybe more like an inverted pyramid? My buddy went to Puerto Rico on vacation and he showed me some pictures of this crazy satellite dish they have there. It's so big, it's not freestanding but dug into the ground like a big basin. You know what I'm talking about?"

"I think so, yeah. It was in some movie I saw a million years ago maybe."

"So it's a little like that. But then, with our blueprints, there are the weird little details. There are all these weird little intricate details, you know? Designs. Symbols. Whatever they are."

"Maybe they're somehow functional."

"Functional how?" He finishes buttering the second slices of bread just in time to flip the sandwiches. He can't find a spatula so he uses his hands and winces at the heat and licks some melted cheese off his finger.

"This isn't my area of expertise," she says. "But a lot of electricity needs to get poured into this facility. I can only guess it has something to do with lasers or sonar or projection of some sort. Whatever ways they study the atmosphere."

The microwave beeps. He pulls out the mugs, plops in tea bags, and sets them on the table to steep. She leans into the steam.

"You mean sky science?" he says. "Studying clouds and holes in the ozone and stuff?"

She hugs her hands around the mug, taking in its warmth before she tries for a sip. "I did some sleuthing when I first took the job, and Alaska seems to be a hub for that kind of thing, I guess because of the dark skies or the lack of pollution or I don't even know."

"Normally, when I build something, I like to imagine what will go on there. Here's where a family will live, for example. Or here's where cars will be produced. Or whatever." Bryce plates the sandwiches and takes a seat across from her. The smell of toasted bread gives her a surge of good feeling. "But what's going to happen here? What am I supposed to imagine taking place six months or a year from now?"

"Every time I try to get some more information out of the bosses, you know what they tell me?" She tears the sandwich in two, and strings of cheese ooze between the halves. "Don't concern yourself with that. Just do the job." She pops a bite in her mouth and makes a happy sound.

Bryce watches her eat with a small smile. "Then I guess that's what we'll do."

They finish their meal and put away the food and wash the dishes. She opens her laptop. Bryce fiddles with the cell booster and router, but the internet connection remains glacially slow.

"I can't work in here," she says. "And I can't work out there. So . . . fuck it. You want to go explore that old lab?"

. . .

They check the soldiers' trailer first, confirm that it's empty. The sky is quiet, but two inches of sloppy snow have accumulated. Their boots trudge through it with a squeaking crunch. Joanna feels lighter and fuller than she did before. It's easy to forget for a second that they're on a job. "I always like walking through fresh snow," Bryce says and she says, "Yeah?"

"Yeah." He watches his feet as he takes a few more steps. "It's kind of like writing on a fresh pad of paper."

"You're funny," she says.

"Why am I funny?"

"Because you look like some big dumb construction guy who can only grunt out monosyllabic thoughts about football and hunting."

"Me like ball. Ball good. So is dead things me shoot and eat."

The laugh that tumbles out of her mouth surprises her.

"I don't think I've ever heard you laugh."

"I laugh."

"No, you actually don't." They walk a few more steps, and she struggles to respond, so he makes it easier for her. "You should do it more. You're good at it."

"Yeah?"

"Yeah."

"Prove it."

"Prove that you're good at laughing? Oh, jeez. Okay." He clicks his tongue until he figures out what to say. "Okay. So sometimes, when I'm walking around, I like to imagine I'm building a life."

"Building a life? What's that supposed to mean?"

"Building a life. Like building a building, except it's a life."

"For example?"

"Maybe I see this nice house. Big Victorian. All lit up. Roses in the garden. Pool in the back. I might be like: *That's my house. I live there.*"

"You live there? In that big Victorian?"

"I live there. In that big Victorian. That's my house. And I have a room that's full of books and DVDs and it's got two big comfy chairs and a minifridge full of beer. And there's a secret panel that leads to a staircase that leads to the roof. And on the roof I've got a telescope set up and I look at the stars every night."

"This sounds like some house."

"Also, just down the street there's a coffee shop. The barista knows my order. His name is Sam and he has a man bun and a tree tattoo on his forearm."

"Is Sam the one who sits in the second comfy chair?"

"Nope. That's for somebody else."

"I see. A girlfriend?"

"If I had one, sure."

"I thought you were trying to make me laugh."

"Wasn't that funny? The things my stupid brain comes up with?"

"No, it was sweet."

They make their way down the old road through the broken, fallen trees and find the abandoned facility waiting for them. The brutalist architecture lends it the air of a tomb. Dark hollows stare back. When they get closer, they can see the vines veining the structure and the sections where the concrete has chunked away to reveal the ribs of rebar beneath.

"Last I saw the guards, they were walking in here."

The glass entryway to the building was long ago shattered by weather or vandals. A few dusty fangs still hang in the framing. Anything could have taken up residence inside, and indeed it smells pungent within, like a wet dog digging a hole. They take a dozen or so steps into a reception area bottomed with dirt and stone and brush. Each of them carries a Maglite and they look at each other and nod before clicking on their beams.

Here is a reception desk. Here is a door hanging from a splintered hinge. Here is a sign on the wall that says PASSES MUST BE PRESENTED TO GUARDS. She sweeps the area and something briefly flashes its reflection. She crouches to find a framed photograph half buried. She sweeps off the dirt and reveals the faded face of Harry Truman.

Bryce has a few odd tics to him. In the time she has known him, whenever the subject of dancing came up, he immediately said,

"You know, I'm not a terrible dancer," and then his eyes darted about as if he were searching for the truth in this statement. "I'm okay. I'm not bad actually." It is obviously a subject he is wrestling with. He also has the strange habit of calling out emotions as if they are steadily building orgasms. If somebody in the crew starts telling jokes and the jokes continue to grow in humor and frequency, Bryce will say something along the lines of "Oh, yes. *This* is funny. *This* is so freaking funny. This is hilarious, guys. We need to laugh like this. It's good for us. It's good medicine." His searching earnestness eventually takes all the humor out of the situation and results in people wandering away from him.

He is doing something similar now as he and Joanna move down a windowless concrete hallway. Shadows dance on the walls. Their footsteps and voices echo. The occasional mouse scurries underfoot. Something brushes her cheek and she startles and swings the flashlight only to realize there are roots dangling from the ceiling like hair.

"Huh," Bryce says. "This is kind of scary. This is getting scarier by the minute. This is definitely creepy. I am officially creeped out. I'm—"

"Bryce."

"What?"

"Can you stop?"

"You want to stop? For a water break?"

"No. I want you to stop."

"Stop what?"

"Narrating. Pointing out how something obviously creepy is creepy."

"Oh. Okay."

"It's annoying."

"Sorry."

They continue a few steps and she can tell he's gone rigid with embarrassment and she says, "I'm the one who's sorry, okay? I'm just exhausted. I don't do well without sleep."

They find a room as big as a lumberyard full of what she initially mistakes for cabinets. But when they get closer, she recognizes them for what they are: Computers. Wall-size units with buttons and what must have been blinking lights. Rust stains bleed from the controls. A yellowed scroll of paper featuring dozens and dozens of columns of numbers still spools from a printing slot. The floor is speckled with guano. Gray, empty birds' nests wig the tops of the units.

Pipes and cables run along the walls and ceilings of the hallways. Nothing is pretty. Nothing in this place was built to be welcoming or pleasing to the eye. It was all industrial efficiency, a big box mazed with hard angles. People lived and worked here, but even without the winter wind funneling through it, it was a cold space.

She and Bryce don't have a good system for navigating the facility. They go up and down stairwells, open some doors and ignore others. They find a cafeteria with all the tables pushed off to the side. They find an office with the drawers of the desk and filing cabinet hanging open. They explore dormitory rooms, one with a cross on the wall, another with a violin lying neatly on a pillow. Here is a closet full of janitorial supplies, still smelling faintly of bleach after all these years.

They cough. They swipe away old cobwebs. They run their hands through thick layers of dust. Bryce steps in something that makes his foot slide—a smeared pile of what he hopes isn't bear shit. "But I think it might be." He scrapes it off and stomps his boot. The shit is gray and viscous and looks like something a sick animal might cough up. "At least it doesn't smell. Or does it?"

They come to a place where the walls and ceiling have collapsed. They nudge at the rubble and wonder aloud if the ruin came from age or something else. They're on the first level at the center of a rectangular building built on flat ground. The edges of the structure would have been much more likely to decay first, unless . . . what? Maybe some pipes broke and gushed a few thousand gallons? But they're not seeing any water damage. Bryce delicately clambers up the pile of crumbled stone and digs around and reveals a steel support beam. It's bent toward them. "Maybe there was an explosion?"

"There are a lot of downed trees outside. I was originally thinking they might have got knocked down in a storm. But maybe not. What if . . ."

"What if indeed," he says.

They backtrack and find a parallel hall, but the way there is blocked by debris as well. "I want to get on the other side of that," Joanna says.

They try another door and it creaks open on a lab. Their flashlights can cut only through patches of the dark, so exploring a room is like putting together a soft yellow puzzle piece by piece. A flash of a counter. A spotlight of equipment. The bright hollow of a cabinet. She doesn't understand what they were studying here. There are stations of machines that look like salvaged-metal art projects. This one resembles the rim of a tractor wheel set on its side; it is busy with valves and dials and hoses and what looks like a numberless calculator. There is another that looks like the pipes of a church organ but the keyboard has been replaced by something like thin, tight-knit saw blades.

In the dust of a desk, she draws nonsense. Her name. A heart. Then she wipes her scribbles out with the palm of her hand. Her fingers find the handle to a drawer and she pulls it out with a rusty screech. Inside is a black leatherbound book the size of a Bible. She thumps it onto the desk and flips it open to the first page. "'Logbook,'" she reads aloud. "'George C. Warnok.'"

It is then a growl sounds—so deep-throated that it is beyond bass; it's like stone shifting—and something rises up on the other side of the desk. A dark bristling shape twice as wide and nearly twice as tall as she is.

20

◎

The two old men hike through the White Mountains. Their feet chuff rocks and slide on pebbly grit when they make their way down a slope, and then a carpet of fallen fir needles softens their passage when they travel through a thick section of forest that gives way to a pond. Everywhere there is fog clinging to branches and brush like torn cobwebs.

Moses asks Rolf how his bum leg is holding up.

"Holding up about two hundred fifty, last I checked the scale."

Moses goes slower now, and Rolf manages to move along steadily, even with the pained limp. They enter a meadow with a creek silvering it. Chimneys of steam rise off the water. Fog oozes out of trees and softly collars the clearing. When they get to the other side of it, a pond waits for them.

Moses has a canteen on a strap and he unshoulders it now and takes a swig. He offers it to Rolf, and the water is clean and cold and good. He settles his bulk onto a boulder and takes another drink and fights the urge to drain it dry.

"Well," Moses says.

"Well what?" Rolf says.

Moses's beard folds against his chest when he bends his chin, nodding at the water.

"It's a pond. What about it?" Rolf asks.

"That ain't no pond."

"That ain't no . . ." Rolf says, a quiet echo. He understands now, but his eyes are having trouble focusing, like when you've been reading hard for a few hours and then try to eyeball something across the room.

He hands the canteen back to Moses. He stands. He wobbles a few steps forward.

"I wouldn't get much closer," Moses says. "Not with you unsteady on your feet."

The mist-laced water isn't water. Not exactly. He feels like he's looking into the top of a slowly bubbling cauldron. Rolf points at what he's seeing, shaking his finger in an almost accusatory way, then runs the hand along his mustache, neatening it, because what else is he supposed to do?

Moses fetches a stick the size of a femur off the ground. "This'll do." From his belt he unclips a buck knife. He runs the blade along the wood, forcing two white notches into it, forming an X. "Now watch this."

He walks carefully up to the shoreline. Or maybe *border* is a better word. He holds out the stick. And releases it.

A few seconds pass. And Rolf curses. Because a stick falls from the sky and hits the dirt beside them. Moses picks it up. He holds it out for Rolf to see. And there it is. The freshly notched X.

Rolf looks up, then down, then up again. He grabs the stick and turns it over in his hands. "It's a trick. You swapped out the stick. You planted that there to make a fool of me."

"I can tell by your voice you don't believe what you're saying."

He almost angrily snaps the stick over his thigh. Then he studies it further. A whorl here. A spot of lichen there. The white X. Then he marches up to the shore and holds out his hands and drops the stick. Maybe thirty seconds pass before it falls with a thwap from the sky and strikes the ground beside him.

What he first believed to be mist-laced water is sky. He's looking down into a cloudy sky. Down is up. Up is down. Another broken mirror.

"I dropped it there," Rolf says.

"And it fell from up there," Moses says, pointing a finger.

"So the elk."

"The elk fell from up there too."

Rolf shouldn't be willing to believe what he's seeing. He's always had an obsession with facts, an allergy to the unknown. This is what kept him out of church even when Doreen made a habit of going to Mass every Sunday. This is what kept him on a case until it closed even when a lead went cold.

Maybe this getting-old game has made him soft in the brain. Maybe losing Doreen opened him up to the possibility of something else. Or maybe it's the woods.

When you're in the woods, there's always this sense of mystery and make-believe. That's why Grimms' fairy tales spilled out of the Black Forest of Germany. The light is different. Sound is different. And no matter how hard you look, even in a square acre of land, you can't see it all. Beneath the bark of that pine, a novel's worth of beetle-bitten cursive is etched into wood. Beyond that cluster of manzanita, a mule deer is nestled down. Twenty yards overhead, a squirrel is worrying over a spruce cone and a woodpecker is spearing a moth, and six feet below your boots, a toad is settled in his muddy burrow and fungal networks are lapping up minerals with their gray tongues. A spattering of lichen on a boulder takes on the shape of a witch. A rotten log gives off the smell of sex. The half-buried rib cage of a dead animal whitens the forest floor like a grin. Something is always watching you. The birds chatter about you. Ferns shake as hidden things scurry away. It is a place where language doesn't matter, where you don't matter, and where secret things happen that the rest of the world doesn't know about.

He can feel Moses watching him. "Just because you don't know what it's called or how to explain it don't mean it ain't real."

"That's an easy thing for you to say," Rolf says, his breath coming out ragged and damp. "You got faith in the Good Book."

Every now and then, as sheriff, Rolf rubs up against a chaos machine or reality breaker. A guy who tears off his clothes in the middle of a gas station and declares himself the lizard king and tries to claw out the clerk's eyes. A guy who drives a hundred and fifty miles an hour down a highway, bumper-bashing and side-swiping folks, with the metal cranked up and a bottle of Old Crow tucked in his crotch. A guy who shoots up a hardware store and holds a customer hostage and demands a golden helicopter and a Tahiti mansion. These folks are operating so far outside the bounds of normal that you have to rewire your brain to deal with them. Rolf is more accustomed to this than most, but the laws of human behavior are easier to think of flexibly than the laws that govern reality. The sky is blue; the grass is green; water keeps you hydrated; you fumble a ball, it's supposed to drop. What in the hell. What in the hell indeed.

Rolf stares at Moses for a long time. "You better help me understand what's happening here or I'm going to check myself into a clinic and ask them to pump me full of the drugs that cure the crazies."

"I got a few ideas. But ideas is all they is."

"Let's hear them."

"The first is God."

"Okay."

"The next is man."

LOGBOOK: GEORGE C. WARNOK

ENTRY 61

April 7, 1944

For a good month now, Dr. Devinor has been shadowing us in the lab. He wears the same gray suit and red tie every day. His knuckles are cubed with arthritis, and his back is hunched, and he winces sometimes at a pain in his left knee. He wears glasses and takes them off regularly to clean with a handkerchief. A cloud of cigarette smoke follows him. His fingertips and white mustache are stained yellow from tobacco. He does not go out of his way to instruct or correct our work. He is more of a silent editor. He will make notations in data reports. He will restart a computer with a variant algorithm informing its programming. He will say of a certain X-ray machine that for it to make any bit of difference, we need to increase the magnification fiftyfold.

There is a chalkboard hanging on the lab wall. One day he walked into the room, picked up a piece of chalk, and, in quick slashing strokes, etched out a formula. He departed without explanation. We spent the better part of two hours trying to decipher his hieroglyphics—and then everything crystallized. I clapped my hands and said, "We need to make an adjustment to the gravitational lensing."

One time, when he lingered by my desk, I set aside my work and said, "Dr. Devinor? May I ask you something?"

He had a hangdog face. Every part of him drooped as if from exhaustion except for his thin silver eyebrows, which raised now as he waited for me to continue.

"I'm sorry if this seems rude of me. But why don't you simply tell the men what you know? Why make us work so hard to figure out these hints and clues?"

"Because what I know isn't correct. My way failed. You need to go your own way." He placed a hand over his heart, a gesture I thought indicated he cared for us, but he was only searching in his breast pocket for his cigarettes and matches.

"I heard you mention something the other day in passing when you were meeting with the major general. *Tunguska*, I believe the word was. You referred to Tunguska as a failure and a disaster. Is there any chance you could elaborate on that?"

His entire body stiffened and he looked at me severely. "I must be going."

His favorite spot was the roof. Day or night, you could find him up there. He enjoyed the isolation, I'm sure. But I noticed his head often tilted up, as if he were seeing something in the sky the rest of us didn't.

Spring came late here. A damp chill seemed to soak into the very bones of the building. Boots tracked mud through the halls. The windows fogged over. Coughing barked down hallways, and every drinking fountain was oystered with phlegm. Given the close quarters, everyone was soon sick. Wiggins joked that the permafrost up here had released some ancient virus. Kubert joked that the gamma rays were rotting our lungs, and nobody laughed, maybe because we had heard rumors lately of our brothers and sisters at Los Alamos falling ill from their atomic research.

Most of us didn't need more than a hot shower and a few aspirin to feel better, but Dr. Devinor was frail and fell especially ill. For several weeks, he was pale and feverish with a deep-chested cough that sounded pneumonic. We did not have a doctor on-site, only a guard who had been trained as a field medic. There was a very basic clinic with medications and bandages and a bed for observation or an emergency operation, if need be.

A few months back, a researcher named Bunker had had severe abdominal pain that turned out to be a burst appendix, and they shipped him down the mountains to Fairbanks for treatment. He returned a week later with an angry red stripe of a scar along his belly.

I believe there was some anxiety about sending Dr. Devinor away for medical care, given his sensitive political status, so a doctor was driven to us. I happened to spot his arrival, and when the guards escorted him out of the Jeep and through the halls of the building, he was wearing a blindfold.

I stopped by the next day to check on Devinor. The door was half open, but I knocked at it anyway. I found him awake and propped up by three pillows. He wore an undershirt that didn't hide his stick-thin arms and yellowish skin dotted with moles. I noticed some scarring along his shoulders and wondered if he might have been whipped. His glasses were off, folded.

"You," he said in a whisper. "What is your name again?"

"George Warnok, sir."

"Yes. They took away my cigarettes, George. Will you fetch some for me?" He began to cough then, hacking into his hand. His eyes closed painfully. Once finished, he swallowed down a whimper.

"Is that a good idea?" I said. "The cigarettes?"

"Don't condescend to me. You could be my grandchild's grandchild. You're a sperm in a lab coat. Do what you're told, boy. Get me my cigarettes."

"Yes, sir," I said and followed his instructions on where to find them—inside the closet, back of the shelf, on top of his folded shirt and pants. I realized how weak he must be then. A walk of ten paces was too much for him to manage. I brought over the pack of Lucky Strikes and the matchbook and settled onto the stool at his bedside. I knocked a cigarette out of the pack but I didn't offer it to him just yet.

"Well? What are you waiting for?" he said, holding out his hand.

"The other day, when I heard you arguing with the major general?"

"Oh, not this again."

"You mentioned Tunguska."

"So I did."

"Please. What were you talking about?"

"If I tell you, you'll go and tell the others. And I certainly don't need Major General Tusk accusing me of rabble-rousing or mutiny. He might send me back to . . ."

"You don't want to go back to the Soviet Union?"

"No. God, no."

"But you don't want to be here either."

"No. I don't want to be here either. This is true."

"Then where do you want to be? Ideally?"

"Are you really not going to give me a cigarette until I answer your inane questions?"

"No, I am not," I said.

He brought his chin sharply to his chest as if to lock his voice down. But after a few moments he studied me again. One eye was filmed over with a cataract. "A long time ago, when I was your age, I worked on a farm. My parents' farm. We grew wheat and barley and potatoes mostly. It was what my father had done. And my father's father before him. And my father's father's father before him. They lived in the same house, and they worked the same land. I saw my fate as akin to the wheat itself. I would be ground down by our windmill in a crushing familiar cycle.

"So one night I left. This was toward the end of March, approaching the Easter holiday, and I suppose I had rebirth on my mind. I did not say goodbye, in part because I knew my father would forbid me to leave, and I did not want to defy and embarrass him. I hitched a few short rides on wagons, but mostly I walked. For five days. Until I arrived in Moscow. Everything was gray at that time of year, so you can imagine the sight of the bakery. With its bright light and its pink, yellow, and blue confections, it appeared like a portal into a summer garden.

"I stood before the window for a long time. There was a tray of paskhas on display for Easter. Each was thickly topped with whipped cream and dotted with cherries. I did not have much money saved. It was foolish of me to waste it on the paskha. But I was nothing if not rash then. I went into the warm bright bakery that smelled of sugars and spices. A smiling girl at the counter wrapped the paskha for me in paper and I walked through the cold streets until I found a place to sit, a bench in a churchyard. Easter Mass was taking place, and I ate the paskha and I listened to the voices singing an Orthodox chant, and I thought about what else might be possible."

His eyes had grown distant, but they focused on me again now, returning to the room. "You asked where I would like to go? I would like to go there again, I think. I would like to sit in that churchyard and taste that paskha while beautiful music pours over me."

We sat for a time in silence, both of us transported.

"What if I promise not to tell anyone?" I said. "About Tunguska. Will you tell me then?"

"Oh, for God's sake, boy."

"You were brought here for a reason," I said. "What did you do? What did you learn?"

"Give me that cigarette, will you?"

I lit the cigarette and brought it almost to his lips, but not quite. The smoke drifted around his face and he took a greedy breath of it. "Closer. Please."

"If you tell me."

"All right. All right, damn you!"

I placed the cigarette between his lips and he drew on it and held the smoke in his lungs as long as he could before releasing it in a sputtery cough.

And then he told me about Tunguska.

21

◉

Sophie is the vanguard for an operation known as the Collectors. She founded it soon after skyfall, when the meteors changed the geopolitical reality of the world.

Her first recruit was a German, a KSK soldier named Hans Muller who had been a whistleblower on the far-right beliefs expressed by many in the special forces. After he went to the press, he faced scathing denials from high-ranking officials; his apartment caught on fire, and several videos of him engaged in sex with other men were released online. She found Hans alone, drunk in a bar in Munich, and she slid into the booth beside him. "I have a proposition for you," she said and he stared at her blearily and said, "You're not my type, fräulein," and she said, "As a matter of fact, I think I am."

One by one, they grew their operation. Their recruits were ex-military, mostly. Some CIA and SVR and MI5. A few hackers. One failed Vegas magician. Mercenaries. Together they formed a kind of orphan family.

They study the feeds. They study maps. They pay for tips from reporters and politicians and military insiders. They run surveillance on phones, security cameras, satellites, social media. They run predictive algorithms and consult psychics and numerologists and metal-eaters. Then they put the data into action.

They dive into deep-sea trenches. They canoe and bushwhack the Amazon. They snowmobile to Siberian outposts. They drive ATVs into the Sahara, and they climb the Dolomites, and they spelunk in the New York City subways. They chase leads. And they collect. Even before the comet, a meteorite could be worth a thousand dollars per gram. Omnimetal is an even richer strike.

They don't feel allegiance to any country; they are loyal only to themselves. They don't care about politics; they only want money.

Their work is too risky for a permanent address, so when they aren't in the field, they generally stay on a boat—a Metal Shark Defiant 165—that cuts through international waters. They have safe houses and storage bunkers throughout the world containing their finds. They have samples of the alien fungus that gripped Seattle. They have an herbal accelerant that seems to speed up both cellular growth and time itself. They have ice that freezes at seventy degrees. They have a man who can seemingly control flora, and a boy with omnimetal impossibly woven into his skin. The archive of auction items is long.

But Sophie is here in Alaska for something else. Something incalculably valuable.

She has a list of 152 people. That's how many are on the passenger manifest for the 737 that flew from PDX to FAI. She crosses them off name by name. More than half came here for tourism or business. Some rented cars to visit Denali. Some transferred to a single-engine plane to Barrow. Some have already finished their business in Fairbanks and returned home. The rest live in the city or within a hundred-mile radius.

She rings bells and knocks on doors. Sometimes a dog barks. She waits for the doorknob to rattle or the shades to be drawn aside. She arranges her face into a smile. She presents her badge and introduces herself as an investigator. At first they think that they've done something wrong, that they're in trouble, but she assures them that no, that's not it at all. They're good. She's simply following up on the in-flight disturbance they unfortunately experienced. She is gathering witness testimony as the DOT decides which charges to file and determines whether the crew followed protocol. Oh, and she's happy to report that the airline will be giving everyone a thousand bonus miles as an apology and a thank-you for their willingness to participate in the investigation.

Some people speak to her through a crack in the door, but most invite her inside, apologizing for the mess. She sits on couches and La-Z-Boy recliners in living rooms and on wooden chairs at kitchen tables or barstools at granite islands. She pretends to drink the coffee and water they offer her. The walls are pine-paneled or sheeted with bear-patterned wallpaper. There are lacquered fish and mounted antlers and family photos and football trophies and crosses and wooden signs that say LIVE, LAUGH, LOVE. The carpets are brown or the floors are salt-stained hardwood. Sinks stacked with dirty dishes buzz with the last flies of the year. TVs play constantly in the background on mute. Babies cry. Dogs eye her suspiciously. Phones ring. But please, she says, she only needs a few minutes of their time. She takes notes on a legal tablet that she pulls from a portfolio that carries the DOT emblem. "Do you mind if I smoke?" some say, as if this were her house. And no, of course she doesn't, as long as they keep talking through the clouds of menthol.

Tell me about what happened on Delta Flight 3469, she says.

One man, Josh Cassara, lives in a trailer with four other men. They're members of a construction team working on a pipeline. His knuckles are stained with grease. He wears a Colorado Rockies ball cap that's so filthy, she can't be sure of its original color. On the flight he was watching a movie, a really good movie, one of those action movies starring the Rock. He can't remember the name of the film, but there were at least four helicopter explosions, and it was awesome. She should totally watch it. But yeah, sorry, he's got nothing. The movie screen kept glitching, though, toward the end of the flight. Maybe twenty minutes before they landed? Maybe ten? The screen glitched and went dark and he was like, *Fuuuuuck.* The sound got all weird. Like the Rock was whispering something to him. But then he poked and punched the controls a few times and it was all good. Honestly, whatever else was going on, the dude going crazy or whatever, Josh didn't even realize anything had happened until the cops boarded the plane and dragged him away.

Cory Smith works in insurance and lives in a Colonial home in a development called Polar Heights outside the city. Soft rock plays from built-in speakers while they talk. He wears a collared shirt under a gray knit sweater. He says that yes, he was aware of the passenger causing a scene—he was a rangy man with a big beard in a corduroy jacket and a Hawaiian shirt. He remembers the man running down the aisle. At first Cory assumed the guy had to use the restroom. But then he began hollering about the clouds, the clouds. Something crazy like that. He pounded on the door of the cockpit. That's when several people unclipped their seat belts and charged forward and brought the man to the floor. "Here," Cory says and digs out his phone and swipes through his photo album until he comes upon the shaky video. "I was a little slow on the draw. But I got the end of it. Just to give you, like, a vibe."

The video is seemingly worthless at first glance. Shot from twenty rows back, jerky and unfocused. Seat backs and heads. Glimpses of what's going on at the front of the plane, where a small crowd has gathered and a desperate voice can be heard bellowing.

"Do you mind if I take another look?" Sophie says, and Cory says, "Knock yourself out," and she takes the phone and toggles the video slider. Here is a glitch, a glitch, a glitch. Second-long breaks in the footage when everything goes grainy black. Her hands move without pause as she flicks her finger and thumb outward, zooming in, finding a cabin window. She edits, clarifies, changes the color gradient, and screen-grabs a shot of the sky outside, where the clouds appear to be sculpted into monsters.

"What is that?" Cory says, leaning in.

She uploads the video to her own device before deleting it from his. "Evidence," she says and hands the phone back to him.

"You hear all about stuff happening on airplanes these days," he says. "If you fly enough, I guess it's only a matter of time before you rub up against something crazy."

"Indeed," she says.

Mary Poole lives in a brick ranch with a chain-link fence collaring the yard and last year's Christmas lights still dangling from the gutters. Her couch has cup holders built into the arms. Mary remembers everything going dark. "It's like when you stand up too fast and all that blood rushes around your body in weird ways and the edges of your vision blacken like curtains are getting pulled on you." She remembers seeing the man charging down the aisle, and then she remembers nothing else. The next thing she knew, one of the flight attendants was gently nudging her, telling her it was time to deplane. Everyone else was gone at that point. She had evidently fallen asleep. "But I haven't felt right since. I keep having these spells. I keep . . ." Here her voice falls off a cliff.

Sophie notes the yellowish cast to her skin and a plummy purple bruising around her eyes. "Is it just that you feel faint or are you having other problems?"

"Everything's off."

"I think you should see a doctor. I think you should insist on a full-body MRI."

"Why would you say that?" Mary grips the arm of the couch tightly as if she might be dragged into another faint.

"Just a hunch."

"What did your airplane do to me?"

"Go to a doctor. Okay?"

Kristi Pursell lives in a condo near the university. She drinks from a coffee mug that says RX. Her pants are coated with the white fur of her huskie. Her eyes settle on the traffic passing by the window. Her voice sounds slurry and slow when she speaks, and at first Sophie wonders if she might be drunk.

"I was scared," Kristi says.

"Scared he was going to hurt you?"

"No."

"Why not?"

"Because he didn't look angry. He looked scared. He was scared and so I was scared too."

"What was he scared of."

"I don't know. Something out the window. At first I thought maybe an engine was smoking or a bolt had come loose on the wing or what have you." She sips from her coffee cup. "But it was something else."

Sophie notices something then. In addition to turning her face away, Kristi is stiffening her upper lip unnaturally. She's shielding the right side of her face. She did the same when she answered the door, tilting her head when she said hello and invited her visitor inside.

"Kristi?"

"Yes?"

"Will you look at me."

With slow reluctance, Kristi turns her head. Her mouth is pinched shut, but noticeably sunken along the right side.

"What's wrong?"

"My teeth fell out."

"When?"

"I don't know exactly. Maybe on the flight. Maybe then. I was just so distracted and upset, I didn't . . . I didn't notice it until I was waiting in baggage claim." When she opens her mouth to speak, Sophie can see the black gap and the raw pink line of gum. "I feel ugly."

Sophie visits the hotel of a businessman named Todd Marston who never checked in. She visits the ex-husband of a woman named Sandra Basso who was supposed to come for their kid's birthday, but she never showed up.

She visits the addresses of Darren Shan and Vernon Ponsoldt and Pattie Gleason and Nick Faucher and Bernie Peters, and when nobody responds, she goes around the side yards and peers in the windows and breaks in the back doors and finds their dead swollen bodies, the same story at every house. For each one, she removes a bottle of Vicks VapoRub from her coat pocket and smears a line beneath her nose to help fight the smell. Then she pulls on a set of surgical gloves and pops the blade on a knife. Field autopsies reveal that one of them is missing her left eye. One is missing his liver. One is missing the majority of his lower intestine. One of them has left behind a drawing on a piece of paper. It looks like a tangle of vines or tentacles with an eye at the center of it.

Their blood is too coagulated to draw, so she clips off the ear of one, the finger of another, and seals them in labeled Ziploc bags to examine later.

At the Klondike Motel, she sets up an ad hoc lab in the bathtub with the flesh samples laid out on paper towels. She takes the iron from the closet and slices the cord off with a knife. She peels back the rubber casing to reveal the wiring beneath. She plugs the cord into an outlet and spits on the frayed end of it, causing it to sizzle. When she jams the live wire into the flesh samples, they crisp and blacken. The smell of scorched meat makes her curl her nose. But then she sees what she's looking for: Faint blue sparks. Like when you bite into a Life Savers wintergreen candy in a dark room. Omnimetal. They all have faint tracings of omnimetal in their blood.

She gets on her burner phone and punches the U.S. exit code of 011 followed by a long series of numbers. There is a buzz before a connection is established. No one answers but she can hear breathing on the other end of the line. In Mandarin, she says, "Activity confirmed. Stage two, location and acquisition of the sample, under way."

A male voice responds in German. "I have the coordinates on where the plane disappeared. You'll find them uploaded to the chat. Along with the flight path of the three charter planes that went missing last month."

"I take it they're not in the same place."

"Negative. We've got either a roaming entity or variable expulsions."

"But there's a source."

"There's a source. Find it. Fast."

With that, the line goes dead.

The room stinks so she flushes the flesh samples down the toilet and opens the door and windows to air the place out. She stands in the parking lot staring up at the sky for a long time. A few flakes swirl down and melt on her face.

Her eyes settle on the hill nearby. There is a giant building castling the ridge with what looks like a UFO atop it. This is a huge satellite dish aimed at the sky. The architecture stands apart from anything else in the community; it appears to be a Cold War relic. A quick Google search on her phone reveals it to be the Geophysical Institute at UA Fairbanks. If anybody is paying attention to what's going on in the sky, it's them.

She is about to head back inside to fetch her car keys when she notices movement in the front office. She looks that way without looking that way, her head tilted only slightly. The bulky slumped silhouette of the clerk has been replaced by a man wearing military fatigues.

She crosses the ice-scabbed parking lot and returns to her room, not appearing in any sort of hurry. But as soon as she closes the door, she moves with controlled speed. First she goes to the edge of the window, barely nudges the shades, and scans the area. There is a black SUV in an alley across the road, and she'd bet a million dollars it has government plates. There are also the humps of two heads poking above the roof of a nearby duplex. She should have been paying closer attention.

She drops to her knees and rips the silver briefcase out from beneath the bed. Her laptop goes into her satchel. Her suitcase she'll have to leave behind. She has only a few minutes now.

In her jacket is a hidden pocket. From it she slips an object shaped like a thin black brick. It weighs close to five pounds. She places it in the center of the floor. The control panel allows her to set a delayed timer. In three minutes, it will be motion-activated.

She goes to the bathroom and wraps a towel around her hand and punches out the window above the shower. She scrapes the rim, making sure all shards are swept away, and lowers the suitcase and then the satchel through it. She is small enough to follow.

She's two blocks away when she hears the detonation thunder behind her. She doesn't look back.

22

Moses says what's happening in the White Mountains is either an act of God or the work of man.

Rolf keeps staring at the hole in the ground—the hole full of clouds—that seems to be behaving like a passageway between above and below. "Any theories you got, Moses, I'd sure appreciate hearing. I'm in desperate need of an education."

Moses starts to walk again, more slowly this time. The two old men hike side by side as Moses shares the story of his father, who owned this land and who had served in World War II. Originally from Alabama, Samuel was stationed here during the war and fell in love with the wildness of this place. So with the help of the GI Bill, he claimed this small piece of it, a hunting retreat that later became Moses's homestead.

When Moses's father was drinking, he sometimes got a faraway look in his eye and spoke of his time in the war. He hadn't fought on the front lines. He had never felt a bullet ping his helmet or been showered with dirt by a mortar round because he had been Stateside, a guard stationed at a lab. A top secret government facility located somewhere in these White Mountains. He supposed that meant he was lucky. He had lost a lot of friends in the European and Pacific theaters. But mostly he felt sickened and guilty, especially in later years, when he fully understood the devastation of Hiroshima. He felt complicit, because he believed he had been guarding something that was, if not directly, then diagonally connected to the bomb. A secret weapon. The soldiers were housed separately from the scientists, and their posts remained at the perimeter and entrance of the facility. Whatever happened in the bowels of the lab was kept from them. But they heard things. They saw things. The scientists were building something atomic.

There was communication with the lab in Los Alamos. There were signs on doors warning of radiation exposure. The scientists sometimes wore space-suit-like outfits meant to protect them from gamma rays. There was the usual emergency pump and hose on-site for a fire, but there was also a hose that blasted foam meant to blanket and neutralize radioactive contaminants.

Despite the danger charging the air, it was a rather boring post. At first Samuel studied the skies for planes and the shadowed trees for spies and bent his ear to the road, wondering if he might hear an enemy motor tooling their way. But over the three years he was stationed there, his focus drifted, his nerves relaxed. He could spend an hour watching a squirrel working its way from branch to branch, knocking pine cones to the ground. He could lose an afternoon snapping down a stream of playing cards in a never-ending game of solitaire. He could, in his free time, fly-fish in a nearby river, soaking up the sun on its banks and feeling perfectly content. So he wasn't ready—nobody was—for the day when everything ended.

He had been down in Fairbanks on a supply run. This usually happened once a month, and the soldiers always fought for the job. They tore up pieces of paper and put black Xs on two of them, then drew, and this time he and Scott Beem had been the lucky ones. They drove the two-and-a-half-ton GMC CCKW with a canvas-topped bed down from the mountains to Ladd Field, where a shipment of groceries and supplies were waiting for them.

The soldiers on the run were supposed to return immediately, but they always tarried as long as they could, driving by the swimming pool for a glimpse of skin, maybe even risking a visit to a bar for a beer or three. That's exactly what he and Scott did that day. The day of August 6, 1945. They had passed a few hours at a bar, drinking, dancing with some girls, and now they were laughing and passing a bottle back and forth as they drove to the lab. Samuel remembered the windows were down, and it was cool out, the first breath of fall in the air. They sang a Perry Como song—"Till the End of Time"—and the engine groaned as they worked their way up the steep, rutted grade.

They were maybe a mile away from the lab when the hillside flashed red. They caught only a glimpse of the flash before their windshield shattered and their tires popped. It sheared the tops off trees and seemed to shake the very foundation of the Earth. At first Samuel believed it was a volcanic eruption. But it was the lab, he soon realized. The lab had exploded. He had always expected a threat that came from outside, not from within.

What burst out of the building—what escaped upward and into the sky—looked like a rocket the size of a city. Like the vault of heaven had opened up its doors. Like a comet was being born. It roared upward and left a cindered trail in its wake. They watched in awe for many minutes until it escaped the atmosphere and appeared as a glowing track among the stars.

"What in the name of Jesus, Joseph, and Mary was that?" Samuel said.

"It looked like the biggest firework there ever was."

"What should we do? Nobody could have survived that."

"I think we're obligated to go and see."

Smoke filled the air and made night of day. They hiked the rest of the way to the lab. They climbed over the fallen trees and walked through the wrecked building and found everyone gone. Not dead, not buried in rubble, but gone altogether.

"But where could they be?" Samuel asked, and they both looked up.

It was only later—after Samuel was interviewed by the MP, after he was reminded that if he spoke to anyone about what happened at the lab, he would be court-martialed—that he learned about the bomb dropped on Japan.

The date had been the same, August 6. Was what happened at the Alaska Project a retaliation? Or a synchronized experiment? Where did all the scientists and the other guards disappear to? He didn't know. He would never know. But that's what haunted him on the nights he took to the bottle. Everyone else in the world was reeling from the assault on Hiroshima, but he was one of the only witnesses and survivors of a simultaneous disaster. The weight— and unanswered questions—of that private trauma took a toll on him.

Moses finishes telling Rolf this, and the two old men continue to hike for some time in silence. Rolf finally asks Moses if he believes there is a connection. Between what happened then and what is happening now.

"Can't say for sure," Moses says. "But some eighty-odd years ago, my old man saw a light in the sky, and the world changed. And some five years ago, I saw a light in the sky, same as you, same as everybody else. And the world changed again. A comet, they called it. Well, what if they weren't right to call it that?"

"I don't understand."

Moses stops walking and lays his hand on a tangle of vines. He rips at the vines, pulls them away to reveal a rusted fence and a sign that reads GOVERNMENT PROPERTY. NO TRESPASSING.

"What if the blast that came out of this lab," Moses says, "came circling back to us all these years later? What if we're the author of the comet? What if it was us all along?"

LOGBOOK: GEORGE C. WARNOK

ENTRY 62

April 9, 1944

Dr. Devinor laid his head back, denting his pillow, and began to speak. He did not take many breaks except to beg for the occasional sip of water or puff of cigarette, which I hurried to provide, hoping to keep him awake, alert, and willing to share. His voice kept on at an even pace, a creaky music I nodded along to.

I wished desperately for a pen and paper, but I tried as best I could to commit as much of this to memory as possible.

His research into what he called "the mirror theorem" began when he was a professor at the Swiss Federal Institute of Technology in Zurich. It was there that he began his first experiments and failed one of his brightest students. "And now? The student has outpaced the professor. I understand the U.S. government has hired the patent clerk."

"I'm sorry?"

"He's down in Los Alamos now, is he not?"

"You can't mean Einstein?"

"The very same."

"Hold on. You were Albert Einstein's professor?"

"For a short time, yes," Dr. Devinor said. "A short time that has become a very long time. We are both old men now. Since our days in Zurich, Albert has been in the spotlight, and I have been in a dark cell in a gulag. He went one way, I another. But now we are in similar places working on similar tasks, yes? Such is life."

He spoke of how in 1905, the revolution brought him back to Russia, where he was tasked with applying his scientific knowledge to the future of the country. They wanted innovation, breakthroughs. The light bulb, the telephone, the steam engine, the camera all belonged to the West in the late nineteenth century. The wonders of the next century should belong to the Soviets. "And, as you may have guessed, it was weaponization that interested my leaders most. And my focus was the atom."

Much of what Dr. Devinor told me, I already knew, but I was not about to announce my precociousness to a wizened man who seemed to once again be teaching. I could imagine a younger, crisper version of him pacing back and forth at the head of a classroom, sharing some of the same thoughts on physics.

"When most people think of a black hole," he said, "they think of something round. A ball. A dot. But the math seems to indicate that a black hole would be crushed down into the shape of a ring. Do you follow? A ring that spins. Spins. Yes. You heard that right. This is the other misconception about black holes. People think they're stationary. But they move! They're a place where things move.

"So let's say you are drawn toward this black hole, this gravitational nexus, yes? This ring. And let's say you fall through the center of the ring. Where will you go? What is on the other side?" His eyebrows bobbed up and down with every sentence. "There are those of us who believe you go backward in time or forward in time. And there are those who believe it is the entry to a parallel universe. It is hard to know for certain. It is merely a theory, after all, until proven." And here his eyes sparkled and the corners of his mouth twitched in a faint smile. "But what matters most is its potential as a conduit." His studies focused on the possibilities of this conduit. The journey it could offer.

"Now the patent clerk, little Albert, he is thinking about atoms as a blunt instrument. Because that's what America is. America is a blunt instrument that wallops everyone and gets its way. But I was thinking about atoms very differently in 1917."

"In Tunguska?" I said.

He nodded. "In Tunguska."

They had a lab there. An underground lab. To keep their work sacred and secret. Not so dissimilar to this one. A windowless lab in a cold, forested place. "You know what that's like? Don't you, my boy?"

Coming here to Alaska certainly felt like a form of time travel for Dr. Devinor. In both instances, he was to oversee the building of a machine. "Not to split the atom, but to crush it and to rotate it." When he said this, he closed his hand until the knuckles whitened. "Because I wanted to create a small but controllable black hole." Weakly, he lifted his fist and opened it slightly and brought it to his eye and peered through the tunneled gap. "A conduit. A gateway. A door. You could call it many things, but I always favored the term *mirror*. Because a looking glass—a mirror—was what Alice stepped through on her way to forever, yes? Through the mirror, then. That is where we hoped to travel."

He let his hand drop to his chest. For a time he made a muttering sound deep in his throat and it seemed he was trying to hold down a cough. Then he continued. "Electrons can be in two places at the same time. When we talk about machines powered by quantum mechanics, we speak of harnessing that energy. Now, if this can be true for electrons, why can't it be true for a cigarette or a baseball? Or a tank? Or a soldier? Or even one of the patent clerk's bombs?"

All we needed to make that happen, he argued, was a looking glass.

A mirror.

"Can you imagine the power?" At this he shook his head. "If you had a conduit such as this, and if you could control its locational-ity, you could move from point A to point B just like that." He tried to snap his fingers but the skin just made a papery noise. "What if I put an atomic entrance here and an exit in the Hotel Metropol in

Moscow? You could roll my bed out of this godforsaken place and into their restaurant. We could be dining by candlelight! Stuffing our faces with caviar!

"You could watch the sunset one minute and the sunrise the next. You could march an army from Saint Petersburg into Washington, DC. You could step out your door and onto the surface of the moon. Or farther. Farther still. As long as you could find a way to control the coordinates of the conduit."

So that was what Dr. Devinor built in Tunguska. A black mirror.

It took five years to construct—and five seconds to destroy. "We activated the power from a bunker twenty miles away, but that wasn't nearly far enough. There was a white flash that expanded into something red and terrible, a hellish fissure in the night sky. The sound was beyond description. A heavenly artillery. Really a feeling more than a sound. Deep in my guts, deep in my marrow. A force. It made me fall to my knees and piss myself and pray to a God I didn't believe in." A single tear dropped from his eye and trickled down his cheek. He made no effort to wipe it away. "A hot wind tore through forests and boiled marshes and ripped apart farms and collapsed our bunker. Many died that day, including several military commanders overseeing my experiment.

"It was the very definition of a *cataclysm*, and I was responsible. That's what I believed. That's certainly what my country believed.

"The blast was detected in Germany, England, America. They were told that Russia had suffered a natural disaster. A meteor had fallen from the sky. Yes. That was the explanation for Tunguska. The spy planes that later circled the area had little to observe beyond devastation. I had succeeded even as I had failed.

"The blast zone was over two thousand square kilometers, but unlike a bomb, this was not a round crater. The shape was later described as being like a butterfly. This, I believe, was caused by the spin of the black hole. The *wormhole* is the term we are using now. When it spun, it had a kind of infinity effect."

Dr. Devinor fell into a coughing fit and even after it had silenced, he kept his hand over his mouth.

"Are you all right, Dr. Devinor?"

He held up his hand, and it was bright red with blood. "I am dying, I think. I survived all that time in the gulag by dreaming about life after my escape. And when it comes, my lungs give up on me." He snorted a laugh. "Ah, but that is the way of things."

Before his eyes fluttered shut and he drifted into a deep sleep, he said to me, "I am convinced we almost destroyed the world. You must be careful not to make the same mistakes that I did."

23

At the Grizzly Hangover—a dive bar with walls built from railroad ties and no windows—the four of them sit on high stools at a table: Theo, Jackson, Little Head, and Diane the Port Authority officer. The table has a round wooden top scarred and oily from years of use. A chandelier made of antlers hangs over them and gives off beer-colored light.

Diane asks the boys how much money they have. Everybody looks to Theo. "This is your mission, dude," Little Head says.

Theo pats the pockets of his army jacket and finds his wallet and unpeels twenty-three dollars in wrinkled fives and ones. "That'll do," she says and scoops the money toward her, taps it into a neat pile, and tucks it away in her purse. "If I'm going to lose my job, the least I deserve is a pitcher of Hamm's and a bacon cheeseburger special."

The air smells like creosote and stale beer. The floor is dirty with peanut shells and bottle caps. Country music plays from the jukebox. A pinball machine occasionally lets out a cheery fountain of notes. A mustached man in a vest with no shirt underneath plays pool, the balls clacking and humming.

Diane refuses to say anything until the food arrives, and even then, she requires a pint of beer to loosen her up. They watch a television over the bar that is playing a show about sport fishing until she is ready to speak.

"We found him in the hall," she says.

"What?" Theo says.

"We had him locked in a holding cell. Six by eight foot. Bunk and a toilet. Nothing for long term—usually nobody's in there more than a few hours. There's the door and there's the toilet and there's a vent. Nothing else going in or out otherwise. But we found him *in the hall*." She fills up her pint glass again, tipping it to keep from foaming over on the pour. "He was lying there. On the ground of the hallway. Shaking, sort of. Breathing heavy. Touching himself all over. Like, making sure all his bits and pieces were there.

"Not sure how long he'd been there, but he sprang up when I turned the corner and said, 'Hey!' He looked at me in a panic, but he didn't try to run or nothing. I remember his eyes was all bugged out, white as peeled eggs. I radioed for Ted-O to come on the double and then unholstered my Glock and told him the business. *Hands behind your head, get down on your knees,* and all that. But it's like he wasn't hearing me. He kept running his hands along his body and then along the walls and even the door to his cell. Pushing and poking. Like you would if you were looking for a secret passage or such.

"When we sat down with him before—for the interrogation—he was drunk. Stupid drunk." She makes eye contact with Theo. "Sorry, kid."

"It's okay. He liked to drink. Keep going."

"So, like I said, when we were interrogating him, he stank to high hell of booze. He must have emptied every little bottle on the Delta snack cart. He was drunk, but he made sense! Even when he was talking nonsense about monsters in the clouds and such, you could follow him."

"Wait," Theo says. "What do you mean, *monsters*?"

"Monsters." Diane sips from her beer and dirties her upper lip with foam. "That's why he freaked the fuck out on the plane. Am I allowed to say *fuck* around you? You're old enough, right?"

"Fuck yeah," Little Head says, and Jackson says, "Fucking A."

"Anyway, he freaked out," she says, "because he thought he saw something. In the clouds. Monsters."

"No," Theo says. "You must have misunderstood him. The whole reason he traveled to Oregon was, he thought he discovered a new cloud formation. He's completely obsessed with it. He's been trying to talk to scientists about—"

"I talked to him. I know what he told me. I'm sorry, kid, but I'm one hundred percent on this." She knocks on the table to punctuate the thought. "He thought the plane was flying into a monster. He thought they were all going to die. That's why he got up from his seat and made a fuss. He was being a hostile dumbass, but he was at least a hostile dumbass with, like, charitable intentions."

"You said he was drunk," Theo says. "I believe you about that part. He does that. But usually when he gets drunk, he falls asleep on the couch. Maybe he just had a nightmare, and everybody over-reacted or something."

"If he was having a nightmare on the plane," Diane says, "then he never woke up from it."

"What about when you found him in the hall? You said he wasn't making sense anymore?"

"Right. At that point, he was completely unhinged. Loco-coco-nutso. Off his rocker. I figured he'd either gone off his meds or popped a pill we missed when patting him down, one or the other. Because this wasn't nobody you could talk to reasonably.

"I tried. I asked him what in the hell he was doing and how in the hell he got out. 'I don't know,' he said. 'I don't know, I don't know, I don't know.' He just about I-don't-knowed me to death, number of times he said it in this voice that barely rose above a high-pitched whisper. His face didn't have any color to it. Pale as can be. And he was soaked in sweat. 'I don't know,' he kept on saying. 'I don't know.'

"Ted-O came along shortly. That's my partner. Your father was a big boy, but Ted-O, he's bigger. He rag-dolled your old man. Slammed him against the wall, then the floor, then held him there. Cuffed him tight. I went to open the door of the holding cell, but the knob wouldn't turn. You hearing me? It was locked. How in the hell did he get through a locked door, I want to know?

"That's what I ask him, but all he can say is 'I don't know, I don't know, I don't know.' And then he goes quiet except for this gaspy breathing. And then he starts to heave and retch. Pukes all over the floor. Big splattery sheets of it. It's in his beard. It's on his clothes. It's running down the hall. The smell was something else. And in between all this puking, he says how dizzy he is, how he can't tell up from down, left from right.

"Ted-O, he wanted to just toss your old man back in his cell, but with the way he was breathing and sweating and twisting around, I was worried he might be having a heart attack or a brain event. My grandpa died of a brain bleed on Christmas morning, and I remember he started talking in tongues before he puked gingerbread cookies all over his Santa Claus sweater. That was some pretty traumatic shit. I'm still processing it, you know what I'm saying? To this day, I can't smell gingerbread without reliving it all again. But anyway, back to your old man.

"'Aw, he's just drunk,' Ted-O says. But I call an ambulance anyway. Course, you can't just send somebody in handcuffs on his way. You got to escort him. So the EMTs show up and check his pulse and blood pressure, both of which are through the roof. The EMTs hoist him onto the gurney and roll him out the door and I follow. Because Ted-O, he's done. He thinks this hospital thing is a waste of time. But I'm willing to see it through.

"The whole way to the hospital, you know what I'm thinking? I'm thinking, *How in the name of sin did he get through that locked door and end up in the hallway?* And then—then maybe I get the start of the answer." Diane lowered her voice here, and the three boys leaned in to hear. "He started coming apart. Not just mentally. Physically."

Theo says, "What's that supposed to mean?"

"It means I'm looking at him one second and he's a man. It means I'm looking at him a second later and he's veins and muscle and bone. It means I'm looking at him a second after that and he's gone altogether. But before I can blink twice or say *Holy merciful Jesus,* he's back. It's like he's sinking. It's like he's unraveling. It's like he's gone and here at the same time."

The shirtless guy in the vest strikes the cue ball and the break shot is loud enough to nearly startle Theo off his stool.

"This is when most people would say, *You're talking crazy, Diane.*
But from the way you're taking this in, seems you're already fluent
in crazy yourselves."

"We don't think you're crazy."

"Good," she says. "Because I'm not. Those EMTs saw the same
thing. Not just with your old man. With others. Others they were
shuttling to the hospital."

"How many others?"

"That I don't know. I just know there's something going on here
in Fairbanks, God help us. Maybe in the water. Maybe in the air.
Maybe in the goddamn clouds. Whatever it is, it's wrong enough
that the government's investigating."

"I saw them," Theo says. "I think I saw them."

"Where?"

"At the hospital. I saw a guy in, like, an army uniform."

Diane nods. "Department of Defense, actually. This guy in fatigues,
he came to the airport, asked me what happened on the plane. And
in the cell. And in the ambulance. You'd think I was the one under
arrest, the way he was talking to me. Little punk. Looked like he was
twelve years old. But he sure wanted me to know he was in charge,
the bossy son of a bitch."

"What was his name?" Theo says.

"Colonel Purdin. Not sure about the first name. Cheese Dick,
probably."

Jackson laughs and Theo gives him a look and he says, "Sorry."

"What did Colonel Purdin say to you?"

"He asked me not to say nothing. Not to no one. On account of
it being a matter of national security. So you can see why I hesitated
when you showed up on my doorstep. But fuck that guy. Is it con-
tagious? I'm asking him. Do I need to worry about being exposed?
I'm asking him. He says not to worry. I'll be fine, and he'd take care
of everything from there. Meaning your old man. The DOD was
officially taking him into custody. And since then, this has all been
festering inside me. Making me feel sick. Making me feel like I did
something wrong. When I seen you there outside the airport, when

I learned Chuck Bridges was your old man, I knew I had to say something." She holds up her hands as if to show she has nothing to hide. "And now I have. Now I've done and said it."

Her voice has begun to rasp, and she drinks in silence for a time, wetting her throat. Then she inclines her head toward Theo. "Well? What are you thinking, kid?"

He's thinking about how, over the past year, year and a half, the worst thing anybody could say to him was *You're just like your dad*. Maybe they were talking about his build or the color of his hair or the way he walked with a stoop, angled at the waist, as if he were fighting against a hard wind. And now here Theo is, behaving exactly like his father too. Medical conspiracies? Top secret military operations? It's hard to accept this whole story, but not because it breaks the rules of reality. It's hard to accept because it feels *exactly* like something his father would have ranted about on the radio or at the dinner table. But now it's Theo's turn to chase the truth. Now it's time for him to take over where his father left off.

"The hospital told me my dad is dead," he says.

"But you don't believe it?"

"I guess not. Not for sure, anyway."

"I don't know what I believe either."

"What would you do?" Theo says. "If you were me?"

"If you were *us*, you mean," Little Head says.

"Yeah, us," Jackson says.

"This is starting to get kind of scary," Theo says to them. "You guys don't have to keep going if you don't want to."

"Shut up," Little Head says, and Jackson says, "Yeah, shut your hole, asshole."

"Okay," Theo says to Diane. "What would you do? If you were *us*?"

"Nobody's dead without a body." Diane picks up her meaty, oozing cheeseburger with two hands and before she snaps a bite out of it, she says, "I were you, I'd go straight to the morgue. If he's there, he's dead. If he's not there, you're being lied to and your old man needs your help."

24

◎

Rolf drives down from the mountains. He has the radio set to the classical station and the piano music comes in snatches broken by static. His foot hovers over the brake, pumping it now and then on hard turns. His wipers knock the slush off his windshield, but the way is blurry and the asphalt is wet and his tires slip out with quick kicks until he can steady the truck. The trees blur into a wall of wood. He loses thousands of feet in elevation every few minutes. His ears pop. He feels like he's getting heavier, like he's gaining speed, even if he keeps the needle around fifty, forty-five. It's the truth of what he's seen. It's a weight he now carries with him. What's he supposed to do with it?

Of course he's read the news over the past few years. He understands that people *believe* the comet changed the world, that the meteor shower was a trigger event that *supposedly* shook up the economy and the political theater. But to him it's always seemed like a bunch of overblown hooey.

Every night, when the world sleeps, people lose touch with reality. Their minds invent things that aren't there. They see things that aren't real. Rolf always felt like if you spend half your time on Earth in a delusional state, that will sure as hell carry over to your waking life occasionally. He observes this all the time. The community-college professor who shot his wife because he thought she was cheating on him. The lady at the local Walmart who ripped masks off people's faces during COVID because she thought the government was poisoning folks with CO_2. The dummy at the convenience store who week after week thinks he has a shot at winning Powerball. The kook DJ on 93.3 the Grizz who thinks Sasquatch lives in the woods. They're all dreaming with their eyes wide open.

Until Rolf lost his wife, he didn't remember his dreams. He believed that was because he didn't have room for nonsense and saw life straight. He prides himself on being as rational as a ruler.

A bunch of shit from outer space changed the world? Yeah. Sure. Whatever you say, buddy. That's just people being people. Inventing conspiracy theories or loving juicy gossip or politicizing some bullshit or getting lost down internet rabbit holes. Where's the evidence? Show him the proof. Over the past five years, the comet hasn't changed his life. The comet hasn't changed Fairbanks.

Things that happen to people faraway honestly don't matter much to him. Sounds harsh, but it's true. There's a riot of some sort happening where? Wildfires are raging because why? There's an authoritarian dictator in South America who did what? There's only so much he can give a damn about. Worrying about somebody a thousand miles away makes as much sense as worrying about a rock on Mars. He's concerned with whatever is in his orbit. This county. His county. When people talk about the weaponization of omnimetal or about some secret lab in the Gobi Desert, or about some alien fungal contagion or blah-blah-blah, that's no different than when they're talking about plural pronouns or trigger warnings or defunding the police. It's a foreign language he doesn't speak and doesn't want to learn. That's one of the reasons he knows it's time to retire. He just doesn't feel like he's in touch with the conversations people are having anymore.

Or at least, that's how he used to feel.

He doesn't have the words for what he's witnessed in the White Mountains. He also doesn't have the first notion how to handle it.

"You should call the FBI," a voice says.

He looks over at his wife sitting in the seat beside him. She wears her favorite green cardigan with a black turtleneck and a pair of jeans ironed crisp like she always liked them.

"FBI, my ass."

Doreen reaches over and pats him on the thigh. "This isn't a time to be defensive. You're way out of your league. It's okay to admit that."

"Don't tell me—"

"This isn't a problem you can handcuff and lock up, Rolf. This isn't like anything you've dealt with before."

Rolf's wife wears glasses. She takes them off now and puffs out a breath and diligently cleans them. This was her habit at the end of every day before bed. She called the fog on the glass the ghosts of an exhausting day. That's how he feels now. Like he needs to pull out his eyeballs and wipe the ghosts from them.

She puts the glasses back on and studies him steadily with those jade-green eyes that always made his heart hurt. "Let me remind you of that elk you found on top of the Westmark Hotel. Whatever's happening here isn't isolated to the woods. It's bleeding into the city. You've got to protect your people. You've got to ask for help."

"I'll call Emily Katoo."

"And what's she going to do?"

"She'll hear me out without calling me crazy."

"You're not crazy. Moses isn't crazy. *The world*'s gone crazy."

"I'm talking to you, aren't I?" Rolf says. "Most people would call that pretty goddamn crazy."

The passenger seat is empty now. There's only the heater blasting and the sleet-rippled window and the forest beyond.

He aches for company. Someone to talk to. He tried to get Moses to come to town with him, but the old man wouldn't leave the woods. He was going to keep searching and studying, because he believed there was something sacred taking place there and he wanted to bear witness to it. "Some are saying we're living in a time of miracles," he said. "Maybe we saw a little bit of that today. The beginning of something miraculous."

The Bible has been telling Moses all this time that there's another reality stacked on top of this one, and now here it is—evidence of *something else*. Who wouldn't want to look a little closer?

Rolf realizes then that he has rolled into Fairbanks without any memory of the last twenty minutes. His body has been on autopilot while his brain churns through all this trouble. The air is gray but absent of sleet. He's outrun the weather system. He sits at a traffic light. The person in the car beside him is staring at him.

"I'm talking to myself, aren't I?" he says and gives a sad chuckle. He tries to camouflage the fact by tapping at the steering wheel and pretending to sing. But the song dies in his mouth when a brigade of military tactical trucks roars past him, ten of them, heading in the opposite direction. Toward the mountains. Their engines are loud enough to shake the air. They are painted the same camo color as the fatigues the soldiers inside them wear. "Shit," Rolf says and thinks about pulling a Uey to follow them. He supposes they could be here for a routine exercise, but—

A honk sounds. The red light has changed to green. He gives an apologetic wave to the car behind him and motors up to speed— and then crushes his brake halfway through the intersection as a cream-colored Ford Explorer roars out of the cross street and screeches past him, a narrow miss. He and several others lay on their horns.

This is not his job—and especially not the kind of thing he wants to deal with right now—but this one is too ugly to ignore. He watches the SUV go weaving in and out of lanes, its brake lights flaring erratically. No doubt the driver will stumble through a so-briety test before blowing a .30 or will stare slackly at him, his eyes swimmy with fentanyl.

He has some light bars hidden in his grille and he switches them on now. He cranks the wheel and pushes through the cross traffic and chases the Explorer for two blocks. The pulsing blue light of his LEDs reflects off the rear hatch of the SUV as it slows and then crookedly pulls onto the shoulder.

He steps out onto the street and belts on his holster. He can make out two, maybe three, figures inside the vehicle. The window drops as he approaches. He slows and puts his hand on his pistol butt and cranes his neck. He pauses a moment before saying anything because he can't quite make sense of what he sees.

He's looking at a kid, clearly, but he doesn't look put together properly. An elementary-school head rests on top of a high-schooler's broad neck and shoulders. "What's up, my man?" the boy says in a screechy, reedy voice.

"I—" Rolf says. "Do you know why I pulled you over?"

"Honestly? No idea." It's difficult to tell if he's hearing sarcasm or obliviousness. But he doesn't smell weed or whiskey. And though the boy's eyes bulge unnaturally, the whites aren't bloodshot and the pupils aren't dilated.

Rolf peers into the vehicle and spots two others. Unlike the driver, they appear scared shitless. They could be fourteen or they could be eighteen. He's lost touch with how to pin down an age. Everybody under thirty looks like a baby to him.

"Shouldn't you boys be in school?"

So quickly that Rolf almost believes him, the driver says, "We were on a field trip, actually."

"That right? Where to?"

"It was a cancer-awareness field trip. We were visiting kids. With cancer. At the cancer ward. And trying to make their day a little better. A little brighter. Because those kids, they're really sad. They needed a pick-me-up."

"Uh-huh."

"The doctors like it when I come in, because I was one of those kids. I graduated, I guess you could say, I'm what you call a survivor. But you know what? Seeing all those bald, sick kids and smelling all their bald, sick smells—it brought back some terrible memories. I'd really, really, really like to get home to my family now. And hug them. And rest. I could use some rest."

Rolf thinks he hears a voice hiss, "Will you shut up?" from the back seat, but he can't be sure over the highway noise.

"Can I see your license and registration?"

"Sure thing, Officer." Again, that tone. Just a little bit of a knife blade beneath the surface of his voice. This kid is clearly a special sort of pain in the ass. He digs into his butt pocket and pulls out his wallet and hands over the plastic card with complete confidence—even though it's clearly a permit. "There you are."

"Junius, huh?" Rolf taps it in his hand.

"Yeah. Now you know why my friends call me Little Head."

"They call you Little Head?"

"Right. Because otherwise I'd have to listen to them call me Junius. Which sounds like a term for a vitamin deficiency."

"This your dad's car, Junius?"

"You can call me Little Head. But no—it's mine. I mean, my father paid for it, but it's mine."

"How do you think he'd feel about you joyriding in it?"

"Joyriding?" The boy puts up his hands in mock offense. "Sir, did you not hear me talking a moment before about the field trip? To the children's cancer ward?"

"Do me a favor."

"For you, Officer? I'll do anything."

"You can call me Sheriff. Now cut the engine and get out of the vehicle."

The boy digs around in his wallet. "What if I gave you ten dollars? No, eleven dollars!" He peeks the cash out from the lip of his wallet. "Could we just make this all go away?"

"Cut the engine. And get out of the car."

"The thing is, we're on a really important mission. I know that sounds made-up, but it's true. Something really messed up is—"

Rolf opens the door for him. "Out."

"Okay, okay."

"The rest of you knuckleheads too."

Another minute and all three boys are standing on the shoulder, sullen and flinching against the cold wind pouring down from the mountains. One of them wears a camo jacket and looks like a linebacker. The other kid wears a tracksuit and might be seventy pounds sopping wet. A few snowflakes whiten the air. "Everybody get your asses in the back of my rig."

Turning his back on them is a mistake. But his mind is only half plugged into this current bit of trouble. The rest of him is still up in the White Mountains. He hears the rattle of keys and a voice call out, "Go, Theo!"

Before Rolf can spin around, he feels a sharp pain in the center of his spine as someone tackles him from behind. He is facedown in the gravel and cursing at the weight on top of him. One kid flops over his back and the other tangles up his legs, trying to hold on. "You stupid little shits! Do you realize how much trouble you're going to be in? Let go of me!"

"Go, go, go!" the one named Little Head yells.

A husky voice, presumably belonging to the kid who looks like a linebacker, yells, "But I barely know how to drive!"

"Just do what I did! It's easy!"

"I've only done parking lots and country roads!"

"Get off of me!" Rolf tries to push himself up without any luck. The gravel bites into his belly. A mix of snow and rain patters on the back of his neck. He can't see much more than the front grille of his truck. The blue LEDs flash in time with his pounding heart. "You're being really goddamned stupid right now."

"Just go!" Little Head says. "You need to go! Or it'll be too late."

The tiny kid in the tracksuit says, "This is awesome!"

"I don't know what the hell you kids are up to," Rolf says, "but this is going to get very, very ugly for all of you."

Suddenly there is hot breath in his ear. "Sorry, old-timer." A mouth smooches his cheek. "But government conspiracies are more important than a date in juvie court."

Behind them an engine roars and tires screech as the SUV takes to the road.

LOGBOOK: GEORGE C. WARNOK

ENTRY 73

May 14, 1944

I met with Dr. Devinor on only one other occasion before our short time as colleagues concluded. In the night, I awoke to find him standing over my bed. I almost shouted at the sight. His breath rattled in his chest and his features weren't immediately distinguishable, so my dream-addled mind understood him to be a specter until he spoke in his raspy, thickly accented voice: "Why is it that you do what you do?" That's what he asked.

"Dr. Devinor." I sat up in bed and kneaded the sleep from my eyes. "What time is it?"

"Don't avoid the question. I asked why is it that you do what you do? Here. At this facility. With your research."

Slowly my mind was waking up. I could see now that he was dressed in his gray suit and red tie and I assumed this meant his health and energy had improved. "I suppose I . . . well, Roosevelt talks about the arsenal of democracy, yes? How we're all freedom fighters? How we all need to do our part, whether on the battle-field or the factory floor, to end tyranny? The work I'm doing, if successful, will hopefully help the Allied effort? It will keep the world safe?"

"Why is it that you sound as if you're asking questions instead of giving answers? And how does building something dangerous keep things safe?"

"Well, sir. I suppose it's a matter of balance." The fog was lifting from my brain and the words came easier. "Our reports tell us that we're not the only ones working on splitting the atom. So it's very likely that we're not the only ones working on rotating it either. The Manhattan Project and the Alaska Project undoubtedly have foreign competitors. It's a race, I guess you could say."

"A race to ruin the world."

"To ruin it?" I said. "Why not to save it?"

"Bah. You've got a savior complex, then."

"What do you think Hitler would do with this technology?"

"Nothing good. But what makes you think America would do better?"

"I believe in this country. I really do. Maybe we haven't always been this way—and maybe we won't always be this way—but right now we are *united* states. We're all in this together. And I think we want that for the world as well. A united world."

"Pfft. You're at once a patriot and a globalist. Make up your mind."

"Why can't I be both if America is the vanguard for a democratic world?"

"Oh, please. Such youthful optimism. Such empty-headed nonsense. You're avoiding the fact that you're building machines that will result in widespread death."

"With respect, sir, I would like to argue a counterpoint. You referred to Einstein's work as a blunt instrument. Splitting the atom can kill, yes. But doesn't nuclear energy also have the potential to power cities?"

He made a disagreeing noise, but he stopped barking insults at me, so I kept on.

"By the same token, let's talk about the Alaska Project. If we are building an atomic rotator, or a turnstile, or a gate, or what you called a black mirror—well, sure, you *could* weaponize that. But that's kind of a limited way of thinking in my mind. Because isn't this black mirror actually the way to make us *one world?* If we could create and control wormholes, we would all be neighbors. It would revolutionize trade and transportation and more. So much more."

"You will see," Dr. Devinor said. "When you get older, you won't be as hopeful. Because you'll see what man is capable of."

"I know you've had some ugly things happen to you. I know you're carrying around a lot of anger and regret, but . . ."

"But what?"

"I am hopeful. I am. Or I wouldn't be here."

"Hmm. Hmm—hmm—hmmm." He stood there for a long time, readjusting his posture now and then to keep his unsteady self balanced. Then he reached into his mouth. I presumed he had a piece of celery or meat trapped between his teeth and was trying to dig it out. I found the sight rather ghastly and rude to look at, so I averted my gaze. But then he began to gag and retch, and I said, "Sir? Dr. Devinor?"

Half of his hand was lost from sight, his fingers searching for something. He pushed at his elbow to help in his foraging. His eyes were closed in seeming pain. There was a popping, sucking sound. And then a muddy *rip*. And he finally withdrew his hand, now gloved with blood.

He held out something to me. What looked like a gory gem. A tooth, I realized. "They didn't put me in the gulag right away. I had several days to assess the damage I had caused. And this. This is what I found at the center of it all. This is what I found in the crater of Tunguska." He opened up my hand and placed the tooth in my palm. "There. I kept it hidden and safe all these years."

"I'm sorry, Dr. Devinor. But . . . a molar?"

He spit some blood on the floor. "Look closer, boy."

I climbed out of bed and stood by the window and wiped away the blood and saw that the tooth was made of metal. A silver-blue metal, the shimmer of which reminded me vaguely of the colors seen in the northern lights.

"It's metal," I said.

"The ninth metal," he said.

"Why the ninth?"

"There are eight noble metals. Gold and silver and the like. They are called noble because they are rare and precious. Because they resist corrosion and have unique properties that make them valuable as jewelry or useful in technology. Now there are nine. And this ninth metal is the summit of the galvanic series."

"What are its unique properties?"

"It can absorb an enormous amount of energy. On a quantum level."

I couldn't help but laugh. "On a *quantum* level?"

"Subatomic absorption, yes. But also expulsion. Whatever it soaks up, it can spit right out."

"Why haven't I heard of it?"

"Are you not paying attention, boy? You haven't heard of it because it is not of this Earth. And it is not man-made. There is no place for it on the periodic table."

"If it's not of this Earth, where did it come from?"

He touched a finger to his temple. "Alice went through the looking glass, yes? But did you ever think how the story might have been different if someone in Looking-Glass Land had come to Alice? The looking glass works both ways."

"It worked, then. Your machine in Tunguska?"

"It nearly blew a hole through reality."

"But it worked! You opened up a wormhole! And this is what was on the other side!"

"It is more than evidence of another world. I found this at the very center of the blast crater. It survived what I believe was the equivalent of a cosmic forge. A refiner's fire."

"How do you know all of this for certain?"

His eyes took on a faraway focus. "The metal has been with me for a long time. I have listened to it."

"Listened to it?"

"Do you think you're strong? Up here, I mean?" He reached out and poked a finger into my forehead.

"I believe so."

"You have to be strong. Or it might corrupt you."

"What do you mean by that?"

"I mean exactly what I say. It whispers. It seduces. It corrupts."

I assumed he was being metaphoric in ways I didn't fully understand. He seemed worried about my integrity, so I said what I felt was true: "I want only what's best for the world."

"Hmm," he said. "Let us hope that is true. Now, when I say this metal can absorb and expel energy, I mean that in ways that are beyond description."

"I don't understand."

"What if a battery could take on more than electrical charge? What if it could contain memories? Or even life itself?"

"I still don't understand."

"No. And sometimes neither do I. But you will. Soon. I might as well be telling you about a song or a poem I heard instead of letting you experience it firsthand. Keep the metal close. Keep it secret. The truths of another world await you. It is a key."

"My God."

"As I said, it corrupts. So it could very well be your god," Dr. Devinor said. "Or your devil."

He left me then and I settled back into a restless sleep and learned in the morning that he had gone to his favorite spot on the roof and thrown himself from the building.

25

oanna runs through the lab. She can't keep her flashlight steady; the beam cuts wildly through the dark, giving her brief, dizzying bursts of clarity. Here is a desk. Here is a fallen chair. Here is stack of moldering papers. Bryce is behind her. So is the bear. It is not a bear, but that is the closest word Joanna has for it. A bear that is not a bear. The huff and roar and scrape of the beast is close behind them. She risks a look backward. The shape of the thing is generally familiar—a big shaggy body, a broad triangular head—but it seems to be made of mist. Mist that trembles and flows. And from inside this mist, strange details burn into the view of her flashlight's beam. A muzzle that appears like slick bone. A tongue that splits into gloppy tentacles. Too many marbled eyes. Wherever the bear travels, it leaves behind a second or two of steam, like a fleeting contrail.

She barely has time to recall last night. But the memory of what happened is in her prickling nerves. This *thing* is what stalked her through the rain and the mud and the dark. This *thing* is what she saw in the rear camera of the truck. Her mind moves swiftly from denial to acceptance: *That's impossible, it can't be, it is.* You don't sit around and debate the plausibility of what's trying to kill you.

They run. They try to hide behind a desk, but the desk gets knocked aside. A cabinet tears from the wall. A machine that looks like a giant camera topples. Glass shatters. Metal shrieks. Wood splinters. Claws scratch concrete. Wherever they go, breath follows, panting and chuffing and staining the air, hot and rotten.

Then they find the bodies of the two guards. One of the men appears to have had his face snatched off like a mask, revealing a gnawed skull beneath. The other is little more than a rib cage and boots ribboned in the remains of a tattered, bloodied uniform.

They scream, and between their screams, Joanna manages to say, "Over here," and grabs Bryce by the arm and drags him out of the lab and into the hallway. She slams the door shut behind them. Seconds later there is a scrape and a shuddering boom that tests the hinges. Then another. Then another. They make it ten steps before the door splinters and the bear that is not a bear crashes into the hall and lets out a gruff moan.

She dares a look back. Her flashlight makes its many eyes glow like a galaxy of stars. The surging bulk of it approaches fast. She can't possibly outrun the thing. She slows and readies to either curl up or take a swing.

But this time Bryce grabs hold of her and pulls her through a doorway. He claps the door closed just in time for the bear to hit it. A *doom* sounds. The door is metal, not wood. *Doom.* Joanna doesn't know if it will hold forever, but it holds for now—*doom*—as they scramble up the stairs, trying to find their footing in the shaky beams of their flashlights. *Doom.* The concrete walls are cracked, and through the cracks, occasional snatches of wind and gray light seep in. *Doom. Doom. Doom.* It is difficult to distinguish the pounding of the door from the pounding of her heart.

On the fourth floor, they hurry out of the stairwell and into the hall. Here they wait, their throats tight and searing from their labored breathing. Bryce leans against a wall. Joanna bends over her knees. "Okay," she finally says. "You saw that, yes? You saw what I saw."

"I saw *something*."

"It wasn't a bear?"

"It most definitely wasn't a bear."

Her breath settles to a slight wheeze. She straightens. Somehow she is sweating and cold at the same time. "You believe me now? About last night?"

"I didn't not believe you before."

"What should we do?" she says and then realizes he's looking at her expectantly. Like she's the boss. She is the boss. "Here's what we do," she says. "We try to go down another way. Another part of the building. Another staircase. Hopefully find an exit."

"Roger that."

She realizes she's still holding the ledger, the one she fished out of the desk drawer in the lab. Her fingers have dug into the binding so deeply that they've dented it. She tucks it inside her jacket and zips it snug.

The building is a rectangle. Like most government buildings, it is extremely boring and predictable in its design. Three hallways run the length of it. These are interrupted every fifty feet by a hallway that divides the width. The structure should be easy to navigate. Except that it isn't.

The ceiling has collapsed here, blocking the way. Down this other hall, the floor is cracked and bowed, and when they step on it, a groaning complaint sounds, the tile cracking and vibrating. A wall has opened up here, rough-lipped by broken concrete, allowing in a shaft of weak moonlight. The ceiling is mudded with dormant wasp nests.

And then there is the poster of the pinup girl. Joanna doesn't think much of it at first. A yellowed, ragged piece of paper tacked to a dormitory door. On it is an image of a woman in a high-waisted bikini lounging on a beach towel, her smile a crescent moon. They keep moving. But then Joanna spots the pinup girl again. And again. And again.

"The hell?"

"What?" Bryce says.

"Either everyone in this facility was lusting after the same woman or we're going in circles."

"We're not going in circles."

Joanna studies the pinup girl another second before tearing away her bottom half, shearing her at the waist. She lets the legs flutter to the floor. "We'll see."

They start to navigate the hallways once more—and up ahead, the door with the pinup girl appears, the picture torn in two.

Bryce picks up the bottom half of the poster, stares at it dumbly, and tries to fit it back together with the top. There is nothing to say except "I don't understand." They try three different routes, even speaking them aloud—"Left, right, left"; "Left, straight, left, straight, left"; "Right, left, straight, right"—but always end up in the same place, greeted by the torn-up pinup girl.

This time they try the knob of the door the poster hangs from. It opens to a room like all the others. Single bed, the sheets made. Clothes still folded in the bureau, hanging in the closet. A small desk. A mirror mossy with age. A rotten curtain hanging from a rod at the shattered window.

She looks out the window, which is several stories up, and debates whether she can jump without breaking a leg. Then she sits on the bed and the springs chirp. A musty smell puffs up. She wants to lean back anyway. Lean back and shut her eyes and will herself into a dream or out of this nightmare. Anything to escape this place.

"What are you thinking?"

She's the boss. He's looking for direction, and she's the boss. But she doesn't have the energy to be anything but honest. "I'm scared," she says. "I'm so, so, so scared."

"Yeah," he says and steps to the window and looks out it. Sleet gathers on the sill. "Maybe this is a little embarrassing to admit, but when I was a kid, I was scared a lot. Of the dark. Of other kids at school. Of my parents getting divorced. Everything, pretty much, scared me. And you know what I used to do? And you know what I still do?"

She knuckles a tear from the corner of her eye. "What do you do?"

"I danced. I dance."

She snorts, then studies his face. He isn't smiling. "Oh, you're not joking."

"I'm actually a pretty good dancer." He holds out a hand.

"No," she says. "No. Uh-uh."

"Come on."

"I am not dancing. What are you even—this is absurd."

"You're smiling, aren't you? That means it's already working."

And he's right. Her cheeks are bunched up in a smile she can't make go away.

"This is dumb," she says, but she takes his hand. The calluses on his palm are thick as bark, but his grip is gentle. He tugs her up into a standing position and puts his other hand on her waist.

"What are we—it's not like there's music."

But he's humming. A waltz. She recognizes it but doesn't know the name until he tells her. "The Blue Danube." Strauss. Somehow she is moving, following his lead, their bodies spinning slowly, their feet squaring out patterns.

"I always thought," she says, her face turned away from him. It's hard to look into his eyes when they're this close.

"What?"

"I always thought, when you said you were a good dancer, you were talking about—I don't know, rock or hip-hop or something."

"Those are okay too. But I always liked ballroom dancing best. Because you don't have to guess. There're rules. There's, you know, blueprints you follow."

"Rules would be nice about now."

"Right?" He keeps humming. They keep turning, twirling around the small room. "There's a ballroom-dance club at the community college."

"And you belong to it?" Her voice is somewhere between curious and teasing.

"Sure. Don't you do other things besides work?"

"Actually, no. Work is pretty much it for me."

"Well, that's no fun."

"You're probably right."

"You want to go sometime?"

"Um."

"No pressure. Just an idea. For some, you know, extracurriculars you seem to be sorely lacking."

"How about this—if we live, sure. Yes. We will go." It feels good to imagine. A well-lit space, a gymnasium, with other smiling bodies whirling across the honeyed hardwood.

"Feel better, don't you?" he says.

"I do, actually."

He spins her out with an extended arm and she feels something slide past her belly and out the bottom of her jacket. The ledger. It clunks onto the floor between them. The pages open to a sketch.

Bryce stops humming. Their hands release. They stare at the diagram penciled onto the page. Slowly she scoops up the ledger and holds it toward the light.

"But that's—" Bryce says. "That's what we're building. Isn't it?"

The specs are different, but the shape is the same. It looks like an elaborately designed door.

His finger taps the top of the page. "You see the date, 1943?"

"I see it."

"What were they doing here?"

She thumbs through the pages, letting them riffle by, a blur of entries. "I think we're about to find out. Let's see what George Warnok has to tell us."

LOGBOOK: GEORGE C. WARNOK

ENTRY 90

October 20, 1944

I haven't written much here lately. I haven't had the time or, honestly, the presence of mind. But I feel compelled to get my thoughts straight because everything . . . feels rather messy right now.

At first I didn't know what to do with the tooth Dr. Devinor had given me. It sat on my desk for days, a disturbed and doomed token. I considered sweeping it into the trash and wiping away the stain it left on the wood. I felt rather haunted by the thing, to be honest. The man had thrown himself to his death right after giving it to me, after all. Maybe I was a fool to believe everything he told me the night of his suicide. Maybe it was just the ramblings of a mad, demented mind.

Religion has never been a lens through which I understand the world, but even if I did not regard his suicide as a sin, it was still an offense. Like the war itself. If I ever spoke to God, I would simply say, "Show me Your face. Come down here and explain Yourself for all this pain and ugliness."

We buried Dr. Devinor in the woods. There was no casket, no traditional service. I placed a wildflower bouquet on his chest. One of the guards—a red-haired man named Samuel Lavender—had a wonderful baritone, and he sang "How Great Thou Art." Wiggins played a bugle song. And then we shoveled the dirt onto the body and rolled some rocks over the grave to keep the wolves from digging him up. Major General Tusk refused to come to the service, disgusted and furious at Dr. Devinor for giving up on life and on the cause. "Do you realize how much fucking trouble it was to get him out of that gulag?" I heard him say. "What a waste of time and resources."

I didn't tell the major general—or anyone else—about Dr. Devinor's final visit to my room. Maybe the tooth was just a tooth. Made of silver. But he had believed it to be so precious and cardinal that he'd secretly banked it in his gums for decades. He gave it to me and me alone. That had to mean something.

What that was, I didn't know. I had to get over my misgivings first. About the man, yes, but also about the slippery science. A major explosion had occurred in Tunguska. He claimed it was because he had successfully rotated the atom and created an unstable wormhole. But what if he was wrong? Any detonation will result in debris, and perhaps this tooth was merely a melted bit of steel beam. How could I determine that it was indeed as special as he claimed? I'm very glad I keep this logbook, because memory can't be trusted. I reread and reread my chronicle of his nighttime visit. It was imperfect but as close as I had to data. He had referred to the metal—the ninth metal—as a key. That's what my eyes kept coming back to.

Eventually I cleaned the tooth off and marveled at its sheen and coloring. Not quite silver and not quite blue, its own special shade, an otherworldly hue. There was a curious weightiness to it, as though it were ten times its actual size. Lost in thought, I tapped it against the desk in an idiot rhythm for a minute, maybe more. But I soon realized that it was glowing—giving off a spectral light—and I set it on the desk to observe more closely.

There was a tinny humming in the air, something I felt as much as heard, almost beyond the reach of my ear. Vibrations that pulsed off the metal. The glow and the sound eventually subsided. I tried the experiment again, this time making notations and keeping time with my wristwatch. As Dr. Devinor indicated, the metal appeared to be absorbent, a sponge or battery for kinetic energy at the least.

I clasped it in my hand and squeezed. It was but a pebble of warmth. But I felt in it the possibility of a volcano blast of heat. The ninth metal, he had called it. The greatest of metals, the product of the ultimate refiner's fire, hammered into shape at the eight-hundred-square-mile cosmic forge of Tunguska. Yes, I was beginning to believe.

I felt more than protective of my secret. I felt paranoid. Certain someone else would toss the metal away in error. Or steal it for his own use. So I kept it hidden beneath my pillow or in my pocket. My fingers often caressed it. And later on, I secreted it away in my mouth. Sucking it, rolling it around on my tongue, fitting it between my lip and gum. It made me feel full and bright.

People began inquiring about me, asking if I was okay, asking if I was getting enough sleep. Perhaps they meant well, but I found their questions aggravating and I couldn't help but feel that they wanted something from me. The truth. My secret. My metal.

I began to have the most vivid waking dreams. In them I saw things. A recurring image was of wires or roots or tentacles spilling out of a lit doorway. In the same way that I might plug a toaster into a wall, they plugged into my flesh. Into my eyes and ears and mouth and belly button. They fed me as if through an umbilical cord, and I felt sated. I heard often a whispering, and though I could not discern the words, I knew they were welcoming.

I was soon taken by an idea. After dinner each night, rather than retiring to my room, I returned to the lab. Sometimes—I know this from a childhood spent in piano lessons and recitals and composition courses—you hear a snatch of a new song in your head, and if you don't rush to the instrument or scratch it down on paper, you will lose it forever. I felt similarly now. There was a music in me waiting to be brought into the world.

Do you know how many physicists are musicians, by the way? Many. Einstein himself plays the violin. There is something to be said about finding harmony and order in all the chaos of the universe. In our facility alone, more than ten of us play. Often, in the afternoon, before dinner, you can hear a bugle tooting or a clarinet hooting or a violin whining through the walls. Sometimes on weekends when it's warm out, we gather on the lawn of the grounds and set up a half-moon arrangement of chairs and put on a concert. One time we looked over to discover, at the edge of the woods, a moose studying us. Its great antlered head was cocked, its ears perked. It listened a full ten minutes before shambling off into the brush.

I was trying to do something similar now. I was trying to entertain wildness. There was a chalkboard in the lab I used to write on, but lately I make my notations on paper, paper I keep hidden from others so as to avoid questioning, derision, or outright plagiarism. Up to this point, I worked in a lab with an open floor plan, but I asked to be transferred temporarily to a private room, and that is where I began an experiment I referred to as the Looking Glass.

The metal is mine. The coming breakthrough is mine. My country's flag once inspired me, but I no longer feel walled in by borders or constrained by a constitution. What I'm imagining is far vaster and more timeless than this speck of a moment in man's history. When my fellow scientists ask at the sinks in the restroom or over hurried meals in the cafeteria what I'm up to, I tell them they'll have to wait and see. They are suspicious and frustrated. Kubert says, "You're behaving very strangely." I imagine myself as one of the heretics burned centuries ago for claiming the Earth revolved around the sun. I am ahead of them all, and I have no doubt they will hate me for it.

If what I was doing before was more classical composition, this is jazz. I don't know exactly where I am going. But I feel caught up in an improvisational frequency. I call it my Looking Glass, but it is the size of a door, five feet wide, seven feet tall. There is something industrial and biological about its appearance. I wield an arc welder and a soldering iron. I apply a screw here, a magnet there. A sickle-shaped setting mechanism and a toothy gear train. A fifty-amp cord. A transmitting antenna with a gain of 50 dB. I meticulously fit together thousands of pieces of copper and iron and nickel in a steel frame marbled with wiring. A piece of quartz here, an agate there. I laser-etched ciphers onto the sculpture. I don't know how to pronounce them, but I understand them like a language learned in my sleep. Several wider channels lined with magnets merge into a circle at the center of it all.

Within this circle there is a mechanism that looks like a cross between a solar-system model and a grandfather clock's guts. When I place the omnimetal key here, the mechanism ticks and churns at a blurring speed.

This happened around two a.m., and I was so tired from my work, I collapsed into a chair. My body hunched with a weariness I suddenly felt all the way down to my marrow. *I should drag myself off to bed,* I thought, but I couldn't muster the energy.

It was then I heard—no, felt something. Like a window had been left open and a breeze snuck through. I lifted my head from my hands and saw something I at first did not believe. The frame of the structure remained but everything within that rectangle had vanished, replaced by a faint light silhouetting a figure. I don't know how to describe him or her or *it* except as a cold shimmer. It was in a seated position, but when I rose, it rose. When I lifted a hand, it lifted a hand. I took a step, it took a step. Backward, forward, side to side.

A mirroring. A misty reflection of myself.

I laughed—and then the laugh became a scream as the thing launched itself at me.

The next morning Wiggins woke me. I rose blearily from the floor and then, remembering what had happened, double-checked my pockets. They were empty. As was my mouth. I looked wildly about. "Where is it?"

"Where's what?"

I saw then that the Looking Glass had collapsed in the night, shattering some of its pieces. There was a scorched ozone smell to the air, and I realized my skin was red and peeling, and my eyebrows had been burned off my face. The floor had cracks in it. A desk had been knocked over.

Amid the debris, I saw a silver-blue spark. I fell to my knees and thanked God, for here was the omnimetal. I hurried it into my pocket and looked suspiciously at Wiggins.

But his attention was focused on the fallen and shattered Looking Glass.

"So this is what you've been building," he said.

"What are you doing here?" I said.

"We were worried about you when you didn't show up for breakfast."

"I'm fine," I said.

"You don't look fine," he said.

"Get out! Get out of here!" I said and he did not argue with me.

I rubbed my eyes so hard that ghost colors smeared across my vision and their afterimages played across the lab as I studied it carefully, searching for any transparency or light or movement. I walked to the place where the structure had stood, trying to imagine crossing an invisible border to somewhere else. When I got close, every hair on my body sizzled briefly, but I dismissed the reaction as psychosomatic. Maybe nothing had happened, I thought. Maybe it had all been a dream.

But I should not have been so dismissive of dreams, because it was in them that the truth eventually revealed itself.

I soon gave up on sleeping with any regularity. The combination of the windowless labs and the endless sunshine pouring in my dormitory window interrupted any possibility of a reasonable circadian rhythm. I was exhausted, but I was wired. What little sleep found me was fitful and made me feel like I was dipping my face in and out of a warm pool of paint that streamed half-realized visions across my eyes.

In one of my dreams, the other scientists and I sat on the lawn outside the building, listening like a congregation as Dr. Devinor stood on the roof and held up his arms in benediction and said, "I warned you! I warned all of you!" The sky above him churned black and tendrils dropped from the clouds to entwine him. He was ripped upward, vanishing from sight.

And then there was the bridge. The Bering Land Bridge that once connected Russia to North America. I saw it as clear as day. Ice-coated so that it appeared like rough spine. I was among the many crossing it. There was a long line of us. We were huddled into our furs, impervious to the hard, snow-bitten winds. I sat on the back of a lumbering mastodon. I was one of the first men. And now it was here, once again, that we would bravely cross a bridge that led to an unguessable future.

There is a left-right symmetry to everything we know in nature, and I began to think of these dreams as the sideways or upside-down version of the waking world. The metal carried knowledge that it was passing along to me. It was a battery of not just kinetic energy but soulful energy, a battery unlike any other. And it would serve as the great beating heart of the machine I was going to build.

This first experiment was exactly that: A rudimentary test. A clumsy prototype. What I was going to build next—with the help of my colleagues—would be a hundred times the size and power.

26

◎

Sophie's mission to Alaska began close to a year ago, when, over the city of Hiroshima, Japan, the sky rained bodies. Several hundred of them. They all wore black, and some people described them as looking like crows and others said they were like shadows and still others said they looked like rips in the fabric of the sky. They crashed through roofs and they exploded on streets and sidewalks and yards. They were estimated to have fallen from a few thousand feet. There wasn't much left to examine. But eventually it was determined—through dental and fingerprint records—that they were, by and large, Americans. And further inquiries revealed that they belonged to a cult of metal-eaters based in northern Minnesota. Their blood was found to contain toxic levels of omnimetal.

One of the cult members was identified as Nico Frontier, a member of the Frontier mining dynasty in Northfall, Minnesota. Some speculated that the metal-eaters were victims of a mass suicide. Since they worshipped the sky, why not make that their grave? But no plane had appeared on radar or satellite that day that could have carried them.

The vanishing—or what some called the ascension—of the members of the cult in Minnesota had not gone unnoticed. Some religious leaders reported on the possibility of a celestial doorway, a vault of heaven. Perhaps these metal-eaters had been cast out at the gates for their heathen ways.

Sophie and Hans showed up at Hiroshima and, soon thereafter, the compound in Minnesota. Because the Collectors were particularly interested in this seeming way to travel across the world in an instant. If they could track down the element or tech that made such a thing possible . . . well, they could sell the shit out of that on the black market. Hans called it the hunt for the suicide teleporter. She referred to it as the quest for mirror matter.

In Minnesota, there was a man-made monolith erected at Gunderson Woods. It was the supposed site of the ascension. Nico Frontier built it. His family and friends reported that he'd constructed it over the course of several months. It consisted of tens of thousands of interlocking parts. Its inspiration and specifications, he said, came from the voices and visions he had when smoking space dust, the resin of omnimetal.

Sophie and Hans led a nighttime raid on the property and helicoptered the monolith out. From Minnesota, she and her crew traveled by semi to a warehouse in Kansas City, where they hired three physicists and two computer scientists and a symbologist to figure out what made the thing tick.

A month later, they understood it to be a door or a window or a gate or a highway or a trampoline or whatever you wanted to call it—a conduit to someplace else.

When the team powered up the monolith with electricity, it glowed brightly and took on a translucent quality, like the sheen of a sunlit bubble. They pushed GPS transponders through it. A transponder would ping in Kansas one minute, Hiroshima the next. Another transponder would ping in Kansas one minute, Vesuvius the next. Kansas, then Area 51. Kansas, Kilauea. Kansas, Bermuda. Kansas, Fairbanks. Kansas . . . nowhere. Sometimes the transponder went nowhere, blinking out of existence. They couldn't figure out a control system at first.

Then they recognized that all of these exit ramps aligned with volcanoes, nuclear explosions, or asteroid strikes. They were frail spots between this world and something else. The monolith was connected to all of them, the entry to a hallway of half-open doors.

The only location that didn't make sense was Fairbanks. It was the anomaly, if their disaster theory held true. What had happened there that allowed for the fissure in space-time?

They wanted to know if the directionality of the conduit could be controlled. Because if so—if you could watch the sunset in Rio and the sunrise in Tokyo, if you could haul a payload of titanium off the Kuiper asteroid belt and deliver it directly to a processing mill in Gary, Indiana—then you owned a key cut with a trillion teeth.

The symbologist pointed out to Sophie and Hans a series of ciphers etched in a looping braid around the monolith: A glyph with three slashes. A twinned series of circles. A rune shaped like five flagged and beamed musical notes linked by a single semibreve. And so on. A different one lit up for the various locations. They could be manipulated by touch.

But what happened when all of them were lit up? they wondered. What appeared to be fog poured out of the monolith, spilling across the floor like slow milk. One of their crew—an Australian named Tim Taylor whom they all called Dingo—stepped toward it curiously. What could only be described as a tentacle unfurled through the doorway. It was gray and fibrous, as thick as an arm. It wrapped around his ankle, and before he had a chance to scream, his legs were pulled out from under him. The back of his head hit the floor with a sickening crack. The tentacle retracted, dragging him away with it.

Sophie killed the power. The monolith solidified as suddenly as a door that had been slammed shut. The fog burned away, vanishing the same as Dingo. The only evidence of him was a slug's trail of blood reaching across the floor.

"What was that?" she said, but a better question was *Where was that?*

Farther, they guessed. They had gone someplace farther than before. Beyond that hall of half-opened doors. Beyond the reaches of this world, even.

Hans remained in Kansas, and Sophie traveled with a team to Bermuda. They chartered a boat and followed the ping of the transponder seventy kilometers off the southern shore. They dropped anchor. Waves slapped the boat. The sky was a painful blue and sunlight diamonded the water. They didn't know what they were looking for. They knew only that the transponder was pinging a few hundred meters below them. Sophie put on scuba gear and dropped into the water. There she found nothing but lazy pods of grouper, bright curtains of angelfish, and the silver dart of a barracuda.

It wasn't until the sun began to set and the blinding brightness of the Caribbean softened that they noticed the anomaly. The sky and the sea darkened, except *there*. It was like a shimmering crack. It began in the air and ended a few meters above the surface of the sea. It was, by their best estimation, several hundred meters tall and fifty wide. To look at it was to look at a drapery of faintly rainbowed cellophane. They motored up near the edge of it, giving it a wide berth.

She called up Hans in Kansas and asked him to power up the monolith under the Bermuda heading, then throw something through the portal. "Like what?" he said and she said, "Anything." A few seconds passed before a pencil arced through the crack and plopped into the water. "Did it work?" he said and she said, "Try again." She heard the flap and ripple of paper and a moment later an airplane glided through and skimmed the waves before soaking and sinking. Then came a stapler. Then a basketball, which splashed out of sight and popped back to the surface.

Sophie had the phone pressed to her ear. "I feel like if I got a little closer, I could see you."

Hans said, "If you could, you'd know I'm smiling right now."

"I wonder," Sophie said, standing on the deck of the rocking boat, "if we can somehow collect it?"

"Collect what?"

"Do you remember when we were in Myanmar during that monsoon?"

"I've never seen so much lightning."

"And after it passed, we went to the beach. The sand had been struck over and over and turned to rivers of glass."

"Sophie?"

"Whatever the sand that makes up this glass is, that's what I want. The mirror matter."

Now, in a first-floor hall at the Geophysical Institute on the University of Alaska campus, Sophie waits. There is a window in the door across from her, and through it, she can see Professor Butler. He is teaching his last class of the day, a thirty-student seminar called Atmospheric Dynamics II.

He wears a tweed jacket and jeans. He has a salt-and-pepper beard and constantly pushes his glasses up the bridge of his nose. He looks like a man who doesn't own a hairbrush. He paces when he lectures.

Every now and then she hears something—the squeak of a sneaker, the click of a door—that catches her attention. But no soldiers rush her. She feels relatively safe here among the thousands of students. She has spotted at least three other twenty-somethings wearing military-style jackets like her own, thrift-shop chic; she thinks she can pass for an undergrad or a TA.

Finally the door opens and the students file out. Professor Butler finishes tidying his notes, fits them into a leather satchel, and heads for the hall, only to find her blocking the way.

"If this is about adding the course, I'm afraid it's far too late for that."

"I'm not a student, and this isn't about adding the course." She flashes her Department of Transportation ID. "I want to talk to you about what's happening in the skies over Fairbanks."

"Oh?" His body stiffens. "Okay." He pats his pockets, pauses on the bulge of a cell phone. "I wonder if you could meet me at my office in a few minutes? It's just down the hall. I need to use the restroom." His voice quivers, so different than it was in the excited, booming lecture he delivered only minutes ago.

"No," she says. "I think we need to speak here and now."

"There's a class," he says and clears his throat. "There's a class coming in here. They'll be here any minute."

"There's no class coming in here. I checked the schedule. Yours is the last of the day."

"Oh," he says and gives a soft choking chuckle. "My mistake."

"Are they here?" she says.

His glasses have nearly slipped off his nose and he hurries to push them back up. "I'm sorry. Who?"

"The people who told you to look out for me, who told you to call if I showed up."

"I . . ." he says, his face steadily reddening. "I . . . I . . . I . . ."

"It's okay," Sophie says. She steps all the way into the room, closes the door, and punches the lock. "We can be honest with each other. How about this? I'll tell you the truth, and then you'll tell me the truth. It will be a trade."

"I—"

"I bet you'd be more comfortable if you sat down." She nods toward the desks. "There are plenty of options."

He looks vaguely around the classroom and nods and shuffles toward a desk and lowers himself into it. His satchel sits in his lap.

"I'm not with the DOT. There. I told you a truth. Now you do the same for me. When did they talk to you?"

"I don't. I can't."

She reaches into her pocket and his eyes track the gesture and widen.

After being dammed up, his words spills out in a rush. "He showed up yesterday."

"Who?"

"Colonel," he said. "Colonel Purdin."

"Was he alone?"

"No. He had others with him. At least two others. They stayed in the hall."

"Go on."

"Purdin had photos. Photos from the airport. Surveillance-camera footage. Of you. They wanted to know if I'd seen you, and I said no, and they said if you happened to show up asking questions, I should give them a call."

"That's better. Good job. What kinds of badges did they show you?"

"Department of Defense," he says. "Are you a terrorist?"

"I could see somebody calling me that. But I'd say no. Not the kind that blows up government buildings and hijacks planes, anyway."

"Then what kind are you?"

"The kind who makes money."

"I don't . . ."

"There's no political cause here. There's no religious fundamentalism. I don't care who you vote for or worship. All I care about is money, man."

"Oh," he says with some relief. His posture slackens and he smooths his beard with his hand. "Okay. But—what does that have to do with me?"

"I want to know what's happening in the sky. You know about what's happening in the sky."

His voice is now exasperated. "Why does everyone want to know about what's happening in the sky all of a sudden?"

"Do you mean Colonel Purdin?"

"Among others."

"Tell me about the others."

His hands slap the desktop and his fingers drum out a nervous song. "Yesterday morning I received a voice mail from a police officer named Emily Katoo. She asked if I had ever heard of animals raining from the sky! A few days before that, I received a call from a reporter over at KTVF asking if the locals were talking about any weather anomalies. When I asked what kind of anomalies, the reporter said shapes. Disturbing shapes in the sky. Maybe a month ago, a former student of mine—I believe she's in construction now—called me and asked me a litany of questions about lidar and atmospherics. And to top it all off, I've been routinely harassed by a local DJ who believes he's discovered a new form of cloud!"

"And then Colonel Purdin came around."

"And then he came around!"

"And now me."

"And now you!"

"Tell me more about Colonel Purdin."

"How long does it take to achieve that rank? I don't know. I'd guess that you'd have to be in your late thirties, but he could have passed for midtwenties. He wore military fatigues. He had a pistol on him. He was extremely rude and bossy. He also . . ."

"What?"

"This isn't relevant, I'm sure, but it's a weird detail that kept distracting me. He had his phone out the entire time. He had his phone out and it was as if someone else was on the line, listening to us. I could hear something, something like breathing, but it was upsettingly loud, like heavy static."

"All right, Professor Butler. You've been doing great so far. Now let's switch gears. Because I don't have a lot of time. Pretend I'm a bad student. Give me the CliffsNotes version of your research and tell me if you've noticed anything anomalous lately."

His gaze leaves her and finds its focus in the three windows running along the wall. The glass is spotted with moisture. Clouds hang low over the city, where streetlights are beginning to flare.

"Professor Butler?"

"We're being honest? Isn't that what you said?"

"I did."

His eyes remain on the windows, the city. "I've seen some things. Things I haven't told anyone about. Because I worry they might take me away and throw me in a cell with padded walls."

"You can tell me anything. Anything that's true. What kinds of things have you seen?"

"Do you know what lidar is?"

"Kind of. But tell me."

"Lidar transmits pulses of light into the sky. It measures the echoes to make a profile of the atmosphere."

"And the profile has changed lately?"

"My experiments are now revealing . . . things I haven't seen before." His voice becomes soft and dreamy. "Things I'm quite honestly scared to show people."

"Like what?"

"You can imagine you see anything in the clouds, right? Dragons or turtles or . . . maybe I'm just like a kid. Maybe I'm just pretending and projecting too much. That's what I want to believe. But I think not." He shakes his head. "I think not."

"What do you see in these lidar readings?"

"Oh . . . well, would you like to see for yourself?" He reaches for his waist. "I can show you."

"Slowly," she says and puts her hand in her pocket.

He stiffens. "Slowly. Of course." He removes the phone from his jeans and she nods and he sets it on the desk. "May I?"

"You may. But if you try to place a call, I can promise you'll regret it."

"Understood." He pooches his lips and activates his screen and opens up his photos and thumbs through them until he finds what he's looking for. "See here?" He holds up the phone, angling it toward her.

She sees grainy, gray images that look somewhere between a photograph and a painting. Tentacles. Eyes. Mouths. Madness. Things beyond description.

Butler glances at her and then away. "But maybe most upsetting of all . . ."

"Yes?"

He presses a button and the phone goes dark. "Maybe most upsetting of all is how some of the lasers don't bounce back."

"Where do they go?"

"That's the question. I sometimes feel like I'm looking . . ."

"Yes?"

"I sometimes feel like I'm looking through a keyhole into another world." He glances again at the window, and the clouds there reflect off his lenses. "I don't know why I'm telling you this. You're exactly the sort of person I imagine locking me in a padded cell. I guess all of this stuff has been dammed up in me too long."

"I'm the last person you need to worry about locking you in a cell."

"No? You prefer shallow graves?" He gives a hollow laugh, then leans forward eagerly, hugging his satchel. "Let me ask you something. A truth for a truth."

"Okay."

"Do you believe in God?"

"That is not the question I expected you to ask."

"But do you?"

"Do you mean, do I believe in a Christian God? Do I believe in the Bible?"

"God. Buddha. Allah. Krishna. Whoever."

"I do not."

"Not any kind of God?"

"No."

"What about any kind of . . . *other*. Other than all this."

She doesn't hesitate. "Yes."

"Yes." He nods for a long time. "Yes. Then we have that in common."

"You're sounding more like a philosopher than a scientist, Professor Butler."

This makes him smile, revealing crooked, coffee-stained teeth. "Does God exist? Do angels exist? Do leprechauns or ghosts or werewolves exist? I would have told you no before. But now I say maybe. A lot of scientists are saying maybe right now. They never used to be so squishy. But we've all gotten very, very squishy lately."

"Because of the comet."

He throws up his arms. "All bets are off. Everything changed when the comet came. It was like somebody showing you that two plus two no longer equals four."

"Then why are you afraid to share what you've seen in the sky? Why not be part of that conversation?"

"Aren't you in a hurry? You're asking very roundabout questions for one who's in a hurry."

"I am in a hurry. But you've aroused my curiosity, Professor Butler."

"Okay." His thumb traces his lips. "Bear with me a moment. How . . . no. Perhaps I should say . . ."

She makes a small noise of impatience.

"Okay. So we claim we know things about the universe beyond our planet, yes? But we've never actually *been* there. I shine my lidar into the sky and the lasers bounce back, reflecting a shape. The James Webb telescope does some approximation of the same with deep space. We look, but we don't go, not very far. We've got our telescopes and our spacecraft and our probes and our rovers, sure. They do their flybys and their orbits and their soft landings on Venus and Mars and Mercury. But no human has actually left low Earth orbit since 1973. Our passport is barely stamped. So what do we have? We have some data and a lot of *guesses*." He makes a dusting-off gesture with his hands as though dramatically cleaning something from them. "And then the comet shows up and proves those guesses wrong."

"Like what?"

"The periodic table, for one. That's supposed to be it. That's the memoir of the universe. That's all the existing elements. Some were created by fusion reactions in stars. Others were formed by novas, supernovas, and collisions between stars. And some were created in labs and linear accelerators. But these elements—they're all built from the same stardust. We're all built from the same stardust. This solar system, these galaxies, the universe—the same stardust. But now all of that's being revised. Because of the comet."

"So?"

"So? *So?* This is like fundamentalists realizing they've been worshipping at the wrong altar their whole lives!"

She glances at the door. "Keep your voice down."

He shifts in his seat, no doubt wanting to pace about. "Listen. I'm not the only one who has this theory, but I might be the only one who's on his way to proving it."

"Which you'll do how?"

"You said you believed in something *other*, yes? Look up at the clouds, then. There's your *other*."

"Explain it better. CliffsNotes, remember?"

"The comet didn't come from the Oort cloud. Or another solar system. Or another galaxy." His voice rises in volume again but then he catches himself and says in an almost whisper, "It came from another dimension. That's why some of my lasers aren't bouncing back."

"Is there a concentrated location for these anomalies?"

"No. Which is all the more maddening. I can't simply point to a hole and say, *There. There it is. The rift.* These anomalies—as you call them—travel with the weather. They're like a roaming system."

"Something is in flux here, in other words."

"Yes. Yes, I believe that's true."

"And where does the . . . *weather* come from? We could conclude that's the source of the flux, couldn't we?"

"With the wind patterns here, the weather typically comes down from the mountains. The White Mountains."

"Do you know of any meteor strikes in the mountains?"

"No. Alaska was mostly spared any debris during skyfall."

"Do you know of any other activity in the mountains?"

"Like what?"

"Private or government labs."

"We have an atmospheric sciences lab in the foothills called Poker Flats, but I can assure you, nothing fishy is going on there." Here his voice rises in pitch and he puts a finger to his mouth. "But then again . . ."

"What?"

"Do you remember how I mentioned my former student calling?"

"The construction worker."

"Contractor, yes. She was working on something in the mountains."

"Working on what?"

"She didn't say. She was rather coy. But she wanted to know the same thing you want to know. About other labs that might exist up in the White Mountains. I mentioned to her something I heard once. An anecdote, really."

"About?"

"There was indeed a lab operating up here, but way back during World War Two. There wasn't any real press about it, not like Los Alamos. Top secret stuff, maybe. Or maybe nobody knew about it because it was of minor importance. For all I know, they were training rabbits and chipmunks to navigate minefields. But it's defunct now. I'm sure if you did some digging, you could find something more useful than what I'm telling you."

"I'm good at digging."

"I believe that."

"Did Colonel Purdin mention this lab?"

"He didn't. But he seemed . . ." His voice fades.

"What?"

"He seemed like he knew everything." He takes off his glasses and stares at her plainly. "You said we were being honest."

"Yeah."

"What are you after? Who are you? Really, I mean."

"I'm a collector."

"A collector?" His eyes drop to her silver briefcase. "What is it you collect, exactly?"

"I collect things of great value. And then I sell them."

"What are you looking for here in Fairbanks?"

She gives him a small smile. "Thank you for the talk, Professor Butler."

Again he shifts in his seat. "What now?"

"Give me your phone."

He pinches his mouth, but nods. He knew something like this was coming. He holds it out to her and she drops it on the floor and stomps on it several times with the heel of her boot until it cracks and shatters.

"What's next?"

"What do you think is next?"

"I certainly hope you're not going to kill me."

"No, I don't think so," she says.

"Oh, good." He titters in relief. "Because, well, you have that look in your eye."

She pulls a gun out of her pocket, just to show him, and slides it back into place. "It's a good thing you turned out to be such an excellent conversationalist." Her hand moves to another pocket. "But I'm afraid I can't simply let you go."

He flinches as if he's about to be struck. "Not even if I promise not to say anything?"

"It's hard for people to keep promises, I've found."

She duct-tapes his mouth closed, then zip-ties his ankles and wrists to the desk. She pats him on the back and leans toward his ear. "The next class in this room is at eight a.m. tomorrow. That should give me all the head start I need."

27

heo stands in the parking lot staring at the fortress of the hospital. The wind knocks his hair about. It's only four o'clock, but night is coming fast. The clouds seem too low, like if he reached up, he could pull down a handful. A flurry of snow makes soft sounds like moth wings in the air. In his hand he holds the ID badge and key card belonging to Little Head's mother, Mrs. Castor. *Dr.* Castor. He shivers from the cold or from nerves. He starts and stops a dozen times; after five minutes, he hasn't made it more than ten feet from the SUV. It isn't until the lamps in the parking lot buzz on that he finally hurries inside.

He might as well be caught in the blaze of one big spotlight as he moves through the hospital's fluorescent-lit halls. He cringes every time his wet shoes squeak. He keeps near the wall when he can, trying to be as unobtrusive as possible, dodging around wheelchairs, carts, and gurneys. At first he wears his hood up to hide his face, then he pulls it down because he worries it will make him more conspicuous, then he pulls it back up again.

At one point a nurse calls out to him, asks if she can help. He sputters out a string of nonsense words that end with "Restroom?" and she sends him in the right direction. At another point an orderly asks what he's doing, and Theo decides to be honest: "Looking for my dad." Nobody seems to suspect him of anything except being lost.

He turns a corner and stops so suddenly he almost falls over. Up ahead is an officer dressed in fatigues. The same officer he spotted in the ER yesterday. Theo knows from all of the Call of Duty he plays that the man's rank is colonel. He has a young face, but he's clearly in charge. A doctor nods her head, widening her eyes as she listens to him list off a series of instructions. Theo might hear the term *martial law*.

Beside him is a reception desk for the oncology department. Nobody is stationed there at present. He spots a phone and something occurs to him. He digs into his pocket and removes the piece of paper with the 317 number from the Defense Switched Network. He selects an outside line and punches in the digits and waits.

A second later, a cell rings. Not twenty paces away. The colonel excuses himself from the doctor and pulls out his phone. "Yes?" he says.

Theo has a thousand questions he would like to ask, but he remains silent.

"Who is this?" the colonel says, his voice edging toward irritation. "Hello? Hello?"

Theo lowers the pitch of his voice and says, "Sir, I need you outside ASAP. It's an emergency."

"Who is this? What's the—"

But Theo has already hung up.

The colonel excuses himself, telling the doctor something has come up, and walks at a fast clip down the hallway.

Theo doesn't know where the morgue is, but on TV, it's always in the basement, so he uses the key card to access a stairwell that leads him belowground. He knows he'll be more conspicuous down here, so he peers out a crack in the door before entering an empty corridor that smells of bleach and detergent. He passes by a laundry facility. Some people are folding sheets. Others are pushing gowns and towels in and out of giant washing machines that bank the far wall. Steam clouds the air. Dryers rumble. Theo spots a rack of white lab coats, snatches one from a hanger, and hurries on.

He tries to straighten his posture and neaten his hair. He has his costume, but he isn't stupid enough to think he can pass for a doctor. Maybe a medical student? He knows there's a difference between what happens in his head and what happens in reality. In third grade, he had a vivid scene in his mind of a knight battling a serpent-necked dragon in a charred and flaming forest, but when he crayoned it onto paper, his teacher mistook it for a boy playing with a dog. In seventh grade, he put on a Spider-Man costume for Halloween—he puffed up his chest, fired off some invisible webs, felt invincible until he stepped in front of the mirror and saw the baggy fit of the mask and the too-tight groin that clearly revealed the tiny curl of his penis. A thousand times over, he's experienced this, but he's also witnessed it, sadly, in his father. There was the time his dad was convinced they could get rich off Amway, the time he tried to stage-dive at a Journey concert at the state fair, the time he started building an underground bunker in the back-yard before giving up, and the time he thought he'd spotted Chuck Norris at the pharmacy. "That's not him," Theo said and his father said, "It is. It is him. It's totally him," and Theo said, "Why would Chuck Norris be at a Walgreens in Fairbanks?" and his father said, "Alaska is a major tourist destination. Huge. You don't realize how lucky you are to live here. And what, you don't think celebrities get heartburn? I'm just going to go talk to him. It'll be great." It was not great. It was also not Chuck Norris. But his father refused to believe it and kept pestering the guy for an autograph until the man who was not Chuck Norris finally shoved him into a shelving unit stacked with laxatives.

So Theo does not have great expectations for himself. A security guard is probably watching him through a ceiling-mounted camera. Any minute now he's going to get Tased in the balls and handcuffed and dragged out of the hospital. The cops will throw him in the same cell as Little Head and Jackson. He's never going to find his father.

Then again, he had spent his whole childhood afraid of Chris Peters and the other day in gym, Theo somehow managed to pick him up and hurl him to the ground. And he had always considered himself a terrible driver, but this afternoon he somehow managed to navigate the Explorer across town without a single person honking at him or any rack lights flashing in his rearview mirror. And his father's wacko theories about the sky over Fairbanks might somehow actually be true.

The *somehow*s are all working out. Maybe his luck is changing. Maybe Theo has a chance.

That's what he thinks when he stands outside the morgue. There is a small square window that offers a view of a desk and a counter and cabinets. He wishes he could see more but he supposes you don't exactly want a picture window looking in on a bunch of naked people with their guts and nuts hanging out.

He looks over his shoulder, checks the hall, and swipes the key card at the sensor. There is a buzz. He tries the door handle. It rattles but won't give. He slides the key card again, taking extra care this time. There are four small lights at its edge. They don't flash green. Instead, when the buzz sounds, they blink red and yellow three times before going dark. "Shit." He tries again and gets the same response. "Fuck." Mrs. Castor must not have access to this area.

He's about to try again when he catches some movement through the window. He dodges away, flattens himself against the wall. A few seconds later, the door opens and a man in green scrubs steps out and hurries down the hall. His head is inclined down; he's studying a chart.

Theo snatches the handle of the door just as it's about to close. He slides inside and it's only then that he breathes. The air is cold and tastes heavily of chemicals. The light feels paler. He creeps forward, unsure what he fears more, the sight of a body with its chest split open or the sight of a coroner slashing the air with a bloodied scalpel.

Neither awaits him. On a stainless-steel table lies a body, but it is shrouded beneath a sheet. The gray-skinned feet of a man poke out, a tag tied to the big toe. All around him are scales and surgical lamps and tools laid out on a tray and bins with BIOHAZARD labels. There is a wall of coolers that look like oversize versions of the safe-deposit boxes at the bank. But Theo takes this all in hazily. His eyes can focus only on the corpse. He's seen a few dead people in his life, all at open-casket funerals. He remembers feeling disgusted but hypnotized by what little parts of them were visible, their faces waxen, their hands folded like napkins on their chests.

He grabs the edge of the sheet and lifts it an inch and for a moment can't go any farther; it's as if it is suddenly weighted. He looks more carefully at the feet now and sees they are veined purple and striped with white hair and this gives him the courage to look under the sheet. Not his father. An old bony man of maybe eighty. His jaw hangs open and a gray tongue is visible behind the notched edge of his teeth.

There must be a list somewhere that says who is here, but Theo feels rushed, knowing the man in the green scrubs might return at any moment. So he stands before the wall of coolers and takes a deep breath, and, one by one, he unlocks the latches and slides them open. An old woman. A young woman with needle marks in her arms. A boy with a dent in his head. An old man. An old man. An old man. A man whose face sparkles with the broken glass embedded in it. A man whose body ends at the roughly cleaved waist. A fat man who looks like a half-melted candle.

There is one more locker to try. His hand shakes when he places it on the latch. The cold of the metal soaks into his skin. His father once told him that most laugh tracks for sitcoms were recorded over fifty years ago. So chances were, if you were watching a show, you were listening to dead people chuckle and howl. He also said there were signals ghosting through space that were broadcast back in the sixties and seventies. And sometimes a phone buzzed with a voice mail from three years ago that had only just arrived. The air is haunted. That's what his father said, and now that feels like a self-fulfilling prophecy. The last time he saw his father was in the hospital surveillance video, and he was there but not there, past but present, not exactly alive or dead.

He yanks open the locker—and finds it empty. The relief of not seeing his father there makes him giddy.

He pushes out the door and sprints down the hall, not knowing where he's going or what he plans to do next, just wanting to get away from the morgue. He forgets to keep track of where he is—a left here, a right there—because distance is all that matters. If he turns around, he feels certain he'll see all the bodies staggering after him. Maybe the man cleaved at the waist will crawl, leaving a red smear behind him.

But all these thoughts are banished when he sees a man in military fatigues cross the hall in front of him. Theo skids to a stop. He questions for a moment whether he saw what he saw. The effect was like a crow passing by a window.

He is ten paces away from the intersection of two halls. A temporary sign on the wall reads WARNING along the top in orange lettering. It takes a few more quiet steps for him to read the rest: QUARANTINE IN PROGRESS. Below this is a slot for a start date and an end date. The start date was three days ago. The slot for the end date is empty.

He settles his breath and peers around the corner. Two soldiers stand beside the swinging double doors of the temporary quarantine ward. Theo can tell from the clear plastic tubing that they're wearing earpieces.

Theo pulls back. He waits a beat, readying to run, but hears nothing. A minute passes and his mind begins to chug through the possibilities of what's next. He got lucky at the morgue. That's not going to happen twice. He considers his options. Marching up to them and pretending to be a doctor will never work, but if he finds the right gear, would he be able to pass for a janitor or orderly? Or maybe he should scout the surrounding halls and hunt for another way in? Is it possible to worm his way through a heating duct, or does that only happen in the movies? Even if he fit, would the air duct hold his two hundred plus pounds or send him crashing through the drop ceiling?

His eyes settle on a red fire alarm anchored to the wall. In middle school, Little Head forgot to study for a math test, so he yanked the lever to get out of it. It was a stupid move, but he was smart enough to wear a mitten when he did it. The ink blast that would have identified him splattered all over the mitten instead. He slipped it off and tossed it in the trash. All the students filed out of the building and gathered in the parking lot, and ten minutes later a fire truck came roaring up. By the time the firefighters inspected and cleared the building, third period had ended. There's no way a hospital would do the same—they wouldn't evacuate patients who just got their spleens scooped out—but an alarm would certainly create some sort of distraction.

He spiders his fingers in the air in front of the alarm and whispers an apology to all the babies in the maternity ward and yanks the lever. What follows isn't the ringing he expects. Instead, there's a pulsing electronic whine, a *woop-woooop* that sounds like a sound effect from his PS4 console indicating an alien invasion. Lights flash on and off, strobing the hall.

He spots a storage closet and darts inside. He keeps the door cracked to a yellow line to watch. A moment later, the two soldiers appear. They appear unhurried but intent. Their heads swivel in opposite directions, taking in the length of the hall. Then they look at each other, mutter something, and part ways. Soon, Theo can't hear them, but he imagines their black boots clicking out the same rhythm.

When they round the corners of distant hallways, Theo charges forward. He remembers Mr. Reuben encouraging him to go out for football, and he finally feels confident of the power the coach saw in him. Puberty has bulked him up with muscle, squared his jaw. He seems to outgrow his clothes every few weeks. Sometimes he barely recognizes himself in a mirror, but he knows who he is now. He feels cranked up with adrenaline and strong enough to kick through concrete. He shoulders through the double doors of the quarantine area with enough speed that the doors swing back on their hinges and slap the walls to either side.

This might once have been a conference room. The floor is carpeted. Some folding chairs and tables are stacked along one wall. A ficus tree rises from a pot in the corner. But it has been transformed into a ward. Over twenty beds are staggered throughout the space. On each of them lies a body. The beds are bare of any sheets or blankets. The patients are covered only by flimsy hospital gowns, possibly because their arms and legs and necks need to be exposed. Wires taped to their skin feed into bleeping monitors that project streams of numbers. Thin tubes run fluids into their veins; thicker tubes curl out of mouths and come from under their gowns, feeding and draining. At a glance, they look like grotesque marionettes at rest.

Then he sees something. A blur. A glitch. Like when you look through the blades of a spinning fan. A woman's face peels back to muscle and then bone. A man's arm becomes a yarny twist of ligaments and veins. Maybe Theo sees other things too. Like the hint of a tentacle licking beneath a gown. Or a cloud of steam blasting from someone's mouth. But the main thing that defines them is that they flicker. They are here and they are not here.

It's not as constant as it was with the businessman rolled into the ER or his father in the surveillance video—both of them seemed to be barely holding on, like a radio signal that fritzes and fades the farther you drive into deep country. The flickers happen now only occasionally and not to everyone. He wonders if the tubes connected to the bags and pumps are feeding some sort of stabilizing medicine into them or if they've naturally shed some toxin as they rest and heal.

He spots who he's looking for in a far corner of the ward. The black beard gives him away, but otherwise his father is barely recognizable. *Small* is never a word he associated with his father, but that's how he looks as Theo stands next to him now. Shrunken. Weak. The smell of urine and iodine puff off him. "Dad!" The alarm blares. The lights flash. But his father doesn't stir except to breathe. "Dad?" he says, touching his shoulder. "Dad. Please. Can you hear me? I'm here, Dad."

His father's eyelids twitch. He rolls his head back and forth. He opens and closes his mouth. He's deep asleep. Drugged, no doubt. Theo isn't sure which of these tubes and wires he can rip off without hurting his father, but if they're going to escape this place, he needs to be unplugged.

A voice sounds behind him, yelling over the alarm. "What are you doing?"

Theo doesn't turn around fully, relying on the lab coat to shield him from further suspicion, but he angles his head enough to address the soldier. "We've got to get them out of here!" he says.

"So there's a fire?" the soldier says.

"Even worse," Theo says. "A gas leak! This place is gonna blow!" He isn't sure where this lie came from, but he likes it. He toes up the locks on the wheels of the bed. "Grab a gurney and get rolling. I've got this guy," he yells to the soldier, then whispers softly to his father, "I've got you, Dad."

28

◎

Joanna reads aloud the logbook entries in the failing light of sunset and then in the yellow beam of her flashlight. She sets down the ledger. She and Bryce sit there for a long time with the wind gusting and the building creaking around them. There is everything to say and there is nothing to say.

"I want to see it," she finally says to Bryce. "I want to see what he built."

"I want to see it too."

They stop trying to find their way out of the building and start trying to find their way in. They're quiet at first but soon feel assured they're alone on this upper floor. Another thirty minutes of searching, and she and Bryce locate the machine that George C. Warnok referred to in his journal as the Looking Glass. It is situated at the rear of the building in a room the size of a gymnasium. They observe it from the fourth floor, where the wall has crumbled away to reveal the cavernous space.

The ceiling is mostly gone. Night has come, but there are no stars. The beams of their flashlights faintly reveal the low-hanging bellies of clouds. She can see from the structural damage—the location of the rubble, the twist of exposed rebar—that the roof blew off.

"Do you see it?" Bryce says, pointing. "It's different but the same. As our blueprints, I mean. It's like a smaller cousin, maybe half the size of what we're supposed to build."

The machine is recessed into the floor like an inverted pyramid. The tiered levels might be thirty feet wide and fifteen feet deep, one after the other after the other; they go steadily lower to a bottomed center. And here, in the middle of the structure, is a raised dais that looks almost like the antenna you would find mounted on a satellite dish. Upon the dais sits a sort of centrifuge with many rotational layers of axes.

But maybe most striking of all is this: The machine is functional. Lights flicker. The centrifuge spins slowly. There is an engine whine punctuated by the occasional screech of a rust-clotted joint. Joanna remembers the security cameras blinking red at the gate and near the construction site. She remembers Thaddeus Gunn saying he had turned the power back on. Electricity has been flowing into this place, and the broken parts of it have groaned to life, albeit barely.

"Is there a way to get down?" Bryce says and leans out over the broken lip of the floor. "There." He shines his flashlight on a half-ruined stairwell, two walls of it torn away. Bryce swings out and finds his footing. Then he offers her a hand; she takes it. Loose chunks of concrete scatter beneath their feet as they pick their way down. They step gingerly and occasionally grip each other for stability.

The clouds she noticed before hovering over the destroyed roof seem to have lowered to the floor. She walks through a dense patch of fog that clings to her like wet fabric. Something seems to lick her neck and she swings the flashlight to find a thin, gray channel of mist rivering the air. Rusted ladders are bolted to the tiered platforms, and they descend, going down and down and down again, moving toward the center of the structure. Years of dirt and rubble hide much of the flooring, but they appear to be walking on patterned metal. She pauses to swipe away a half-moon of dirt, revealing glyphs, ciphers. This one looks like an eye inside of an eye inside of an eye. Another one looks like hair or waves or tentacles.

At last they get to the dais. It reaches twenty feet high and thirty wide. Atop it is a massive metal skeleton of a globe, its center full of spinning ribs on competing axes. She remembers Warnok describing it in his logbook as a combination of a solar-system model and the inner workings of a clock, and that seems right. Even from here, she can see a faint silver-blue glow flashing in the middle of it. Its heart, she knows, must be cored with omnimetal.

But the air is obscured by fog. She was wrong before. The clouds aren't descending; they're ascending. They're being born right here, rising out of the machine. She tracks a long curling wisp and a jellyfish-looking cloud. They billow off into the dark. *It's leaking*, she thinks. Like a faucet that isn't fully on or off.

Joanna remembers a time—she might have been six, might have been nine—when Uncle Harry woke her in the night and told her to hurry and put on her jacket and mittens and hat and meet him outside. She flipped on the porch lights and tromped down the steps and onto the snow-carpeted lawn. Her uncle was standing in the middle of the yard and he waved her back in irritation. "No," he said. "No lights. Not inside. Not outside. Turn them all off." She trudged back up the steps tiredly and hit the switch and returned. The air swam with color. The artificial light had been replaced by the ethereal glow of the northern lights. "How does it happen?" she said and he said, "I honestly can't give you the specifics. Something about solar flares. I guess the mystery of it is why it seems so magical." The possibility of another world, of magic, was available to her with the flip of a switch.

She snaps off her flashlight and tells Bryce to do the same. When the artificial light is gone, the otherworldly and inexplicable take over. She stares for some time at the glowing blue pulse of the omnimetal and the shadowed sweep of the metal ribs rotating around it. Every now and then there is a flare, like the gas flame on a stove. A white-blue light. And the air above them shimmers like water on the verge of boiling.

"Let's get out of here," Joanna says.

"I'm not arguing with you."

Minutes later, they find their way outside through a crumbled section of wall. The sleet has stopped. Their boots slop in the mud. The air has warmed slightly, and a knee-high layer of fog drifts up from the ground, churned into a swirl by their legs. A column of gray surprises them when it twists up like a sudden sprout, reaching higher than they can see. And then they spot another, and another, all as thick as tree trunks. The air they breathe—cold and clammy—suddenly seems suspect. Joanna imagines a gray sticky porridge bowled at the bottom of her lungs. Are they breathing in the exhalations of another world?

She and Bryce return to the construction site and stand over the quarter-dug foundation. They don't talk, because they don't have the words yet. She toes at the spray paint on the basalt ledge indicating where they're supposed to dynamite the rock, and her feelings grow clear. She was brought here to build another one of those things. A more advanced, twenty-first-century version. Joanna isn't sure how someone who works in a bullet factory feels, but a few must wonder uneasily if any of the cartridges they're packing will one day punch a hole in a beating heart. In this case, the weapon would punch a hole through reality.

Warnok could live with that. But she can't. Dr. Devinor's warning reaches across the centuries and finds her. She puts a hand on the small of Bryce's back and this time it's she who leads him, as if in a slow dance, to the trailer full of dynamite.

"What are you thinking, boss?" he says.

"You know what I'm going to say."

He takes off his hat. It's the first time she's seen his bare head. His scalp is nakedly bald. She can tell from the open expression on his face that at this point, there's no reason to hide anything between them.

"I know we've been hired to build something," she says. "But what if we blew it the hell up instead?"

LOGBOOK: GEORGE C. WARNOK

ENTRY 91

February ?, 1945

I requested an audience with Major General Tusk. I didn't have a choice; what I needed to happen next would require an influx of funding and approval from the higher-ups. In his office I showed him my diagrams and equations. I told him about my discussions with Dr. Devinor. And I shared with him the metal, the omnimetal, the alpha metal.

The whole time he sat at his desk while I stood. His face had the look of a clenched fist. He always appeared on the verge of growing a beard even when clean-shaven, and his arms were as heavy as his legs. He listened to me, saying hardly a word, and when I finished, he seemed to enjoy the long silence that followed. I tried not to fidget my hands or shuffle my feet, but his kind of stillness is difficult to replicate.

"Where is this alpha metal or whatever you call it?"

"Someplace safe." In fact it was in my mouth, lodged beside my upper left molar. "I can of course arrange for it to be shown to you."

"You can arrange for it, huh?"

"I'm happy to show it to you."

"I could make a call right now and have you arrested and tossed in a military prison for what you've been hiding from me." He rose from his chair, rounded the desk, and sat at its front edge. He was close enough I could smell the pipe tobacco on his breath. He could have grabbed me by the throat if he wanted. "Devinor has been dead for months. Why in God's name didn't you tell me any of this before, Warnok?"

"I wanted to be certain. Dr. Devinor was, shall we say, unstable. Everything he told me could have been the product of a deranged mind."

"That word—*unstable*. You know your colleagues say the same of you?"

"Who says that?" My voice was shriller than I would have liked.

"They're worried about you. They say you've been holed up in your lab. They say you won't speak to any of them."

I mellowed my voice to what I believed to be a thoughtful tenor: "I needed to be alone to find the focus required of this work."

"I'm no General MacArthur. Would you agree?"

"I'm sorry, sir?"

"Do you know why they sent me to this godforsaken place?"

"No, sir."

"Because ten years ago, I had an affair with a woman whose husband ended up becoming the Secretary of Defense. And so here I am. At a remote outpost. Doing my time. This is punishment."

"Oh."

"Do you know why you're here? And not in Los Alamos?"

"I—"

"You're smart, Warnok, but not genius-smart. We're the JV squad. Get it? They don't really think we're going to succeed, although they'd love for us to prove them wrong. But that's why Los Alamos gets all the press."

I must have appeared surprised, because he laughed and said, "What? Did you think this place was special? Top, top, *top* secret maybe? No. The *Times* and the *Post* cover Los Alamos because the brass expect Einstein and Oppenheimer to actually deliver. Bombs, our country believes in. Big atom-splitting bombs are something the American government can understand and get behind. But atom-spinning conduits? Who the hell ever heard of that shit? That's a little too Flash Gordon for your standard senator or American citizen to wrap his brain around. Are you hearing me, Warnok?"

"Yes."

"So I'm no General MacArthur." He reached out a hand and tapped my chest hard enough to knock me back a step. "And you, Warnok, are no Einstein. You're not even worth a whisker in his mustache."

"I—I never claimed to be." My left eyelid began to twitch.

"But you *want* to be. Don't deny that. You want to be the guy with the big balls and the big ideas. Same as me. You think there's a day that goes by I don't wish MacArthur could kiss my ass? We're the same in that way. So no more secrets between us. No more working alone, jealously guarding your little math equations. This is bigger than just you. Understand?"

I massaged the spasming eyelid, and when that made no difference, I angled my head in such a way as to hide the palsy. "I understand perfectly, but I'm hoping—given the work I've already done—I might vie for the position of lead scientist."

His gray eyes were folded downward at the corners, almost piggish. "Between you and me?"

"Yes, sir?"

"By the end of this summer, nuclear war will be a reality."

"Is that a good thing or a bad thing?"

"It's a good thing, as long as we're the country to pull the trigger. A quick, decisive win. In the Great War, I was in France. Commanded a battery of artillery units. I've seen people—Krauts and Brits and Americans—ripped to shreds over months and months and months. If we can end this with the snap of a finger, I say terrific."

"If you say so, sir."

"But that would be a Los Alamos job. And the Manhattan Project already gets all the sunshine and press, right? Einstein and Oppenheimer are our star quarterbacks. But fuck those guys. I don't want them getting all the credit. I can tell you feel the same."

"What are you saying?"

"I'm saying I want to get out of this fucking place, and I want a promotion. I'm five years overdue for lieutenant general. So let's say August. By August, I want results. I want to pull my own trigger. I want the Alaska Project to win the war. Then we both get our time in the spotlight. Can you do that? For us? And for our country?"

"I can try."

"Trying is bullshit. Four months. Tick-tick-tock. August, Warnok. You promise me August, and I'll make some calls. I got a good feeling I can get you your funding and your title of lead scientist."

"August it is, then."

"All right," Tusk said. "But just you fucking remember—you're no Einstein. You answer to me. You work with your team. We're only going to win if we do this together."

"Yes, sir."

Construction began almost immediately. There were no budget constraints. The major general had made a big promise to Washington based on my reports, and we now had the full financial support of the American War Machine. Whereas before we'd had supplies delivered maybe once a week, now not a day passed without a brigade of trucks growling up the road from Fairbanks and dropping off piles of steel beams, spools of copper wiring.

We always knew we'd need space for the machine we hoped to build, and up until now, the rear of the facility—a kind of hangar bay—had been vacant. With the constant noise of wrenching and hammering and parts clanking into place, and with the sporadic blaze of welding torches and spark-haloed circular saws, the high-ceilinged space now had the feel of a factory.

29

One time, fifteen years ago, Rolf was off deer hunting alone when he lost his footing, slid fifty yards down a scree slope, and popped two tendons and three ligaments in his knee. There wasn't a signal for his cell. He didn't have any other option besides yelling for help or hoping somebody might stumble across him, so he staggered and crawled the five miles back to his truck.

Self-reliance. That was the Alaskan way.

This morning he saw things in the White Mountains that either defied the laws of physics or revealed a demented mind. And this afternoon he was tackled by a pair of needle-dick teenagers and held down until some passerby called the department and two deputies showed up with their guns drawn.

Maybe the universe is telling him to tap out, cry for mercy. He's done. Past his expiration date. He can't protect his community, let alone himself. There are plenty who have been waiting on him to retire so they can have their shot. It's time to hang it up.

His secretary, Aimee, seems to have trouble hearing him when he huffs his way up to her desk and says, "Call the FBI."

"You want me," she says, "to call the FBI?"

"That's right."

They are in the reception area of his office, and she is wearing a sweatshirt silk-screened with the image of a kitten dangling from a branch. HANG IN THERE, the purple puff letters underneath it say. "I been working for you for two decades, Rolf Wagner, and not once have you ever voluntarily called the FBI."

"Don't rub it in. Get the Anchorage office on the line."

"But I—"

"Just do it."

"But Rolf," she says, pointing at his office door. A light shines through the frosted glass. "If you're looking for the government, they're already here."

"What?"

"I said the feds—they're already here."

Department of Defense, it turns out. They commandeered the office about two hours ago and declared it their command center. Aimee has been trying to call him, but he never answers his gosh-darn phone.

Rolf pulls it out of his coat pocket and studies it absently. There are over twenty missed calls and five voice mails. Only then does he remember the military brigade he passed on the way here.

He goes to the window and sees the Humvee and tactical trucks parked in the lot. He didn't notice them earlier because he was driven to the station by one of the deputies and spent most of the drive stewing with embarrassment and yelling at the teenagers cuffed in the back seat.

"The hell are they doing in my office?" Rolf doesn't wait for a response. He goes to the door, but just as he's about to throw it open, the knob turns, and a boy stands before him. That's what he looks like to Rolf, anyway. Like a child with peachy cheeks and a buzz cut. Wearing a uniform a size too big for him. "Sheriff Wagner? I was hoping it was you I heard. My name is Colonel Purdin. Come in."

Rolf barely knows how to respond to an invitation into his own office. Purdin doesn't offer his hand to shake. He turns on his heel and sits down behind the desk. In Rolf's chair. A leather chair worn into the shape of him. Doreen got it for him as a present ten or so Christmases ago.

Rolf closes the door behind him and takes off his cowboy hat and says hello as if he were the goddamn guest. Purdin stares at him with eyes the color of gunmetal. There is a cell phone in a bulky black case wired into his desktop computer. Purdin nudges it over and sets it between them in such a way that Rolf suspects the conversation is being recorded.

He knew a day like this was coming. He had put off announcing his retirement in part because he hated the idea of some young buck sitting behind this very desk and calling the shots.

"You're bleeding," Purdin says.

Rolf's clothes are scraped and filthy, and his cheek and hands are bloody from getting tackled by the side of the road. "Got into a scrap."

"You've had quite the day. And it's not over yet," Colonel Purdin says and lays his hands flat on the desk. "Martial law has been declared."

Rolf can't help but laugh. Then he hesitates when he sees Purdin isn't smiling. "Martial law . . ."

"I'll need your help communicating this to your deputies and the city of Fairbanks." He pauses for a beat. "Please."

Rolf's voice is mean-friendly when he says, "From the sound of it, you don't need my blessing."

"I don't, actually, but I've always believed in good manners."

"This got something to do with what's happening in the White Mountains?"

The colonel's cheek spasms. "How much do you know?"

"You first."

"Have a seat, Sheriff."

"Think I might prefer to stand."

Again his cheek tics. "I belong to a unit devoted to cosmic threats. The fallout from the comet known as Cain. As you know, a great deal has changed about the world since the meteors rained down. We've received some manna from heaven, you might say, but we've also gotten our share of Revelation." He motions to the graying sky out the window. "Fairbanks is suffering from the latter condition and we hope to contain the problem before it spreads."

"The problem with the clouds, you mean."

THE SKY VAULT | 241

"That is the simplest possible explanation for what is happening, but yes. As of thirty minutes ago, all flights at Fairbanks International Airport have been grounded. No one will be taking off or landing for the immediate future. Additionally, the Alaska Highway and the Parks Highway have been or will be blocked off imminently."

Rolf feels as though he's been socked in the stomach. "You've quarantined us?"

"We're working on it. I need you to start thinking of this county as a Superfund site."

"Jesus H. Christ on a stick."

"Rest assured, we will do our best to keep everyone safe and manage the situation accordingly. I'm sure you saw the news about Seattle. A year ago, they were quarantined as well. The operation was successful. The danger was contained and the city was cleaned of the fungal contaminant."

"This ain't Seattle."

"No," Purdin says. "It *ain't*."

"What I mean is, the people here don't eat kale. And they own a lot of guns. And they aren't going to tolerate a government lockdown."

"They will if *you* tell them it's in their best interests."

"Convince me it is."

There is a crackling sound that comes from the phone. Like someone breathing through pneumonic lungs. Purdin glances at it and then sits up a little straighter in the chair. "First I need you to tell me what you know."

Rolf thinks about holding back information and decides there isn't much point. He avoids all mention of Moses but speaks freely otherwise about the elk on top of the Westmark Hotel and the herd up in the White Mountains and how they appeared to have fallen from above. He talks about the hole in the ground that seemed to loop into the sky. He talks about the World War II lab and what he knows of the disaster that befell it. "You ask me what I know. I don't know nothing. I only seen some things. So maybe you can tell me what in the name of God is going on?"

"I already told you that I belong to a unit devoted to the fallout from the comet Cain."

"This ain't about the comet. It's about that lab up there."

"What if they're not mutually exclusive?"

"Mutually what?"

"What if, when we talk about the comet and we talk about the lab, we're talking about the same thing?"

Rolf takes this in before saying, "What did you all do?"

"I?" Purdin says. "I didn't do anything."

"What did your people do, then? What did our country do?"

"There's no point in me apologizing for what happened a long time ago. The past belongs to people like you. I am responsible for the present. Something is broken—"

"What's broken? The goddamn sky?"

"We're going to fix it."

"How old are you, anyway?"

Purdin seems pleased more than offended by the question. "George Armstrong Custer achieved the rank of brigadier general at the age of twenty-three. So far, he is the youngest to do so. If everything goes according to plan here in Fairbanks, I hope to give him a run for his money." He blinks several times. "I imagine this must be difficult for you to accept, given your age, but . . . you work for me now."

"And who do you work for?" Rolf almost tacks on a *son*. "And I don't mean the Department of Defense. I want a name. If you're a Boy Scout, who's your troop leader? You answer to somebody."

Another crackle comes from the phone and Purdin's eyes once again study it.

"I said, who do you work for?" Rolf says this at a near shout, directing his voice at the phone. A sizzle issues from it and then an electrically charged voice says, "Show him the monitor."

Purdin shifts in his seat. "We aren't required to tell him anything more than we have."

The voice grows louder, corrupted in static: "Show him the monitor."

Purdin obliges, reaching across the desk and swiveling the computer screen so that it faces Rolf. At first it appears black and vacant. Then small flashes of digitized code spark here and there, like stars being born. And eventually they take the general shape of a face. Nothing distinct, the features smearily implied, like a constellation seen through crying eyes.

"What am I looking at?" Rolf says.

A voice—a voice garbled by interference and varying in volume—says, "My name is Thaddeus Gunn, and I am the director of this operation."

Rolf cocks his head as if that might make him see better through the dark veil of the screen. "And where is it you're calling from?"

There are a few staticky pops that follow before he replies. "Someplace far away and very close. I guess you could say I'm standing on the other side of the Looking Glass."

LOGBOOK: GEORGE C. WARNOK

ENTRY 92

June ?, 1945

One day, as the construction of the Looking Glass neared completion, Tusk took me aside. "Just so we're clear," he said. "The plan you and I had going before . . . well, things have changed."

"Changed how?" I asked.

"We're good. Everything's good. Just keep doing what you're doing. But it turns out . . . the Office of Scientific Research and Development, they've been talking to MacArthur. And the thing that really got their attention was this omnimetal stuff. That's the only way I could get them to hand over more money."

"What does that mean?"

"It means these portals or wormholes or bungholes or whatever you're talking about—that's great and all. But . . ."

"But what? That's the very basis of all our atomic research. That's the reason the Alaska Project exists at all. When we spoke about rotating the atom, we imagined a turnstile that would allow us to jump from one part of the world to another. March a platoon directly from Fort Bragg into one of Germany's concentration camps. Push a bomb from Los Alamos directly onto Hitler's Führerbunker."

"Right," Tusk said. "And don't get me wrong—that would be amazing. Obviously. We're not ruling that out. But just to be a bird-in-the-hand kind of guy for a minute. That metal—a metal that can absorb and blast out energy on a quantum level—that would be a real game changer when it comes to the future of the energy and weapons sectors."

"So—hold on. Are we not even talking about the war anymore?"

"We're going to win this war. Oppenheimer's nukes are going to drop and that'll be it. That's a guarantee. I've come to terms with that. But the good news for us is, the brass is thinking long-term. They're not just looking at 1945. They're looking ahead to 20-fucking-45. America's got to keep winning, right? If we can get hold of more of this omnimetal stuff, we'll be heroes too."

"All wars are fought for money," I said.

He appeared confused.

"Socrates said that."

"Sure he did." He slapped me on the shoulder. "Keep up the good work, Warnok. Get me a big old pile of that omnimetal and the two of us still go home winners. They'll put us on the front page. They'll throw us a ticker-tape parade. Okay?"

I couldn't stop thinking about that conversation. It was, I suppose, the same impulse that drove men to follow the cry "Go west!" and make their way across the uncertain plains and mountains in search of gold and silver. But it felt so myopic. And vulgar. Here I was, talking about opening the doors to the multiverse . . . and they wanted a mine.

My mental and physical condition rapidly deteriorated. My skin yellowed. My tongue dried. My nose bled frequently. I suffered from kidney stones and my guts were cemented with constipation. Sleep was a rarity, and when it did come, so did the nightmares.

In one, I lifted up my shirt to find my stomach bloated with some growth, and when I prodded my belly button, it split open and a long black tentacle wormed out. In another nightmare, the facility began to move, to turn one way, then another, so I was standing on the floor and then the wall and then the ceiling, sometimes falling through doorways as the world swiftly rearranged itself. Then there was the nightmare in which I heard a terrible knocking; I couldn't locate the source of it until I stood before my shaving mirror and saw it shaking.

I suspected I was going mad. I remembered what Dr. Devinor had said about the metal's ability to corrupt. I was not as strong as either of us had hoped. I thought I could hear a voice in the metal. Sometimes it sounded like the voice of Dr. Devinor. In his thickly accented baritone, he barked warnings in one ear. But then . . . then another voice would take over. This voice was different. Softer, silkier. It whispered encouragement. It promised me delights beyond imagination. It told me to hurry, hurry, hurry. It told me everyone was waiting. I didn't know who or which or what to listen to—and my thoughts had all the substance of torn-up cobwebs.

One night—or was it day? I know only that I was in my bed at the time with my sheets tangled around me in a cocoon, and another dream came to me, this one the most vivid of all. I was walking through a black void. There was no noise, no temperature, no gravity, no sensory experience at all beyond my forward movement. It was a place of vacancy. Up ahead stood a freestanding door that I recognized as the one that led into the hangar where the machine was being built. A blinding light glowed around the seams of it. I reached for the handle—opened it—and a white blast hit me, tearing the skin and muscle off my bones.

I woke up with vomit spackling my cheek and urine pooling on my mattress and the second law of thermodynamics at the forefront of my mind. A balloon loses air. A cup of coffee cools. A car plows into a tree and transfers that kinetic force into a splintering crack and shivering leaves. Dr. Devinor's body rots down into energy for plants and worms. There is a transference of energy, both gentle and violent, going on constantly, and this guarantees that everything will eventually deflate, cool, decay, rust, die. Everyone will die; everything will die. Entropy owns us, and death and disorder will come for us all—including the universe.

I had stopped considering the consequences of what we were doing. My work had become more of a compulsion, or even possession. But the conversation with Major General Tusk invited me into a larger cemetery of vexing questions.

Where did the omnimetal come from? The metal communicated with me almost as if it were an antenna. Did it indeed come from another world, as Dr. Devinor suggested? If so, why did this other world seemingly want me to build the gate? Why was it channeling through me instructions I barely comprehended?

The multiverse is too incalculable to fathom, so let me boil our situation down to something more simple. There are two worlds. There is our world. And there is the world that slipped through the portal in Tunguska.

Why do we want to enter this other world? One could say knowledge and curiosity, but exploration is more often driven by the good old colonial desire to exploit resources and people. Omnimetal. The OSRD wants omnimetal. General MacArthur wants omnimetal. Roosevelt wants omnimetal.

But why does this world want to enter ours? Does it hope to exploit us somehow? Is there a resource here they covet? Gold? Oxygen? Water? Human flesh?

Or maybe . . . maybe their situation is desperate and they are driven by need.

Consider the following possibility: If another world was dying right now, what would happen if it was offered an escape? Just as exhaust pours out of a tailpipe and a bullet speeds down the barrel of a gun, it would race to the gap. In a violent transfer of energy. Like the Tunguska event.

I was not the same man I was when I began to work for the Alaska Project. Then, I was thinking only about America. I was thinking only about how atomic travel could win the war and unite the world.

But if we open a conduit . . . while it is true we can step through it, we also invite others to do the same. As Dr. Devinor said, Alice stepped through the looking glass, but someone in Looking-Glass Land could have done the same. We create, with these conduits, an opportunity for trespass. The Tunguska event was not an explosion; it was an expulsion. And if we were already staggering before the breath of another world, what of its teeth?

I had been a fool. A puppet. What is the old adage? Some people are so excited by and impressed with their ability to do something that they never stop to ask whether they should.

I shouldn't. We shouldn't.

I realized this too late.

My thoughts were so wild that I felt separate from my body. Somehow I found myself no longer in bed but standing half dressed before the machine. I grabbed the first tool I could find—a weighty crescent wrench—and climbed onto the atom spinner. I struck it—once, twice. It was a childish, impotent gesture. The force of the blows sent a pained shock down my arm, and I nearly dropped the tool.

Others gathered at the base of the dais. "What's gotten into you, Warnok?" Kubert said. "Get down from there."

"We can't do this," I said, brandishing the wrench. "We're going to . . . we need to . . ." Their faces gazed up at me and I realized the futility of explaining myself further. I had started this, and I should end it. I crawled deeper into the atom spinner, moving toward the capacitor at its center.

I don't remember what happened next, but soon there were arms knotting around me like ropes and faces that no longer seemed familiar snarling at me to *stop, stop, stop, you fool, you mad fool.*

"Yes! Yes, exactly!" I cried. "We need to stop!"

I was put on temporary leave—to rest and heal. This meant I found myself in the very same bed once occupied by Dr. Devinor. My wrist was cuffed to a bolt in the wall, and the door to the medical bay was locked from the outside. The omnimetal had been fished from my mouth when they examined me. I no longer heard the voices, and I already felt sedated, but they dosed me with quaaludes and I fell into a deep and dreamless sleep for the first time in a long time.

Maybe we will be safe, I try to reason. Maybe there will be no expulsion the way there was in Tunguska. Maybe the atom will spin and create a clean conduit. Or maybe whatever seeps into this world will simply spread harmlessly through the far reaches of space like dandelion spores.

Maybe.

But August is coming. The bombs will soon be shipped off to the Pacific theater—the war will soon be over—and Major General Tusk is tapping his foot impatiently. He won't speak to me. He doesn't want to be dissuaded. So we will know soon enough who's knocking at the other side of the Looking Glass.

30

◎

The Explorer is parked with three wheels on the driveway and one on the lawn. In the house, in the living room, Theo's father lies on the couch. He still wears the hospital gown; they've covered him with an afghan. Short lengths of IV tubing dangle from his inner elbows. On one of his fingers, a sensor is clipped. He's not fully awake. His eyes are open but unfocused. Drool dampens his beard. His breath rasps, his throat raw from the nasogastric feeding tube Theo yanked out like a slick organ.

"Mom," Theo says. His mother, hovering over his father, ignores him. "Mom." Theo has a cup of water he wants to try to get his dad to drink, but she won't move away. She keeps saying the same three things over and over again, though not in the same order: "You're alive" and "Thank God" and "I love you." Her forehead presses against his. She isn't a natural crier. She always seems embarrassed by her tears. She wipes them off her cheeks and his as they fall.

"Mom!"

Finally she stands and makes a full circle of the room while pulling her hair back from her forehead. She wants to know what's happening. And now the relief in her voice is giving way to a wild and desperate anger.

Theo tries to explain as best and as quickly as he can while he nurses his father. He props the old man up with a pillow. He gets some water to his lips, even if most of it spills down his beard. He removes the IV tubes and tosses them on the coffee table and fits some Band-Aids over the wounds.

"What you're telling me doesn't make sense, Theo," she says, almost yelling.

"That's what everyone said to Dad too. Before he left for Portland. But he was right. There's something in the clouds here—something dangerous—and the government is trying to cover it up."

His father's eyes keep rolling back in his head, and Theo knows he should let him rest, but they don't have that luxury. "Dad," he says, patting his cheek. "Come on. I need you here. We've got to focus."

Sometimes his father pops caffeine pills, the kind they sell at truck stops. He says they help the words come faster when he's on the air. Theo seeks out a bottle in the bathroom cabinet. He shakes three pills onto the kitchen cutting board and places a flour-sack towel over the top and uses a meat tenderizer to mash them down to powder. Then he sweeps them into the water cup and stirs it with a spoon. Again he tries to get his dad to drink. The old man sputters and gags but manages to get down half a glass.

Theo and his mother speak another five minutes before his father says, in a froggy voice, "I was right."

"Dad?" Theo says at the same time his mother says, "Chuck?"

He has what can only be described as a shit-eating grin on his face. "I was goddamn right, wasn't I?"

"Yeah," Theo says. "You were right, Dad."

He blinks at them and rubs his hands against the fabric of the couch, orienting himself. He speaks slowly, as if trying to recall a dream. "The last thing I remember, I was in a room. A windowless room. There were beds all around me. With patients in them. Soldiers were holding me down. A doctor shoved a needle in me."

"That's where I found you. In the basement of the hospital."

His father shakes his head and his mouth hangs open. "How did you get me out of there?"

"Short version?" Theo says. "Lab coat. Fire alarm."

"I don't know what to think of any of this," his mother says. "I don't even know how to participate in this conversation. I feel like everybody is suddenly speaking a foreign language."

"My son is brilliant." His father laughs, and the laugh turns into a cough. His chest hitches. Theo helps him drink more water. He sputters out, "My son is brave."

Theo's at that curious age when you're no longer a kid but not quite an adult. He feels on the inside like Little Head looks on the outside. A body that's still got a grip on two worlds. The borderlands of life. A time for trying out different attitudes, distancing yourself from your parents. That's what he's been doing the past few months—distancing himself. He was embarrassed especially by his father's weirdness, which makes him feel sickened with guilt now that he almost lost him.

"I'm sorry, Dad," he says.

His father tips his head in confusion. "Sorry for what?"

"Sorry for . . . not being the best son."

His father seems genuinely bewildered. "But you *are* the best son."

His mother's hands are on Theo's shoulders, massaging him. A week ago he would have shrugged away her grip. But he puts a hand over hers now. In his throat is an ache he tries to swallow down like a hot walnut.

His father's eyes find a new focus. "They're going to come for me, aren't they?"

"I think so."

"That means you're not safe." He looks wildly at both of them. "Neither of you."

"We're past that, Dad."

His father nods sadly. "Yeah. Okay. How much time do we have?" He's looking for guidance.

Theo doesn't want to let him down, but he's not sure he has the answers they need. "Minutes. Hours. I don't know."

"We should call the police," his mother says, biting at her thumbnail. "I'll try them."

"No," Theo says, and his mother says, "Why not?"

"Theo's right," his father says. "You can't trust them. We can't trust anybody right now." He tries to sit up but doesn't make it and falls back with a cry.

Theo and his mother call out to him, touch him gently, ask him if he's all right. He holds out his hand as evidence of his pain. Theo's mother gasps. The skin is gone, as if the hand had been ungloved, replaced by something gray and vaporous with the quality of an X-ray.

And then, a second later, it's just a hand again. Long-fingered. Black hairs bristling along the knuckles.

His father turns it one way, then the other. He flexes it into a fist. A knuckle cracks. "It's in me," he says.

"What's in you?" Theo's mother seems afraid to touch him, but she does, a testing nudge, as if to make certain he's actually there.

"I can feel it." He licks his lips. "I can hear it too. It sounds like . . ." His face slackens with a faraway look. "Whispers."

"What's in you?" she says again. "What's in you, Chuck?"

"When I was on that plane . . . I went somewhere else. I went someplace that wasn't this place. When I came back, I brought some of it with me. And maybe . . ." His eyes widen. "Maybe I left some of me behind too. Maybe I'm not quite anywhere anymore. I'm in different places at once. I fell through a broken mirror."

"You're crazy," she says. "You're talking crazy."

"No, Mom." Theo grips her by the upper arms. "The world's gone crazy. Dad's the one who's finally making sense."

"We need to do something," his mother says. "He's sick. He needs more of whatever medicine they were pumping into him. Maybe we should go back to the hospital."

Theo and his father both shout, "No!" and she puts her hands over her face, walks out of the room, and returns a second later. "Then what?"

"Help me up," his father says and puts out his arms.

"Do you need to use the bathroom?" Theo says. "Because—you've still got a catheter in your D—and I'm not touching that thing."

"I've got a very bad feeling that this city is about to go dark. I need to finish what I started. The world needs to know the truth of what's happening before we fall off the map. Get me to the radio."

31

◎

Before she zip-tied Professor Butler and abandoned him in his classroom, Sophie stole his car keys. The green Prius is parked in a nearby ramp, and it has a sun-faded Nader sticker on its rear bumper. She beeps the fob and climbs inside and tosses her briefcase on the passenger seat. She finds a thermos in the cup holder, and Starbucks cups are rolling around on the floor and stuffed into the side panel of the door. Caffeine is apparently the drug of choice among academics.

She pulls out her Blackphone and transmits a message to Hans. "Government lab. WWII. White Mountains of Alaska. Red-flag recon. *Danke schön.*"

Barely a second goes by before a message buzzes in return. "On it. *Bitte schön.*"

The sky is darkening, the sunset muted by the clouds rolling thickly down from the White Mountains. This is the direction she aims the car. Even with the gas pedal crushed, the Prius has trouble getting past fifty, the engine whining. This is one of the older models, before omnimetal batteries became the standard.

"Come on," she says through gritted teeth. "Come the fuck on." She is so close to what she has come for.

Sophie has always slept fitfully. The slightest sound wakes her, makes her reach for a knife strapped to her thigh, a pistol tucked beneath a pillow. Maybe this is why she rarely dreams—because even when she's curled up in bed, she always has one foot fixed in reality.

But soon after she and Hans set up the monolith in the Kansas warehouse, she began to experience the most vivid nightmares of her life. In one, the sun had been replaced by a pyramidal blue eye with tentacles dangling from it, and when it rose every morning, the world fell to its knees in worship. In another, she felt her vessels pulsing—pulsing so violently that she could see them moving beneath her skin. At her wrists and along her forearms, they swelled and twisted and surged with every heartbeat. She pulled up the cuff of her pants and found the same at her ankle and along her calf. She checked her reflection in a mirror and gasped. Her neck and temples throbbed with vessels engorged to the size of hoses. Finally her skin split and she screamed as the vessels slithered out of her, gray and fibrous.

Sometimes she stood in front of the monolith and felt certain she could hear a whispering. She couldn't make out individual words, only a rustling babble. When Hans caught her there, frozen before the sculpture with her head cocked, he asked her if she was okay.

"No," she said. "Not really."

One of their consultants was a metal-eater, a guru based in India who went by the name of Ram VII. Sophie often conferred with him about their missions and he had successfully directed them to an omnimetal score deep in the Amazon, in exchange for which he received 20 percent of the black-market sale. He seemed plugged into an invisible circuitry. He would have answers about her current . . . struggles.

She flew out to see him in Mumbai. He lived on a fifty-acre estate and owned a thousand white peacocks. His followers were mostly white as well, and Sophie discovered many of them lounging on floor pillows in smoke-filled tents or wandering paths cut through tropical gardens. The spicy smell of space dust dirtied the air, and all of their eyes glowed a silver-blue.

Ram VII greeted her by taking both her hands in his and saying, "Metal is." He had white hair and wore a black sherwani studded with jewels that sparkled with all the light of the galaxy when he moved. He invited Sophie out to a stone patio and here they sat in wicker furniture and listened to the peacocks wail as the sun set. A servant came with a tray of chai. They drank from their steaming cups as she described her dreams. He listened in silence until she said, "What's wrong with me?"

"There's nothing wrong with you," he said. "You're just beginning to wake up."

"Wake up from what?"

"The fantasy that *this* is it." He scraped a finger along the wicker arm of his chair when he said *this*. "Most humans suffer from some version of the same myopia. They never really grow out of the child's perspective that the planet, if not the universe, spins around them." His eyes were an impossible color to pin down—silver, red, blue, green, purple, like the aurora borealis. "The sun is merely something to set their clocks by. The stars beyond are as insignificant to them as the grains of sand on a beach. When you begin to wake up, Sophie, it can be beautiful, but it can be frightening. Is there something that might have triggered such a change in you?"

She explained what the Collectors had learned so far. She described the monolith—not only its creation by Nico Frontier, not only its seeming ability to portkey across great distances, but its hypnotic pull.

Ram VII nodded and said that he too had built such a design, the blueprints of which he'd sourced from deep meditation, but he destroyed it before it became operational.

"Why would you destroy it?" she said.

"Because heaven and hell share the same gate."

She had no response to this.

He set down his tea and dragged his chair around to face her and focused his radiant gaze upon her. "I too have been having dreams of late," he said. "Disturbing dreams."

"About what?"

"About Alaska."

She had mentioned Fairbanks as one of the unaccountable rifts they had discovered through the monolith. Every night over the past few weeks, he had traveled there. To the skies over the

White Mountains. Something was calling to him. Something that burned in his mind and in the dark woods like a star. He referred to it as the alpha metal. An impossibly rare and refined form of omnimetal—the equivalent of the Hope Diamond. He felt it pull at his blood like the moon commanded the tide. It was a prime source of energy and the ultimate engine for a conduit that could crack open the boundaries of worlds.

"So it's a weapon?"

"In the wrong hands."

"You want me to do something."

"You came here for a reason, I see now. This alpha metal—it will be found. And if it is found by the wrong people . . ." He closed his eyes for a long moment as if to shut out the possibility of such a thing. The wicker complained when he stood from his chair; he walked to the edge of the patio and stared off into the deepening gloom as night threw its cloak over the world. She followed him there.

"Do you know what a Janus word is, Sophie?"

"No."

"It is a word that has two contradictory meanings. *Overlook*, for instance." He motioned to the gardens, where fires burned and laughter could be heard. "It means both 'to study something carefully' and 'to miss something altogether.'"

"Okay."

"In a way, *omnimetal* is a Janus word. I teach my followers to worship it, but they should fear it as well. They should taste just enough of God so as not to be swallowed by Him."

She needed to go to Fairbanks. She needed to recover the alpha metal. And she needed to keep it secret and safe, he told her. "I'm not really into the whole altruism thing," she said.

"Maybe not."

"I'm running a business here."

"Maybe so." The Collectors might be a rogue operation, he said. But that didn't mean they were nihilists. They had a code—a code driven by profit, yes, but a code nonetheless.

"You think too highly of me."

"Would you sell a nuclear missile?"

She sighed. No, she would not.

"Then you would not sell this."

The Collectors wanted to game the world, not watch it burn. They didn't want geopolitical chaos, just a little unrest so countries and business would vie against one another, because that made for the best market. "Think of it in terms of dollars and cents if that makes it easier for you." He put a hand on her shoulder and it felt as heavy as stone. "I know you will do the right thing."

She almost spit her response: "The *right* thing?"

"The right thing."

She wasn't so sure. His words felt far away now. And the alpha metal that supposedly waited for her inside the wreckage of this World War II lab would be the endgame of almost nine months of research and footwork. The ultimate score.

On the Alaska Highway, the traffic is spare, but she notices up ahead several taillights flaring red. Five cars come to a halt. She strains to see, wondering if there has been an accident. Flares spit sparks. A barrier has been set up. Three military trucks are parked beyond them and soldiers wave flashlights, directing the cars to turn around and find an alternate route.

But Sophie parks and drops her window. One of the soldiers approaches. "Let's go!" he says. "Turn around!"

"Hi!" she says, brightening her voice to a Pollyanna pitch. "I'm so curious what's going on!" She gives her widest smile and he seems to finally see her. He sloughs over for a chat.

"Hey, miss? I'm sorry," he says, placing his arm on top of the Prius and leaning in. "But we can't let you through."

"Ugh. No exceptions? Pretty please? With sugar on top?"

He's probably twenty-five. His tallness and sandy-blond hair and blandly handsome features make her think of Nebraska. "Would if I could."

"I'm so nosy, I know," she says. "But can you at least tell me why?"

"Would if I could," he says again. He sighs as if he really regrets it. "We're not supposed to talk about it right now. But trust me when I say that Fairbanks is going to get pretty hairy pretty fast."

"My house is right around the corner. I need to feed my cat. You can see my place from here. Look." She points and he follows the direction of her finger. From her jacket she removes a pistol and shoots him behind the ear.

The other soldiers are slow to respond, confused by what this tiny woman in this tiny car is doing as she walks toward them and fires, fires, fires, dropping them before they can even reach for their holsters. One of them continues to squirm on the ground and she finishes him with a shot to the eye.

The road behind her is empty. She returns to the Prius and retrieves her briefcase. She abandons the car with both of its door hanging open, the dome light glowing in the deepening gloom. She checks the rear of the MZTK and finds several lockers containing hazmat suits and weapons, including a flamethrower.

The keys are in the ignition. The engine growls to life and she roars up the dark highway. She pulls out her Blackphone and makes a call. A familiar voice says, "*Guten Morgen.*"

"Not here, it's not."

"*Guten Abend,* then."

"I'm close, Hans."

"I expected as much or you wouldn't be calling me on a restricted line."

"Things are going to shit here. Heavy military presence. Lockdown. This will be my last transmission. So what do you have for recon?"

He speaks quickly, his accent making his words crunch, like he's taking fast bites from an apple. "The lab in the White Mountains was known as the Alaska Project. It was running concurrently with the Manhattan Project in Los Alamos."

"They were building another bomb?"

"*Nein, fräulein.* Something else. Something atomic. Top secret. Very little information remains, but it appears the program was shuttered by the government after a disaster. What few documents there are refer to it as a failure. All scientists and military personnel—including a major general—are listed as MIA."

"MIA?"

"MIA. Not deceased. That's correct."

"Well, where the fuck did they go?"

"That's an excellent question. There's no one left to answer it. The lab was considered a total loss and viewed as not only an embarrassing mistake but a potential hazard. The gates were locked. The war ended. The world moved on. But—and here is where your ears should perk up, my dear—the Department of Defense turned the power back on a few weeks ago."

The road begins to rise into the dark-shouldered foothills of the White Mountains. "I'm less than an hour out."

"If the alpha metal is there . . ." Hans says.

"If it's there, let's sell it for a billion dollars and retire."

"I'm game. I've always wanted to buy an island in the South Pacific."

"If all goes well, we'll rendezvous later tonight."

"Your tonight will be my afternoon."

"*Guten Tag,* then."

"See you soon, dear. Don't die."

"No promises."

32

◎

olf wavers in place a moment, taking in the shadowy image of Thaddeus Gunn on the computer monitor, before he says, "I think I'll sit down after all." He lowers himself heavily into the chair opposite the desk.

Colonel Purdin rips a sheet of paper out of the printer and holds it out to him.

Rolf takes it with a shaky hand. "What's this?"

"A press conference has been arranged. It will take place an hour from now. This is your script. You'll be our spokesman, but please let us control the conversation. Do not deviate from what is on this paper. When the time comes for questions, I will answer them."

Rolf glances at the paper without reading the words. Then he crumples it up.

"What are you doing?"

"Shit is what I'm doing. Until you tell it to me straight what's happening here."

"Let me remind you that under martial law—"

"You can shove your martial law up your diapered ass." He tosses the crumpled paper onto the desk. "You think you can scare me with legal threats or a spooky face on a screen?"

There is a dissonant shriek. On the computer monitor, two digitized eyes seem to flare.

Rolf continues: "See, there are some benefits to being old as dirt. One, I got nothing to lose. Two, I been the face of this community for as many decades as you've been alive. You need me. If I tell these folks to get their guns, you're going to have a revolution on your doorstep."

Purdin pinches his lips together so tightly, the color drains from them. He is about to say something when a voice crackles from the computer. "Let's not be unreasonable," Thaddeus says. "We'll tell you what you want to know, Sheriff. But first . . . I'm very curious what *you* believe is happening to Fairbanks."

Rolf settles back in his chair. He can feel his pulse beating behind his eyes and the rhythm of his breath feels off. "I guess the simple way to put it is this: Seems like somebody punched some holes in the sky. And there's stuff leaking through them."

"Let's take that idea a step further," Thaddeus says. "Try to imagine an old dam. There are cracks in it, and the force of the river is pushing through them and crumbling the concrete. If we ignore the problems with the dam, the town below could be flooded. We need to build a new structure to harness all that power into something we can use."

"Except we're not talking about a river."

"No, Sheriff. We're talking about another dimension."

Rolf shouldn't believe what he's hearing. He should spit out a laugh at this Twilight Zone bullshit. But he's past that. The last two days have overwhelmed his rational mind. Somebody could tell him the moon was a dragon egg and he wouldn't argue. "And that's where you're at right now? Another dimension?"

The image on the screen shifts as if Gunn is leaning closer. "Right now, yes." His voice has a tinny echo. "But I'm hoping to return home very soon."

Rolf tugs at his mustache. It's difficult to make the words come. "How did you get over there? To this other dimension?"

"This isn't the only place where there is . . . leakage. Thin spots between this world and the next. We've discovered they are aligned with volcanoes and nuclear explosions and meltdowns. Mount Vesuvius, for instance, is a hot spot. So is Kilauea. So is Chernobyl. So is Hiroshima and Nagasaki. So are the Nevada and Utah deserts where so many nuclear tests took place, particularly the skies around

Area 51. The same can be said of asteroid strikes. You are no doubt familiar with the meteor that struck sixty-six million years ago, the one that took out the dinosaurs? The Chicxulub impact crater reaches from the Yucatán into the Carribean, which we believe accounts for all the planes and ships that go missing in that area. Some people call it the Bermuda Triangle. Energy blasts are responsible for opening up these seams. I myself was caught up in an incredible, concentrated, violent blast that transported me . . . abroad."

"Where? In Fairbanks?"

"Not in Fairbanks, no. I assume you're familiar with the omnimetal mines of northern Minnesota?"

"Everybody knows about omnimetal."

"It happened there. And now I'm trying to find my way home. With the help of friends like you."

"You're talking about volcanoes and nuclear bombs and meltdowns and such. What about the explosion that happened in the White Mountains in 1945? Is that the cause of all this trouble in my backyard?"

"I said there were other frail spots in the world, but this is the greatest of them all. What you've been observing in the White Mountains is the waste of a failed wormhole. The litter. The debris. The sky around the laboratory is swirling with disturbances. We flung open the door to another world and never managed to fully close it again."

Rolf's mind churns with a thousand questions. He's torn between asking more of them or getting the hell away from here. "When you were talking before? Metaphorically? You said there was an old dam with cracks in it. And you needed to build a new structure."

"Yes. To properly harness the power. To take advantage of the resources offered by an unclaimed geography."

"What kind of power and resources are you talking about?"

"Omnimetal, for one. There is omnimetal in this computer. There is omnimetal in that phone. There is omnimetal in the batteries of your squad cars. In just a few short years, omnimetal has become the greatest source of energy in this world. But its supply is limited to a few hundred square miles in Minnesota."

"And you've got the keys to the vault. And you're jingling them at the U.S. government. That's why you've got your little army here, following orders and snapping off salutes."

"A condescending but otherwise accurate assessment."

"This country fucked it up the first time. What makes you think you aren't going to fuck it up again?"

"Science and technology have improved a great deal since 1945, Sheriff Wagner."

"This sounds a touch more complicated than anything Silicon Valley's pumping out."

"I know things."

"You know things, huh?"

"I have"—and here his voice yawns wide and becomes like a thousand voices—"become *more* here."

"And what exactly does *here* look like?"

"You'll see soon enough."

Rolf nods for a long time. Then he slaps his hands down on the arms of his chair. "Well, nature's calling. Happens a little too often when you're my age. Hope you don't mind if step out for a minute."

When he stands up, so does Purdin. "Wait."

Rolf waits for him to draw the pistol at his belt or insist on an escort. "You'll be at the press conference?"

Rolf brushes some lint off his hat. Gives Purdin a nod. And heads for the door.

On his way out, he nearly runs into Aimee. She was eavesdropping and hurries three quick steps back and places her hand over her heart. "Rolf?"

He closes the door behind him and drags her away from it, saying, "I know, I know."

"What are you going to do?"

He looks into the hollow of his hat as if the answer might be there before popping it on his head. "I don't think there's much I can do, honestly. Future's officially caught up with me. Way they're treating me, I might as well already be out to pasture."

"What have we been exposed to?"

"You get home to your family. Okay?" He almost says that's what he'd be doing right now if he had anyone to hold close.

She scoops up her coat and purse. "What about you? Rolf?"

He tilts his head toward his office. "Not sure it matters what I do."

"Don't say that. You're the sheriff. Even if you think things like that, you're not supposed to say them."

He can't argue with that. Everybody hates a goddamn whiner. "Maybe I just need a minute to get my head straight."

"You want a cookie?" Aimee says. "I brought in a plate of chocolate oatmeals today. Think there's still a few in the break room. Cookie will always make you feel better."

"Guess I can start there."

She takes her keys out of her pocket and rattles them. "I know what you should do. You take care of people. That's your job. So you go on and get those little shits back to their parents."

"Aimee. My goodness."

"What?"

"Don't know that I've ever heard you swear."

"Well, I've got a few in me, I guess."

"Where did the deputy end up stashing them?"

"Interrogation room. I gave them some root beers and chips out of the machine. I hope that's okay."

"As long as the root beers were flat and the chips were stale."

"Also, I know you won't like this, but I gave them their phones back." She cringes out a smile. "They just seemed so scared. And those phones are like pacifiers for teenagers."

He shakes his head but says, "Guess it don't seem so important now."

She gives him a tight, teary look before starting down the hallway. "Are we going to be okay?"

"Can't tell."

"I'll pray on it, then."

"Do that. Can use all the help we can get."

33

◎

Joanna stands by the trailer packed with dynamite. The taillights of Bryce's truck flare as he backs up slowly. She guides him with a wave of her hands, then holds out her palms flat. "Good." He stops and climbs out and joins her. Together they lift the coupler on the trailer and line it up with the hitch and lower it onto the ball. They crank the latch, attach the chains, and retract the jack.

"Ready?" Bryce says, but she doesn't answer, distracted by her phone buzzing in her pocket.

She pulls it out to silence it, but somehow a voice addresses her. She can't make out any words, only a garbled noise. "What?" she says, bringing the phone to her ear.

"What are you doing?"

"Who is this?" she says, though she knows the answer.

Thaddeus Gunn's voice warps into something much larger than anything that could be broadcast from a man's throat. "I said, what are you doing with that dynamite?"

She looks up and sees the blinking red eye of a camera, one of the many stationed throughout the construction site.

"I don't want to be part of this," she says.

"You already are."

"I quit."

"You're a wrench, a screwdriver. Your opinion is irrelevant. You signed the contract—now do what you're told. Build."

"I know what happened here."

"Do you, now?"

"I learned from Dr. Warnok himself."

"Everyone who once worked at that lab is gone. What they learned and what they did is gone."

"I read the logbook."

"What?"

"I told you I know what happened here. I know you're trying to make it happen again. I've got Dr. Warnok's logbook. The lead scientist for the Alaska Project."

Gunn was spitting his responses now. "That lab is in ruins, and you mean to tell me you found a logbook?"

"You want to rotate the atom. You want to open up a wormhole."

"You're not educated enough to understand what you're saying."

"I understand enough. And I think I might share it with some reporters. How would you feel about that?"

When he speaks again, the sharp condescension in his voice has given way to something like warm reason. "If this is a negotiation, I admire your tenacity. There's more money. We can get you more money if that's what you'd like."

"I don't want your money. I'm going to make sure you don't repeat some terrible mistakes."

"The mistakes of the Alaska Project can't be undone."

"Then why are you so desperate to stop me?"

Silence.

"I know I'm supposedly not *educated* enough to understand all this," Joanna says, "but I got a feeling that it's a lot easier to open a door if the lock's already jimmied."

Now his voice is raw and deep-throated: "Take the money or you're going to find yourself in prison. Or worse."

"I'm making the call. This has turned into a demo project."

"No!" The word comes at her with impossible force, and it sounds like not just his voice, but many. A legion of voices layered on top of each other and not quite finding their harmony. She remembers what Warnok wrote about the voices—the voices that spoke to him through the metal—and she wonders who or what she is actually talking to, if there is even a man on the other end of the line. She knows Thaddeus Gunn existed, but she feels more and more like she's talking to an angry ghost rattling around in the closet and envying the living. Her ear is hot. Her palm is hot, as hot as if she's suddenly holding a brick pulled from a fire. She cries out and throws the cell to the ground. It bounces twice and comes to a flat rest. There is a short fountain of sparks and then the device catches fire and melts into a black bubbling puddle.

She drags her collar over her nose to muffle the stink of burned plastic, and Bryce puts a hand on her shoulder. "I think we better hurry."

They haul the trailer of dynamite down the road, going slow over the ruts and rocks, navigating around the fallen trees. Brush scrapes the undercarriage of the truck. The wheels slip in the slush but don't bottom out. There isn't a way to drive around the old lab, so they park out front and click on the fog lights.

"What about the bear?" Joanna says.

"Yeah," Bryce says. "What about the bear?"

"Keep a stick of dynamite in your pocket. We see any sign of that thing, we light one off. The sound alone should scare it."

They open the doors to the trailer and get to work hauling dynamite. Every case holds eighty sticks and weighs around forty pounds. She feels as though she is carrying something alive, a sleeping infant with a terrible temper, and she walks with great care. She and Bryce start off hauling the cases separately, but after three runs, they work together. It's slower and more awkward, but their backs won't survive the night otherwise.

It takes an hour to stack the crates inside and another hour to arrange the bundles throughout the space, each with its own blasting cap.

"That's the last of it," Bryce says.

"We have to go, but I just need one more minute to take this in."

They've been moving so constantly, it feels strange to sit. But that's what they do, at the lip of the machine, their legs dangling over the edge of the first recession.

Trees calendared their lives with rings. Her uncle Harry marked his with buildings constructed. He would often park outside of a structure—a hotel built ten years ago, a mall built twenty years ago—and say to her, "That's me." That was the merit of a life. The proof of a life. The work. He often mentioned how even after he was gone, the buildings would endure. She imagines him now at the nursing home. He's likely already tucked into bed and sleeping. For once she's grateful that the stroke ruined his mind. He'll never have to learn what she's about to do.

"This was supposed to be it," Joanna says.

"What?"

"The thing that saved my uncle's company."

"You mean *your* company," Bryce says.

"It was never really my company." Her voice almost echoes in the big space; there's a slight reverb. "Now it's all about to go up in flames."

Bryce scratches his beard. "I maybe got another take on that."

"Yeah?"

"Yeah." Bryce tells her a story about his childhood home. One terrible winter when there were over thirty subzero days, the family was feeling dark and depressed and sick of being cooped up. So they decided to host a party and invite everyone they knew. They had a barn on their property, and they swept and polished the old wide-board floors. They strung up Christmas lights and lanterns. Everybody who came brought every kind of food. Wood-fired pizzas and fried chicken and venison sausages and garlic potatoes and cold salads and pecan pies. Beers were shoved into buckets of snow, and the bottles glowed gold like candles. A band—a fiddle and guitar and drums and sax—set up in the loft. His parents took the first dance, knowing that their guests would shuffle and shove their hands in their pockets if they didn't show them how the evening was supposed to work. Then everyone joined in, couple by couple, and they danced so hard and hot, they had to throw open the doors and let the arctic air cool them. It was twenty below that night, but everybody was soaked in sweat by the end of it.

"If you want to offset the dark times," Bryce says, taking her hand, "you've got to bring a lot of light." With his other hand, he holds up the detonator. "That's what we're going to do now. Some version of it, anyway. Bring a whole lot of light to fight whatever dark was conjured here."

"The way you think sure is different," she says. "But I like it."

They start to stand, groaning at their soreness. Bryce grabs a metal bar to hoist himself up, and it slides several notches down and lets out a rusty shout.

"Oh, shit," he says.

"What?" she says, but her gaze has shifted to the dais at the center of the structure. It was moving before but with grinding hesitancy. Now the many parts of it are steadily speeding up, whirling and shrieking dangerously.

"I think I accidentally turned up the volume on this thing."

"Well, turn it off!" She hits him on the shoulder. "Turn it off!"

He's already got hold of the lever, and he pulls—once, twice. "It's stuck." He jams the detonator in his coat pocket. He rearranges his body, squats down, and yanks up with a two-handed grip. His face reddens. There comes a snap. He staggers back, almost falling. Then he holds up the broken lever. "Sorry."

The centrifuge spins faster and faster, its layered parts like many clock wheels and dials wound on differing timelines. The metal scrapes and yowls, but there is a whirring noise beneath all of that. The pulsing light they witnessed before grows brighter and brighter even as the atmosphere of the room grows thicker, like a cloud is being born. She hears something beyond the screeching of the metal, and it sounds like voices. It sounds like Thaddeus Gunn did on the phone. And maybe, if she looks closely, she sees something like a face staring at her from inside the center of the machine, a shimmering face with tentacles spilling out of its gash of a mouth.

"What do we do now?" Bryce says.

"We run."

34

◎

The interrogation room at the station has whitewashed cinder-block walls and a thin gray carpet dirty with stains. Little Head sits, arms crossed, sullen. His phone is on the table before him, playing a video. The other boy, Jackson, paces in circles while licking the crumbs from a snack-size bag of Doritos. Rolf watches them through the window for a minute before cracking open the door.

They both freeze, their eyes sharp on him. Whatever guts they showed earlier are long gone. They're just a couple of scared kids. The people maniacally laughing on the video are silenced when Little Head reaches out and hits Pause.

"How are you dumb shits doing?" Rolf says. His knees and belly are bruised from their scuffle, and he might still have some road-side gravel embedded in his cheek, but he's not angry with them. He's more amused and disappointed. He always tries to give kids a second chance. And with the DOD in his office and the news of the lockdown weighing on him, he just wants to do one good thing and get their asses home.

"Sorry about earlier, man," Jackson says. "We didn't know you were the sheriff—"

His fast flow of words stops when Little Head gives him a one-armed shove.

"What?" Jackson says.

"Don't say anything," Little Head says. "I've watched lots of *CSI* and *Law and Order*. You're not supposed to say anything until they get you a lawyer."

Rolf comes in, lets the door close behind him. He bristles his mustache and rocks back and forth on his heels. "Oh, so I've got an expert on my hands. Good to know."

"They try to trick you," Little Head says. "They give you treats." He motions to the soda and chips. "They're suddenly all nice. Then—they bring down the hammer."

Rolf's voice is not unkind, just genuinely curious, when he says, "What in the name of God were you boys thinking, anyway? Joyriding without a license? Tackling a police officer?"

Jackson says, "We didn't have a choice. We needed to help our friend. His dad is—" Again he's silenced by a shove.

"Lawyer," Little Head says.

"Maybe I won't report you to juvie," Rolf says, "if you tell me the truth."

"See? Like I said," Little Head screeches. "Being all nice. I'm not falling for it. No way."

"What about our parents? Would you not tell our parents?" Jackson says, and Little Head says, "No! No. Stop. You saw those soldiers. We can't trust him."

Rolf pulls out a chair on the other side of the table and tiredly drops himself into it. His brain isn't quite processing what he just heard. "Hold on. What did you say?"

"I saw the soldiers. You're working with them."

"Them?"

"The window on this door is tiny, but we've seen things, my friend. The Department of Defense is marching in and out of this place. That means you're one of the bad guys."

"You think the DOD are the bad guys?"

"Yes. Lawyer."

Rolf raps his knuckles on the table. "Why would you say they're the bad guys?"

"Because they are. Lawyer."

"Seriously, kid." He leans forward. "If it helps you to hear, they pulled rank on me and stole my goddamn office. I'm no friend of theirs. Now, if you know something about what's happening here in Fairbanks you should tell me."

Little Head studies him for a long beat. Then he waves Jackson over and whispers something in his ear and both boys nod before returning their attention to him. "This conversation can continue," Little Head says, "only if you bring us another round of sodas and four bags of Cool Ranch Doritos. Not Nacho. Cool. Ranch."

Five minutes later, polypropylene bags are crinkling, mouths are munching and slurping, and both boys are talking over the top of each other, explaining exactly what happened at the airport and in the hospital. Rolf mostly tracks it all, but he holds up his hands at one point to silence them. "You say he disappeared in one place and appeared in another."

"Yes."

"And these soldiers—they took him away. They said he was dead. But he's not."

"Yes," they both say.

"How do you know that, though? Wasn't your buddy headed to the hospital last we saw him? Maybe his dad was dead after all?"

Little Head gives him a withering look and holds up his phone, where a message reads *Got Dad. Home now. Thank u 4 everything. Srsly. U guys ok?* He clicks the side button and the screen goes dark. He taps the phone against his temple. "Your move, Sheriff."

35

Theo gets on one side of his father, and his mother gets on the other. They hoist him up and crutch his arms, helping him forward. His hospital gown billows behind him, his ass hanging out, as they cross the kitchen and enter the garage.

The air is cold here, and his father steps gingerly on the concrete with his bare feet. They help him onto the padded stool. Before him is a bench with radio sets tangled in nests of wires. There are soldering irons, sockets, wire cutters, strippers. and crimpers. The day the RadioShack closed in Fairbanks, his father wouldn't stop shaking his head and saying, "It's a damn shame," as if someone he knew had been felled by a heart attack.

He's taught Theo about it all—ham, solid state, tubes—and together they've taken apart and built dozens of units. He powers them all on now, turning dial after dial after dial. Their faces glow. A whining undertone electrifies the air and makes the hairs rise on Theo's arms.

His father drags several microphones toward him, checks their plugs, neatens the cords, and says, "Get me the FM transmitter."

He's referring to a device on a shelf above them. He built it himself, following instructions on a YouTube tutorial. It was part of his prepper plan, along with the stockpile of water purifiers, canned goods, prescription drugs, ammo, toilet paper, iodine pills for radiation. He wanted a way not to just communicate with others when the cell towers went down but to jam and override other frequencies in case misinformation and propaganda was being spread. He considered himself more than a DJ; he was a trusted voice, an ambassador. For some people, he might be their only source of information for news and weather in a day. He kept them entertained, but he also kept them informed. He always felt he had a responsibility much greater than hair metal and butt rock, and if things ever went dark, he was determined to stay on the air.

Now is his moment.

If he can manage to hold on. He hunches over in pain again. This time his face flickers its way down to bone—for an instant Theo can see the gray wrinkled mass of his brain—before reconstituting itself. A brief mist pours off him. Theo and his mother want to hold him but hesitate, wondering what they've exposed themselves to. She chokes out a sob.

"Hurry," his father says, his eyes shut. "Please."

Theo hauls down the bulky transmitter. He plugs it into a power strip and cables it to the radios. "Done."

"Good. Now get another stool." He puts a hand to Theo's cheek. "I need you by my side, copilot. I need your help on this last broadcast."

Joanna and Bryce run. She's sick with adrenaline. Her stomach is a bag of acid. Her legs are heavy, and every step is a slippery uncertainty. The fog is thick enough now that she would lose all sense of direction if not for the truck headlights burning in the distance. Somehow they manage to make it. They walk the final few yards to his Dodge, catching their breath.

"How far you figure we should go?" she says. "Before we punch the detonator."

"With all that concrete, we might run into a little bit of interference with the remote signal. I say we try for two hundred yards or so."

She's about to say *Let's do it,* but a figure steps into the yellow haze of the headlights. A woman. She carries what appears to be a briefcase. Joanna can't see her clearly because she is backlit.

"Who are—"

But before Joanna can get the question out, the woman raises a pistol. The muzzle flares. A gunshot shouts. And Bryce falls to the ground with a scream. Joanna goes to him. He seethes his breath and clutches his thigh. A hole has been punched through the denim and blood gurgles from it.

The woman steadily approaches, the pistol extended. The fog swirls around her passage. She comes into focus now. Black-haired. Asian. Compact, no more than five feet tall. She wears a military-style jacket with many pockets. She stares at Joanna over the sights of the gun. Her expression isn't angry or wild but purely indifferent, and that's scarier somehow. "Where is it?" she says.

Outside the sheriff's office, the press has gathered. Reporters from KTVF, the *Fairbanks Daily News-Miner*, even the campus newspaper, the *Sun Star*. Several of Rolf's deputies have joined them, no doubt frustrated and wanting to know what exactly is going on. The media people set up cameras. A podium has been carried out onto the sidewalk. Several microphones are wired to its top. A directional light is arranged on a tripod to brighten the scene since the air has blackened, the sun now nothing more than a red hint on the horizon.

Rolf can see all of this through a station window. Beside him stand Little Head and Jackson. When he let them out of the interrogation room, he told them to stay quiet and not to do anything foolish. But he's not sure if he's capable of following his own advice.

In his pocket is the folded sheet of paper he's supposed to read from—alerting the residents of Fairbanks that martial law has been imposed, that a quarantine is in effect, that they should obey and trust the government to look after them, and that everything will be fine as long as they cooperate.

"What's going on out there?" Little Head says.

"I'm supposed to lead a press conference," Rolf says.

"Supposed to?" Little Head says.

Rolf takes out the speech, studies it a moment, then tears the paper in half and in half again and tosses the shredded pieces in a trash can.

"That's awesome," Jackson says.

Rolf pats the boys on their shoulders. "Let's go out the back," he says. "And let's hurry before I end up locked in a cell."

Once outside, Little Head shouts, "Shotgun!" and Rolf hushes him. There are two sodium lamps burning and he feels naked in their light. They cross the parking lot and climb into his truck without incident. He breathes a sigh of relief when he claps the door shut and cranks the engine and says, "All right. Let's get the hell out of here."

At first he believes the windshield is clouding up with their breath. But when he runs the defroster, nothing changes. He realizes that a fog has rolled down from the White Mountains. He clicks on his headlights and reveals what looks like a wall made of phantoms. It is so easy to imagine anything out there—a face, a mouth. He shifts in his seat, checks the rearview and side mirrors. Then he drops the locks.

"What's wrong?" Little Head says.

"I don't know. I've got a bad—" Rolf starts, but before he can finish, something slams against his window.

A hand, splayed out like a pale starfish, appears suctioned to the glass. Behind it is the face of Colonel Purdin. "Sheriff?" he says, his voice muffled. "Where are you going?"

Behind him stand two soldiers, their hands on their holsters. They haven't drawn their pistols, but Rolf watches as they pop the retention straps. The fog eddies around them, so thick it might be made of muslin, and their faces ghost in and out of view.

"Can you please get out of the vehicle? The press is waiting. Fairbanks is waiting."

"Go," he hears Little Head whisper. "Go. Go, dude."

"Sheriff?" The engine idles. His hands are on the wheel. His foot is on the brake. He hasn't decided whether he's staying or going when something shifts in Purdin's face. It's like watching a hand make a fist. "It doesn't matter, really. You would have made this transition easier, but you're ultimately irrelevant. It's too late for you. And it's too late for Fairbanks. In a few hours the cell towers will go down. The TV and radio signals will be jammed. This city won't even exist anymore except as a laboratory."

"Fuck you, then," Rolf says, and the two soldiers step forward.

"This was known as the Last Frontier, but that's not true anymore. Alaska will be the first frontier just as soon as we open—"

That's when one of the soldiers screams. He reaches his arms back as if trying to knock away something that has stabbed him, but before Rolf can register anything more, the soldier is gone. Ripped upward. The fog churns where he stood a moment earlier.

"Go!" Little Head's voice is louder now.

The other soldier seizes his gun and aims it—at what, he doesn't know. He pivots and calls, "Miles? Miles!" and then something coils around his leg and rips his feet out from under him, and he falls flat on his face. The gun discharges and strobes the fog. And then he too is gone.

Colonel Purdin watches all this happen with a paralyzed stillness. Finally he seems to realize he is alone and backs up until he's pressed against the truck.

"Go!" Little Head says to Rolf again. "Go, go, go!"

Purdin must hear him because he whirls around and smooshes his face against the glass in his panic. But now he doesn't want Rolf to get out—he wants Rolf to let him in. "Open the door! Open it!" He bangs at the window with the meat of his fist and then rattles the handle. "Sheriff!"

There is a dark flash as something falls from the sky. The whole truck shakes with the impact. The hood dents. Blood splatters the windshield. It is one of the soldiers, the one named Miles, but he is missing half his face, and his arms and legs are bent at bad angles.

Purdin stumbles away from the truck, calls, "Sheriff?" Rolf isn't sure what he's asking for—answers, assistance—but his voice has gone high and his cheek is twitching and he looks very much like a lost little boy. "Sheriff!" he cries out again.

"Goddamn it," Rolf says and pops the lock and opens the door and says, "Come on! Get in already!"

But it's too late. Something comes out of the fog—a shadow twice the size of Purdin—and swallows him up. It's like watching a body fall back into water. There is a quick dissolve of his figure and then nothing but roiling froth.

Little Head is screaming and Jackson is screaming and Rolf is screaming too as he slams on the gas and goes tearing off into the night with a dead body on the hood and the wipers smearing a fan of blood across the windshield.

Theo knows what's happening all across Fairbanks. Rock music is dying. Country music is fading. Piano music is sizzling off. People are fussing with their dials, thinking they've lost their station, but they've got the right number. Whether they're listening to KLEF 98 or 93.3 the Grizz, they're all about to hear the same thing.

The static drops and a voice fills the silence. A booming, jocular voice with a fast-paced cadence. The voice of a practiced DJ. Theo's father introduces himself. "My name is Chuck Bridges, and I'm going to tell you something extraordinary." He clears his throat and nudges Theo with his elbow. "My son and I are going to tell you something extraordinary. But before we do, I need you to get out your phone. Open up GarageBand or Voice Memos or whatever app you're familiar with and hit Record. Because I'm going to repeat this message as many times as I can, but I don't suspect I'll have long. They're going to silence me. They're going to cut me off. They already killed me once, and I doubt they'll hesitate to do it again. But before that happens, everyone needs to know what's going on here. Share this far and wide. Okay? Okay. Here we go."

If you turn to another radio station, and another, and another, it won't matter; wherever you move the dial, the voice will be calling out, sharing a story that needs to be heard.

His is the voice of revolution. "They're making us into their science experiment. It's happening right now. If you don't believe me, go to the hospital yourselves and see. But this isn't just about me or those other poor souls. This is about Fairbanks. This is about Alaska. Do you think it's a coincidence this is happening here, in a state that's so far away from the mainland, the state with the fewest government regulations? If we're not disposable, then we better be controllable." He has the voice of a jovial maniac. Spittle flies from his lips when he leans into the mic. "We've always been on our own up here. We're on our own now. This is all happening really fast. If the airport isn't already locked down, I'd be surprised. If the city isn't already locked down, I'd be surprised. This is the last frontier. Let's keep it that way. Don't let them take Alaska."

Sophie feels like she's moving even though she's standing still. That's because the fog moves, coursing out of the lab, past the truck, through the trees, down the mountains. A constant, thick flow. The truck's headlights create an uncertain tent of light the three of them gather in. At first she believes these two to be terrorists or competitors. "Who are you?" she says, staring down the line of her pistol. "Who do you work for?"

The man can barely speak, sickened by the bullet wound to his thigh, and the woman squeezes her eyes shut and holds up her hands. "North Pole Construction! We work for North Pole Construction!"

A demo crew, then. Sophie relaxes slightly, but clearly something is off, given the hour and the weather.

The man lets out a choked scream of pain. Blood darkens the length of his jeans. "Please," the woman says. "Please let me help him."

Sophie sets down her briefcase and digs into her coat pocket and tosses her some zip ties. "Strap one around his thigh," she says. "The other around his wrists."

The woman's hands are shaking, and it takes her a stupidly long time to accomplish this task, despite Sophie telling her to hurry, *hurry.*

"I'm trying!" The woman wears canvas pants and steel-toed boots and has the build of a rugby player. She could do some damage if she wanted to charge Sophie, but she appears legitimately terrified.

"What's your name?"

"Joanna," the woman says.

"Joanna, you keep on behaving, and you'll live. Now you're going to do the same thing to yourself that you just did to your buddy. Understand?"

Joanna nods, some tears leaking down her cheeks.

"Ankles first," Sophie says and tosses her another zip tie.

Joanna gets down on the ground beside the writhing man and binds her legs. Then she puts out her arms and Sophie secures them with a hard tug of plastic, lassoing them at the wrists. "I'm going to search you now," she says. "If you do anything stupid, I won't hesitate to kill you both."

Joanna nods. "Okay." Her face pinkens in teary frustration.

Sophie pats them both down and takes the detonator and their wallets. She looks at their IDs. Joanna is the woman's name; she wasn't lying. Bryce is the name of the other. They each have flashlights, and Sophie tapes one of them to the nose of her pistol. She examines the detonator, then chucks it over the truck.

"Do you work for Thaddeus Gunn?" Joanna says.

"Who?"

"I thought you might be with the Department of Defense. I thought you might be coming to arrest us. For what we're about to do."

"I'm no friend of the DOD."

Joanna's face crumples with relief and confusion. "Then who are you?"

"I'm a Collector," Sophie says. "And I'm here to collect. Now, where is it?"

Joanna stiffens. Clearly she knows what Sophie's referring to: the alpha metal.

"Where is it, Joanna?"

Everything is soaked with the cold moisture of the fog, and when Joanna shakes her head, her hair flings droplets. "You don't want it."

"I assure you, I do."

"You won't be able to resist it," she says. "It corrupts people."

"Thanks for your concern." She jams the gun against the side of Joanna's head. "Last chance. Where is it?"

"Back of the building," Bryce says, speaking in staccato bursts. "There's a machine. There's a platform in the middle of it. That's where. Now, please. Don't hurt her."

Sophie hears something then, like a giant mouth opening and closing with a crackle of saliva—followed by a guttural muttering.

It seems to come from above and around and below all at once. She studies the fog. "Did you hear that?" she says, but Joanna is busy comforting the gunshot man, whispering, "What can I do?"

Sophie remembers when the monolith spilled fog across the floor of that Kansas warehouse, when the tentacle snatched the leg of Dingo and yanked him into the ether. Her hand tightens around her pistol. She starts toward the ruined building, barely visible through the thickening fog, like some English castle in the haunted moors of a BBC drama. Joanna calls after her, "Whatever you're planning—don't. It needs to be destroyed. It's the right thing to do."

"The right thing to do," Sophie repeats, remembering that Ram VII said he was sure she would do the right thing. She turns to address them once more. "What do you mean by that?"

On her knees, with her hands bound together, Joanna looks like she's praying. Her voice is desperately strained when she says, "We keep making the wrong decisions over and over. For money. Or for power. Or for a flag or for whatever. It's just in us. This stupid human thing is in us. We can't just live—we've always got to be greedy. We've always got to destroy everything."

"You were the one with the detonator, Joanna."

"I'm trying to stop people *like you* from making things worse."

"Worse than what? The world's a pretty fucked-up place right now."

"I'll take fucked-up over the alternative."

Again there comes a sound from the darkness. A sound like tongues or worms or toads or sex. A moist movement. Sophie feels something at the back of her neck. A cold, damp lick. She swings around in a fast circle, her finger teasing the trigger of her pistol. The mounted flashlight on it doesn't cut through the fog so much as illuminate it. She might as well be caught up in a vast breeze-blown cobweb. "What's wrong with this place?"

"It's spilling over," Joanna says.

"What is?"

"The place the comet came from. It's coming through. It's bleeding over. Because the sky—or *reality* or whatever the right term is—has been punched through so often, it looks like swiss cheese. We were trying to stop it. Let us stop it."

Sophie snatches up her briefcase. She can barely see ten yards ahead of her. She follows a track of muddied, sleet-laced footprints. They branch off in two different directions. One goes around the building; another goes toward an open door. Here a rusted sign warns her of radiation, but she thinks that's the least of her concerns.

She approaches the entrance just as something charges out. She barely has time to register the chuffing breath or hulking size of it—*A bear,* she thinks, *a bear made of clouds*—before it takes her into its jaws.

Theo's father begins to cough again. The nasogastric tube shredded his throat; talking hurts. He started off strong at the radio, but now he's having trouble getting his words out. Theo helps when he can, filling in the gaps of his father's story, but he knows his voice sounds comparatively halting and uncertain.

His mother goes to fetch another glass of water and when she comes back, she is rushing and the water slops over the rim. "Somebody just pulled in the driveway," she says.

"Don't answer the door," his father says, taking the glass from her with two hands.

"I think it's the police," she says.

"They're here to silence us."

Theo slips off his stool and goes to the doorway between the garage and the kitchen. At the front of the house, he can hear fists knocking and the doorbell dinging. He takes a few cautious steps forward. The porch light is on, and when Theo leans his body toward the window, he catches a glimpse of someone standing there. An old man. With a walrus mustache. Wearing a white cowboy hat. The sheriff.

Theo pulls back with a gasp. Half of his brain is convinced he's about to be dragged off to juvie for what he did earlier today; the other half knows it's stupid to think that at a time like this.

Then comes movement at the window above the sink. Somebody's face pushes into view. It looks at first like a bug-eyed infant.

Its gaze locks on Theo, and the screechy voice of Little Head yells, "Let us in, you stupid fuck!" He bangs at the glass with both hands. There is fear in his face.

Theo runs to the door and twists the lock and tugs it open. The sheriff bulls forward, pushing Theo aside, saying, "Move! Hurry!" Jackson and Little Head follow, backing inside, staring out into the night.

It is then that Theo sees the white tide of fog. It reminds him of when he accidentally knocked a gallon of milk over, but it's slower and more spectral, foaming down the street. The clouds have descended on Fairbanks.

Theo slams the door. Together, the four of them hurry to the kitchenette, where a picture window affords them a view of the neighborhood. The fog rolls across the yard, the porch, the hedges. The crest of it hits the glass and he almost expects it to crack. Instead, there is a smothering hush as if a blanket has just been thrown over the world.

"We got ahead of it," Little Head says, his voice an uncharacteristic whisper. "But just for a little while."

"This isn't good," Jackson says. "This is seriously bad. Not awesome. Not awesome at all."

"Where are your parents?" Sheriff Wagner says, his eyes still sharp on the window.

Theo says, "Garage," and the old man limps his way there.

The vapor swirls and flows, almost hypnotic. He and his friends stare in silence—until Little Head says, with a sharp intake of air, "Do you see that?"

There is an eye and then no eye. A face and then no face. An eely ripple. A pinwheel swirl. The fog is alive.

A second later, the front door shudders. A tentative knocking at first, then hard enough that the hinges complain. Theo hurries to it and twists the lock just as the knob turns.

On the roof there is a creaking. Their faces swing upward, though there is nothing to look at. There's a sound like something heavy is being dragged. Or maybe *slithering* is a better word.

"Dudes," Jackson says and Theo follows his gaze. Some tendrils are visible in the fireplace.

"Close the thing," Little Head says. "Close the chimney fucking thing."

"The flue," Theo says and slides the iron handle, clapping it shut. Maybe it is just the metal complaining, but he could swear he hears an animal mewl.

Little Head snatches a poker from the fireplace stand, and Jackson grabs the hearth broom. "What are you going to do with a broom?" Little Head says and Jackson says, "What are you going to do with a poker?"

Theo pulls the curtain in the living room, blacking out the sliding glass door.

His father's voice can still be heard in the garage, steadily running through what's happened to him, what might be happening to all of them.

"Keep going, Dad," Theo says to himself. "Don't stop."

And then his father's voice rises in volume as he says, "You've heard from me, Fairbanks. And maybe you don't know quite what to think. Because this is a lot, I admit, *a lot* to process. But I have a special guest with me, Sheriff Rolf Wagner, a man you all know and trust. And he's going to take it from here. Consider this a press conference. Sheriff Wagner, the mic is yours."

"Thank you, Mr. Bridges. I'm here to sign off on everything you've just said but also to issue a stark warning. All residents of Fairbanks should shelter in place for the time being. The fog you see out your window is a threat. And so are any soldiers you might encounter. I am advocating resilience and resistance among our population. Consider yourselves deputized. Martial law will not stand, because they brought this disaster on us, and these troubles aren't going anywhere else if they have their way. Our city is being treated as an experiment. We are on our own, but we are ready. People around here don't believe in taxes or fences, and they've been getting ready for the end of the world their whole lives. So here we go. This is it."

Rolf continues to speak, but Theo is no longer listening because something topples over in the basement. From the rattle and bang, he can picture what's fallen—a shelving unit stacked with paint cans. His eyes go to the heating ducts, where tendrils can be seen spilling upward and creeping across the carpet.

Gunfire fills the night. Joanna can't see much through the fog except five quick globes of light that collapse instantly into darkness.

"What's happening?" Bryce says. His skin is as pale and clammy as a mushroom, but his breathing has found a regular rhythm. He's far from fine, but he's come to terms with the pain.

"I don't know."

"What's she shooting at?"

"I don't know!"

Joanna wills her ears open, trying to divine any sound. The distant screeching and grinding of the machine is the only thing she can hear. The building is barely visible, but the sky above it now appears crowned with a wavering blue-silver light.

"I've got an idea." She finds an exposed rock and rolls over onto it. The jut of it prods her ribs and she worms herself back and corrals it with her hands and begins to saw the zip tie back and forth. This isn't a neat process—the rock scrapes and shreds her forearms—but the plastic finally gives way. She doesn't have time to try the same with her ankles. She military-crawls forward, looking for the detonator. The woman who called herself a Collector tossed it over the truck.

"Joanna?" Bryce calls.

"Just give me a minute." She keeps her head angled sideways, away from the Dodge's fog lights, trying to preserve her night vision.

"Joanna, whatever you're doing, you need to do it fast."

She reaches out blindly, patting the ground, cutting her palm, scraping her knuckles, bending back a fingernail. She stops once, goes still and silent, because she thinks she sees something drifting through the fog. There is a chittering sound. She waits for it to pass and begins again. She believes she finds the detonator twice—a spruce cone, a rock—before her hand actually closes around the cold square of plastic. "Got it!"

"Then hit it!" he says.

She won't. Not yet. Not until she's back breathlessly beside him.

"What are you waiting for?" he says.

She almost says she doesn't want to be alone when the detonation happens, but instead she says, "Are we going to die here?"

"If we don't, we're both going to be filing for unemployment."

"That's a fact," she says.

"But that's okay, right?" Somehow he manages to smile through the pain. "We'll find a different way than the one we planned. We'll figure out a new way forward."

"*We* will, huh?"

"Yeah. Sure. *We* will."

She touches his beard. "It's softer than I imagined." Then she kisses him. She wants it to last longer; she wants their lips to stay sealed forever, the two of them sharing their breath. But she pulls back, studies him for a few loving seconds, and says, "Ready?"

"Ready."

They align their thumbs and hit the button together.

Whatever the thing is, it bleeds. Sophie pumps several rounds into it and it lets out a shriek. She is blasted with the wind of its breath. Its jaws hold her aloft, swinging her left and right, but there is more gripping her than teeth, something like roots or tentacles that slime and sting her. She fires again, and the pressure at her abdomen releases. The thing drops her to the concrete floor. She fires again and again, and this time it shrinks away from her and disappears down a dark hallway.

She keeps the pistol aimed in that direction another few seconds before checking her body over. She is covered with blood, some of it her own. There is also a kind of phlegm that glistens near the bite marks puncturing her hips, stomach, and back, where the thing's jaws closed around her.

She collects her briefcase and tries to find her balance. She follows the other path of footsteps, the one that leads through the slush, exits the building, and goes along its outer wall. Every breath comes with a hot hitch; she believes most of the ribs on her right side are broken. Her legs obey her commands, but something feels off about her left hip; there's a spur grind with every step. She isn't sure if she walks a hundred yards or a hundred miles before she finds the back of the building.

Here is a broken wall of concrete that flashes with a familiar light. The light of eyes soaked with space dust. The light of omnimetal charged with kinetic energy. The light of the powered monolith. The light of another world.

She steps inside and feels as though she has entered a planet made of storming gas. The fog gushes around her. She has no real measure of where she might be beyond the pulsing light. She follows its brightness.

Rotten concrete rubbles the floor. She works her way through debris and across metal tile encrypted with alien designs. She recognizes some of them—a runic curl here, a linked series of circles there. This is the machine Bryce referred to; she is inside it already. She comes across ten bricks of wired dynamite as she descends a series of circular platforms, climbing down and down and down ladders until she stands at the center of it all.

A platform rises up with ladder rungs bolted onto it and dynamite tucked into its base. At the top of the structure, maybe twenty feet above her, is the wavering star, the source of light and fog. She doesn't know if she hears whispers or simply the hissing of the moisture itself, expelled as if from the bottom of a balloon. She studies the flashes of light broken every second by an ecliptic dark and begins to understand the design of what might be described as a giant planetary model, heliocentric ribs of metal that swing and rotate with a rusty screech—not so different from the center of the monolith she spent weeks studying. She understands that hacking the core of the machine will be impossible—she will get ground up by its many moving parts. She sets down her briefcase. She pokes around in the debris until she locates a spear-like length of rebar. And then she begins to climb the ladder.

She focuses only on the steadying grip of the ladder until she reaches the top. The light is blinding here. She shades her eyes and notes a swivel at the base of the machine. She stabs the rebar into the mechanism.

The metal clangs and rains rust as the gears grind to a halt. The platform shakes and she nearly falls. But the rebar holds.

The fog stills. And the bright light of the core—the battery of alpha metal—softens to a flickering blue.

In one way, with the machine suddenly silenced, everything is quieter. But that yields to another sound. The whispering grows louder and louder, taking over her mind like a howling wind as she steps inside the globe of ribbed metal. She hears garbled jabbering madness, but she also hears layers of Russian and English, the voices of scientists rattling out formulas and a military commander barking out orders. She tries not to listen and she tries not to look as shapes warp the air all around her. Gaping melted faces. Flowing streams of tentacles. *This,* she thinks. *This is a God machine.*

The alpha metal is no bigger than a pearl, a pebble, a tooth. It is difficult to imagine that something so small can generate so much power. It rests on a pedestal at the center of the structure, locked into a wired brace like a jewel set in a Gothic wedding ring. She uses a knife to dislodge it.

When the metal falls into her palm, she feels a surge down her arm as if she were holding a downed power line. Instantly, she vomits and wets herself. Her vision blackens around the edges. She has no real thoughts during this time. She is a collection of shocked nerve endings. But one word possesses her: *down.* She needs to get down. She staggers and falls more than jumps off the dais.

She isn't sure how long she lies on the floor trying to find the breath that's been knocked out of her. Her hand hums with energy that palsies her arm muscles and might be baking the very marrow of her bones. Her mouth tastes like tinfoil. Her ankle is probably broken. Her nose is bleeding.

She hazily registers other lights flashing. The red lights of the remote charges tacked onto the dynamite bundles. They blink with increasing speed, counting down the few seconds before detonation.

She lurches toward the briefcase, defying all the pain in her body. She shoves her thumb against the sensor. The locks pop. She rips the shell open, hoping it's not too late.

The fog doesn't seep or spill or flow now. It crawls. It scrabbles and slithers. Theo and his friends retreat from it until their backs hit the sliding glass door. They pull at the curtains in their panic, and the fabric rips away to reveal a long gray face smeared across the glass. It reminds Theo of a whale skull he once saw at the Museum of the North. The boys have been shouting and cursing up to this point, but now their screams find a kind of harmony.

The sliding glass door isn't locked, and it's ripped open so hard and fast that it jumps its tracks and falls onto the deck with a shattering boom. The fog pours inside and several tentacles lash forth. One of them curls around Little Head's arm. Another grabs Jackson around the waist. The boys lean back, clawing and punching, jerking their bodies against the pressure that pulls them. Still they slide and stutter-step across the carpet. Theo says, "No!" and grabs them, yanking at their arms, their clothes, but he isn't strong enough. He remembers the fireplace poker then. He stations himself before the taut lines of the tentacles and raises the poker above his head and swings it down as hard as he can.

The tentacle holding Jackson tears in half, expelling a curdled substance that splatters on the floor. Jackson has the beginning of a smile on his face, but any celebration is cut short when three other tentacles come snapping out of the dark. Jackson is seized once more. So is Theo, the feeler curling around his neck. The more he struggles, the more the grip tightens, his breath choked away, his veins and arteries pinched so that a blackening pressure grows behind his eyes.

The sheriff blunders out of the garage and into the house again. In his hand is a pistol. He fires, fires, fires, fires as he continues forward. The sound is enormous inside the house, a painful applause clapping at Theo's ears. But the gun finds its mark. The tentacles loosen and withdraw, and the boys collapse to the floor just as the sheriff empties his clip.

"Get back," he says and pops the clip and removes another from his belt and slams it into place with a click.

Theo's throat burns as he finds his breath again. His head thuds with a sudden rush of blood and he almost passes out. He and his friends are islanded by fog now, and they turn one way, then another, unable to go anywhere except up. The sheriff backs into them, saying, "Cluster up around me, now," and together they climb onto the couch as the billowing gray closes around them. Jackson whimpers and Little Head unleashes a torrent of obscenities.

And then—it stops.

Theo holds his breath until he's certain of it. The lips and tongues and fingers of fog closest to them disperse into wisps. The bulky mass begins to pull back, as if the air suddenly reversed its draft. This reminds Theo of when he brings the blow-dryer to the murky mirror after taking a shower to burn away the condensation. Through the heating vents, at the seams of the doors and windows, through the hole where the sliding glass door used to be, the haze retreats.

Theo goes to the kitchenette and stands before the picture window. He cups his hands to the glass and peers out through the frame of them. The fog steadily departs. He watches the grass and the driveway and the streetlamps solidify. The Ford Explorer reveals itself. So does the sheriff's truck.

"What's happening?" Jackson says.

"It's going. It's gone."

He realizes then that he could say the same thing about his father's voice. "Dad?" The garage has gone quiet except for the sound of his mother's weeping. "Dad!"

The client is known only as X. He wears a Tom Ford Windsor base sharkskin suit. His fingernails are manicured to a pearl glow. His hair is slicked back from his forehead in a rich, oily pompadour, but his face is hidden behind a white mask. He uses a cane to walk but presently sits in a folding chair at a card table in an empty warehouse in Bangkok. The air stinks of the fish market that was held there earlier that day. Scales still speckle the floor and catch the light in flashes.

Beside him sits a heap of duffel bags. Four altogether, each one bloated with cash. Behind him stand a dozen men, all of them also wearing white expressionless masks. They openly brandish pistols and Uzis. They dress in grays and blacks. If he says to kill, they will kill.

Across the warehouse, maybe thirty yards away, stands an opposing line of men and women. These are the Collectors. They are not uniform in their appearance. A red-haired woman with a mohawk wears a white linen suit. A black man who might stand seven feet tall wears a flowing gown. A white guy in a cardigan sweater and khakis appears unremarkable in every way except for the angry red scar that runs across his face. Others wear tactical gear, sports jerseys and high-tops, or khakis and polos. One of them steps forward now.

His name is Hans. His shoulders are thickly muscled and his waist is wasp-thin. He wears a tan suit, and his mouth has a faint trace of a smile. His hand grips a silver briefcase. About five paces away from the card table, he stops, sets the silver briefcase on the floor, and places his thumb on the sensor pad, unlocking it.

They wait. Five minutes. Ten minutes.

X pulls back his sleeve, revealing a Cartier wristwatch.

Hans says, "It won't be long now."

Another three minutes pass before the suitcase shudders. The seam splits and the two sides flop open like a book. A silver-blue light emanates from within. Then a shadow darkens it. An arm reaches forward, a hand gripping the edge of the briefcase. A body follows.

Sophie Chen crawls out, emerging from the briefcase like something freshly born. Her clothes are ragged and blood-soaked. She sprawls out on the floor, resting her cheek against the cool of the concrete.

Hans swiftly closes the briefcase and crouches beside her. "Are you all right?" Hans says in German.

"I'll live," she says in Mandarin.

She allows him to help her up. She stands unsteadily. Blood patters the floor. But her face does not flinch when she walks to the card table and drags out the folding chair and takes a seat across from X.

He studies her with black eyes. "You have the asset?" he says in Mandarin.

"I do."

X motions to the duffel bags. "Here is the first part of the payment."

She nods to Hans. He picks up the four bags and, his shoulders bowed with their weight, carries them back to his team. The Collectors proceed to unzip and count the bundles of yen, U.S. dollars, euros, and rubles. "We're good."

X says, "The rest will be processed in crypto upon delivery." He holds out his hand, palm up.

Sophie doesn't move. "What are you going to do with it?"

His head tilts in seeming amusement. His eyes glitter behind the mask. "I thought you were interested only in how much I was willing to pay?"

A steady trickle of blood hits the ground.

Her silence clearly bothers him, and X laces his fingers together and studies her over his hands. "What do you want me to say? That I'm going to use it to fight world hunger? Or save all the world's orphans?" He puts out his hand and motions with his fingers. "We have fulfilled our end of the bargain. Let's close this sale."

She can hear footsteps approaching behind her. Hans stands beside her and lays a hand on her shoulder. "Is everything all right?"

"I don't know," X says and the men behind him take a step forward.

"I recognize that voice," Sophie says and her eyes drop to study the cane at his side. "Does it still hurt? Where I shot you?"

He stiffens at this, then says, "Only when it rains." He pulls off the white mask and sets it on the table. His acne-pitted cheeks hold shadows. His rosebud mouth curves in a small smile.

"Huang Lixin," she says.

"Chen Sū fēi," he says.

"I should have killed you in Tanzania."

"Yes. You should have."

"I heard you're a colonel with the PLA now."

He extends his hand farther, palm up, demanding the metal. "Soon to be a general."

She can feel blood running down her legs and filling her shoes. She's got blood on her belly. Blood in her mouth. She's ripped open in two dozen places. The outside of her is hot. The inside is cold. "The asset is no longer for sale," she says.

"Enough." Lixin stands and smacks his cane against the floor and now everyone in the warehouse is drawing either a gun or a sword. Sharp sounds busy the air. Charging handles scrape and click. Blades slide out of sheathes. "Give it to me. Now."

"Sophie." Hans's voice is urgent in her ear. "What are we doing?"

"The right thing." Her hand reaches slowly into her pocket and closes around the alpha metal. "This is what you want?" she says, holding up her fist with blue light leaking through the fingers. "Here you go."

What happens next is difficult for her to track. She's lost so much blood and her vision shakes at the edges and the metal's energy is coursing through her arm when she slams a fist into Lixin.

The world and her body seem to suffer the equivalent of a seizure. There is a shock of light. The air shakes with a concussive blast. Lixin dissolves in a screaming flash of blue light. She is vaguely aware of her eyes rolling back in her head and all the spit drying in her mouth. Her teeth click and gnash. At the height of the explosive spasm, she dissolves some. It's as if she is sinking—as if reality is water and she is drowning and then sputtering to the surface again.

She's shoved one way, pulled another. Guns shout. Swords slash. She hears Hans call her name and then darkness swallows her.

Theo finds his father on the floor curled up in the shape of a shrimp. Every few seconds, he shudders as if run through with electricity. His mother hovers over him, her hand out but not touching him, as if she is afraid he might crumble at her touch.

"What happened?" Theo says.

"I don't know. He stopped talking midsentence and collapsed."

"Dad!" Theo drops to his knees and checks his father's pulse. The skin of his neck is cold and slick with sweat but a heartbeat thuds through it. "He's alive," he tells his mother, who calls out his name in an intensifying spiral: "Chuck? Chuck? Chuck?"

"We just got you back, Dad," Theo says and props his father's head on his thigh. "You can't go now."

"Chuck?" his mother says, not slapping his face exactly but roughing it, pulling at his beard, forcing him to wake up.

"Dad, talk to us."

His eyes open halfway. "Hey."

"Hey," Theo says. "Hey, how are you doing? Are you doing okay?"

"Yeah," his father says, managing a smile. "I'm fucking great. How are you?"

Theo is vaguely aware of his friends and the sheriff excusing themselves. Jackson and Little Head need to check on their families. Rolf will take them where they need to go and then he has to get to work because there's going to be a hell of a mess to clean up out there. "I don't know how many of the old rules apply. I don't even know if I'm sheriff anymore. But this old dog isn't ready to fall asleep in a sunbeam yet."

His father isn't capable of walking, so Theo picks him up. It hardly seems possible that the man who always seemed like a giant to him is now a weighty bundle in his arms. He carries him to the ruined living room and sets him down on the couch and draws a blanket over him.

"You want to hear something weird?" his father says.

"I think I might have had enough weird for one day."

"This is the good kind of weird," his father says. "I was just thinking about Teddy. Do you remember Teddy?"

Teddy is a stuffed animal. *The* stuffed animal. His father won it at a carnival at one of those booths where you toss darts at balloons. Theo dragged it with him everywhere for five years. The fur rubbed off in places. It lost its left eye. The stuffing poked out of a seam on its back. And then, on a road trip to Juneau, he lost it. Maybe in a gas station or a hotel lobby or a McDonald's. Theo cried so hard he threw up. In a way, it was his first taste of death. He had lost a companion. Someone he loved truly and deeply.

"We looked everywhere for that stupid bear," his father says. "We drove a hundred miles, circling back everywhere we had been, asking cashiers and hotel clerks to check their lost and found, even digging through trash cans and dumpsters. You were inconsolable. It was kind of funny but really depressing too. This stupid teddy bear, it meant so damn much to you." His voice peters out and he coughs into his fist.

"It's okay, Dad. You don't have to talk. You should rest."

"No, I want to." He clears his throat. "That's what I do best, right? Talk."

"Yeah. Okay. Go on."

"So you kept saying, *Teddy, he's lying in a puddle somewhere. He's lying in a puddle.* I don't know how you got that in your head. But I had to do something."

"So you wrote me a letter," Theo says.

"Yeah, I wrote you a letter."

"From Teddy."

"In the letter, Teddy asked you to please not cry. He was fine. He was just off on an adventure. You had to take adventures sometimes. So he had gone off to see the world. But he would come home. He promised. You always have to come home to the ones you love."

His mother speaks now, her voice thick with emotion: "I actually wrote the letters because Chuck's penmanship was so bad. But he dictated them."

"We wrote a lot of letters," his father says.

"Maybe one a week," his mother says. "For a year?"

"Teddy was in Japan, visiting Tokyo, climbing Mount Fuji."

"Teddy was in Hawaii, wearing a lei and dancing the hula."

"And then," Theo says, "Teddy finally came home. On Christmas morning. Even though Teddy was clearly not Teddy."

"But!" his father says. He coughs some more and puts a hand over his chest to settle it. "But he came with another letter that explained everything."

"The last leg of his world tour had been the North Pole," his mother says, "and Santa had fixed him up. Because he was in pretty rough shape after all those adventures."

"I still have that letter," Theo says.

"Yeah?" his father says and his mother says, "Do you really?"

"The new Teddy had a zipper in its back. I put it in there. And I can recite from memory what the last line says."

"It says—" His father's eyes close. "It says, 'Every time you lose an old love, you'll find its reflection in a new love.'"

"Yeah," Theo says. "That's right. That's it." They're quiet for a moment until Theo says, "What made you think of that anyway?"

Suddenly a huge grin cuts across his father's beard. "Check this out." Some vapor escapes his mouth as if he's outside on a cold day, and then his eyes and ears begin to expel chimneys of steam.

"Dad!"

"Chuck!" Theo's mother says. "Chuck, no!"

And just like that, he's gone. The blanket collapses into the couch, empty of him. Stupidly, Theo rips it away as if he might be hiding under it. He cries out, "No!" He finally finds the tears that he couldn't shed before. "No, Dad. No. Come back."

But then he hears a familiar voice say his name. "Theo."

He looks up and through bleary eyes sees his father limp around the corner of the kitchen and into the living room. "I'm still here, buddy," he says.

"Oh, thank God," his mother says.

"Or am I?" His father vanishes again with a swirl of steam and this time reappears behind them. His words come in a manic rush when he says, "Before, it was like I was being torn in different directions. But I'm here now." His foot stomps the ground. "I'm here and I can control it." He holds up his hand and snaps his fingers and blips out of existence; a moment later, he reappears on the couch. "I'm just like Teddy. I've been gone for a while, but now I'm back. A reflection of me is back."

"Stop," Theo says.

"Yes!" his mother says, putting her hands over her face. "For the love of God, Chuck, stop! Stop it!"

His father can't suppress his smile. "What?"

"Just stop, okay?" Theo says. "I just want things to go back to being the same."

"I don't think anything's going to be the same anymore."

"Maybe not, but for right now, can we please, please, please just be a family?"

"Yeah. Of course." His father holds out his long arms, inviting them into a hug. "Let's just be a family. For a little while, anyway."

EPILOGUE

On the outskirts of Mumbai, the peacocks strut across the gardens and roost in the trees as Sophie and Ram VII walk the grounds of his estate. When several of them cry out, wailing together, she says, "I don't know how you can stand the noise of them."

"I like the sound, actually."

"They sound like they're mourning."

"Sad songs are often the best songs. They remind us of what we've survived."

He walks with his hands folded behind him. She has trouble keeping up, and he pretends not to notice her injuries. She is the one who now walks with a cane. Her bandaged arm and spinal brace are mostly hidden beneath the jacket she wears in spite of the heat of the day. The pebbled path crunches beneath their feet. Insects drone. There is no breeze, and the air seems to drip. Even when they move through the shade of teak and sandalwood trees, the sun still seems to find them. Some men and women are gathered on a blanket near a pond clouded with mosquitoes. They look up with glowing eyes when Ram passes by. All of them chant "Metal is" as if with one voice.

Sophie follows him, with some difficulty, as he climbs the mossy stone stairs that lead to his patio. "I would offer my arm," he says, "but I doubt you would take it."

At the top, they can see the high-rises of Malabar Hill and the glittering sea beyond. A servant approaches, asks if they would like a bowl of fruit chaat or anything cool to drink, and Sophie says, "No."

Her voice is clipped enough that Ram dismisses the servant, indicating that they wish to be left alone. The man bows and his footsteps swish away. A door clicks closed.

Only then does Ram say, "Why did you come to see me, Sophie?" His hair is as white and downy as the seeds of milkweed. His eyes swirl with curious color.

She looks around to make certain they are alone. Then she reaches into her jacket pocket and removes a small box, the sort you might keep an engagement ring in—except this one is made of lead.

"What's this?" he says, taking it from her.

When he pops the latch, light streams out, enough light to make the sun seem dim. He stares at the metal for a long minute before he says, "Why did you bring this to me?"

"Because I don't want it."

"I told you to keep it secret. I told you to keep it safe."

"I did."

"You must have misunderstood." With that, he shoves the metal into his mouth and swallows with a starved gulp. He bends over and shudders his breath and when he looks at her again, jets of blue light pour from his eyes and mouth. "I meant from me."

ACKNOWLEDGMENTS

I owe a debt of gratitude to the work of Dr. Michio Kaku, especially *The God Equation*. His brilliance as a researcher—and his ability to give a layman's explanation of incredibly complex theories in physics and multiverses—helped me enormously. I know I have broken some rules here—with my slippery science—and I hope the PhDs out there are willing to give me a hall pass for the sake of story. My father, Pete Percy, is also a giant physics and space nerd—and over several years and several bourbons, he helped talk me through the science behind some of these bonkers ideas.

Thanks to Helen Atsma, the first believer in the Comet Cycle. Thanks to Jaime Levine, Mireya Chiriboga, and Jessica Williams at HarperCollins for ushering *The Sky Vault* from first to final draft. For their superheroics in publicity and marketing: thank you to Eliza Rosenberry and Kelly Dasta. Tracy Roe is the greatest copyeditor in world history; she has worked on all the Comet Cycle books and I kiss the ground she walks on.

Thanks to Katherine Fausset and Jazmia Young at Curtis Brown for their support and guidance as lit agents. Thanks to Holly Frederick, Noah Rosen, and Michael Claassen for their hustle and muscle on the film and television end of things.

Thanks to Jessica Peterson-White and the staff at Content Books—a truly wonderful indie bookstore here in Northfield, Minnesota—for their support and awesomeness. And to all the heroic indie booksellers and librarians out there; you're my favorite people.

I don't know what I'd do without pals like Peter Geye, Dean Bakopolous, James Ponsoldt, James Boggs, Paul and Stacie, and the Fantasy Fathers.

All the love in the world to my wife, Lisa Percy, who is one of the strongest, kindest, most charitable humans on the planet. I'm better because of her.

ABOUT THE AUTHOR

BENJAMIN PERCY has won a Whiting Award, a Plimpton Prize, two Pushcart Prizes, an NEA fellowship, and the iHeartRadio Award for Best Scripted Podcast. He is the author of the novels *The Ninth Metal*, *The Unfamiliar Garden*, *The Dark Net*, *The Dead Lands*, *Red Moon*, and *The Wilding*; three story collections; and an essay collection, *Thrill Me*. He also writes *Wolverine*, *X-Force*, and *Ghost Rider* for Marvel Comics. He lives in Minnesota with his family.